This novel is entirely a work of alternative history. The names, characters and incidents, and even the author himself, belong to an alternate timeline. Any resemblance to persons, living or dead, or events or localities in other dimensions is entirely coincidental.

Xaris Living LLC
Abridged First Edition 2020
ISBN 978-1-7348346-3-5
Copyright © G. K. R. Lindenberg 2020

Cover Design by germancreative @ fiverr.com

Cover Art by pantelispolit @ fiverr.com

Title Page Art by Anna Taubel
in collaboration with
doantran @ fiverr.com
renflowergrapx @ fiverr.com

Praise for *Florenz Nightingale and the Sword of Layban*

"This epic tale of the Tuscoraura Elves manages to pull off a hilarious and insightful parody on our quirks and foibles as Americans while retaining a profound reverence for those values that make us most truly who we are."
~ Sir George Warshington

"...a one-of-a-kind spoof of fantasy tropes mixed with clever plotting, fun characters, and a profound message."
~ Kit Marlowe

"Never could I have imagined that funny and epic could be such perfect neighbors until I met them among the Tuscoraura Elves."
~ Sir Benjamin Franklyn

"A masterclass in American culture."
~ Alex de Tocqueville

". . . the first time fantasy has gone so far as to get so close to home."
~ Sarah Wentworth Mourten

"Lindenberg relies on his extensive experience in real-life medieval combat zones to recreate for the reader a fantasy experience like none other."
~ Dame Frances Marian

Seek, dear Friend, and enter.

Welcome to the world of medieval Vinland before it came to be known as Amerika! In these pages you will find the story of Florenz Nightingale and her quest to find the Sword of Layban.

This book is abridged. What does that mean?

It means that the book *Johnny Appleseed and the Tuscoraura Elves* covers all these same events but goes into much more detail about the various races of the Vinland (elves, dwarves, gnomes, humans, goblins, and trolls) and explores the perspectives of other characters, especially Johnny Appleseed, Dungaree Jeanne, Lynx, Louis, and Clarke.

The next installments in this series will focus on young Louis and Clarke on their adventures leading up to the birth of a new united nation.

Florenz Nightingale

AND THE Sword of Layban

BY

G. K. R. LINDENBERG

Being the Prelude to the

Vinlander Chronicles

of the Clayborn

BY
G. K. R. LINDENBERG

XARIS LIVING LLC

TABLE OF CONTENTS

Please visit our website for more information
gkrlindenberg.com

If you have feedback for the author, catch any typos, or
simply have questions about the clayborn world of
Vinland please contact gkrlindenberg@outlook.com

We invite you to consider supporting the author on
www.patreon.com/gkrlindenberg

Dedication

To David and Louis Mallozzi, who guided and
encouraged the shaping of this text with their brilliant
ideas and enthusiasm over many years.

1st of January, 2021
Feast of the Theotokos

Acknowledgments

First and foremost, I would like to thank my wife for the many sacrifices of time and attention that she made to enable me to write this book.

Thanks also goes to my dear friend Mathieu, who made this project possible on a practical level.

Finally, my gratitude extends to my editor and proofreader, Lee Ann at FirstEditing, who worked with incredible industry and creativity to keep this work innovative without getting too wonky.

Special Thanks to these Talented Artists

Page 1 – *Kings of the Hill* by sabartstudio @ fiverr.com
Page 33 – *Amhirst at Ithica* by pavellog @ fiverr.com
Page 78-79 – *Ambush* by sabartstudio @ fiverr.com
Page 156 – *The Bough Breaks* by pavellog @ fiverr.com
Page 239 – *Sacagawea* by Anna Taubel
    in collaboration with abhay1029 @ fiverr.com
Page 382 – *Johnny Appleseed* by pavellog @ fiverr.com
Author's Portrait by abhay1029 @ fiverr.com
Shentalpee City by Anna Taubel
    in collaboration with doantran @ fiverr.com
    and with renflowergrapx @ fiverr.com

ACT I

KINGS OF THE HILL

Scene 1: A Long-Expected Party

Shentalpee City on Tuscoraura Mountain
Frige's Day Nones. Afternoon, 24ᵗʰ of March, 1283
Eve of the Feast of the Annunciation (New Year's Eve)

As the sun warms the afternoon high in the sequoia treetops, the sweet scent of pine begins to fill the spring air. Red-breasted robins and blue jays flutter in closer to squawk out the tingling tones of their thrill. On this festive day, throngs of well-dressed elves gather in the amphitheater to listen to an odd Christian preacher.

The wood elves are curious but the high elves of Shentalpee City just want to get the New Year's party started. They sit down restlessly and shush anyone who sounds too happy about being here.

The gray-haired umpire-in-chief of the Tuscoraura fire elves, Kibbler Earnestson, walks up onto the stage. Robed in silky green with a red tweed vest and yellow velvet sash, he speaks in Runic, the official language of the high elves. "Mesdames, mesdemoiselles, messieurs, ladies, and gentelves. Four score and seven years ago, our ancestors brought forth upon this Tuscoraura Mountain a new fire elf colony, conceived in hard work and dedicated to the proposition that of all the clayborn in Vinland we fire elves are created better.

"Since then, Shentalpee City's fire elves have become the leader in nearly every industry, from cookie baking to fashion design, and we have made of this sequoia grove a treetop paradise and a worthy home to the Alfheim gods our ancestors brought to the New World from their citadel deep within Mount Ragnarök.

"Up here, high above the forest floor, we touch the friendly skies at the break of each new day and our fingertips tremble with wonder as we reach for something special in the skies."

The high elves, who dwell high up in Shentalpee City, nod with approval at his eloquent flattery. The wood elves, who live on the forest floor below, shuffle in their seats. Few wood elves have the leisure to study Runic well enough to grasp his high-flown speech.

Umpire Kibbler switches to Eldric, their native language, so they can all understand. "Neither the high elves nor the wood elves among us are afraid to ask the deeper questions about life, religion, politics, and philosophy, and so despite the ridiculous tin hat and unfashionable overalls, please welcome the renowned human missionary Reverend Johnny Appleseed."

The high elves applaud coldly and the wood elves are too intimidated to make any more noise.

Johnny Appleseed stands up to shake his hand.

Yikes!

"You're not supposed to stand up next to an umpire in public if you are taller than he is. Look at how short you made him look! Where are your manners?" His translator, Dungaree Jeanne, hisses between clenched teeth. She yanks his hand so hard that Reverend Appleseed tumbles back and flips over his chair. His tattered pant hems and dirty bare feet stick straight up over his head.

You see, the truth is that elves were always rather short, despite their schemes to appear otherwise.

Contrary to what Professor Tolkien and other prominent historians of elves would have you believe, elves were never taller than humans, even in their so-called Golden Age. Elf skeletons discovered from archeology sites dating back to the thirteen century reveal that most full-grown elves, like gnomes and dwarves, averaged around four and a half feet in height back then, as they do today.

To avoid the humiliation of appearing short, Umpire Kibbler dashes to his chair, but even with Johnny Appleseed sprawled out backwards on the wooden stage, the missionary's long toes, bony ankles, and hairy legs whirling around high in the air nearby have a way of making the proud elf appear small and insignificant. Kibbler is not just an umpire among the fire elves, he is *the* umpire-in-chief over all of Shentalpee City. And yet, for all his posturing and anxiety, he cannot add an inch to his stature.

In the back row, the umpire's daughter, Florenz, buries her face in her hands. Florenz inherited her mother's dark elve features. As you can guess, in a society where image is everything, standing out from the crowd is not highly esteemed and Umpire Kibbler has already spent a lot of his political clout keeping bullies away from his daughter.

The umpire-in-chief has many rivals, but not one has ever dared criticize his love and care for Florenz. He has always been one of the most devoted fathers an elve could wish for. He attends all Florenz's archery tournaments and helps her with her alchemy projects. Every morning he combs through her thick curls—dyed blonde, as is expected of a proper high elve—and he cooks dinner with her after work.

For now, poor Florenz can only hope this preacher man has something clever to say or the backlash could spell the demise of her family's political fortunes.

4

Once Umpire Kibbler is safely back in his seat, Johnny Appleseed calmly rolls around onto his feet, clears his throat, and starts to preach. "It's mighty kind of y'all to invite me here to this New Year's Eve party. For Christians, each calendar year starts with the Feast of the Annunciation. On that day, almost thirteen hundred years ago, an angel appeared to a young girl from Nazareth and started the story of our salvation."

Fire elf society here is segregated—high elves on the right, wood elves on the left. Johnny Appleseed looks them in the eyes one after another. Suddenly, he chokes on some phlegm. The wood elves look ordinary enough, but the uncanny uniformity among the high elves strikes him as odd, almost creepy. Except for Florenz, a dark elf on her mother's side, the high elves all have light skin, blond hair, high cheeks, wide foreheads, sculpted chins, pointy ears, celestial noses, and blue, green, or violet eyes.

Not a single scruffy or laid-back high elf in sight: all he sees are overdone hairdos, elegant ball gowns, silk shirt collars, and dapper waistbands. The view is picture-perfect—disturbingly too perfect.

Johnny Appleseed hocks up a wad of cud from the back of his throat and attempts to spit it out discreetly behind the polished hardwood stage so no one notices. They do. The elves all gasp and groan.

Florenz nearly faints. This bumpkin's act is spiraling out of control. She's already lagging in the polls. Her father would take it hard if she loses in the upcoming elections for the next umpire-in-chief. She's got to get him off the stage by hook or by crook.

Gizzard and mind cleared, Reverend Appleseed resumes his sermon in Aenglish, which Dungaree Jeanne translates into Eldric with a loud, assertive, and confident voice. It goes something like this: "Oooooh, the Lord is good to me, and so I thank the Lord for giving me the things I need; the sun and the rain and the apple seed. The Lord is good to me. Amen! Amen! Amen! Amen! Amen!"

Johnny Appleseed sings this prayer with amazing enthusiasm. He slaps his knees and stomps his feet in perfect harmony while his hips do a little jig.

Apparently, the prayer's rhyme scheme gets lost in translation, or something like that, because the elves in the audience just sort of wince. For Johnny Appleseed, that good, old-time rhythm lifts his soul toward spiritual realms above. For the high elves . . . not so much. They purse their lips and roll their eyes, keeping their souls bound to the material world below.

Florenz bites her nails and rocks back and forth. She looks at her best friend, Zena, sitting next to her and gasps. "How can you be giggling like that? He's making my father look ridiculous. Your mother's the one who invited that preacher man. You're supposed to be my best friend. Can't you make him stop?"

Zena shrugs as if she doesn't care. "That's how it goes in the game of politics. As the wood elves say, 'If you want to look good, just smile.'"

Florenz glares. "Is that what this is all about? Do you really think that pulling a stunt like this'll make you the first umpire-in-chief of wood elve heritage?"

"I'm gorgeous, smart, and athletic. I can pull it off."

"Oh really? When my father told me I had to run in the elections, I only wanted to find a way to bow out gracefully. But on second thought, I think it's time for Shentalpee City to elect its first umpire-in-chief of dark elve heritage."

Zena's carefree giggle turns into a sly grin. "All right, then. Game on."

Scene 2: The Lake Woebegone Effect

Port of Cayuga. Northern tip of Lake Cayuga
in the Confederacy of the Seven Nations
Frige's Day Terce. Morning, 24ᵗʰ of March, 1283
Eve of the Feast of the Annunciation (New Year's Eve)

A-CHOO!

"A kerchief for your nose, my lord?" asks Brother Curtal Tuck. The cleric with smart eyes and hard-earned wrinkles digs into his waist pouch for a clean rag. "You should tend to that sneeze before it gets serious. It's been bugging you for weeks."

"Bah humbug," replies the baron of Amhirst as he blows his nose on the friar's kerchief. Though surrounded by a cleric, two sorcerers, a physician, and three heralds, the baron does not stop straining his voice and shouting out orders. "I want those horses and wagons loaded onto the boats immediately!"

The baron's chief herald, Sir Sean Madigan, objects. "My lord, the camp is rife with disease. Several horses have already gone blind."

The baron of Amhirst rages. "Don't worry about the horses being blind; just load the wagons!"

Two prison guards drag the defeated Frankish viceroy of Vinland, Samuel de Champlane, in chains down the paved path along the lakeshore. A few Frankish merchants peek out from their moored vessels to see for themselves the sad fate of their beloved "Uncle Sam." His haggard face, bushy, white eyebrows and scraggly, white beard remind them they should have joined the army when they had the chance.

New Frankland has recently suffered a total defeat in a war against the Aenglish Crown, and now it's too late for good intentions, especially where the former viceroy is going.

An Aenglish knight gives the command to load up the wagons and board the boats, but the bleak looks on the faces of his men spur him to relay their complaints to the baron of Amhirst. "My lord, the men are beginning to grumble. They keep asking why they have been forced to rush all the way to this dismal Irokian port on a lake no one has ever even heard of, after we have endured so many woes for you at Montroyal."

The baron of Amhirst forces a smile on his face. "Tell the men that this is Lake Woe-be-gone! Our hardships will end somewhere over this lake."

Uncle Sam mutters, "More like somewhere over the rainbow."

The Aenglish knight slaps the defeated Frankish viceroy for his cheeky comment. Weak and maltreated, Uncle Sam stumbles and falls into the lake. The knight seems ready to let him drown but the water is barely waist-deep, and the handcuffed prisoner manages to stand up on his own. The knight complains, "Zounds! Am I supposed to fish you out of Lake Woebegone?"

Uncle Sam replies, "Do not ask what you can do for me. Ask what you can do for my country."

"New Frankland is gone. This is all New Aengland now. You have to stop living in the past and start thinking about getting out of the deep waters."

"Let every Aenglishman know, whether he wishes me well or ill, that I shall pay any price, bear any burden, meet any hardship, support any friend, oppose any foe, to assure the revival of New Frankland."

Annoyed at his lazy knight and the prattling prisoner, the baron points at the knight and says, "I want you to pull him out of the water." Then he points to Uncle Sam and says, "I want you—"

HA-TISH-OO!!!

His violent sneeze sends snot everywhere.

"Bless you!" his entourage calls out politely, pretending not to notice how gross the baron looks.

The baron resumes his thought and points at Uncle Sam. "I want you to keep your mouth shut."

Amhirst's personal physician, Doctor Estrange, analyzes his illness with the best explanation medieval medicine has to offer. "Clearly, my lord, those pestilential Kaybec marches, along with significant sleep deprivation, have trapped a bitter rheum in your spleen, ascending into your nostrils. A few leeches in the right place will clear that up for you."

The baron of Amhirst waves his hand vigorously, but the snot still dangles from it as he speaks. "Nonsense! It's just a cold. Hand me another kerchief!"

Amhirst blows his nose, wipes his fingers, and hands the slimy kerchief to his herald, Sir Sean, who reminds him, "My lord, you were about to inform these troops, who fought so valiantly for you beneath the walls of Montroyal, what we're doing in this backwater village. Not even those of us on your privy council know why we're here."

The baron perks up as he speaks. "Ah, yes! Start spreading the news; we're leaving today!"

Sir Sean's shoulders sag at what he is hearing; he just does not see the sense in it. "But we just arrived last night!" he exclaims. "We are in no shape to leave this morning! Please give the troops a rest."

Doctor Estrange adds his objections. "The troops and horses are exhausted. You are seriously straining their humors. We must rest or else disease will defeat this valiant army, which the Frankish could not!"

The baron of Amhirst raises his palm to stop them. "I haven't slept more than two hours a night for the last month. My eyes burn, my throat is sore, and phlegm fills my nostrils from dawn to dusk. I'm not demanding any more of my troops than I'm demanding of myself. We'll rest once we reach New Amsturldam. It's ripe for the plucking now. We must seize the day!"

Doctor Estrange cannot believe his ears. "Rest in New Amsturldam!?! You're going to wake up in a city that doesn't sleep!"

KER-TI-SCHOO!

"Bless you!" his advisors say in unison.

"My career has languished so far. It's time to make a brand-new start of it in old New Amsturldam."

"But it's a mess over there! Ever since Count Richard Nicolas conquered Thane Petur Styvesant's Vikings, many lords have been battling to be king of the hill, top of the list—number one!"

The baron of Amhirst smiles despite his bleary eyes and reddened nose. "Exactly! I want to be a part of it."

"What claim do you have? The king has only appointed you governor of Fort Pitt and Montroyal. You missed the conquest of New Amsturldam."

"We'll be backing the claim of a trusted friend, Sir Samuel Maverick."

Sir Sean racks his memory. "As I recall, that Maverick is a man who acts with an independent mind. What makes you so sure that as duke of New Amsturldam he'll just hand the title over to you?"

The baron of Amhirst stops his horse suddenly and dismounts. An uncanny silence creeps through the wind as the baron wheels around to gloat over the prisoner. All eyes fall upon Uncle Sam, the bloodied Frankish viceroy of Vinland, sprawled across the gangplank.

With a low voice as if talking to himself, Lord Geoffrey Amhirst announces, "My dear Sir Sean, I have no mind to ask Sir Samuel Maverick to hand over his paltry title as duke. New Amsturldam means more to me than just another city—it is the start of an empire. In return for my support, he will join those who shall proclaim me the first Aenglish viceroy of Vinland."

"Viceroy of Vinland!?!" They all gasp at the notion.

HAT-SCHIII!

"Bless you!" they mumble one after the other, still trying to fathom the baron's ambitions.

The baron of Amhirst continues monologuing away his scheme. "I wrote to the duke of Yourke back in February, informing him that Sir Samuel Maverick had taken New Amsturldam from Thane Petur Styvesant and his Vikings. In the same letter, I explained that those of us who planned the conquest had always intended to rename it New Yourke in his honor, but that we uncovered a plot by the duke of Lancaster to use his toady, Count Richard Nicolas, to usurp his claim and rename it New Lancaster, despite arriving too late to aid in the conquest."

Sir Sean Madigan wrinkles his brow in dismay. "But, uh, my lord . . . Count Richard Nicolas conquered New Amsturldam two weeks ago. Sir Samuel Maverick is the one who arrived too late for the conquest."

"Ah-ha!" exclaims the baron. "That's the beauty of it. Since I correctly anticipated the events, the king will read my version first and he will read Count Nicolas's version several weeks later. When it comes to credibility, Sir Sean, it's first come, first deserve."

"That's a dangerous play, my lord. King Eddard Longshanks is very shrewd. What if he discovers your falsehood?"

"When we were boys, we used to steal apples from a farmer. To catch us thieves, he would smear the apples with red tarberry juice, since the stain is hard to remove. I noticed this and took a bite from the biggest apple I could find using only a leaf to help guide it to my mouth, but I left the apple on the tree. When the other boys tried to steal apples, the farmer made them turn up their palms and caught them red-handed. He looked at me, but I had no red on my palms. I innocently asked him for the big apple off his tree that was already bitten into. As far as he was concerned I hadn't stolen it and it was worthless to him, so he gave it to me."

"So what's the moral of that story?"

"New Yourke is my big apple. I bit into it before Lord Nicolas conquered it. Good timing, combined with tact, gets you far in the game of politics."

The baron's cleric, Brother Curtal Tuck, scratches his tonsured pate. "I don't get it."

A-TCHOUM!

"Bless you!" they say with a little more confidence this time around.

"Listen carefully. King Eddard cares nothing about truth or falsehood. His preoccupation is with finding lords who know how to win. The king feels that his advisor, Earl William Pitt, is a winner. So, when Fort Duquesne surrendered to the Crusade, I offered to rename it Fort Pitt in his honor. That was enough to convince the king to name me governor. As governor of Fort Pitt, I had the right to lead an army, so we set out and conquered Montroyal. The point is, I'm winning. The duke of Yourke is a winner. King Eddard will play along, as long as we keep winning."

Sir Sean Madigan thinks about it for a short while and then squirms. "A very good strategy, my lord; but there *is* one flaw to your plan."

"Oh really? Enlighten me if you would, Sir Sean."

"Although you have conquered several key cities in Vinland, you are only a baron. There are several higher-ranking Aenglish nobles on this continent who have been equally victorious in battle. Count Richard Nicolas won many battles for King Eddard in Welchland before conquering New Amsturldam, and Earl James Wolf has recently taken Kaybec. Viscount Sean Pridow is now master of Fort Niagara. They are all stronger candidates for viceroy than you are."

The baron of Amhirst rubs his chin and says, "All good points, Sir Sean, except that there *is* one item on their résumé that makes them weaker candidates for viceroy than I am."

"What's that?"

"They're all dead."

Sir Sean Madigan scoffs at the suggestion. "They were all in perfect health last I heard. What makes you so sure they're dead?"

HAI-KU!

"With vict'ry at hand,

"they died fighting in battle.

"Trust me. I made sure."

No one says, "Bless you."

Scene 3: The Producer

Amphitheater at Thor's Base, Shentalpee City
Frige's Day Nones. Afternoon, 24th of March, 1283
Eve of the Feast of the Annunciation (New Year's Eve)

Ignoring the elves' flustered grimaces and looks of disdain, Reverend Appleseed preaches on. "Being able to ascend into the trees and visit with the companions to the eagles, friends of the squirrels, and delegates to the clouds, is an honor I would've never imagined available to me in all of God's glorious creation."

Upon hearing Dungaree Jeanne's translation of his flattering and poetic comment, the elves soften their harsh expressions. Florenz breathes a sigh of relief.

"And so I've come here today to offer you a few more marvels of creation so as you can share in his goodness and his providence even better.

"My pappy always told me, 'It's not polite to ask a friend to worship the Lord on an empty stomach.' From that time onward, I decided to make sure everybody in Vinland's got a full belly so as we could sing together songs of praise to our God. Why the apple? Adam and Eve ate apples before getting kicked out of paradise. Since we can't get back in until the Lord comes again, we'd might as well stock up on a few apples out here to munch on while we're waiting."

He reaches behind the chest flap of his overalls and pulls out an apple. He bites into it. Taking his time to chew and swallow that first chunk, he then goes for another bite . . . and another. *Crunch!*

The elves look at him, mesmerized.

He winks back at them and says, "It's healthy for you too. An apple a day keeps the doctor away."

With that, he grabs another apple from his overalls, shines it on his shirt, and says, "Here, Chief! Sink your teeth into one of these and tell me what you think."

He tosses the apple at Umpire Kibbler but Dungaree Jeanne, with quick reflexes, intercepts his pass and says in Aenglish, "Of course we'd all love to sample the fruit of your labors, Reverend Appleseed, but food will be served after your talk. Don't want to spoil anyone's appetite by snacking in between meals, do we?"

Johnny Appleseed shrugs and says, "Suit yourself." He then pulls out a thin sheet of lead and two separate pouches of white powders from deep inside his overalls and dumps them all in a wooden bowl. Immediately, blackflame billows up from the bowl.

"In my travels, I found that oftentimes, people've got plenty of food, but it goes bad before they can eat it. This blackflame chills vegetables, meats, and fruit juices to keep them from spoiling quickly. Stick a little brazier of this blackflame in your cupboard and your food'll stay fresh for weeks.

"It's perfectly safe. It takes metals as kindling, so it won't set trees or living creatures on fire. It burns clean; no smoke. You don't even need to blow on it or stoke it up. Leave a lead plate in here and instead of ashes or soot, you'll find a beautiful piece of stained glass."

Reverend Johnny Appleseed wraps the end of his ragged linen shirt around his hand, using the hem as a mitt, and reaches into the brazier. With a quick snatch, he pulls out a nice slab of crystalline yellow glass.

He draws a few oohs and aahs from the audience.

Umpire Kibbler stands up, clapping deliberately, and calls out, "Cottage humans clap their hands to show appreciation. Let us thank Reverend Appleseed in gestures that his own culture understands."

Warmer applause erupts.

After Johnny Appleseed sits back down, Umpire Kibbler peers over to make sure the tall human is firmly settled into his chair before daring to walk over next to him again. On his way back onto the stage, the high elf leader pauses to unruffle his green robes and straighten his yellow sash, emphasizing his renewed sense of self-worth.

The umpire-in-chief of Shentalpee City concludes the New Year's Thor's Enlightenment Discourse (TED) with a short speech in Eldric. "This blackflame is an intriguing new fire technology. The smith gods, Weyland, Vulcan, and Hephaestus, have hidden the blackflame from the other gods cautiously, and Prometheus seems to have altogether forgotten to distribute it among mortals.

"But this is to our advantage! We get the first crack at it. Not long ago, we felt invincible for having deciphered the code of Athabask fire. After learning about it from the canoe humans, we combined it with Graec fire and perfected it into our own unquenchable elf fire.

"The clayborn of Vinland are forgetting our prowess with fire weaponry. Goblins encroach in our lands, humans rob fire elf merchants, and dwarves cook up new fire recipes in an attempt to vie with us. We must study and unlock the secrets of this blackflame if we are to reassert our military dominance in Vinland.

"Before me, I see row after row of stunningly good-looking, stylishly dressed geniuses. If anyone can master this blackflame it's you, o fire elves of Tuscoraura Mountain!"

The elves rap their knuckles on the wooden benches and clink their silver and gold rings and bracelets for applause, as is their custom. Cheers whistle through the assembly like a howling wind.

Dungaree Jeanne blurs her translation of the umpire-in-chief's words. She's guessing Johnny Appleseed has no intention of becoming an arms dealer.

Meanwhile, Umpire Kibbler carries the wooden bowl of blackflame back to the colossal statue of Thor behind them and puts it inside a brazier. "I hereby dedicate this blackflame in honor of Thor, the chief protector of this treetop colony. Let us all take upon ourselves the sacred duty to analyze its alchemical composition, to unlock its artistic and industrial potential . . . and most of all, to weaponize it!"

The high elves stand up with great enthusiasm and extend their right hands straight up into the air, chanting, "Kibbler, hail! Kibbler, hail!"

Dungaree Jeanne chooses not to translate that last bit of information for Reverend Appleseed either.

Florenz leaps up cheering and joins her father on stage. Meanwhile, Zena stews in her seat, grumpy and resentful. Knowing a good deal of Aenglish herself, Zena mulls over her mother's reluctance to translate accurately for the missionary.

In a flash of inspiration, she hatches a plan to cool the rising enthusiasm for Umpire Kibbler and sap the political momentum he is winning for Florenz.

Grinning wildly, Zena steps over to Johnny Appleseed and drops a pouch of gold coins in his lap. He looks up at her, a bit confused. "What's this?"

Zena answers in her heavily accented Aenglish, "Tuscoraura double eagles—pure gold coins worth twenty dollars each."

Reverend Appleseed is so shocked he barely manages to speak. "Okay, but what's it for? I'm offering you these gifts freely."

Zena gives him a wink. "We call it earnest money. Umpire Kibbler Earnestson has family tradition of holding onto good deal. He not want you to give the dark fire to anyone else. This money to be followed by much more if you keep it our little secret."

Appleseed scratches his ear and tilts his head back. "Tell him that I serve the Lord and not Mammon!"

"You should be afraid to stand up to him and tell him yourself. He is too powerful!"

Without another moment's hesitation, he stands to his full height and hands the money bag over to Umpire Kibbler. "I don't want your hush money!"

Despite his high heels, Umpire Kibbler's head barely reaches up to Appleseed's bushy, gray beard. His shortness is painfully obvious to all the high elves there. The entire audience gasps at a second—and this time, intentional—act of effrontery against their umpire-in-chief's short stature.

Umpire Kibbler shoots an angry look in Dungaree Jeanne's direction. "Madame Dungaree, tell your Christian preacher here that the base ledges tend to be rather low for exceedingly tall men such as himself, and newcomers get vertigo real easy when they see for themselves how high up we really are."

Scene 4: Petals on a Wet, Black Brow

Port of Ithica. Southern tip of Lake Cayuga
in the Aenglish Lordship of Vinland
Frige's Day Compline. Night, 24th of March, 1283
Eve of the Feast of the Annunciation (New Year's Eve)

It is a dark and stormy night. Frigid rain slices through the roiling sky. The haggard and sorely pressed soldiers under the command of the baron of Amhirst disembark onto the slippery docks at the Port of Ithica. Spurred by hopes for warm fires and featherbeds within Ithica's walls, they slosh their way up the cold, muddy roads.

Along the quay, black rain clouds dump sheets of chilled fury across Amhirst's brow like petals of divine wrath. Along the wearisome road, the raindrops slow to a gentle trickle, only to pick up again moments later. The alternation jangles the nerves of the soldiers and horses alike. Both bray like wild beasts as the storm proves itself a more relentless, ruthless, and intractable foe than the Frankish ever were.

Clanging raindrops on the soldiers' metal helmets add a noisy torture to the bitter cold. For the knights and mounted sergeants in mail, the precipitation stiffens the rusting chain links until their arms grow too rigid to even wipe the snot from their faces and soaks the rusty chill deep into their bones.

The baron of Amhirst, past his sneezing fit but still suffering from a runny nose and starting to go feverish, yells out with authority: "Why have we stopped?" *Sniff* "Ithica is right there!"

Sir Sean is quick to answer. "The vanguard is standing before the gates of Ithica now, my lord, but a messenger just arrived saying that the town has barred its gates to our soldiers!"

"What on middle earth are you talking about, Sir Sean? Why are they refusing us entry? This is an army of Aenglishmen. Are the Ithicans not loyal subjects of the Aenglish Crown?" The baron fumes.

"Perhaps if you reason with the captain of the gatehouse, you might rekindle his patriotic fervor . . ."

Amhirst shouts hoarsely, "Patriotic fervor?" *Sniff* "I'll strike the fear of God into that knave's heart!" He spurs his horse to a brisk trot and rides to the front of his halted column of soldiers.

Despite the raindrops splashing in his eyes, he catches a glimpse of Ithica's town guards and identifies which one is the gate tower's captain merely by the way he carries himself. The baron of Amhirst has a knack for sifting out men and women with power. As he yells, he realizes his voice is getting hoarse. "What is the meaning of this?! I am Lord Geoffrey, baron of Amhirst, and commander-general of His Highness King Eddard's expeditionary forces to Montroyal. The king's soldiers have a right to be quartered in any Aenglish town." *Sniff* "In the name of the king, I order you to open these gates!"

Although far away and watery-eyed, the baron imagines he can detect a sardonic curl in the captain's lip. "Begging your pardon, my lord, but them joints on the gate took a hit from, you know, a catapulted boulder during the last siege by those cheese-eating Franks. Now the dang portcullis is all wrecked and our engineers can't fix it until next week!"

With cold rain seeping down his back, Amhirst loses patience. "What sort of tomfoolery are you playing at, man?" *Sniff* "You shall open these gates to my troops at once or suffer the king's wrath!"

"Tut, tut, Lord Jiffy; it ain't gentlemanly to go making threats like that. They're liable to stick to the roof of your mouth!" The captain of the gate tower guard struts around with a show of bravado.

The baron of Amhirst clenches his fists. "Do you realize that there are over five thousand soldiers at my command?! They are soaked to the bone and in no mood to sit here all night. One word from my mouth and they'll unleash a torrent of" *Sniff* "blood!"

"You lot of bed-wetters can unleash a torrent of wee-wee for all I care." The captain of the gate tower guard wags his steel-mailed fanny and saunters away from the wall. In his place, a scholarly looking elder wearing carnelian red and dark-gray academic robes and holding a large, metallic staff with a comfortable, red velvet grip in the middle approaches the wall.

The scholar calls down to him: "Lord Amhirst, you would do better allowing your herald to speak for you. You are losing your voice, and you are about to lose your army as well. You dare threaten to attack Ithica?

"Ithica is home to the Silvermorn College of Sorcerers and I am its grand sage, Ezra Cornwell. We have over three hundred brilliant young apprentice sorcerers eager to demonstrate the military applications of their proficiency with source stones. They could sweep away your iron-clad army with their staves quicker than they could sweep up my study with three hundred bewitched brooms!" Cornwell deftly twirls his staff to demonstrate his skill and awaits a reply.

Amhirst confers with Sir Sean Madigan and then lets his herald do the speaking for him. "The baron of Amhirst has no wish to start any conflicts with loyal subjects of the Aenglish Crown, only to remind you that since we are a royal army with a commission directly from King Eddard himself, we have the right to quarter our troops in Aenglish towns. We are here to exercise our royal prerogative."

"Royal prerogative, eh? We'll see about that." Master Cornwell beckons a large, mail-armored man wearing a tabard with the Aenglish Crown's heraldic coat of arms: three gold lions passant guardant on a gules field along with King Eddard's personal badge consisting of the Queen Mother's Provençal golden rose with a green stalk and his late father's Plantagenet sprig of broom.

The man shouts out authoritatively, "His Royal Highness, Eddard, king of Aengland, prince of Welchland, lord of Erinland, duke of Baskony, duke of Aquatania, and count of Picardy, commands you to hold your peace. The mayor of Ithica reminds you about the atrocities committed by unruly Aenglish soldiers against those loyal to the Aenglish Crown at Fort Bedford. In light of those excesses, he insists that you send your troops in unarmed and one at a time."

Sir Sean Madigan fumes. "We have six thousand soldiers who need food and housing immediately! Of that number, nearly four hundred are sick or wounded! We can't queue up for days waiting to get inside one at a time! The king's commission accords us the right to quarter troops in Aenglish towns!"

The man replies, "The King's charter to Ithica grants the mayor the right to decide how and where

Aenglish troops will be quartered. On the king's authority, I order you to back your troops away from these walls."

The baron trots his shivering horse forward a few more paces and wipes the cold rain from his face. "On the king's authority?" *Sniff* "Who in the wild blue blazes do you think you are?"

"I am Sir Walter Rally, the royal coroner for Ithica," the man replies with a bold air, despite the wet rains lashing against his face and armor.

"Royal coroner? I've never heard of such an office."

"The wise King Eddard has heard too many cases where both sides make claims in the name of the Aenglish Crown, so he has appointed coroners who alone have authority to speak for the Crown."

"Balderdash!" the baron barks out, quickly losing any semblance of patience. "We'll show them who has the Aenglish Crown's authority! Sir Sean, tell the offensive coordinators to ready the battering rams."

Grand Sage Ezra Cornwell calls forth hundreds of apprentice sorcerers to take up defensive positions along the wall. Cornwell holds out his large rod of lodestone. In the hands of this master sorcerer, it becomes one of the most powerful weapons in medieval warfare.

The grand sage pulls down his hood (to protect against the rain—contrary to popular misconceptions, real historical sorcerers only wore hoods outdoors during inclement weather, to keep the rain out of their eyes, and never wore them inside just to appear creepy and mysterious). With his face hooded from the rain, he meditates for a moment. Gradually, he begins to regulate his breathing and pulse until the polarization of his lodestone grows stronger and switches from attracting metal to repelling it. Then, with a flick of the grand sage's wrist, Amhirst and his armored bodyguards go flying backwards off their horses.

Amhirst's tall frame, on top of such a tall horse, makes for a harder fall than the rest of the knights. Afraid his master might have broken his neck, Amhirst's diligent squire rushes to help him to his feet.

Alive but with the wind knocked out of him from the fall, Amhirst still manages to wheeze out his defiance. "Sorcerers, eh? We'll show him what we can do with sorcery! Slingers! Clear the walls! Engineers! Bring forth for the battering ram!"

His squire repeats the baron's command to the heralds. Like opera singers, they use voices to amplify and project sound as far as megaphones.

Sir Isaac Davies, captain of the baron's slinger company, readies his troops in under a minute and lines them up to strafe the walls. Incidentally, this same Davies would organize the first company of patriotic minutemen from the town of Akten in the duchy of Masswachoosut Bay and would give his life heroically for the cause of freedom during the Battle of Lexton and Concord a few years later.

At his command, the Aenglish slingers whirl smooth, round stone pellets over their heads, then launch them at the young sorcerers on the battlements. From a thousand yards accuracy is impossible, but a constant peppering of weighty stones is usually enough to keep a wall's defensive squads hunkered down long enough to bring up scaling ladders and a battering ram.

Usually.

Against Cornwell's apprentice sorcerers, it is another matter entirely. Since lodestones, the source stones for elemental earth, are only effective against metal, sling stones or bone-tipped arrows normally keep battlesages at bay. But the apprentice sorcerers at Silvermorn let their imaginations run wild.

Wind sorcerers blow into pipes of nacre, the source stone for elemental air, also known as mother of pearl, and buzz into pitch-bored conch shell trumpets to whip up gusts of wind at hurricane velocities, shooting the sling stones and bone-tipped arrows back over Amhirst's battle lines with terrifying force.

Water sorcerers with glass-encased salt crystals at the tips of their ivory rods drive the blustery rain out in concentrated streams, power-washing the slingers and archers off their feet. Fire sorcerers with their pyrite-studded canes send whirling vortices of fire blazing through the night and steaming the rain to create a thick, blinding fog.

The baron of Amhirst watches all these developments with grim determination from the sidelines. Sir Sean Madigan comes galloping back to report to him. Amhirst shouts, although his failing voice barely scratches out more than a whisper, "What are the reports from the unit captains, Sir Sean?"

"Not good, my lord. You might not want to hear it."

"Generals have to watch what they don't want to see and listen to what they don't want to hear."

"Right. Here it goes then. The truth is that our center is crumbling from the onslaught of the elements brought on by all those sorcerers, and the reserve teams are refusing to get into the field. The wounded are literally piling up on top of each other from the violence of the wind and the rain."

Lord Amhirst slaps him on the back. "Don't lose courage, man!" *Sniff* "Tell the troops there is pork roasting on a spit and a side of beef waiting for them inside Ithica and I have a plan to get it.

"First, we are going to divide our battlesages into three groups and send them forward there, there, and there," he says, pointing to clusters of apprentices using the less common source stones—wind, fire, water.

Lodestones, the source stones for earth sorcery, have traditionally been the main tool for training battlesages, who specialize in making life difficult for warriors who rely on steel for their weapons and armor. The apprentices equipped with lodestones are wielding them like the savvy soldiers they aspire to become. The wind, fire, and water apprentice sorcerers, on the other hand, prance around with rowdy zeal. Their battle stances are sloppy.

Amhirst observes, "See how they lean over the walls. Our marksmen should be able to pick off a few."

Sir Sean disagrees. "With wet bowstrings and soggy slings, we won't take down enough to turn the tide."

Lord Amhirst does not lose resolve. "Through this dismal rain, the one thing I can see clearly is that those apprentices are having fun. This is a big game for them. We just need a quick kill or two from our sharpshooters to bring home the deadly realities of war. As soon as Cornwell sees a few of his students getting killed in action, he will withdraw them all. Mark my words!"

Sir Sean sends out the marching orders. Soon Amhirst's crossbowmen and slingers move into position behind the battlemages and battlesages. On their mark, the first volley of crossbow bolts and sling stones flies up against the walls.

The Silvermorn apprentices deflect the sorcery, magic, quarrels, and stones aimed at them, displaying true teamwork and skill. Volley after volley, Amhirst's troops fail to hit anyone on the town's ramparts.

Amhirst's own battlemages and battlesages ply their tricks, spells, and cantrips, but the ensorcelled winds and rains from the Silvermorn apprentices lash back at them with overwhelming gale-storm force.

A conjured hurricane sweeps Amhirst's best and brightest off their feet. The plan is not going well.

"Battlesages, rally!" Sir Sean's voice booms.

Wearing armor of horn scales or bone plating, the baron's remaining battlesages slosh through the cold mud to gather up any of the storm-battered marksmen willing to stay in the fight.

Having realized that they are reckoning with a truly powerful foe, one gnome battlesage tries a forgotten tactic using some old kite shields from the reserve wagon. Although kite shields were a valuable mainstay for the Frankish knights who vanquished the armies of Aengland in 1066, by 1283 they have become outdated tech, lacking the stopping power of the new heater shields. Still, by constructing a small kite shield fort she could position her crossbow troops to score a few hits.

With most of the army swept away, and facing overwhelming odds, the brave battlesage straps a kite shield to her back but then gets caught in a tremendous updraft of wind. It lifts her off her feet high into the air. That battlesage, well-known among Vinlanders of all races in later generations as Merry Pippins, happens to be one of my ancestors.

Carried from one current of drafts to the next, she eventually drops face-first in the mud right in the middle of eleven down-hearted crossbowmen. She smears the mud off her face and says, "You see! Flying on a kite can be quite fun."

The crossbowmen laugh. Her pluck and good humor lift their spirits.

With a simple wave of her hand she calls out, "Let's give them a spoonful of their own medicine and make them go fly a kite of their own!"

Something sparks to life inside these eleven muddy crossbowmen and they crawl through the muck and mire on their hands and knees behind her while cowardly soldiers scramble away from the battlefield. Merry Pippins leads them to the supply wagon with the old kite shields. She then pushes on closer to the walls and orders them to set up a shield fort. Once in position, they crank up their crossbows for a volley.

After they have cocked their bowstrings and loaded their bolts, the crossbowmen look to Merry Pippins and await her orders. Merry Pippins explains her plan. "On three, we are going to pull a supercalifacted expialidox on source stones one, nine, six, and four."

One of the crossbowmen, named Bert, interrupts with his terrible cockney accent: "I amn't got um idear whater yikie just said."

A crossbow-dwarf crouched next to him named Ernie, who happens to be his loyal friend, despite his odd sense of humor and an even odder laugh, tells him, "Don't worry, no one ever understands whatever you say either. Just take your shot on three and don't miss."

"Rawtee ho!"

Merry Pippins meditates and focuses her lodestone staff at specific Silvermorn apprentices. Her staff starts to vibrate with a humming noise. She counts out, "One . . . two . . . three!"

From the kite shield fort, crossbow bolts cut through the rain and the night with terrifying speed and strike several hooded young sorcerers with such force that they are carried off the wall back down into the streets of Ithica behind them.

Sir Sean sees it and whoops in triumph, "Whoo-ee! They managed to strike down a few apprentices!"

The baron of Amhirst strains to see. "Where?"

"Over there, behind those kite shields, my lord! You'll see a dozen soldiers all dirty in the mud."

The baron of Amhirst sniffs. "That dirty dozen over there, eh? Let's see what Cornwell thinks about that!"

No mistake about it—Cornwell is devastated. A wrenching knot twists the grand sage's gut at seeing the violence escalate to lethal proportions. He will be delivering eulogies instead of diplomas this year. Not wishing to endanger any more young lives, Cornwell calls them off. "Sorcerers' apprentices! Withdraw!"

Seeing this, the baron of Amhirst exults and shouts with what is left of his voice, "Call up the siege ladders! It looks like meat is back on the menu, boys!" He spurs his horse forward to lead his demoralized troops in a daring charge from the front while Sir Sean Madigan uses his thunderous voice to echo the war cry.

Eeesh!

The baron's optimism is a bit hasty. The death of the apprentices only spurs their mentors to finish this fight with unnecessary roughness.

The instructors at Silvermorn College gather at the top of the gate tower to combine their powers. They wave their staves, rods, and canes with all the focus their disciplined minds can dedicate to the task. Pillars of fire and windy tornadoes descend upon the attacking hosts and spray raindrops, shields, helmets, swords, and spears into the clutter before the walls. A speckled tidal wave of rainwater and discarded equipment crashes down upon the infantry companies surging forward and demolishes their siege ladders.

Together with two highly skilled colleagues, Master Cornwell points his lodestone staff directly at the baron of Amhirst. With a twist of their wrists and a grunt from their guts, the three powerful sages hoist the feisty baron up into the air. The magnetic force of the lodestone staves acting upon his steel mail armor zips him up toward the top of the gate tower.

The captain of the gatehouse guard reaches out to grab him mid-flight with a gloating smile. "Well now, Lord Jiffy, the mayor's puttin' out a cordial invitation for you to sort out this little difference of opinion you been havin' with the coroner. We'll see who really represents the king's authority around these parts."

"Never!" shouts the dangling baron.

"Oh well. The coroner says that if you ain't got a likin' for the king's authority, we could always drop you off the walls and let ya go hash it out face-to-face with God's authority."

The baron of Amhirst retains his composure as he hangs over the tower's edge. "I am God's good servant, but the king's first."

Scene 5: Florenz's Nightingale

Shade Gap.
Five Miles Northwest of Tuscoraura Mountain
Frige's Day Matins. Midnight, 24ᵗʰ of March, 1283
(The medieval new day did not start until sunrise.)
Eve of the Feast of the Annunciation (New Year's Eve)

Two reindeer fly fearless and fleet through the gloom of the moonlit forests around Tuscoraura Mountain. The rush of wind startles a pair of turtledoves from their roost. Having no mind for their cooing, the two dark figures cling to their swift steeds.

As the damp of the river fog drifts over them silently, only the sparks of their steel-shod hooves against pebbles signal their approach to the goblin ritual mounds overlooking the Shade Gap.

The midnight hour is close at hand and goblins lurk. Their demon gods haunt the barren rockface in search of blood. A foul stench wafts through the air and slides down the stony, cold hills at the unwelcome visitors.

A savage place! Unholy and disenchanted as ever the waning moon has spied upon. An evil sanctuary covered in scratched boulders and spilled blood. Here the two panting reindeer come to a stop.

Chilled but unafraid, Florenz dismounts and pulls from her saddlebag a small, cloth-wrapped crate. Tucking it under her arm, she crawls through the underbrush, closing in on the goblins dancing to the sound of their drums. Her dress has ribbons and filigree that the brambles and thorns shred as she moves.

Though the night assails her comeliness, Enganyon follows after her like a sailor after the siren's song.

He takes one peek ahead and tugs at her hem. "Oh, look at that. They're human! It's not a problem for elves to meddle with. Let's go home."

Amid the tattooed and roughhousing goblins, a half-dozen humans wallow in captivity. Stripped down to their undergarments, they are cuffed with rough vines to a line of wooden stakes. Gruff goblins prod and poke at them with stone-tipped spears. Glib goblinesses chatter and chant over them in preparation for sacrifice to the goblin god of death and conquest.

Florenz doesn't back down. "There's a choice we're making by being here and I'm saving those lives."

Enganyon starts to whimper, "What about all those goblins? What can the two of us do against so many?"

Florenz will hear none of it. She scolds him, "We can't just let the other races in our land keep dying a pointless death at the hands of those goblins!"

"Not pointless at all! That goblin chieftain's got a sacrificial dagger with a phoenix talon blade. I'd say their deaths will be very pointy."

"Coward."

Enganyon's voice squeaks despite all his efforts to keep it low. "What is it with you, Mademoiselle Florenz? Isn't being a fairy-tale princess good enough? You're rich, gorgeous, and powerful! You don't have to pretend you're some kind of hero as well."

"So you're saying I'm not really a hero?"

"Yes, no! What I'm saying is . . . to me, you're more than a hero. You're a . . . a . . . a superhero. But we can't just ask all those goblins to stop sacrificing their captives to their god, Poopoo, so why risk our lives?"

"It's Poodoo. They worship Poodoo. And you're right—we can't tell them to stop the bloodshed; but Poodoo can. If a singing nightingale flies over their ritual, they believe Poodoo has sent them a sign to release their captives alive. Here's the nightingale."

She pulls the cloth covering off her crate and reveals it to be a small cage with a nightingale inside.

"How do you know it's going to fly in the right direction and sing on cue?"

"I don't." Florenz looks at the nightingale. "But I have to believe that there's a Higher Power out there guiding nature and protecting the lives of the innocent."

She opens the cage door. The nightingale flies out and swerves off in the wrong direction without a peep.

Enganyon raises his eyebrows. "Well, that was certainly anticlimactic. It's really been a treat playing the good guy with you, Mademoiselle Florenz, but I don't need to be an augur to tell you it's time for us to head home. I'll saddle up Prancer and Donner."

"So you're saying you're not really a good guy?"

"Nope, not with all those bloodthirsty goblins around us and nothing but a few human lives at stake over there. I'll pass on the whole good guy thing, thank you. In general, my personal philosophy is to stay neutral between good and evil. In all of life's straits, I look to steer the middle course. When facing the perils of the high seas, I'm a buccaneer of mediocrity. 'Armed and harmless' is the motto when my flags unfurl. A middling champion for moderation—that's me. I uphold all high ideals but fanatically adhere to none."

"Oh, Monsieur Enganyon, you are ridiculous. If you're going to leave me here alone, do me a favor and cause a big distraction on your way out. Maybe I could sneak up close enough to cut their bonds."

"Impossible, Mademoiselle Florenz! I could never abandon you. Instead, I urge you to join me in the comfortable median and together we'll live a long, happy life. Maybe we'll even rule over the fire elves as husband and wife—with your father's help."

"Don't be ridiculous! Are you going to cause that distraction or not?"

"Sorry, my love, but I can't oblige you on this one. It goes against my principles."

"What principles!?! You sound so indifferent to the sufferings of others that I'd believe you've already filled out an application to become an evil villain."

"You'll find most evil villains are really sensitive, caring people deep down inside. They've just got a lot of angst to deal with."

"What does angst mean?"

"Whether you realize it or not, you know the meaning of angst. Umpire Drayton exiled your mother, and your father only gathered up enough political clout to fight back seven years too late. You grew up unfairly deprived of a mother and spoiled by your overworked father with privileges you haven't earned. You're moonlighting as a do-gooder to make up the difference. I'd say that same angst could push you to commit some evil villainy, given the right conditions."

"Monsieur Enganyon, leave. I'll do this by myself."

Enganyon grabs her hand and kisses it. "No! Not without you! You know I just can't stop loving you."

She pulls her hand away. "Hey! No ring, no touchie. Besides, how do I know you'd still love me if my father lost all his wealth and political connections?"

"See that? That's the angst talking now. You're well on your way to becoming an evil villain after all."

"Never."

"Never say never."

"You just said it, twice."

Enganyon sighs with a playful smile. "I'm just not going to win with you, am I?"

Turning away from him, Florenz starts sneaking in closer to the captives and whispers, "No, nay, never."

"Ahhhhh!" Enganyon screams.

She looks back to shush him quiet, but he's gone.

"Monsieur Enganyon? Are you all right?" Florenz scans the forest anxiously. All the while, she doesn't hear the footsteps creeping up behind her.

She takes three paces forward. Under the moonlight, she sees a sight that almost stops her heart. She tries to scream but terror takes the sound before she makes it.

A goblin lurker grabs her neck and drags her up the rocky mound until they reach the ululating goblinesses around the human captives. They pipe to the foul spirits ditties of no tone and dance with daffodils in their hair.

The goblin lurker hands Florenz over to the green-skinned ladies who snatch her up and start picking off her jewelry, pouches, belts, boots, and knives. After they've rough-handled her in every way possible, they tie her to a stake near the human prisoners.

She is both relieved and disappointed that Enganyon is not with them. Perhaps he's safe, or maybe he's dead. *Oh, Enganyon, where art thou?*

Forgetting her own discomfort at the tight bindings, her mind goes to work coming up with an escape plan for herself and the humans. Suddenly, she sees him. Enganyon's plight ties a knot in all the threads she's been working out.

Across the stony sacrificial mound, just behind the giant slate altar, goblins are crowding around a black cauldron filled with a steaming, white pigment. They are dipping Enganyon's right foot into the white pigment and placing it on their foreheads.

Florenz shrieks, "What are they doing to him?"

To her surprise, one of the human captives answers her in Elvish Runic, "Do not fear, Mademoiselle elve. They do him little harm. They take unto themselves the Mark of the Feet. Goblins like to collect a white footprint on their right hand or forehead from as many light elves as they are able to capture. It is a token of piety and allegiance to their god, Poodoo."

Though she'd said her words in Eldric, the dialect exclusively spoken by fire elves, she switches to Runic, the language common to all high educated light elves.

"How comes it about that thou speakest Runic?"

The human replies, "I am a master silversmith. Whilst I was still a journeyman, I trained with the sea elves of Martha's Vineyard. Any silversmith in Vinland of worth speaks some Elvish Runic, just as any ironsmith of worth speaks at least some Dwarvish Runic."

Florenz is so amazed at how well this human speaks Runic that she forgets about Enganyon momentarily and asks the human, "Who art thou, and how hast thou fallen into the clutches of these goblins?"

"Master Paul Riviere of Baston. Whilst I was stationed at Fort William Henry, we were besieged by the Heron clan and some Frankish insurgents. We surrendered under terms that we should be allowed our weapons. Certain Heron warriors, however, broke the treaty and demanded our weapons. Those who resisted perished. We all ran for our lives, but soon after reaching the forests, I was captured by goblins and brought here.

"May I, in turn, ask thy name and how comes it that thou hast fallen captive, Mademoiselle Elve?"

"I came here with a nightingale to rescue thee and thy companions. Goblins release their captives if a passing nightingale sings. Our bird flew awry."

"My deepest regrets, fair lady, that thy plan miscarried and that now thou sharest our fate."

Florenz leans her head back on the stake in deep frustration and says, "If only I knew some witchcraft to recall that wayward nightingale."

"The best witchcraft is a mind tuned to nature," replies Paul Riviere, and he starts to whistle. Florenz marvels at how perfectly his whistling imitates the intricate songs of a nightingale.

The goblins hush each other and cock their necks, peeking anxiously at the night sky. Miracle of miracles, Florenz's nightingale flies in and lands on top of Paul Riviere's stake, chirps out a quick ditty, then flies off.

A long pause follows but then a larger goblin, whose sun-dried, dark-green skin has enough tattoos, body piercings, and war trophies to leave no doubt that he is a renowned war chieftain, bellows in triumph.

All the goblins on the sacrificial mound overlooking Shade Gap break into a new flurry of chanting, hopping, and chest-beating. The party breaks up soon enough and the yawning goblins pack up their goodies, including all of Florenz's jewelry, and wander off.

All the captives remain tied hand and foot to their stakes except Enganyon. The white pigment on his foot was hot enough to scald all the skin from his knee down. He writhes with pain in such grandiose gestures as not to notice that he is free.

Florenz calls out to him, "Monsieur Enganyon! Are you all right? Speak to me!"

He courteously replies, "Ouch!"

"Can you find a sharp object to free us with?"

He stops groaning and pulls out her silver dagger with a smirk. "You mean like this? A gobliness was toting it around and I figured you'd want it back."

Florenz can't hide her joy at his craftiness. "Yes! Monsieur Enganyon, your sleight of hand has saved the day! You're my hero! Quickly, free us before those goblins change their minds."

"I can't walk, but I can toss it to you."

"So I can free the humans like a hero? How sweet!"

He tosses it within reach of her bare feet. Handling it deftly with her toes, Florenz slices away the vines tying her to the stake. She then frees Paul Riviere and the other humans, but Enganyon continues to sulk on the ground. She offers him a hand. "You big sissy, I'll fetch Donner and you can just ride him home."

Enganyon stays put and starts to tear up. His lips pucker like a child whose candy just got stolen. "No! We can't go back! Not like this! Our jewelry is gone, our clothes are raggedy and . . . and look! My foot is all glopped up and ugly!"

Paul Riviere walks up and hands her the silver dagger. He thanks her in Elvish Runic. "Thou hast our eternal thanks, Mademoiselle Elve, for saving our lives! If there is anything we can do to repay—"

Enganyon butts in. "Actually, thou couldst get us new clothes and some subtle but elegant jewelry—"

Florenz stuffs a rag in Enganyon's mouth and talks over him. "What my companion means to say is that it is highly shameful for elves to be so disheveled. To walk among our fellow elves in tattered garments and lacking jewelry is no less shameful to us than if thou had to walk among thy peers with no clothes at all."

Paul Riviere nods thoughtfully. "Yes, indeed. I have learned as much about ye elves. Never fear! Whilst at Fort William Henry, many of the soldiers had sticky fingers, so I buried three stashes of silver wire and smithing tools. We shall find one and I shall smith thee simple but elegant jewelry to get thee home without disgrace."

Delirious with gratitude, Florenz bows so deeply she nearly kisses the ground at his feet.

Enganyon objects in Eldric. "Hey, you don't have to worship him like that. He's just paying us back for saving his life."

Florenz gives him a sharp look. "Monsieur Enganyon, he is the one who saved our lives by whistling to my lost nightingale. Now he is showing greater concern for our well-being than his own. In my mind, that makes him the truest hero of us all."

Enganyon shrugs. "Yeah, he's a nice guy, but it's not like the fate of Vinland is riding on his shoulders."

"Perhaps," replies Florenz. "Now, Master Riviere, how shall we reach these three stashes of thine?"

"One is by land, and two are by sea."

Florenz replies, "Let us go by sea. My mother was a pirate queen and I yearn for the open waves. Though I love reindeer, I have no more taste for midnight rides."

Scene 6: The Scarlet and the White

Town Hall of Ithica
Frige's Day Compline. Night, 24th of March, 1283
Eve of the Feast of the Annunciation (New Year's Eve)

Standing on the top step of the town hall, Mayor Hiram Ulysses sees the baron of Amhirst, wrapped in chains, approach. He bows. With a gentle motion of his hand, he issues his invitation. "Please, step right up, Lord Amhirst. The coroner believes you might enjoy meeting some of my guests."

Soaking wet, wheezing, and with snot dripping from his nose like a leaky faucet, Lord Geoffrey, baron of Amhirst, commander-general of the Aenglish Crown's expeditionary forces in Montroyal, stands before Mayor Hiram Ulysses with the bearing of a conquered conqueror, no less than Vercingetorix before Caesar after the Battle of Alesia. The captain of the tower guard removes the fetters from the baron's wrists but two Ithican guards stand by close enough that their body odor becomes oppressive.

A detachment of town militia, in soaking-wet padded armor and armed to the hilt with spears, swords, crossbows, and long axes, stand inside guarding Sir Sean Madigan. Lord Amhirst notices his herald sitting on the bench with a dejected face.

"Get up!" Amhirst snaps. "This is no time to be warming a bench, Sir Sean. I need you to get your head in the game. Get up, I say!"

Sir Sean pulls himself together and follows his leader. After Amhirst and his herald walk into the room, Mayor Hiram Ulysses speaks up. "Allow me to commend you, Sir Sean, for your loyalty in turning yourself in as our prisoner. Have a seat and allow me to introduce you to some men whose opinions I trust. Ithica's coroner, the Honorable Sir Walter Rally, and Master Ezra Cornwell, chancellor of the Silvermorn College of Sorcerers. At the end of the table is a very holy Dominican friar, Father Peter Sheen. Father Sheen was recently appointed special inquisitor for the Blackflame Heresy in Vinland."

The baron of Amhirst gathers his pride and nods his head before speaking. "What an august gathering! Now, Lord Mayor, can you please explain to me how you dare refuse to quarter the king's troops in your town as is our right by Aenglish Law?"

The coroner steps right up to field that question. "The king's authority has been abused too often throughout his realms. Law-abiding subjects of the Aenglish Crown cannot be forced to quarter troops without their consent. If we let several thousand armed men run loose in this city, they will begin breaking into homes, roasting chickens and pigs for a midnight snack, taking advantage of the womenfolk, and roughing up anyone who stands in their way.

"Before you attacked this Aenglish city, we offered to ask for volunteers and assign your troops quarters, one by one, in an orderly manner."

"Poppycock! You know full well that we'd never be able to house all my troops if we ask for volunteers."

"Aenglish Law is clear. Maybe you were hoping to find a lawyer's excuse to add Ithica to your conquests?"

"Bah! I don't give a goose quill for lawyers. I act in the king's interest. My troops have had a long march.

44

Many are sick. If they are forced to spend the night in the cold and rain, we won't make it to New Yourke—I mean, New Amsturldam—with sufficient forces."

"New Amsturldam has already been conquered and as far as I know, Count Richard Nicolas intends to rename it New Lancaster. Your little slip of the tongue piques my curiosity. You say you're hoping to bring sufficient forces to ... overthrow Count Nicolas, perhaps, and rename the city New Yourke instead?"

Without batting an eyelash, Amhirst deflects the mayor's accurate accusations in a masterful way. "Regrettably, Count Nicolas had a very unfortunate and untimely accident at sea. Sufficient troops will be necessary to restore order in the absence of his leadership since the Viking population is restive and on the edge of rebellion. Only a firm and steady hand will avert more bloodshed.

"From what I hear, the acting governor, Sir Samuel Maverick, has some ... shall we say, 'unorthodox' methods for dealing with dissent. The situation is grave, and I need to get to the scene quickly and with my troops healthy enough to deal with it."

"Dire situation indeed. Please show us the king's orders appointing you mayor of New Amsturldam."

"The crisis is too new, but I assure you—"

The coroner cuts him off mid-sentence with a raised hand. "Yes, yes, I've heard it all. What we have here is a clear case of yet another power-hungry noble abusing the Crown's authority to trample the rights of the king's loyal subjects. Attacking a town loyal to the king is either an act of treason or rebellion. The punishment for both is death. Do you deny the charges?"

The coroner stares straight into the eyes of the baron of Amhirst, clearly hoping to provoke him to act rashly. The baron of Amhirst does not flinch, but calmly takes stock of the situation. He realizes every man at this table hopes for his death except one—the inquisitor.

"You know, politics is never a good conversation topic at the dinner table." With a show of respect, Amhirst turns toward Inquisitor Sheen. "What we should be discussing is the soundness of our religion in Vinland. Can you tell me now, Reverend Inquisitor Sheen, about this Blackflame Heresy and how I, as a loyal son of Holy Mother the Church, can help extirpate this threat to the faith in Vinland?"

Inquisitor Sheen is happy to oblige. He explains, "Fire promotes warmth, light, and life—all symbols of God's goodness. Heretics go around sputtering on about this new discovery they call blackflame, but it is contrary to nature—it chills, hides, and kills. The Cathars in Europa preached a religion where the soul is good and the body is bad."

"Oh, do tell. I know so little about these Cathars."

"The Cathars take their name from the Graec word for pure, *katharos,* but the Graecs are too orthodox to call them pure so they call them *vrykolakas* instead."

The baron of Amhirst, not much of a theologian, puts on a serious face and nods as if he agrees. "*Piña coladas . . . daiquiris . . .* it's all Graec to me. But I can tell that this is all so very serious. We must do something!"

"Indeed," replies the inquisitor. "They finally developed a spiritual technology whereby they are able to purify their own souls from their bodies in this life. They use the blackflame to accomplish this."

Amhirst's eyes widen with comprehension. "So basically, you are telling me that they want to be dead."

Inquisitor Sheen lifts a finger in the air. "Oh no! Not dead . . . undead!"

The baron of Amhirst rubs his chin pensively as he speaks. "You know, dear Father Inquisitor, that my sword has always been at the service of Holy Mother the Church, but these worldly men around us seem bent upon my destruction. If only the Holy Office of the Inquisition could assert its influence in this matter, you would find in me a worthy champion to combat this Blackflame Heresy."

The coroner and the mayor seethe at Amhirst's attempt to undermine their authority through the Church. Seeing the consternation on the faces of the powerful men around the table, Inquisitor Sheen proceeds cautiously and wisely. "As an inquisitor of the Holy Church of Roma, I have no jurisdiction over secular matters here . . ."

The captain of the gate tower guard snickers with glee at that last comment and makes a gesture as if tightening a noose around his neck, then points to Amhirst. They all look at him with irritation over his indiscretion. The captain fakes a burp, puts a fist over his mouth, and mutters, "Excuse me."

The inquisitor continues. "If you should confess your sins, as a priest, I have Christ's authority to absolve you of them. That would not interfere with any punishment the civil authorities might impose."

Amhirst knows there is a way out. "But . . ."

"But," continues the inquisitor. "If you take up the cross against the Blackflame Heresy as a Crusader, it would grant you a plenary indulgence from all temporal and spiritual punishments due to those sins—including the death penalty."

Trying to repress a smile, the baron of Amhirst lifts his eyebrows in a show of theatrical piety and hopes on his life that the inquisitor will go with it. "Yes, a plenary indulgence is just what my soul needs about now. I confess that I have greatly sinned and I sincerely repent of it all. Before you all, I take up the cross and the Crusader's vow to never return home until the Blackflame Heresy is wiped from the face of Vinland."

The inquisitor holds up his hand to restrain the baron's enthusiasm. "The efforts of valiant Crusaders over the past two centuries have been stifled by insincere oath-takers and weak-willed Christians. Before agreeing to bestow upon you the Crusader's cross, I must put your resolve to the test.

"An informant has tipped me off that a heretic is currently visiting the fire elf community at Tuscoraura Mountain. He goes by the name of Johnny Appleseed."

All the notables in the room gasp. Mayor Ulysses exclaims, "But he's such a kindly old man!"

The inquisitor raises his hand to silence the objectors. "We have many undeniable reports of crazed, undead wendigos infesting the forests around Tuscoraura Mountain. Wendigos arise from blackflame rituals, and Johnny Appleseed is handing out blackflame wherever he goes. He must be stopped!"

Inquisitor Sheen gives out harsh looks. "Not a single one of you gentlemen sitting around this table feels he has the time, money, or manpower to escort me safely through the goblin king's territories between here and Tuscoraura Mountain to investigate. I declare by the authority that Holy Mother the Church has invested in me that if the baron of Amhirst can provide suitable soldiers to escort me safely to Tuscoraura Mountain with haste, I will grant him the Crusader's cross and a plenary indulgence, exempting him from any of the punishments you may have had in mind for him. We must reach Tuscoraura Mountain before Appleseed eludes our grasp once again."

A cunning grin returns to the gate tower captain and he says, "That goblin king, Gog the Destroyer, ain't much of a king, but boy, he's got the 'destroyer' part down all right. Waren't a single goblin who took a liking to Gog in them Magog forests but they's all scared witless of him. Them goblins ain't happy until they got some sicko as king who whips the snot out of 'em day and night.

"Mark my words, you go traipsin' through them irreverent lands with a man of God and you's invitin' a right ugly death. Ain't no army going to save you. I betcha, they ain't enough miracles in the Bible to get y'all there and back again alive."

The inquisitor is unfazed. "Miracles, my dear captain, are God's calling cards. As a man of God, I deal in them every day."

The tough captain chokes out a cynical laugh. "Like I says, sorry I's got to be the one to break the bad news to ya, but miracles ain't good enough—not when it comes to Gog and his Magog goblins."

A loud bang at the door startles the gathering. The captain of the guards races to the door to check out the disturbance. No sooner does he touch the door than it breaks off its hinges and crashes into the captain's face. Sir John Henry, a heavily muscled ranger of Aphrican origins, slams the door clear off its jambs with his massive wooden mallet. He steps inside the room, and more leather-armored rangers flood in behind him.

Master Cornwell quickly lifts a lodestone rod from under his robes to ward off the invaders but his sorcery only sends the steel blades and mail on the Ithica town guards flying backward. The rangers have no steel on them—being clad in leather armor and brandishing wooden mallets, clubs, quarterstaves, and bows with bone or silver-tipped arrows. Having experienced the mayhem caused by three hundred budding sorcerers at the walls, Sir Robert Roger and his rangers are a little worse for wear, but all the wiser.

The brawny ranger Sir Jim Bowey holds a large silver knife, whose sleek design would later become the pattern for his famous line of Bowey knives. Neither source stones nor magica wands have any effect on silver but somehow, silver has a devastating effect upon the undead. Sir Jim Bowey was not the first to discover this, but the silver war knives he would go on to craft after his retirement from adventuring have since become extremely popular with young adventurers.

Capitalizing on the element of surprise and taking full advantage of the agility their light armor affords them, the rangers quickly surround and knock out of the fight any remaining town guards. The Erinish bard among the rangers, Sir Gilbert Sullivan, skilled in *bataireacht*, and hefting a huge blackthorn shillelagh, pounces on Chancellor Cornwell and his battlesage bodyguards, knocking the lodestone rod from the chancellor's hand and kicking the other two over. "Now don't be makin' a fuss, gentlemen. Methinks it wouldn't sit well with the missus to hear that I knocked about such noble bollixes as yourselves."

The mayor and the coroner hardly get a chance to stand up and spin their heads around the room before they find their hands tied behind their backs. Sir Robert Roger shoves them back into their seats and hovers over them menacingly. "Thank you for the warm welcome, Mister Mayor and Honorable Sir Coroner, but I know you have other guests coming. The baron and my boys are sick and tired of crashing parties."

The mayor cries out, "How did you manage to get in here? The only way in is through Easy Street, and I've posted more guards there than along all the other roads in Ithica combined!"

Sir Robert Roger points out the back window. "The road to Easy Street goes through the sewer."

Amhirst twirls his fingers gracefully in the air. "But wait, my valiant ranger captain! The mayor and I have just come to an agreement. You and your company of rangers are about to become the secular arm of the Holy Inquisition to root out the Blackflame Heresy from Vinland."

"Why would setting a different color fire make someone a heretic?" Sir Robert Roger asks, still trying to process why the baron is trying to call off this overwhelmingly successful rescue mission.

"Permit me to explain," interrupts Inquisitor Sheen. "The Tuscoraura elves were using blackflame to dabble in necromancy. Their goal was to raise up an army of obedient thralls. Instead, they reanimated crazed, blood-thirsty undead wights called wendigos who hate life in every form. They kill trees, animals, and innocent travelers. The Holy Office of the Inquisition took all sources of blackflame from the elves to stop them but Johnny Appleseed seems to be offering them a new source of it. He must be arrested and questioned before the elves return to necromancy and stir up any more unnatural troubles in the heart of Vinland."

Sir Robert Roger still cannot believe it. "Why would such a nice old man have so sinister intentions?"

"Under the guise of seeking reform, he has shaken the Church in Vinland to its foundations, claiming to build a New Church. What arrogance and pride! We suspect that he has already seduced the famous archbishop of Fort Detroit to his ways, and he must be stopped before any more important ecclesiastical figures are led astray."

The baron of Amhirst puts on a piteous frown. "This is a grave threat indeed! I put my troops at your disposition, Holy Inquisitor. But alas! A great many of them lie out in the roads and fields around Ithica, exposed to the rain and chill. They are cold, tired, sick, and wounded. If only we could find suitable housing from the elements! Surely then I could spare these dauntless rangers to do God's work."

Inquisitor Sheen announces to the edgy men around him, "David entered the house of God, and he and his companions ate the consecrated bread, which was not lawful for them to do, but only for the priests.

"Vow to send these rangers of yours to Tuscoraura Mountain and I will have the respective rectors open Holy Savior Benedictine Monastery and the Church of the Annunciation to house your troops—after we repose the Blessed Sacrament to a secure location, of course. Your troops will receive protection from the elements, warm soup, and fresh blankets. The monks and clerics will tend to the sick and wounded."

With almost child-like glee, the baron of Amhirst says, "God has answered our prayer for deliverance! Sir Robert Roger, take your rangers to protect Inquisitor Sheen all the way to Tuscoraura Mountain and back."

The coroner interrupts the jubilation of the moment, saying, "One month, Lord Amhirst! If your rangers fail to show up here in one month, we will have the right to nullify your crusading vow—and send your head to the chopping block."

Inquisitor Sheen stomps his foot impatiently. "Enough bickering! The heretic Johnny Appleseed has slipped through our fingers too many times. We will leave at first light in the morning. Rangers, are you ready to take up the cross?"

Sir William McIntosh swipes an apple off the table and tells the baron, "You know, no one could stop us if we decided to just uptail with the wind and blow out of here scot-free."

The baron of Amhirst is having none of it. "I gladly submit to imprisonment at the hands of these men. The delays I face in reaching New Yourke—um, New Amsturldam—are insignificant compared to the blessing of having the Holy Inquisition as an ally."

Scene 7: Mere Magiculture

Reflecting Pool at Thor's Base, Shentalpee City
Frige's Day Evening, 24ᵗʰ of March, 1283
Eve of the Feast of the Annunciation (New Year's Eve)

A harmonious female voice in concert with her harp resonates high on Tuscoraura Mountain with a purity and range that would make the best practitioners of Celtic music tear up with awe at its beauty. Sighing elves listen and watch as Zena treads lightly across the aromatic pine boards in her flowing, white evening gown toward the colony's only magica tree.

Sprouting from a large, ornate ceramic pot, the magica tree sits in the middle of a reflecting pool wide enough that no one can approach within ten feet of the tree without climbing into the pool. Its stem is dark blue and the innermost leaves are a lush green. As the branches unfurl farther from the stem, the leaves yellow out a little until they start blending into a Halloween orange. The outermost leaves are bright red with violet tips, like fireworks. Hanging beneath the most mature branches are tiny golden fruit buds.

Five feet above the magica tree, an aqueduct curves past the colossal statue of Thor that overlooks the outdoor theater. Cool, clear mineral water springs from the heart of Tuscoraura Mountain and cascades down the aqueduct into the reflecting pool. A rainbow weaves in and out of the mist as it showers the pool with its glowing crystal droplets.

With a gentle, graceful motion, Zena steps up onto the ledge of the pool, singing and playing the harp.

Her music finds the melody that stirs a long-lost dream in Johnny Appleseed's heart. Maybe it was his first love, his awkward eloquence in chasing her with a frog, and her rambunctious innocence in making him kiss it that left such a fond but forgotten memory. Or perhaps it was the day God the Father first lifted his soul up to the seventh heaven and locked inside it the sure faith that good will overcome evil in the end.

Whatever it is that holds him, Dungaree Jeanne's words bring him out of the nostalgic trance. "My dear Zena's teenage years have been bumpy, but she has a good heart and it comes through in her voice. The songs she sings are ancient elf lullabies preserved in our tradition from mother to child, but she breathes a minty freshness into them by her heartfelt passion to cherish the gifts of nature and to use them for the good of all."

Johnny Appleseed feels some culture shock when he sees Zena descend into the reflecting pool, wading her way toward the magica tree. He agrees, saying, "As we say in Kentikie, her voice could soften a hardened criminal's liver like a wad of butter on a hot griddle. Still, that's the first time I have seen a girl in her right mind go sloshing around in a public fountain pool without any sergeants trying to arrest her."

"She has a license to tame the magica tree. Any gruff move or threatening stance toward it makes the tree vanish. A gentle gait, calm demeanor, and soothing presence can get a person close enough to cull one of the branches before it disappears. Mage Nittany, the dean of Pinne Mage University, has witnessed Mademoiselle Zena touch this same magica tree before. She will come back in a few weeks to observe her.

"If Mademoiselle Zena successfully cuts off a magica branch, then Mage Nittany will help her turn it into a magica wand and allow her to start her apprenticeship as a freshman magicultor at Pinne Mage University."

"Good for her. My, my, look how that aqueduct spits out its waters so high above the pool! Every time the wind blows, it drizzles all over the platform."

An immensely proud mother, Dungaree Jeanne cannot help telling him everything she knows about magiculture, even though she has an inkling that Johnny Appleseed might know more about magica trees than he's letting on. "Magica trees only grow beneath waterfalls because they need the rainbow light refracted through the spray. That's why you see all those glass prisms dangling from the sides of the aquifer. Taste and see how refreshing this water is."

Dungaree Jeanne picks up a cup off a small stand with twenty or so white ceramic cups on black iron ring holders around the center staff, making it look like a little black-and-white Christmas tree. She scoops some spring water up to the brim and hands it to Appleseed.

The good reverend takes a sip and smiles with a gleam in his eyes. "Mmmm. 'Whosoever shall give you a cup of water to drink in my name,' Christ says, 'she shall not lose her reward.' I am deeply honored that you invited me and most grateful for your kindness to me. May the Lord bless you and your family."

Out of the corner of her eye, she spots a group of rowdy teenagers gathered around the umpire-in-chief. "I fear our Council of Perfects was more open to your gift of blackflame than to hearing you preach God's word. They're very hostile towards Christianity."

"Saint Paul built tents so he could work and live among those who were not open to hearing God's word. I give out apples and blackflame so every corner of Vinland can hear the good news."

Staring absently at them for a brief moment, Dungaree Jeanne sees Enganyon wearing crutches with a big cast around his foot. He nods to Umpire Kibbler and then starts moving toward them with a purpose, followed by a dozen or more other high elf teenagers.

Dungaree Jeanne instantly snaps out of her trance. "Reverend Appleseed! Permit me to take you on a walking tour of our beautiful city before dinner. It will help you work up an appetite and will leave you with some fond memories to cherish. We get a lot of honeymooners visiting here. They call Tuscoraura's treetop colony the Venice of the Skies."

Reverend Johnny Appleseed thinks about that last statement for a moment. "Venison pies? None for me, thank you. Sounds delicious, but I don't eat deer."

Dungaree Jeanne stops and thinks for a moment. "Oh! Not at all! We don't eat deer either. Deer are sacred in our culture since we ride them."

Johnny Appleseed asks, "Are there many vegetarians in Shentalpee City?"

As Enganyon's teens get closer, her danger instincts set off alarms ringing out loud in every corner of her skull. She drags Reverend Appleseed off in the opposite direction and comments, "Some high elves do refrain from eating meat entirely, but most are out for blood."

They walk quickly and take frequent turns until they lose sight of Enganyon's gang of teens.

Glittering in her misty-moon blue, diamond-studded evening gown, Dungaree Jeanne strides out across a suspension bridge away from Thor's Base. Even as the suspension bridge wobbles under her brisk steps, her gait and upright posture never waver.

Neither rushed nor hesitating, her hips sway on high heels that tread lightly and decisively on the wood planks beneath her. Lesser men would have easily been enchanted by the influence of her unrelenting femininity and fallen on one knee by now to profess their ardent love, but Johnny Appleseed walks behind her with a cheerful innocence.

She glides up a set of stairs with the stamina of a professional athlete, but Johnny Appleseed does not allow her to outpace him. His highly ambulant lifestyle keeps him firm and fit, even in graying old age.

Johnny Appleseed asks, "Who was the boy on crutches following us?"

Although she's been trying to downplay their evasive maneuvers, Dungaree Jeanne is not entirely surprised that he knows exactly why they've been rushing around in their tour of Shentalpee City.

She sighs. "That was the monsieur Enganyon. He's the son of one of the most powerful high elves in Shentalpee City. My dear Zena and Mademoiselle Florenz have been best of friends for most of their childhood, but between the election and the monsieur Enganyon's charms, they've been at odds lately.

"It's really a shame because my husband died before my dear Zena was born and Umpire Kibbler has been the only father figure she's ever known. He's really encouraged her to follow her dreams."

Johnny Appleseed gives her a compassionate nudge. "Believe me when I tell you from personal experience that God makes himself the best Father a child could ever need when we invite him into our hearts with child-like trust and simplicity of heart."

"Yes, I believe it. But my dear Zena never invited God into her heart so it's very empty right now. She's trying to fill it with a powerful boyfriend and an even more powerful position in our government. She wants whatever she can't have and because of it, I'm afraid she'll lose all the happiness I've worked so hard to provide for her."

"It sounds like you've got a lot weighing on your mind. Hope my visit won't make it any harder on you."

"Do you know what I do when I feel the weight of the world on my shoulders? Come, I will show you."

Dungaree Jeanne walks even faster up a long flight of wooden stairs. When they reach the top, she waltzes across a garden patio and sweeps her right arm across the cityscape below. "Perfect peace abides up here. The sky can never belong to despots. People grovel to the powerful and carry out all manner of atrocities, but one hundred fifty feet above the ground their power ceases, their influence fades, their authority disappears.

"Ah, Reverend, to live in the heart of the sky! Let your imagination soar! Set your fantasies free up here where no one can take you down!"

Johnny Appleseed approaches the ledge and looks at the skyline that sets Dungaree Jeanne's fantasy free.

The glowing, red horizon behind the setting sun lends fascinating hues of pastel yellow, deep blue, and purple majesty to the scene. The evergreen sequoias sprout girders and trestles across one base after another like a skyward paradise floating on clouds. The forest floor is so far down he can't even see it in the dim shadows of the rising moonlight.

As he leans on the elf-sized railing gazing out into the picturesque scenery all around him, the high elf teenagers reconvene behind him. This time they have a large dog with them. They giggle and snicker and set the dog loose on him. The dog's body mass and velocity hold enough momentum to carry Johnny Appleseed over the ledge. The good reverend does not seem to notice the dog coming at him.

Dungaree Jeanne hears the heavy thumps of the snarling dog's paws as it barrels toward her guest. She turns her head to look—the dog is about to make Umpire Kibbler's prophecy about tall men falling over low railings come true.

She screams.

Johnny Appleseed's eyes flick over to his screaming friend and follow her panicked gaze to the ferocious dog racing at him. He raises his hands up to the heavens in prayer and the next moment, the dog turns docile, padding up to him at a gentle trot. It starts sniffing his pant legs. Reverend Appleseed pets the friendly animal and it begins to rub its tush up against his knees. The teenagers disappear into the evening twilight.

Dungaree Jeanne stops screaming and swallows hard. Still panting, she asks, "What just happened?"

"Oh, this poor little fellow is just hungry."

"That's not what I saw. I know that dog and he's become quite wild of late. He was about to attack you. With a wave of your hands you calmed him down. Do you have some kind of power over wild beasts?"

"It was just a little miracle. Not to us, O Lord, not to us but to your name give the glory. You could say I'm a Christian druid. I spend a lot of time in the wilderness and often pray the prayer of Daniel in the lions' den. Miracles happen all the time if you have faith enough to notice.

"By the way, you mentioned that you know this dog. What's his name?"

"His name's Fido. He's Old Mother Hubbard's dog. The Hubbard clan was once the wealthiest and most powerful of the high elves at Tuscoraura; now she can't even afford a bone for her dog, so he started going around begging. The high elves don't like stray dogs and treated him roughly. Ever since then the dog has had a mean streak."

Johnny Appleseed rubs the dog's shoulders and chin, asking, "Are there some scraps around here that we can offer our sweet little Fido?"

Dungaree Jeanne finally calms down her breathing and suggests, "Let's head back to the garden party. The Council of Perfects is sponsoring a boar roast on the council chamber's front steps out of the public funds. We could throw him a bone."

Johnny Appleseed shakes his finger at the dog. "Sit here, Fido, and we'll bring you a little treat if you're a good doggie."

Fido sits and wags his tail, licking his lips as if he knows he's won a treat from the tall visitor.

The public festivities to celebrate Appleseed's visit are quite an extravaganza, although the good reverend himself was not specifically invited to the party. To honor their guest's gift of apple seeds, they have placed an apple in the boar's mouth and baked several apple pies. Umpire Kibbler has provided a large number of soft-baked cocoa chunk cookies and spiced chokecherry cider out of his own personal funds. To make the occasion memorable, he has declared the reception dinner open to wood elves as well.

Well-paid, armored dwarves act as elevator operators, courtesy staff, bodyguards, and bouncers all in one, making sure the right people—and only the right people—make it onto Thor's Base without a hitch.

Posh, black-robed halflings with slicked-back, dark, wavy hair and white sashes carry trays with hors d'oeuvres and amuse-gueules, pickled fish eggs, goat hoof paste, and other elven delicacies.

While Dungaree Jeanne asks the caterers to provide her with a spare bone for the dog and a tasty treat for her guest, Johnny Appleseed leans over the edge and swallows hard. Quite a long way down!

She brings him a spinach quiche pie and he nibbles it gratefully. "Thank you, ma'am. As we say in Kentikie, praise the Lord and pass the gravy."

Dungaree Jeanne tugs his arm. "Come! There's one other place you must see. It's called Worship Base."

After delivering the bone to an effusively grateful Fido, they cross a few more suspension bridges and reach Worship Base. Dungaree Jeanne tells him, "The other twelve bases have only one sacred space each, but Worship Base has several large temples. Over there is the Temple of Saturn, which serves as a hub for trading with passing vendors and traveling merchants. My appointment as Dungaree of Foreign Trade entitles me to an office on the second floor.

"That rounded building is the Temple of Bragi, which we call the radial city music hall because of its round shape and the supporting arches that radiate from it. We hold most of our concerts there. Elves are brilliant musicians and my dear daughter, Zena, has perfect pitch, so she is much sought after even at her young age.

"And down there is the Temple of Astrea, which is an observatory for the stars. Oh, look! The first star is starting to twinkle. Make a wish!" she suggests politely.

"I don't see it." Appleseed points up to the heavens, hoping to locate it. "Is it over yonder somewhere?"

Dungaree Jeanne grimaces. "You're not supposed to point at stars. It's bad luck. Just look.

"See! It's that little star twinkling over there, so high up above the world, like a diamond in the firmament. Astrologers say that starlight is the fifth element—

aether—but Christians say that the stars are angels singing God's praises, isn't that right?"

Johnny Appleseed says, "It's true that when Christ was born in Bethlehem, the angels filled the heavens with light and sang, 'Glory to God in the highest, and on Earth, peace to people of goodwill.' As to what the stars are made of, I can only wonder."

"So did you make a wish?"

"Oh, a guy like me does not get wishes from stars,"

"They say it makes no difference who you are. When you wish upon a star, your dreams come true! What are your dreams?" Dungaree Jeanne prods as if to remind him of an important lesson from his childhood.

"Well, I have a dream that one day every valley shall be exalted, every hill and mountain shall be made low, the rough places will be made plain, and the crooked places will be made straight, and the glory of the Lord shall be revealed, and all flesh shall see it together—humans, elves, dwarves, halflings, goblins, and trolls. We are all sons and daughters of Adam and Eve, and Jesus died for us all, light and dark-skinned, green-skinned and pink."

"Wow! What a noble wish! But come, it's getting late. You're invited to stay at Betzy Rose Mansion, my home, for as long as you wish. It's not far from here."

"Thank you for your hospitality. As a rule, I only stay in one place as long as I'm needed, then I have to move on. My hope is to end hunger and spread the good word to all of Vinland. I'll have to leave bright and early in the morning."

Dungaree Jeanne peers out into the forest one more time. "Then please, take a moment to soak it all in. There's so much beauty around us for just two eyes to see. Oh, if I were a painter I don't know which I'd paint—the calling of the ancient aethereal stars or the assembling of the angels above the saints.

"And see there! The mountains are drifting off to sleep with the innocence of children. What a gorgeous evening!"

Johnny Appleseed looks over the ledge with her. "Boy, we're mighty high up. It makes my head dizzy."

"We call that vertigo," Dungaree Jeanne explains. "Live here long enough and you'll hardly feel it."

Just then, the rowdy group of teenage elves reappears. Though hobbling on crutches Enganyon manages to strut forward, showing off his fancy white tunic and blue denim pants with black boots. His slicked-back, half-braided, platinum-blond hair sparks envy and awe within the gang of teens.

Dungaree Jeanne greets him in Runic to keep it all very formal. "Good evening, Monsieur Enganyon, so nice to see that thou art wearing the blue variety of my denim pantaloons. What service might I render thee this fine evening?"

Balancing on one foot, Enganyon slaps his hip and replies in the common tongue, Eldric, "Yeah, I'm wearing my blue dungaree's for you, Jeanne. Blue is your favorite color, right?"

Dungaree Jeanne maintains her speech in Runic. "Thou shalt address me as Madame Dungaree, young elf. Now, if thou hast no further business with us, please step aside."

Enganyon snickers and says in Eldric, "Me and my buddies here just wanted to personally extend a few words of welcome to your Christian guest. It's very nice of him to give us all that blackflame for free."

She sighs and says with one-half exasperation and the other half sarcasm in Runic, "How courteous of thee! But unfortunately, thou hast never bothered to learn Aenglish."

Enganyon just smirks and hops over to Johnny Appleseed anyway. "No worries, Madame Dungaree," he retorts. "There's always the universal language of friendly gestures." With that, he lurches off his crutches and swings around delivering what is supposed to look like a heartfelt pat on the back but ends up being a hand-whipping whack.

The less-than-gentle blow propels the good reverend forward over the ledge, giving him a truly breathtaking view of the one-hundred-fifty-foot drop as he plummets downward.

Enganyon leans over the railing and mumbles out loud, "Oops, that's gonna hurt—if he survives . . ."

ACT II

WEE WEE WEE
ALL THE WAY HOME

Scene 1: Woolly Monastics

Juniata River Bend
Twelve Miles Northwest of Tuscoraura Mountain
Spy Woden's Day Prime
Early Morning, 5th of April, 1284

"Ite missa est," concludes the white-robed Inquisitor Sheen. His eyes convey sincere piety but also carry a war-weary pluck of worldly pragmatism. Having celebrated Mass on a tree stump, he reads out the psalms from his breviary to three odd-looking friars.

Several rangers who attended the inquisitor's Mass stand up and ready their gear for another day's march. Sir Kip Karlson, the only halfling ranger in the company, remarks to his companions, "First time in my life I get to hear the Bible every day."

"Yeah, almost heaven," replies Dame Frances Marian, the only female ranger in the company. She surveys the area with one hand on her brow. "We'll need all the prayers we can get. See the blue streaks on those mountain ridges across the Juniata River? Those are goblin territorial markings, older than the trees. They'll be lurking behind us soon enough . . ."

Sir Robert Roger did not attend the Mass but comes striding over quickly and barks, "Get ready, Priest; we have a long march ahead of us today."

"Thank you, Sir Ranger. My companions and I will finish reciting the psalms shortly," replies the inquisitor.

Oddly for this epoch, his three companion friars are mismatched in color, but they are all even more oddly mismatched in their backstories. The inquisitor himself is a somewhat tallish dwarf, a hair above five feet tall, conventionally handsome by any standard with a plain but dignified gray beard. His white robes signify membership in the Dominican order of preachers.

His first companion, Brother Umbert, is an unusually short halfling Franciscan friar, a gnome of mixed Lutin and Folletto ancestry, standing barely three and a half feet tall. He wears reddish-brown robes. The halfling serves as the inquisitor's scribe, traveling magicultor, and scholar of ancient lore.

The inquisitor's second companion, Brother Indigo, is a giant from the Mohawk Nation, standing an inch over seven feet high. Missing his right arm and wearing a patch over his right eye, he is dressed in the purplish-gray robes of the Tironensian order. His role as porter technically makes him the spokesman for the group, but his actual job is more eloquently summed up in the bulging muscles on his left arm and the huge club tucked just beneath it.

The inquisitor's third companion, Brother Crowe, is an average-height Aenglish human monk wearing the black robes of the Benedictine order. He serves as the group's cook and purser. At one time a thief himself, he guards the group's purse from his former colleagues.

Brother Crowe's transition from the streets into the monastery was not a smooth one but thanks to patient mentorship, this man's talents now serve the Lord well.

The four clerics of the Inquisition, though different in so many ways, stand together firmly.

Sir Robert Roger fumes. "We don't have time to wait around for you to babble on with your prayers. We have to cover ground quickly to avoid the goblin wildhunters lurking in these forests."

Brother Umbert interrupts them. "Excuse me, Sir Robert Roger, but you always seem to rush us when it's time to pray, saying we have to avoid goblins. But I don't think you even know where the goblins are."

Brother Umbert's balding head retains only a thin wisp of bright-red hair that dangles in the middle of his forehead, but it is enough to call him a fiery redhead. Gnomes average about four and a half feet in height but a Folletto, a gnome from the island of Sycilie, normally only reaches about four feet when full-grown. At three and a half feet, one might say that being extra-short among a tribe of extra-short people has added an extra layer of spunk to Brother Umbert's temper.

"Of course I do! Just follow those country roads and they'll be all over you lickety-split." Sir Robert Roger waves his hand off to the south.

Brother Umbert rubs his chin. "Hmm, all my memories tell me we've been heading down those same country roads for the past two days. If I didn't know better, I'd say you're leading us right to them."

Inquisitor Sheen raises his voice. "That's quite enough, Brother Umbert! I am sure the rangers have an adequate defensive plan in place. How many more days before we reach the elf settlement, Sir Ranger?"

"Don't worry, Priest. I'll get you to the place you belong," Sir Robert Roger mutters.

Brother Umbert pipes up again, his face turning red. "You know what I think? I think you have no idea where Tuscoraura Mountain really is!"

Sir Robert Roger shoots back, "The whole point of a hidden elf colony is that it's *hidden*. You don't just walk in the front door over the welcome mat. They know how to keep outsiders out."

"So you keep interrupting our prayers just so you can blow around like a breeze, hoping to stumble upon a hidden elf colony?"

"Brother Umbert, silence!" Inquisitor Sheen cuts him off. Turning to Sir Robert Roger he says calmly, "Sir Ranger, Johnny Appleseed has eluded us time and time again. We are eager to reach Tuscoraura Mountain before he leaves, but prayer is essential to our mission. Please just tell us how you plan to get us to the elf colony without being attacked by goblins?"

Sir Robert Roger shrugs his shoulders. "We'll send out scouts to pinpoint exactly where to head next. It's typical military strategy."

Brother Umbert starts getting personal. "Your knowledge of military strategy is quite shabby if you plan to send your troops out to get hacked apart by goblin lurkers piecemeal."

Sir Robert Roger walks over to him and invades the halfling's personal space with his tall and muscular physique. "For your information, imp, I wrote the book on military strategy for rangers."

Brother Umbert snarls, "Yeah, I know. I read it, and I wasn't impressed."

"You think you're so smart, don't you?"

"Let me put it this way. Have you ever heard of Plato, Aristotle, Socrates?"

Sir Robert Roger narrows his eyes. "You're a moron if you think you're smarter than those guys."

Brother Umbert pushes the tall ranger back. "Well, this moron has read them all in the original Graec. I even reconstructed Aristotle's second book of the *Poetics* from the fragments at a cemetery in Praga."

Inquisitor Sheen steps in sternly. "Whoa! That's quite enough out of you, Brother Umbert. How many times must I echo that warning from the book of Proverbs: pride comes before the fall? Instead of arguing about how smart you are, you should keep a humble silence. We're going to pray for guidance by the Holy Spirit to show us the way."

Sir Robert Roger throws his hands up into the air with outrage. "Oh, come on! This is ridiculous! We don't have time to waste with saying prayers! I am the military professional here and I give the orders."

Inquisitor Sheen shakes his head and calmly replies, "We are not military professionals, so we cannot risk a confrontation with goblins. When your scouts find a safe route to Tuscoraura Mountain, we'll follow your lead. In the meantime, we'll plan on staying here and praying for God to send us guidance."

Sir Robert Roger says, "You go ahead and wait for a miracle. But as for me, I'm going to put my faith in a keen eye and sound military tactics. We'll see who gets us there first."

The inquisitor resumes reading the psalms to his companions while Sir Robert Roger organizes teams of scouts to search for the elf colony.

About an hour after the ranger scouting parties have departed, Inquisitor Sheen sends Brother Indigo, the Mohawk giant in purplish-gray robes, to refill their waterskins at the Juniata River. Once a famous warrior, Brother Indigo lost his right arm and right eye in battle. Lacking depth perception and having to relearn to handle a weapon with his left hand sent him into a deep depression until he turned to prayer. He realized the glory won by following warlords into battle in this life is of little worth compared to the glory of following Christ along the way of the cross into the next.

That spiritual revelation pulled him out of his depression and led him to join the Abbey of Tiron near his home village of Ossernenon. Years later, the abbot received orders from one of the Lord High Papal Inquisitors in Vinland, Maderno Cardinal Orsini, to release Brother Indigo from the abbey to serve as porter for Inquisitor Sheen. Nobody had to guess why the Mohawk monk had been singled out for service.

When he reaches the river, he puts the waterskins down and dips them one by one under the water.

A gray-haired elf strolls up next to him and says, "You don't want to be drinking out of the Juniata River. It's dark and dusty. I can show you some real potable water, blue as if it were painted on the sky."

Without looking up, Brother Indigo says, "I am a stranger to blue water."

The elf kneels down to scoop a handful of water from the river and tastes the water with a big slurp. "Hmmm, told you so. It's got that misty taste of moonshine, so bitter that it puts a teardrop in the eye. How about you give me a few biscuits from your pouch and I'll show you where the sweet water is?"

Ignoring him, Brother Indigo stands up and starts to tie the waterskins together. The hungry old elf tugs on the sleeve of his only arm, begging silently. Brother Indigo asks him, "Can you take us home?"

"And where might home be?"

Brother Indigo says simply, "Home is the place where you belong. We have plenty of food to share."

The gray-haired elf snaps his fingers. "Come to think of it, these mountains remind me that I should have been home yesterday. All I need are a few loaves of bread, a slab or two of meat and some cheese . . . oh, it's been quite a while since I've had any cheese."

Instead of negotiating, Brother Indigo just picks up all four waterskins and walks back to the camp.

The elf takes fright seeing the armed rangers and runs off to climb a tree. Brother Crowe hears the rustling in the trees and spots him immediately. With the excitement of an answered prayer, he points up with his finger and shouts out, "An elf!"

The inquisitor's party follows his finger with their eyes up to the gray-haired elf sitting on the branch of a large elm tree above the rangers' campsite, like a wise old owl ready to offer advice on taking licks at life.

"So you want me to take you to my home?" the elf says in fluent Aenglish with a distinct Elvish accent.

Inquisitor Sheen smiles at him. "Ah, welcome, sir elf! Yes, we are hoping to visit Tuscoraura Mountain."

The elf returns the smile like a merchant used to charming customers. "Tuscoraura Mountain, is it? Your purple-robed giant of a monk asked me about taking him to my home but he never asked me where my home is. As a matter of fact, it is quite a chore to get him to say anything at all."

"The friars on my staff have taken a vow of silence. Brother Indigo is our porter, so he is allowed to offer introductions and extend words of greeting to guests." Giving Brother Umbert a dirty look, the inquisitor adds, "Unfortunately, he is the only one in our brotherhood with a penchant for silence."

The elf snickers. "So he's a one-eyed, one-armed, giant purple people greeter who doesn't like to talk?"

Dame Frances Marian peers over her lunch and sees Inquisitor Sheen talking up into the trees. She spots the elf that managed to sneak past the rangers' lookouts. Alarmed at the security breach, she yells. "To arms!"

Hearing the call, the startled rangers drop their stew and scramble for their weapons. They lick the grease off the tips of their fingers, string their bows, and notch their arrows, pointing them at the elf. Sir Robert Roger is outraged and shouts, "Who let him in?"

Seeing all the fuss and the arrows pointed at him, the elf swings down from the elm tree and hits the ground with amazing agility for his age. He swiftly rolls behind Brother Indigo and begs, "Please, Mister purple people greeter, don't let them shoot me!"

Inquisitor Sheen is quick to respond. "Sir Robert Roger, order your rangers to stand down."

Sir Robert Roger snorts. "It's just a short, pigeon-toed, undergrown elf. He's no threat to us."

The gray-haired elf swaggers and struts over to Sir Robert Roger as if he just won a bout of armed combat. "You're not so tough!"

Seeing trouble brewing, Brother Crowe hurriedly whisks the elf away from the ranger captain and offers him some stew. The elf takes the stew and gobbles it down as if he has not eaten in a week. "Mmm ummm. This sure is some fine eating. But that's not the reason I came down to land in your camp. I can guide this ragtag band of yours to the Tuscoraura elf colony—for a price. Can you pay?"

"Well, bless the Lord my soul!" Inquisitor Sheen proclaims. "You are the answer to our prayers. May I ask your name, kind sir?"

"Master Shoemaker Gulliber Swiffson of Clan Adidazar, at your service. I can guide you to the Tuscoraura elves if you bag up some of this delicious stew for me and my party of adventurers over yonder."

Inquisitor Sheen is more than happy to oblige. "Indeed, this is our bursar and our cook, Brother Crowe. He will pack some up to bring to your friends."

"Much obliged; but what's a bursar?"

An unremarkable man of average build, most people find Brother Crowe's long, jet-black hair greased back and thin goatee more creepy than charming. Even the way he wears his Benedictine robe with its large, black cowl gives off the impression of a shadowy hood rather than a prayer shawl. Some habits die hard.

Inquisitor Sheen explains, "Our vow of poverty requires us to share all our wealth. As our bursar, Brother Crowe carries the communal purse. He handles the money and provisions for our brotherhood."

Master Gulliber squints at the slick-haired bursar with the curly handlebar mustache and the pointy chin puff. "He sure looks strange to me . . ."

Inquisitor Sheen adds, "All the same, he is one of us. You and your party can share our food and we will pay you a fair wage for acting as our guide. Now, can you take us to Tuscoraura Mountain?"

"Well, the Tuscoraura elves are a private people," says Master Gulliber as he gobbles down a second bowl of stew. "Technically, it's against the law to lead an outsider in without a formal invitation from the Council of Perfects. But I think we can work something out. As my wife always says—actually, I hear her voice now, she's calling me. Gentlemen, begging your pardon, but I must take my leave. I'll talk it over with her and let you know our answer in the morning."

Brother Crowe hands him a medieval doggie bag to carry out the stew. Master Gulliber bows and says, "Much obliged, Frater."

To celebrate the miraculous appearance of the elf, Inquisitor Sheen pulls out his rosary beads and invites the company to pray together in thanksgiving to the Lord for hearing their prayers.

Sir Robert Roger interrupts the celebration abruptly. "Okay, Priest, your friar just unwittingly led an elf straight into our camp. We need to tighten up security and implement some new procedures if we are going to make it to Tuscoraura Mountain alive."

Brother Umbert, his face reddening with anger, speaks up instantly. "You just saw how our prayers were answered. Instead of apologizing, you become even more insufferable."

Sir Robert Roger puffs out his chest. "So what about this vow of silence I keep hearing about? How's that working out for you, Brother Umbert?"

Straightening his back, Brother Umbert squeaks out in his nasally, lisping tone, trying to sound assertive, "You are a bully, and I have always made a point of standing up to bullies."

"No wonder it worked! At your height, they must have thought you were kneeling to them."

Inquisitor Sheen intervenes. "Brother Umbert!"

Brother Umbert looks back and forth from Inquisitor Sheen and Sir Robert Roger as if struggling to control his temper when suddenly, his eyes bulge wide open. "Uh, Father Sheen . . ."

"Brother Umbert, I order you to keep silence!"

"But this is an emergency."

"What? You mean you have to relieve yourself in the woods?"

He stutters. "No, too late for that!" As the midsection of his brown robe trickles with a growing dark spot and yellow liquid drips down his legs, his lips quiver and he whimpers, "Goblins! Everywhere!"

Scene 2: The Great Raspberry

Wood Elf Village Leading off Fennel Base
Spy Woden's Day Terce. Morning, 5th of April, 1284

Along the forest floor, tucked close to the trunks of the sequoia trees beneath Thor's Base, a happy-go-lucky young elf dressed in a green shirt and light-brown Dungaree trousers strolls up to a fruit and vegetable stand waving his hand and greeting the pretty young vendor. "Health and happiness to you, Miss Buttercup."

A bright, cheery smile greets him in return. "Welcome, Mister Lynx; you bring sunshine to this place. Can I interest you in some apples? Reverend Johnny Appleseed's visit has really sparked interest in planting apple trees. You can eat these delicious apples and there are free seeds inside to plant your own apple trees if you wish."

Even at ground level, it is a prestige item to own real estate attached to a sequoia tree. Slate shingles testify to the success of Buttercup's family fruit and vegetable business. Her charm and feminine wiles have played a part in their recent upturn in sales. Lynx chuckles to himself awkwardly. "Actually, I'm here to talk about a bad apple."

Buttercup instantly erases any friendliness from her face and switches mode to a blank expression of bureaucratic impartiality. "I'm sorry, but we don't offer refunds on bad apples. We cannot put them back, since even one rotten apple spoils the bunch."

"Yes, so I've heard . . ." Lynx picks up one of her apples and polishes it on his shirt. "Actually, I was speaking about one of your customers metaphorically."

"I don't seem to recall a customer named Metafor Ickly or anything like that. Do you have a civil dispute with him or is this a criminal case?" she asks in a standoffish manner.

"Neither, it's just a personal matter. What can you tell me about Monsieur Enganyon Gandorfson?"

The expression on Miss Buttercup's face darkens to a mien of cruel calculation that would pluck the feathers off an angel's wings. Nervous and intimidated by her sudden rush of anger, Lynx accidentally stumbles back into the apple cart and tips it over. "Sorry," he says with a troubled grin. "I didn't mean to upset the apple cart. I'll pick those up for you."

As he gathers the apples that fell on the ground Buttercup comes over with a bag and puts the dirty apples in it. "You are going to have to pay for those. That'll be two farthings for the apples and the sack."

Lynx takes out two silver quarters and tucks them in her palm. She snatches them away and parades back behind her stand like a bully who just shoved over a little kid. Resentment at her treatment builds inside his chest until Lynx decides to press on so as to get his money's worth out of this confrontation. "So now, you were going to tell me about Monsieur Enganyon."

"Was I? I don't recall promising you anything. But since we are in a democracy, you have the right to hear my political opinions. Monsieur Enganyon is the best choice for umpire-in-chief and he would be on the ballot if it weren't for that brat, Mademoiselle Florenz. Her father is rotten to the core."

Lynx is suddenly confused. "Wait, Mademoiselle Florenz is a nice girl. She's nothing like her father."

"The apple rarely falls far from the tree."

Lynx cannot believe how confused this pretty fruit seller has become. "Yeah, maybe for green apples; but look at this orange apple here. You don't let something like this just fall on the ground. You pick it off the tree and put it in a basket. It's the same with Mademoiselle Florenz. She's handpicked, kind, and respectful. She would make a great umpire-in-chief. But Monsieur Enganyon just causes trouble for no reason, like a rebel without a cause. I don't get why all the girls dig him."

Buttercup huffs. "You are comparing apples and oranges. Monsieur Enganyon has the appearance of being cool and rebellious but he is a good elf deep down inside. But Mademoiselle Florenz puts on this act of being oh-so-sweet and charming but she is a snake born from a brood of vipers."

Confrontation is not Lynx's specialty, out of sheer nervousness he picks up a small bucket of beans and starts fidgeting with it. "You sound so sure of yourself but I think I know a little something about Monsieur Enganyon that might change your mind."

"What would you know of Monsieur Enganyon? Look, are you going to spill the beans or buy them?"

"You might be surprised to know that he meets up with Mademoiselle Florenz at the Shade Gap often."

Buttercup just shrugs. "So what? That's where the goblins do their ritual sacrifices. Maybe they're trying to get the drop on the goblins there."

"Oh come on! You can't seriously believe that!"

"I have no doubt they're going to hit pay dirt."

Lynx cannot fathom why Buttercup is changing her tune so suddenly. "You seriously think Mademoiselle Florenz and Monsieur Enganyon are going to figure out a way to eradicate the goblins from the hinterlands?"

"No, the beans!" shouts Buttercup. "The way you're holding them like that they'll all fall out onto the dirt and you're going to have to pay for those as well."

Frustrated at her stubbornness, Lynx gets even more truculent. "You should be happy about that. It seems to be your favorite way to make a sale."

"I don't need your money. What were you doing spying on them at the Shade Gap anyway? What legitimate business could an elf like you have over at that goblin sacrificial altar?"

Lynx takes up the challenge to justify himself. "Well, you know Dasher and Dancer and Prancer and Vixen, Comet and Cupid?"

"Yes, they are some of the most famous war reindeer in our colony. So what?"

"But do you recall the most famous reindeer of all?"

"Maybe Donner or Blitzen, I guess—why?"

"It ought to be Rudolph! He has a shiny, red nose; it's very sensitive. Last Saturn's Day, the League of Licornes was holding a recruiting tournament. Thanks to Rudolph I won the race, but they didn't award me a free commission as a junior cavalry officer."

"No one has ever heard of a red-nosed reindeer named Rudolph. I can assure you of that much."

"That's because until last Saturn's Day, they never let poor Rudolph participate in any of the reindeer war games. On that foggy tournament morning, the sandman said to me in a dream, 'Rudolph's nose is so bright, he'll guide your way, Lynx.'

"When I woke up I harnessed him, and all of the other reindeer riders laughed and called us foul names when we lined up at the starting gate. Then we were off, and the fog was so thick that even the adjudicators got lost. Rudolph seemed to smell every tree and branch and shrub that I could not see. He galloped onward at full tilt, even though we were all blinded by the mist. He carried me across the finish line a full half-hour ahead of the first adjudicator. After no one showed up for a while I started to doubt, so I scouted ahead until I found myself at the Shade Gap.

"When the fog cleared, guess whom I saw running around out there with Mademoiselle Florenz?"

Buttercup waves him away. "Oh, Mister Lynx, don't even go there. Everybody knows you are jealous because Mademoiselle Zena likes him instead of you."

Lynx gets so upset at the accusation that his hand knocks some beans all over his shirt. "For your information, it was Monsieur Enganyon running around with no splints on his leg, getting all lovey-dovey with Mademoiselle Florenz! He's faking his injuries and playing two ladies at the same time. You need to help me warn both elves about his character before he breaks their hearts."

"Look, Mister Lynx, you are full of beans."

"Fine, don't believe me, but I need you to explain to Mademoiselle Zena what kind of elf Monsieur Enganyon really is so that she won't have the same terrible experience with him that you had."

"How obnoxious of you! I had a wonderful experience with him. Monsieur Enganyon was nothing but a gentleman to me while we dated."

He takes a bite from one of his newly purchased apples that fell on the ground. "If you keep quiet, he is just going to hurt other maiden elves. I hope you can live with yourself." Lynx scrunches his face and realizes that the apple is riddled with worms. He spits out his mouthful and wipes off the rest.

Buttercup gives Lynx a spiteful glance and sneers. "How do you like them apples?"

Lynx looks down and sees the figs in front of him. "Can I have a fig to get the awful taste of the worms out of my mouth? That was gross!"

"I don't give a fig. Look, Monsieur Enganyon and I found true love together but we realized that we just couldn't be together for reasons beyond our control, okay? It's complicated."

"That kind of love is only true in fairy tales."

"You can go now, Monsieur Lynx. I guess true love is meant for someone else, but not for you."

Lynx stomps off toward his home with his bag of dirty apples, not even bothering to pay for the beans he spilled on his tunic. He finds a secluded spot behind some shrubbery and falls to his knees. On the forest floor one hundred fifty feet beneath the grandiose network of platforms supporting the high elf colony among the giant sequoias, the young wood elf weeps.

Grief surges through him in waves and he prays, "O Lord, show me what to do. Love is out to get me. Disappointment haunts all my dreams."

Then he sees her face.

"Ahh! You scared me!"

"Mister Lynx, are you all right?" Zena bends down and puts a hand on his shoulder. "It looks like you were crying."

"Oh, me? I'm not crying. No, I was just snacking on some apples and it turns out one of them was actually an onion. It's fine; I was hoping to make a garden salad later on. What can I do for you, Mademoiselle Zena?"

"Okay, whatever. My mother asked me to fetch you because you are the only wood elf on Tuscoraura Mountain we know who speaks Aenglish. My mother got the council's permission to invite a Christian missionary named Reverend Johnny Appleseed to deliver the Thor's Enlightenment Discourse for New Year's Eve and he accidentally fell over the edge of Worship Base."

Lynx's red eyes glaze over in total bewilderment. "Wait, what?"

"Well, Monsieur Enganyon sort of slapped him on the back too hard and Reverend Appleseed is so tall that the railing didn't do its job."

"So Monsieur Enganyon killed him?"

Zena starts pulling Lynx up onto his feet. "No, no, no! Monsieur Enganyon would never intentionally hurt anyone. One of the lower branches caught the missionary, but he hurt his leg pretty bad. Now he is lying in our guest room all by himself. My mother is very busy organizing her next trade convoy and she was hoping you would pay him a courtesy visit so he will not have to be alone all the time."

Lynx gets annoyed at all the excuses she makes for Enganyon and says, "Do you realize that the Major Leagues are all holding tournaments this month? I should have won the League of Licornes tournament, but I finished the race before even the adjudicators got to the finish line. So they used that as an excuse to deny me a commission. Now I have to try out for the Justiciar League right after lunch, and my main competitor is none other than your slap-happy friend, Monsieur Enganyon. Maybe he should be babysitting your missionary instead of me since he's the one who almost killed him and all."

Zena pushes Lynx a few feet forward, not taking his attitude. "Monsieur Enganyon already went over to apologize but he doesn't speak any Aenglish! Besides, his leg is in terrible pain. He can only stay out of bed for so long before the pain becomes unbearable."

Lynx doubles back and folds his arms, ready for a confrontation. "On that subject, I was just telling Miss Buttercup over there that after the League of Licornes refused to award me the commission I won at their tournament—"

Zena grows furious and interrupts him. "Mister Lynx Cougarson, excuse me if I interrupt your rant, but you can't feel sorry for yourself just because the League of Licornes treated you unfairly. Self-pity is toxic, and the more you indulge in it, the easier it will be for every little setback to tear you down.

"Now get up off your behind and go compete in the Justiciar League Tournament! You are a better shot than Monsieur Enganyon. I've seen you both shoot myself. You'll win; I'm sure."

The expression of shock on Lynx's face slowly drifts into a warm smile. "Thank you for that vote of confidence, Mademoiselle Zena. I...I don't know what to say—"

"You never do, Mister Lynx," says Zena. "Just smile and keep on the sunny side. See you after the tournament!" She places her Thor's Hammer pendant around his neck and kisses him on the cheek.

She walks off and he just stands there in stunned silence until after she is out of sight. And that's when he finally lets the words drip off his tongue like a glob of honey, "I love you, Zena . . ."

She pops her head back around the corner and with a snide grin calls back to him, "I know!"

Back up on Thor's Base, you would have thought you were at a fashion show, so chic and dapper are all the high elves in the outdoor amphitheater. On the stage sit Florenz Kibblersdottir and Zena Jeannesdottir, extravagantly dressed as if their lives depended on it. Makeup, jewelry, lace, frills, and glass slippers are not good enough for them today—both candidates have calculated every detail to look like the kind of leader the Tuscoraura elves want for their future.

Although she has Drowish (dark elf) lineage on her mother's side, Florenz has dyed her curly hair extravagantly blonde, full of body and volume. Her dress is an amethyst satin with lavender highlights. All her jewelry is platinum or silver, in a bold statement about the temperature of her skin. Deep-blue gems, black pearls, red and violet precious stones are inlaid sparingly but impart a grandiose look in both size and luminosity. The centerpiece is the famous Star of Corundum, fashioned after the one worn by Helen of Troy when she first met Paris.

Zena walks over to the front stage and bows to the audience in a showy gesture of respect. Although her black dress and vest have the same high-quality satin glow as Florenz's and a lusciously glamorous design, her jewelry lacks the zing and surprise that Florenz's arrangement delivers, especially since Zena is without a centerpiece. Her budget simply could not tolerate the kind of extreme makeover Florenz's team has put together. Still, Zena's poise, confidence, and studied movements capture their attention.

Zena hopes to make up for Florenz's budgetary head start with a stirring and bold speech. "This election year, I would like to change an unfortunate trend in our democratic system. Instead of bashing and criticizing each other, I propose that we simply share our views on how we see ourselves fulfilling the role of umpire-in-chief. I am sure Mademoiselle Florenz has the same mindset as I do on this one and that we can keep this debate polite and positive.

"In the Magnificent Charter that they left for our guidance to preserve the prosperity and the racial purity they brought with them from Alfheim, our Founding Mothers and Fathers state emphatically that true excellence is as rare as a pearl in an oyster shell.

"Prodigious parents do not necessarily produce prodigious children. Here I quote our Magnificent Charter: 'Nepotism and primogeniture always bring about decay in political, social, and economic structures when institutionalized by law or unofficially condoned by the customs of a people.'

"Mademoiselle Florenz Kibblersdottir indeed has the advantage of growing up in one of the most illustrious high elf families in Shentalpee City. Her ancestors have managed the same businesses, have led the same social clubs, and have controlled the same governmental posts for generations.

"My mother's pedigree, in contrast, was hard-won through her resourcefulness, talents, and dedication. Many of you still remember her as the young wood elve who earned her status as a high elve by taming a unicorn. Shentalpee City has always counted its unicorn honor guard as the emblem of its vitality and the resourcefulness of its citizens.

"My mother's ingenuity restored our pride in our traditions, revived our enthusiasm for the Magnificent Charter, and set her up for success in the business world. Creativity has been her hallmark and innovation her calling card. When you care enough to wear the very best, you wear a Dungaree.

"But I do not stand here before you today asking you, o brilliant and gorgeous elves of Tuscoraura, to vote for me because of who my mother is but because of who I am, thanks to her. The Magnificent Charter of Tuscoraura Colony forbids us from instituting any form of dynasty in our selection of leadership but instructs us to elect the umpire-in-chief who is the fittest to rule.

"My mind is fit. My memory holds word for word the poetry of all the Runic sagas and wisdom sayings of elf lore that define our cultural heritage. In school, I worked out all the propositions in the geometry of Euclid and Apollonius on my own with only the five postulates. Not only do I speak Aenglish and Gnorrachi but my literacy in Dwarvish Runic, Latin, Avrith, and Nabotean has enabled me to read the works of more philosophers, historians, and orators than most garden gnomes even own in all their impressive libraries.

"My body is fit. I have won every competition in archery, running, reindeer riding, and wrestling that my high school ever set up. My title as Miss Tuscoraura has held for the last two years and my first entry in the Saturnalia fashion contest this year met with rave reviews both as a model and as a designer.

"My spirit is fit. The muses inspire me in every art. I love to draw, compose poetry, dance, and gaze at the stars. When I sing or play flute, I have perfect pitch. My love of music has been the entryway to taming this magica tree you see behind me. It is with great pride that I can announce in three weeks' time, Mage Nittany will observe me cull my first magica branch as an apprentice magicultor at Pinne Mage University.

"Looking out before me at this crowd of smart, athletic, and artsy elves, I know that our Founding Mothers and Fathers would consider you fit in mind, body, and spirit to carry on the ideals they described in the Magnificent Charter. Only by returning to those ideals can we make this colony great once again and bring about a new Golden Age for Shentalpee City.

"This is my vision for the chief umpirage, with your vote. May the gods bless you all with prosperity, insight, and good health for many years to come."

Fervent applause erupts as Zena sits down and smiles. By their reactions, she has no doubt she'll be able to keep her lead over Florenz in the polls.

Now the pressure is on for Florenz. Though innately shy, Florenz is no stranger to public appearances and approaches the stage with an arsenal of smiles and poses. "As you all know, Mademoiselle Zena and I have been best of friends since childhood. In the electoral debates, we hoped to focus our discussions on policy and avoid personal attacks or mudslinging— but I cannot. This latest scandal runs too deep."

Flabbergasted, the high elves stare at Florenz in disbelief. Political discourse in Tuscoraura has always been in the gutter but to hear the sweet, mild-mannered Florenz jump straight into the slime hits them all from left field. They would have assumed that the overweening ambitions of the misfit, Zena, might drive her to aim below the belt, but not Florenz.

Still, Florenz is presenting them with a chance to hear some dirt on Zena, and none of them has any intention of passing up on the offer. They tune their pointy ears in.

Florenz looks at them wide-eyed, almost as if horrified to hear the words coming out of her own mouth, but she has their attention and does not waste a moment of it. "It has recently come to the attention of the Council of Perfects that Madame Jeanne, the dungaree of Foreign Trade, has a halfling stewardess named Bartlebee who has sold the alchemical plans to our top-secret weapon, elf fire, to the renowned dwarf mercenary Master Chief Engineer Tom Thumb.

"The investigation is likely to drag on for months, but I believe you all have the right to know this before the elections. My father has worked day and night over the past twelve years to rebuild Shentalpee City's military infrastructure. If Zena's umpireship squanders our military edge in fire technologies, a disaster worse than the eruption of Mount Ragnarök could befall us right here on Tuscoraura Mountian.

"The Justiciar League is currently conducting a full investigation of Bartlebee's betrayal and will ascertain whether or not our monopoly over the colony's top-secret elemental weapon remains intact. Any evidence of collaboration—or even negligence—on the part of Madame Jeanne Ranglursdottir in allowing this elf fire leak could brand her a traitor. My sincerest hope is that this is all one, big misunderstanding and that we can clear our dungaree of Foreign Trade from guilt and seal up the leak.

"If not, may the gods help us."

Florenz steps down from the stage. The crowd sits in stunned silence at what they just heard.

Zena's face drains white like spilled milk.

Conviction for treason will result in the confiscation of all her family's goods and property by the Council of Perfects, permanent exile for herself, and execution for her mother.

Worst of all, Zena could never marry Enganyon with a scandal of those proportions weighing on her dowry. Zena's mind stews. *This is not over, Mademoiselle Florenz! If you think I won't fight back, you are mistaken — gravely mistaken!*

Scene 3: Genesis

Shade Gap.
Five Miles Northwest of Tuscoraura Mountain
Spy Woden's Day Terce. Morning, 5th of April, 1284

A muscular, five-and-a-half-foot-tall, green-skinned goblin with a stone-tipped spear charges at Sir Robert Roger from behind. Brother Umbert pulls a magic wand from up his sleeve. "Alakazam!" He shouts his magic word out, loud enough to give away their exact location to every goblin within a hundred yards.

Suddenly, the charging goblin loses his spear—in fact, it magically disappears into thin air. The baffled and unarmed goblin keeps running and crashes awkwardly into Sir Robert Roger without doing any real harm. Sprawled in the dirt, they grapple for only a few seconds before the goblin's vastly superior physical strength overpowers the ranger captain. The goblin hoists him over his head, spins him around, and tosses him into a group of nearby rangers aiming their arrows at him. In a trice, the goblin dashes back into the forest.

The rest of the rangers, already on high alert, shoot their arrows and fling their hatchets, but the goblins prove elusive foes.

Barrel-chested, big-fisted, and massively muscular, the goblins have no armor and fight with fire-hardened wood or chipped stone weapons. They compensate for the lack of metalworking in their warcraft with higher degrees of cunning in battle.

Although goblins only tend to reach somewhere between five and five-and-a-half feet tall for adult males and about four-and-a-half to five feet tall for adult females, both goblins and goblinesses are much stronger than the tallest and heaviest humans. By age twelve, a healthy goblin whelp could arm wrestle two muscle-bound humans at the same time and easily win.

In caves deprived of the light of day, their skin turns a pale-gray hue. But when continuously exposed to the sun, their skin tans to a dark green. This adaptation acts as a natural camouflage and helps them blend easily into forests and grasslands.

Their most astounding adaptation to the wild is their regenerative capabilities; healing broken bones, and recovering from serious infections in half the time as other races. Their foreheads are narrow and slope back steeply with thick, bushy brows, long chins, and wide cheekbones. All goblins have a pronounced overbite, which distinguishes them from trolls, whose jaws carry a tusked underbite.

After the initial goblin attack, Inquisitor Sheen remains in prayer but Brother Crowe has drawn two long knives and Brother Indigo holds in his left and only hand the large, knotty club that has been dangling from his rope belt all the while. Brother Umbert skulks around the underbrush with his magic wand, pointing it outward like a viper ready to strike.

After taking a nasty tumble, Sir Robert Roger sets himself back on his feet and readies himself for action, shouting out orders to the rangers. "Form a perimeter!"

Then he turns to Brother Umbert and states, "I owe you thanks for saving my life with that little magic trick, but now you've got to tell the inquisitor and your holy buddies to huddle behind those rocks inside our defensive circle. We can't risk your lives in combat."

Brother Umbert does not retreat. "The inquisitor is praying. God will keep him safe."

Sir Robert Roger yells, "Get the inquisitor behind those rocks or I'll carry him there myself!"

The standoff ends when a skull-sized boulder flies into the ranger camp. Poorly aimed, it does not hit anyone. Sir Jon Stark, the first lieutenant for the rangers, shouts, "Keep your eyes open and shoot at anything that moves!"

When the next boulder arrives, Sir Ethen Allan calls out, "I saw a goblin toss it about fifty yards to the northeast, but he ducked behind a tree before I had a chance to shoot at him!"

"Incoming!" Sir Daniel Boone screams in a terrified then suddenly hushed voice. From the opposite direction of the flying boulders, goblin lurkers rush in at the rangers. The boulders were just a distraction and the goblins are wickedly fast on their feet.

The first ambushing goblin swings a gnarly oaken club at Sir Richard, the ranger posted in the rear. The blow puts the dazed ranger out of the fight and three goblins charge directly into the gap. They quickly reach the middle of the rangers' defensive circle and start swiping at the other rangers from behind.

The rangers a few paces back shoot their arrows at the ambushing goblins. Although the rangers' arrows bite against their flesh, the goblins have an amazing instinct for spinning just before being struck with the rangers' well-aimed arrows. Their spinning motion takes all the penetration out of the arrowheads.

Despite getting all slashed up by the sharp arrowheads from the rangers' longbows, the goblins press their attack. Dame Frances Marian pulls out a long knife but a fat goblin with a scrimshaw ox bone club knocks the knife aside, numbing her hand. Another shorter goblin dashes at her from her blind spot and tries to clobber her with a backhand swing from his heavy ashen spear shaft, but her sixth sense tells her to dive out of the way in the nick of time. She retreats.

Seeing that the tactical situation is lost, Sir Robert Roger blows his horn to withdraw to the river.

With all the rangers' attention on the goblins in their midst, they fail to notice the goblins emerging from behind bushes, trees, and ditches lobbing smooth stones at the distracted rangers. Several rangers get hit from behind and fall to the ground, stunned.

Sir Robert Roger picks up his hatchet and tries to rescue the situation with a daring countercharge, but a short goblin trips him with a whack of his spear behind the knees and the fight is back to square one. Looking around, Sir Robert Roger notices his rangers are badly bruised, but none have received mortal wounds so far. Hoping to keep the bloodshed to a minimum, he shouts, "Don't go for the kill! They are trying to spook us. Keep moving back toward the river and stay alert!"

Meanwhile, Inquisitor Sheen continues praying. Brother Indigo smacks down a goblin with his huge, gnarly club before the goblin can get to the inquisitor.

The Mohawk brother then twirls his club around to deflect a stone ax from a different goblin on his right. Brother Umbert makes the stone ax disappear with his magic wand and Brother Crowe slashes at that same goblin just above the eyebrows. A few heartbeats later, the blood trickles down into his eyes copiously and the blinded, unarmed goblin stumbles off into the forest.

They do not pursue because Inquisitor Sheen has ordered them to avoid loss of life at all times.

Although the three monks are holding their own fairly well, the groaning and stunned rangers lose ground. Three larger goblins decked out with tattoos, body piercings, and war trophies to signal that they are chieftains walk into the combat zone. The first looks older, mostly bald, and with a salt-and-pepper goatee. Dry, dark-green, weathered skin wraps tightly around his bulging muscles. His perfect six-pack abs and the veins crawling all over his arms, neck, and legs bespeak a goblin driven by a life-long obsession for destruction.

To his left walks a tall but less muscular goblin. This one has all the tattoos and body piercings of the other two, but far fewer war trophies hang about his neck or on his belt. Unusual for a goblin, he has a full head of hair. Long and black, his braids dangle down past his shoulders. His fine nose, narrow forehead, and sharp chin give him a ladylike charm.

On the right side of the elder chieftain marches a hulking goblin, just over six feet tall, with a loose-hanging gut and arms so thick he could take down a bull with one hand. His neck is stooped and his back hunches over slightly. The flapping jowls on his cheeks and his pig-like nostrils are both ugly and intimidating.

Apparently, the hulking goblin is looking for a challenge and points to Brother Indigo, saying, "Boom shakalaka do wa ditty diddy dum ditty do!"

Inquisitor Sheen calls out in response, "Gaggle aowl yahoo terwitter whoop!"

Sir Robert Roger grimaces and moans, "Seriously? What is he doing? Calling the birds to help us?"

Brother Umbert responds, "He has the mystical gift of tongues. He's speaking Gobbledygook, the language of the Magog goblins."

The salt-and-pepper-haired old war chief grunts in surprise, then says, "Wiki yootoob amuson paipaal!"

Inquisitor Sheen replies, "Inztagrahm reddet blogsbot lynktyn ne'flicks?"

The pretty boy chieftain asserts himself as a negotiator. "Bing taobao sohu yip baidu alixpriss!"

The older goblin chieftain nods, "Ebaie."

The inquisitor tells Sir Robert Roger, "The Mighty Gog, exalted king over all the goblins in the forests of Magog, has agreed in his benevolence to spare you your lives if you put your weapons down and allow them to bind you."

"How do we know he won't just kill us?"

"The exalted goblin king says he will allow his son, Skaar, to be your personal hostage, Sir Robert Roger, until all your followers are safely returned to you."

"If he's so benevolent, why doesn't he just let us go now? We're not trying to pick a fight with anybody."

"It seems we have trespassed upon their sacred territory. They need to perform a ritual with our blood to cleanse the pollution we have brought. If we give our blood willingly, it only needs to be one drop. If they have to take it from us unwillingly, then they have to pour out all of it."

"Okay, Priest, I'm taking your word for it. Tell him to send us his son first as a ransom and then we will atone for our trespasses."

Inquisitor Sheen tells the goblin king they are willing to give up their freedom for the promise of safety. "Boosh klin'in boosh opama drumb."

The goblin king gives the command to bind them up. "Alecksa!"

The goblins tie up the rangers and inquisitors, then lead them to the top of the northernmost mountain, overlooking the Shade Gap. The site looks like a pile of randomly scattered stones but as Inquisitor Sheen's trained eye surveys the patterns, the ritualistic arrangement of the stones pops out at him like a 3D message suddenly becoming visible in the swirling patterns of an optical illusion design. For all its naturalistic calm and peacefulness, this area is actually an outdoor temple for ritual murder!

Several curved boulders mark off this mountaintop clearing and form a circle of arches around the main altar. The altar itself is just a huge, stone slab that has been tossed on top of the central pile of stones. Its surface is uneven and slightly tilted, but from the layers of dark stains, it seems to be used often. Blood and restless spirits abound here.

A pang of doubt pinches the inquisitor's soul. An unsettling feeling that the goblin king may have lied about sparing their lives tightens his throat.

Their goblin captors arrange them in a semicircle with their right hands on their chests. From the other corner, some goblins carry a wicker basket cage into the semicircle. It holds a teenaged boy dressed as a monk with a strange, hempen halter around his neck.

Sir Robert Roger presses his knife tightly against the throat of his hostage, the goblin king's son. "Tell him no sudden moves. We want the monk boy to go free as well."

Inquisitor Sheen gets worried and asks the goblin king, "Gobble makdoe arbee panda supway dunkin pitsada hut?"

The goblin chief laughs with a deep growl and says, "Chicaboom noon-egg solo manga wookey bantha Poodoo!"

The inquisitor translates. "The mighty Gog says that you were lucky to escape with your lives, but the monk boy will be a human sacrifice to their god, Poodoo."

Scene 4: Poor Richard's Comeback

Town Hall of Ithica
Spy Woden's Day Sext. Noontide, 5ᵗʰ of April, 1284

"Ah, welcome, Grand Sage Cornwell!" The baron of Amhirst puts on his most charming smile. "It is most gracious of you to allow me this opportunity to clear up the misunderstanding between us when we first arrived. Please have a seat by the fire. May I offer you some wine?"

The grand sage wears his academic robe without the hood. His face is stern, and his attitude is skeptical. "The Silvermorn College of Sorcerers deeply mourns the students who lost their lives in defense of Ithica, a town they had called home while studying with us."

"Regrettable," says the baron as his chief herald, Sir Sean, comes over to pour out two cups of wine for the baron and his guest. Cornwell refuses so Sir Sean places both cups on a little table beside the fireplace.

The baron is wearing red slippers and a smooth, red robe that is the closest medieval garb to a roaring twenties smoking jacket. "A tragedy, really. Such bright promise for the future cut short because their leaders failed them. You and I need to put our heads together to make this right. A simple apology, no matter how sincere, just won't be enough."

Grand Sage Cornwell stares Amhirst straight in the eye. "You took the words right out of my mouth."

"It's because we both have the same vision for leadership in Aenglish society." Amhirst stalls, waiting for the grand sage to relax and let down his guard.

"Quite frankly, my lord, your vision of leadership resembles that of a bully on a child's playground."

"That's exactly why I asked you to come. Such misperceptions can only lead to more unnecessary bloodshed. We must come to an understanding before it costs us any more Aenglish lives."

"What more do I need to understand? You attacked the walls of Ithica and my students rallied to its defense. Some of them died."

The baron looks at him with pleading eyes. "Please have a seat, Master Grand Sage. We discuss such weighty issues, and it would only be proper to observe the suitable decorum in our conversation."

Grand Sage Cornwell stiffly takes a seat on the couch and says, "Only because of the grave responsibility on my shoulders of informing the families of those deceased students do I force myself to sit down and hear you out."

The baron of Amhirst sits across from him and stares into the fire as if in deep thought. He says, "Yes, these parents are making great sacrifices to send their sons and daughters to Silvermorn in hopes of ensuring a successful niche for their future. They are immensely proud of their child's talents and accomplishments."

Amhirst looks at Cornwell thoughtfully, but Cornwell keeps quiet.

"I've just heard too many cases of brilliant young sorcerers returning home only to find out that the Sorcerers' Guild demands that they travel farther afield because all the local jobs are taken. Unemployed sorcerers have a bad reputation for causing mischief."

Still no response from Cornwell, but Amhirst can tell he is touching on a raw nerve.

"As a way of putting the past in the past and opening up a brighter future, I'll offer to hire any and all unemployed graduates of Silvermorn."

Cornwell perks up and asks, "At full wages?"

"Absolutely, at full wages."

"Fourpence a day?"

"Thruppence a day starting wages until they prove their worth. I usually pay at least double for competent ones. Several sorcerers at my court are making a dollar and sixpence a day after accomplishing legendary quests in my service. They could retire before forty, but they enjoy the position so much, they stay on."

"And you will put this in writing?"

"Yes, we have prepared a document extending the patronage of my court to Silvermorn College."

"But you have no authority here in Ithica."

"That might change, and soon enough. Believe me—this contract benefits you as much as it benefits me. If my authority were to extend to this region, it would entail a revision of nearly all charters granted by local authorities. Signing this would ensure your educational mission continues uninterrupted."

"May I read this contract you are proposing?"

The baron of Amhirst nods his head gravely, using all the body language of a person speaking to a peer of equal social status. Grand Sage Cornwell is under no illusion that the baron's deference is anything more than a veil for his threats and bullying.

Amhirst beckons Sir Sean, who is sitting quietly in a corner, and he brings the baron's proposal forward with much gravitas.

"Be a good man and wait in the hallway while the chancellor considers this deal, would you, Sir Sean?"

Sir Sean bows and exits the room. The grand sage reads the scroll carefully while the baron waits, sipping his wine.

After a long pause, Cornwell says, "I need you to indemnify the families of the fallen students."

"Agreed."

"And refund them the tuition they paid so far."

"How about we split the refund so we each pay half? After all, the tuition went into your coffers."

"Unacceptable." The grand sage stands up. "You are putting a lot of faith in the Inquisition's ability to bail you out of a very ugly situation. If Inquisitor Sheen fails to return to Ithica from Tuscoraura Mountain, your rangers would find it considerably more difficult to mount another rescue operation before your beheading. We will be prepared the next time around."

Amhirst starts dropping some bigger names. "Not necessary. It's a done deal. Reports are coming in that my rangers have already succeeded in bringing the good inquisitor to Tuscoraura Mountain, and the Cardinals Orsini have already invited me to a meeting in Salim. You no longer have any legal grounds to carry out your proposed execution.

"King Eddard has agreed to expand the role of the Inquisition in Vinland significantly over the next few years and, seeing my devotion and piety, the Cardinals Orsini are offering to put my name forward as Aenglish viceroy of Vinland to oversee the whole process. My policy is that it is better to have more friends than enemies. Surely you see the wisdom in that."

"I have seen little wisdom in your policies thus far. Good evening to you." The grand sage walks toward the door.

Amhirst stands up and calls after him, "There is one other issue I could help you with—Richard Chandler."

Grand Sage Cornwell freezes with his hand on the doorknob. He turns around slowly. "Are you the one that tipped his former master off to his presence here? Leverage, I suppose."

Amhirst puts his hand over his heart. "Never would I dream of such skullduggery!"

"But if someone else should dream it up, you would be game to capitalize on it, I am sure. All right then, tell me how you know about Richard Chandler."

"The crumbs I like to toss for the little birdies outside my window seem to have attracted a few magpies. Across their chatter, I learn a lot."

"Sounds like a bird-brained form of skullduggery to me. What do you intend to do with this leverage you have on him?"

"You have seen how I confront my enemies. I want to show you how well I treat my friends. Call him in, will you, Grand Sage?"

"It's late in the evening, and all the apprentices have gone to bed."

Amhirst calls out, "Sir Sean!"

The baron's herald opens the door immediately. "You called, my lord?"

"Fetch young Richard Chandler, will you?"

"He's right here, my lord. Also, a messenger from the Pony Express has arrived."

"Have Brother Tuck handle it for me."

"Begging your pardon, my lord, but the halfling working for the Pony Express insists the letter is for your eyes only."

"Tell him I will receive him as soon as I have concluded an agreement with the grand sage. Now, please send Apprentice Chandler in."

"Very well, my lord."

Amhirst cannot restrain a little smirk at Cornwell's surprise seeing the jovial young man walk in. His nose is round as a ball and his face plump and smooth. His wavy, brown hair falls back from his high forehead, giving him an air of intelligence and confidence. Richard Chandler shakes Cornwell's hand and says, "Thank you so much for arranging this meeting, Grand Sage Cornwell!"

The baron of Amhirst ushers the young man to the fireplace. "Welcome! Come in, Apprentice Chandler. Have a seat and let me pour you some wine."

Richard Chandler sits right down and makes himself comfortable. "You are too kind, my lord. Your generosity to your friends is legendary, but to treat a runaway slave in the employ of your bitterest enemy with such cordiality defies all comprehension."

"Happy to oblige, Richard," answers Amhirst. "Or should I call you, Benjamin?"

The young man laughs. "Ah! You figured me out. My father always used to tell me, 'Love your enemies, for they tell you the truth about yourself.'"

Amhirst echoes Benjamin's laugh theatrically. "That is precisely why I invited you here—to show you what kind of friend I could be if only we can work out a way to dispel this enmity between your college and my regime. Tell me, Benjamin, about your troubles."

The grand sage gives the young man a look of warning to keep quiet. Benjamin Chandler nods to him as if submitting to his request and then immediately pours his heart out to Amhirst. "My father, Josiah, is a candlemaker from Ecton, a little community of humans within the shire of the Hampton Hobs.

"Life was hard for the family back in Aengland so he came to Baston as an indentured servant. When I was ten years old, he paid for two years of my education at a monastery near Cambridge in hopes of having a son gain prominence in the Church. But when funds ran out, he apprenticed me to my older brother, James, who had set up his own tallow candlemaker's workshop.

"James was jealous of my ability to read and of my natural aptitude for sorcery. He strictly forbade me from reading any more books and promised to hunt me down whenever I tried to sneak off to a monastery library. One after another, I visited every library in Baston, thirsty for knowledge. He became so familiar with all those libraries that the hide-and-seek we were playing ceased to have any sporting fun left in it.

"A friend of mine tipped me off that the law granting serfs freedom after living one hundred and one days in a chartered Aenglish town also applies to contracted apprentices who enlist in a chartered military, academic, or religious institution within Aenglish domains.

"So, I stole away to Ithica in pursuit of a career in sorcery, with the hopes that it would take my brother more than one hundred and one days to find me. Unfortunately, he seems to have gone all the way around the world in eighty days.

"Now that he's here, he'll drag me back to Baston and lock me in a dark, dank room. The boredom of candle making will be the mildest of my punishments.

109

My brother will think up ways to get back at me—and trust me, he has an active imagination when it comes to inflicting misery on others."

The baron of Amhirst listens to the story intently. "How old are you now, young Benjamin?"

"Nineteen, sir."

"How would you like to fulfill your father's dream to make a cleric of you in Brother Tuck's monastery?"

Benjamin puts his fist to his mouth and coughs slightly. "My lord, a very credible astrologer has told me that the stars forbid me to take on monastic vows. I was born precisely between two conjunctions that would really bring disaster upon me and Holy Mother the Church if I did take the vow of . . . ehem—"

"Your astrologer has perhaps seen a weakness for pretty ladies in your eye?" suggests Amhirst.

"The astrologer was a very pretty lady herself, but she told me I was the sort of rebel destined to transform colonial Vinland. Perhaps we could talk about the dreams I have for my own life, instead of my father's dreams for me."

Amhirst snaps his fingers and sits up excitedly. "She has seen the fire in your eyes, Mister Benjamin Chandler, and I have seen it too! On that desk there I have a document declaring you a frankelyn in my court. The moment you sign it, you will be free from your apprenticeship to your brother by your oath of civic service to the barony of Amhirst.

"Naturally, you'd be able to pursue your studies here at Silvermorn. Your aethereal experiments in harnessing the power of lightning with a kite and a key have already gained notoriety among your peers. All I ask is that you go on a quest or two, if needed."

Ebullient and optimistic, Benjamin Chandler turns to the grand sage and asks, "What do you say, Grand Sage? This seems to me like the opportunity of a lifetime—the answer to all our problems."

"It's your life, Richard. No doubt we would be thrilled for you to continue your studies as a sorcerer's apprentice with us here at Silvermorn. However, I have a feeling your debt of gratitude to the baron of Amhirst will get more and more encumbered with obligations until studies will become impossible."

Amhirst jumps in before Benjamin Chandler has a chance to think it over too much. "The contract stipulates that as my frankelyn, you would be obliged to leave Silvermorn in my service no more than one semester every other year. You would graduate with your Master's degree in Sorcery in five years tops, potentially earlier. We'll even throw in paid summers, whether or not we call you up for service."

"Done," says the apprentice chandler, standing up to shake Amhirst's hand.

The baron of Amhirst turns a triumphant smile to the grand sage. "We can agree on one thing, dear Chancellor—we both recognize talent when we see it.

"Shall we agree to a mutually beneficial contract then? Guaranteed employment for all Silvermorn graduates who seek it in my court. Indemnities and half-tuition refunds for the families of the students who fell at the walls. An official elevation of Benjamin Chandler to the rank of frankelyn in my baronial court. Let's move on with the future, shall we?"

Cornwell looks long and hard at his star pupil. "Throw in Chandler's full tuition and you have a deal."

With a coy smile Amhirst concludes, "You drive a hard bargain, Chancellor, but I'm in no mood to drag this out any further.

"Sir Sean, the document, please."

Sir Sean pops back in with the scroll on a tray, followed by Brother Tuck, armed with a quill pen, inkwell, lit candle, and some sealing wax. Amhirst picks up the scroll and unfurls it in front of the grand sage, then dictates the negotiated conditions for his cleric to write down. Cornwell leans over Brother Tuck's shoulder reading and rereading every word as it goes down on the parchment.

Brother Tuck's penmanship, spelling, and grammar are impeccable and, despite his better judgment, Cornwell can find no technicality for backing out of this deal. A deep sinking feeling warns him that he is heading down a direful path, but he waves it off for the sake of his students and their loved ones. "Mind you, Lord Amhirst, a contract signals a political alliance, not an act of abject submission to your whims."

Amhirst's mind is already elsewhere and he blankly agrees, "Yes, yes, yes. Of course."

Cornwell begrudgingly signs and seals the scroll.

Benjamin Chandler gets up and puts an arm around the grand sage's shoulders as if sharing a family hug. The grand sage is nonplussed by the excessive show of familiarity, but he holds his tongue.

Chandler tries to lighten the dour mood. "What the noble grand sage means to say is that without freedom of thought, there can be no such thing as wisdom. We will always tell you the truth as best as we can discern it. Whether you take that as a token of friendship or enmity depends on the greatness of your spirit."

Amhirst admires the young man's quick wit and feels reassured that the tuition scholarship Cornwell muscled into the deal will be money well spent. "Brilliantly stated, young man. Now if you will excuse me, it seems an urgent message through the Pony Express is waiting for me. Make no mistake about it— in the upcoming days, we will plan a celebration of our newfound accord for all Ithicans: feasts, tournaments, dramas, and entertainers."

Benjamin jumps right into his new role. "As your new frankelyn, I would be honored to serve on the planning committee for this celebration, my lord."

Ushering them out, the baron concludes with a grandiose swirl of his arm, "As my frankelyn, you shall be the head of that committee. Good evening, Grand Sage! Adieu!"

With an almost polite shove, the baron steers Cornwell out of the room and waves his herald and the halfling messenger waiting at the door to come inside.

The messenger hands him a sealed letter but Amhirst does not touch it. He waves to his herald. "Whose seal is it, Sir Sean?"

The halfling courier in long riding boots—about as long as his short legs can fit into—steps past Sir Sean Madigan briskly. "Begging your pardon, my lord, but even the seal is for your eyes only."

"All right, set it on the table," says the baron of Amhirst. "Sir Sean is my most trusted advisor, but your discretion is commendable. Here, let me pour you some wine while you warm yourself by the fire."

"Sorry, my lord, but we have an oath that prevents us from ungodly language and strong drink."

The baron of Amhirst nods. "Yes, that was my understanding. I wanted to make sure you actually are with the Pony Express. Few people know about your special work requirements.

"Several of my enemies have plotted my demise with false letters and poisoned packets. Your insistence that I be the only one to see this delivery came across as suspicious, but you passed the test. Here's a newly minted groat for your troubles."

The halfling postal worker looks at the coin quizzically. "How much is a groat worth, my lord?"

Benjamin Chandler loves math and explains, "Four pennies. He that spends a groat a day idly, spends idly above six pounds a year."

Sir Sean adds, "It'll more than cover a hearty meal and a good night's rest at the Dancing Pony."

Amhirst concludes, "You are dismissed for now. What did you say your name was again?"

"Underhill, my lord."

"Oh, that's a splendid name for a halfling. Mister Underhill, please check back at my door first thing in the morning before you depart, in case I have an immediate response for the sender."

"Yes, my lord." The halfling bows respectfully. His frizzy sideburns sway with every motion of his head. Though his eyes are young, his sun-dried brow and rugged cheeks speak of a rough life in the saddle with few creature comforts.

After the Pony Express rider exits the room, Sir Sean Madigan picks the letter up off the table. "It's the seal of Cardinal Orsini."

Amhirst asks, "Which one? Each of the three Orsini brothers keeps wanting to make his importance felt over the other two."

Sir Sean inspects it closely but looks up and says, "Can't tell. The imprint on the wax is all smudged and fuzzy. My guess is they want you to know it's really from them while still retaining a measure of deniability. One swipe of the thumb would efface it entirely."

Benjamin asks politely, "May I have a look?"

Amhirst raises his eyebrows. "By all means! You are in my court now, Mister Frankelyn—a trusted advisor."

The flattery takes its effect on the new frankelyn. He looks at it carefully and reports, "I'd say this is coming from the office of Maderno Cardinal Orsini, my lord. He has made quite a reputation for himself as being the brains behind their witch trials. Paterno Cardinal Orsini

115

is the ferocious one—the reason the people of Baston have started calling them the Three Bears.

"Actually, if my paltry Italian serves me right, *orsino* is the diminutive form of *orso*. We should be calling the Orsini brothers the Three Little Bears. It's the little one among them, Piccolo Cardinal Orsini, who adds the whimsical unpredictability to the whole operation that makes the very sound of the word *Inquisition* drive terror into the hearts of the general populace."

"Terror hardly begins to describe it, Mister Frankelyn," comments Sir Sean dryly. "It's one thing to be condemned to torture and death for a crime you never committed. It's another thing entirely to be condemned to Hell for a sin you never committed."

Amhirst waves his fingers to shoo away the whole conversation and says, "Putting a little fear of God into the hearts and minds of the Bastonians can be useful. Anyhow, what does the letter say?"

Sir Sean breaks open the seal and unfurls the scroll. "It's in Latin, my lord."

"Let's have Brother Tuck read it carefully. I want to know anything you can deduce from the letter, not just its contents. Was it written with an agitated hand? Is he trying to impress me with the cost of the parchment? Is the tone subtly threatening or is he trying to hide desperation or some less obvious vulnerability?"

Brother Tuck motions toward a seat near the hearth fire and the baron nods. He sits and examines the letter, front to back, turning it over and reading it twice.

The baron's patience eventually begins to wear thin. He asks, "What can you tell us?"

"Without a little more context, it will be hard for me to surmise exactly the implications. But Cardinal Maderno writes to ask for help investigating a very delicate matter."

Benjamin snaps his fingers and calls out, "I was right! It *is* Maderno after all!"

Amhirst commends him patiently. "Very good, Benjamin. Now, let's hear what it says."

Brother Tuck clears his throat. "Uh, yes. After the formalities it says, and I quote, '. . . now that you have been appointed by King Eddard the secular strong arm of the Holy Inquisition in Vinland.' I'm not sure what he means by that."

The baron of Amhirst sips his wine by the fireside. "Yes, yes, in my letter describing our relationship with Inquisitor Sheen, I implied that our patronage might expand by royal decree, without getting into specifics. My contacts at King Eddard's court in Lunden should hammer out something official in a few months. For now, time is of the essence, so until I get a response from the king, I'm improvising as I go along."

"Very well, my lord," says Brother Tuck.

"So what does the Inquisition want of me?"

"It says they had an intruder break into their residence in Salim. Um . . . let's see here . . . yes, so I'll do my best to translate these few paragraphs here:

> Your stay in Ithica has made you the closest friend we have to a very delicate and confidential matter. Upon successful completion of this quest, we will guarantee your appointment as viceroy of Vinland by His Holiness Pope Martin and support any accusation of heresy you make against your enemies.

Last night, a document of inestimable value was stolen from our residence. The Roman Curia has charged Raymond Bertrand de Goethe, the archdeacon of Auch, a powerful and well-connected cleric from Frankland, with the task of extirpating all Cathar heretics from the lands of Oxitania and Longbardia. The archdeacon sent to us a certain Parisian doctor by the name of Georges Faust, asking us to aid and abet him in every possible manner.

As it turns out, his quest was to locate and obtain the lost Sword of Layban. After much diligence, Doctor Faust discovered this ancient artifact in the possession of the Hill Dwarves of Cumorah. The dwarves demanded of him the exorbitant fee of 8,000 gold florins or 2,400 silver marks for this ancient artifact. Reluctantly, he obtained the funds in the form of a banknote from the Knights Templar preceptory in Rofchester. According to the agreement, the Hill Dwarves of Cumorah were to exchange the sword for the banknote after the Templar loremasters had verified its authenticity.

The verification process took several months but on the feast of Saint Mary the Egyptian, documents finally arrived from the Templar loremasters certifying the authenticity of the Sword of Layban. The Templar bankers duly forwarded the payment to the Hill Dwarves of Cumorah and sent Doctor Faust a receipt of the transaction along with a safe deposit slip so that he could come claim the sword from their vaults in the Templar Preceptory of Rofchester.

Upon receiving these documents, Doctor Faust handed them to us for safekeeping in our residence before he went into Baston to purchase equipment and hire adventurers to escort him safely and secretly to Rofchester and back.

That morning before leaving to hear cases, my brother Piccolo put the Templar safe deposit slip to claim the Sword of Layban in a secret compartment in his parlor chair. Under his bed, he devised a trapdoor to conceal the Templar certification of authenticity and the purchase receipt for the sword.

By the grace of divine Providence, all three of us returned home early that day and saw that all our parlor chairs had been tampered with, but that Piccolo's had been completely disassembled. No doubt, someone tipped the thief off.

Fearing the worst, we rushed upstairs and surprised a young girl with curly, blonde hair rummaging through Piccolo's bed. Before we could get a good look at her face, she escaped with great dexterity out the second-floor window and eluded the Swiss guards we sent after her. Fortunately, she did not find the receipt and certificate hidden under the trapdoor beneath Piccolo's bed.

Asking ourselves how it would be possible for an intruder to know precisely where and when to look for these documents, we could only conclude that we had been betrayed by one of our household servants. Normally, we dismiss all our servants while we are away and lock up the residence carefully.

It was Piccolo who noticed that a bowl of porridge had been eaten in our absence. The porridge in the pot was too cold for the cook to have accidentally left it on the fire while away and too hot for him to have extinguished the flame before leaving. Therefore, the cook must have been in the house while we were away and warmed up the porridge for Goldilocks after letting her into the house.

Before he expired, we learned from the cook that although Goldilocks has the safe deposit slip, she does not yet know which Templar bank holds the

Sword of Layban in its vaults. That is why she needed the receipt as well.

Your quest, Lord Amhirst, should you choose to accept it, is to recover the Sword of Layban and deliver it to us in Salim before Goldilocks and her coconspirators can find it. Without the safe deposit slip, you may need to break into the vault and steal it yourself.

If you or any of your agents are caught or killed, the Holy Office of the Inquisition will disavow any knowledge of your actions. This letter is to be burnt immediately after reading it, upon pain of excommunication.

Brother Tuck tosses it into the fire. Quickly, Amhirst grabs a fire poker and tries to rescue the letter but the flames consume it with such a burst of light and smoke as to leave little doubt that it had been brushed with linseed oil before sending.

The baron of Amhirst huffs as he sits back down. "Brother Tuck, your obedience in following instructions is commendable, but if backed in a corner, that letter could have been useful."

Brother Tuck stands up to the baron. "With all due respect, my lord, if you pulled out a letter like that when backed in a corner, you would be dead before you could think of a proper use for it."

"Oh, all right," concedes the baron. "What is so important about this sword, anyway?"

Brother Tuck sits back down and clears his throat. "If my memory serves, the Sword of Layban is used as part of a blackflame ritual in the art of necromancy."

Benjamin Chandler adds, "Some of the students were talking about that the other day. I think it can transform a living person into an undead state. They were calling it a type of evil transubstantiation."

Brother Tuck corrects him. "There is no evil form of transubstantiation. The proper term in theology for that would be *transmogrification*."

Amhirst rubs his chin. "Confusing, isn't it? When I pledged myself to support Inquisitor Sheen, did I not take the Crusader's vow to fight the blackflame heresy in Vinland? Now the Holy Office of the Inquisition is asking me to fetch an artifact that would allow them to engage in blackflame necromancy. Doesn't that violate my own Crusader's vow?"

Brother Tuck tugs at the collar of his monk's cowl and says, "Theologically speaking, we can make a distinction. You only swore to fight the blackflame heresy in *Vinland*. This Sword of Layban will be shipped off to *Frankland*. By removing it from Vinland, you will be keeping it out of the hands of blackflame heretics here and thus fulfilling your vow."

Amhirst pauses, then says, "It disturbs me how easily you are able to convince me that black is white and white is black."

"Both are liturgical colors, my lord."

Amhirst shrugs and turns to his herald, saying, "Sir Sean, what's your opinion? Is it possible to take on this quest without risking war with the Knights Templar?"

"One way immediately comes to mind, if it pleases your lordship."

"Go on."

"Remember that party of adventurers you hired to hunt down the heir of the late Marquis Ducaine? I'm quite sure they don't know they're working for you—at least they've asked no questions."

Amhirst thinks for a moment and replies, "Yes, you sent them out years ago, if I recall correctly. I thought they had abandoned that quest."

Holding up a bone amulet with scrimshaw letters he says, "Apparently not. They brought me this amulet as proof that they succeeded."

"Why didn't you tell me this before?"

"They just arrived yesterday to inform me that their quest has been accomplished. They're waiting for their reward at the Dancing Pony."

"How did they find us here?" asks the baron.

"If they could track down a boy that nearly every Frank in Vinland is trying to hide, how hard could it have been for them to track down your army?"

"Supposedly, they don't know I hired them."

"Don't worry, my lord. They're all hush-hush."

The worry on the baron's forehead visibly heightens. "Their silence doesn't prove their ignorance of my involvement in the plot to assassinate young Laurence Ducaine. They could use it against me."

"Their silence proves they understand the risk of double-crossing us, my lord."

"We'll discuss it later. Right now, we have to decide whether or not to seek out this Sword of Layban for the cardinals of the Inquisition and, if so, whom to send.

"A war with the Templars would ruin us, and I'm not so sure we'll be able to count on your adventurers' discretion or thoroughness on this one. This quest is time-sensitive, and they took years to accomplish the last quest. Besides, this amulet proves nothing. The boy might still be alive for all we know."

"Think of it from the other direction, my lord. Our treasury is full from our recent conquest of Montroyal, my lord. Why risk stiffing these adventurers out of the reward they earned for fulfilling this quest right at the moment when they are our only option to cement our alliance with the Holy Office of the Inquisition?"

"Only option? A whole army is at my disposal."

"You can't send the whole army. Only a small party of adventurers with no formal links to you can complete a quest like this. We don't have time to putz around weighing options and conducting job interviews for qualified but obscure candidates.

"Let's not underestimate Goldilocks. She's got a three-day head start on us. We must assume that she has friends in every town and village from Baston to Oregan. She probably speaks a dozen languages and knows every local custom. She'll blend in, disappear. Unless we send out a crack team of elite adventurers right away, she will have the Sword of Layban before our people even reach Rofchester."

Amhirst shakes his head, gets up, and starts pacing around the room. After a short while he announces, "Sir Sean, I don't like it. I simply don't trust these adventurers. They're sloppy, slow, and inconsistent. A quest of this importance requires someone quick, efficient, and loyal."

"That presents a paradox, my lord. You expect us to entrust this quest to someone who has no association with you but is perfectly loyal and competent."

Amhirst snaps his fingers and stops pacing. "Wait! I have an idea! These adventurers could prove useful if only we appointed a proper leader to keep them in check. We would need someone whose loyalty I trust not to cheat me, but has no known public association with me that could get me in trouble with the Templars if caught, and is clever enough to tangle with sly adventurers. I do believe we have found our man." He and Sir Sean slowly turn their heads to gaze at the youngest person in the room. "What do you say, Benjamin Frankelyn?"

Scene 5: Winning One for the Gipper

Betzy Rose Mansion, Red Giant's Base, Shentalpee City
Spy Woden's Day Nones. Afternoon, 5th of April, 1284

When Madame Dungaree opens the door, joy suffuses her face. "Health and happiness, Mister Lynx! You bring light to this place. I knew you'd come! Mademoiselle Zena isn't home right now but our guest is eager to meet you. Walk this way, if you please."

Clearly making an effort to put on a brave face, Lynx smiles and says, "Health and happiness to you, Madame Dungaree. Please, don't trouble yourself. Bartlebee can show me the way."

A jolt of pain and embarrassment streaks across her eyes. "Oh, um . . . Bartlebee is away on . . . personal leave. It was an unexpected family matter and I haven't managed to replace her yet. I'd be happy to walk with you myself but before we go in, I can't help but notice you look a little sad."

"Not sad, just frustrated. Just before coming here, I won the Justiciar League tournament by one point over Monsieur Enganyon. He was so angry that he left early but when I went up to claim my commission as a Junior Officer, the adjudicators disqualified my last arrow and awarded the commission to Monsieur Enganyon."

"Oh, that's too bad. I'm so disappointed at how they've been treating you. Wait…did you say Monsieur Enganyon left early? Maybe you could argue that he forfeited the tournament by quitting."

Lynx flings his hands out and flops them back to his sides like an elfling that just missed recess. "I already tried. They said his leg injury exempted him from that rule. It's no use, Madame Dungaree. They're always going to find an excuse to keep a wood elf like me out of the major leagues."

She puts her hand on his back and leads him through the corridor to the guest room saying, "Don't give up, Mister Lynx. They think they're so smart, but you'll outsmart them when the time is right."

Compared to the homes of other high elves of her wealth and status, Dungaree Jeanne's residence, called Betzy Rose Mansion, is like a Spartan war camp. Against any other standard, her treetop mansion is no less spectacular than Cinderella's castle at the Magic Realms theme park in D'Isigny World. Magnificent murals, elegant arches, and fancy furniture line every step of the way from the front door to the guest room.

Up in Shentalpee City, real estate is sold by the square inch, not the square foot, so the hallways are just broad enough to let two people pass by each other cozily while admiring the great art along the way. Tables and chairs are recessed into lofted nooks so as not to take up any precious floor space. Not only are the wooden ceiling tiles richly carved, lacquered, and filigreed, but also the wall panels and floorboards make a serious attempt to hold your attention with their decorative ingenuity.

Still, despite all this elegance, Betzy Rose Mansion's décor is staid, almost a bare-bones concept for avoiding extravagance compared to her high elf neighbors.

The fourth door past the waiting room is the guest room. The parlor and the dining room are downstairs so that visitors to the household do not need to go traipsing through the private quarters of the permanent residents upstairs. Bartlebee's room is just past the kitchen with her own servant's entrance across the way.

You cannot see it easily from the bottom of the glittering staircase but once you get to the second floor, the impressive furnishings and refined decorations mellow out significantly to a posh but sparing nexus of bedrooms, the largest of which is currently used as a library and study. The main staircase—complete with the kind of glamorous steps and railings a fairy-tale princess would need to make a dramatic entrance for her suitors waiting down below—overhangs Johnny Appleseed's guest room.

Gently knocking on the door, Dungaree Jeanne hears a muffled hoot from inside and takes it as an invitation to come in. Nearly all high elf dwellings share a wall or two with their neighbors so soundproofing is one of the top architectural priorities. That makes it nearly impossible to eavesdrop in Shentalpee City—I say nearly impossible because Zena somehow manages to overhear every whisper from one end of the mansion to the other.

Anyway, Dungaree Jeanne opens the door and shows Lynx in. Reverend Appleseed seems to be waking up from a nap and gets reminded in the process of all the pain in his leg. The expression on his face lets them all know he is doing his best to endure it bravely.

Lynx extends a hand and says in Aenglish, "Pleasure to meet you, Reverend Appleseed."

Johnny Appleseed takes Lynx's hand and pretends to smile despite the pain shooting up and down his leg. "Are you the young wood elf who speaks Aenglish?"

"My name is Hare Gipper. You say Mister Lynx in Aenglish, no? I am wood elf, like you say. If I speak

Aenglish, you listen and say yes or no." Lynx laughs and when Reverend Appleseed realizes he is trying to be funny he joins in the laughter, just to be polite.

The reality is Johnny Appleseed barely understands Lynx's thick Elvish accent. He sighs with noble resignation. It's going to be a long couple of months up here as the only human in Shentalpee City.

Madame Dungaree backs out of the room, saying in her crisp, fluent Aenglish, "Well, I'll leave you two to get acquainted. If Mademoiselle Zena does return, I'll make sure to send her up to you as well."

The mention of Zena's name spikes a surge of confusion and fear within Lynx's innermost thoughts. He came here intending to tell Zena about Enganyon's relationship with Florenz at the Shade Gap but what if she reacts to the news as irrationally as Buttercup did?

"Pleasure to meet you, Hare Gipper. Do you know about our Lord and Savior Jesus Christ?"

Totally distracted with his own problems, Lynx answers absent-mindedly, "Yes, I do. He is very nice guy, thank you."

Johnny Appleseed says with a fatherly concern, "Something's bothering you, Hare Gipper. It ain't hard to tell. As we say in Kentikie, you look like a cat on a hot, lead-shingled roof."

Lynx confesses at once, "You know Mademoiselle Zena? I love her too much but she love bad elf. His name is Monsieur Enganyon Gandorfson."

"Yes, I've met this Enganyon fellow. You could say he taught me how to fly. Hardy har-har!"

Now it is Lynx's turn to pretend to smile. It is hard to believe even a Christian missionary would take an assassination attempt so lightly. "Monsieur Enganyon is liar and Mademoiselle Zena believe him always. He pretend he like Mademoiselle Zena but he only want to win elve girl who win election. He think Mademoiselle Florenz is better winner so he go to Shade Gap with her. I think to tell Mademoiselle Zena so she see that he love Mademoiselle Florenz but I think she not listen."

Reverend Appleseed rubs his beard and thinks for a while. "Hmm," he says cautiously. "If she has such poor judgment, maybe you would be better off transferring your affections to another young maiden."

Lynx throws his hands up in the air. "But it is not me that I think that I can love other elve! I not choose elve that I love. Mademoiselle Zena is beautiful, smart, and . . . how you say? . . . magical. She soon have magica wand. Her mother is very rich and she tame unicorn! How many Aenglish girls tame unicorn?"

"Most Aenglish girls don't believe in unicorns . . ."

"Wait . . . not believe? What Aenglish girls say when they see pony with horn on head?"

"People believe what they want to believe and rarely allow what they see or don't see to get in the way of that, once they've made up their minds."

"Yes! That is how Mademoiselle Zena do to me! She always believe Monsieur Enganyon and she is mad to me when I say to her that he is bad elf."

Johnny Appleseed gives him a hard but kind look and says, "Let's take a step back for a moment, Hare Gipper. Would you still love her if she lost her good-looks, her wealth, and her talents?"

"I not so sure what you want to say."

"You said Enganyon wants to marry the winner of the election. How different is your love? What I'm asking is this: do you really love Zena . . . I mean,

Mademoiselle Zena . . . for who she is or are you just impressed with all that she has going for her now?"

"I not so sure."

"My intuition tells me her heart belongs to Monsieur Enganyon, but Madame Dungaree does not like him and she thinks you're a better influence."

"Your intuition is good."

"When it comes to winning the heart of a sassy young woman, nice guys finish last, Mister Gipper. I suggest you find a lady whose heart beats at a speed closer to yours."

"But I not let Mademoiselle Zena marry bad elf."

"You have to let her decide that for herself. The more you insist, the worse she will resent you for forcing her to face a truth she's not yet ready to handle.

"Besides, this Enganyon fellow might not be so bad after all. Jonah got angry when he heard God had forgiven the Ninevites after they repented of their sins. What if Enganyon comes around and does some good with his life? Are you going to be able to accept God's mercy for him? Christ came to call sinners, you know."

Lynx folds his arms. "Yes, I know. I am Christian like prophet Healaman. I know that Christians love enemies but Mademoiselle Zena not want—"

Knock, knock!

Johnny Appleseed calls out, "Who's there?"

They hear a muffled voice say, "Hatch."

Johnny Appleseed asks, "Hatch who?"

Zena peeks her head inside smiling and says, "Gezondhide!" When she sees Lynx speaking with Johnny Appleseed, she raises her eyebrows and greets him in Eldric, "Health and happiness to you, Mister Lynx! You bring light to our house! Can I have a word with you for a minute?"

"Sure, Mademoiselle Zena," replies Lynx in Eldric, suddenly turning weak and submissive. "I was just telling Reverend Appleseed I was hoping to see you."

She giggles apologetically and asks in Aenglish, "Pardon, Reverend Appleseed, please give me permission that I speak with Lynx in Eldric for little bit? We have, um . . . family problem."

Johnny Appleseed asks cheerfully, "Are you pregnant? I've placed plenty of unexpected babies in loving families. No need to hide any embarrassments from me. I'm too old to blush at life."

Zena's jaw hangs open for a few moments before she recovers. "Uh, no . . . that is not it at all. I will say it in Aenglish if it makes you feel more comfortable."

"As you wish, my fair lady. If there's any assistance I can provide to you and your mother, I will. Your kindness to me has been overwhelming."

Zena sits down next to Lynx and puts on a serious face. She tells him in Aenglish, "Mademoiselle Florenz has announced to Tuscoraura high elves that our stewardess, Bartlebee, has stealed alchemy for elf fire from my mother and she is selling to mercenary dwarf, who has name Master Chief Engineer Tom Thumb — very famous and very powerful dwarf. We not do it, but Bartlebee is our stewardess and we take blame."

Johnny Appleseed runs his fingers through his beard. "Why would Mademoiselle Florenz say all this about you, if it's not true?"

Zena takes a deep breath. "She wants to win election! Our early fathers and mothers have invented alchemy for . . . how do you say . . . ooze to make elf fire. You throw it at enemy and they go up in big fire and nothing can put out fire, not even water. Elf fire is very important to fire elves. We feel safe because only we know elf fire. If dwarves know elf fire, fire elves feel very scared. We are not special anymore. No one votes for elve who loses elf fire alchemy."

Again Johnny Appleseed nods and comments, "So you have gallons of unquenchable fire ooze up here in the treetops? Not the safest idea, is it?"

Lynx explains, "Shentalpee City is builded on sequoia. Sequoia is fire tree. Fire not harm sequoia. Fire good for sequoia. It make pine cone open and give new seed. Sequoia tree need fire and fire elf need fire."

Turning back to Zena, Johnny Appleseed asks, "Do you need my help to prove that these accusations are not true?"

A worried look settles on Zena's face. "Yes and no. My mother says that Bartlebee stole alchemy to other fire, we call it Athabask fire. Athabask fire not so strong as elf fire and you put salt on it and it goes out. So alchemy to true elf fire is still safe.

"But even so it is still bad. If all world knows that dwarves have Athabask fire, they think that fire elves

132

not so special, even with elf fire. I already tell you that Umpire Kibbler wants that Tuscoraura elves make more weapons so that we be stronger than our enemies. If our enemies have all same weapons—or if our enemies *think* they have all same weapons—they will attack Shentalpee City. And that is no good. The fire elves say best weapon is one we never use."

Tears well up in the corners of Zena's eyes. Lynx puts a hand on her shoulder to encourage her, just as she did for him earlier on. Zena sniffles and pulls out an embroidered silk handkerchief. Without thinking, she switches to Eldric. "If we arrest Bartlebee right away and make sure that Tom Thumb's dwarves don't get their grubby, overgrown hands on that Athabask recipe, the Council of Perfects is willing to acquit my mother of all charges before the case goes to trial.

"If we fail, my mother will be publicly prosecuted for leaking state secrets. If she is convicted, the council could revoke our status as high elves, confiscate all our property, and even have her executed as a traitor!"

Lynx stands up. Striking his most chivalrous pose, he declares in Eldric, "I will find Bartlebee for you, Mademoiselle Zena! I place my bow at your—"

Guessing from his body language that Lynx is about to make big promises, Johnny Appleseed cuts him off and says in Aenglish with a loud, assertive voice, "What young Mister Lynx means to say is that he is flattered by the trust and confidence you have placed in him and that he will give your dilemma serious consideration.

"In the meantime, he has a matter of similar peril that he has to handle at the Shade Gap this very night. Perhaps if you, little missy, could help him with his quest at the Shade Gap, he could help you with your quest in handling all that elf fire business. Isn't that right, my boy?"

Lynx blinks. Suddenly a light goes on in his eyes and he stutters in Aenglish, "Oh . . . um . . . yes, that is right. You can help me with my . . . um . . . quest at Shade Gap tonight, then I can help you with your quest to get Bartlebee."

Zena looks askance at Johnny Appleseed, then nods to Lynx and says in Eldric, "Yes, I agree to help you if you solemnly promise to see this quest for Bartlebee through to the end. If Bartlebee escapes on a swift pony, we may need to take on Tom Thumb and his dwarf engineers."

Lynx puffs out his chest with pride. "Rudolph could run down a halfling pony any day of the week."

Zena smiles with a sly, satisfied grin, convinced that she has thoroughly manipulated every weakness in Lynx's chivalrous nature, and announces, "Very well then, let's get our gear ready. Hi ho! It's off to Shade Gap we go!"

Scene 6: Blasphemous Rhapsody

Shade Gap
Five Miles Northwest of Tuscoraura Mountain
Spy Woden's Day Compline. Night, 5th of April, 1284

Brother Umbert blurts out to Sir Robert Roger, "We can't let them kill him! Show him you mean business. Cut off the goblin's ear or something!"

Inquisitor Sheen interrupts, "Our Lord healed Malchus's ear. We are not to resort to violence except in self-defense."

Sir Robert Roger, holding the dagger to the throat of the old chieftain's son, says, "Sorry, little monk, I tried but it's just not going to happen that way. The deal was to keep my men safe. If I harm his son, he will kill all my rangers." He turns to Brother Umbert. "It's too bad about the boy, but at this point, there is nothing we can do about it."

Brother Umbert squeaks, "We would be material accomplices to murder if we do nothing!"

"All we can do now is pray, Brother Umbert," says Inquisitor Sheen, resigned. "We put our trust in God."

The goblin captors make the rangers and the monks kneel between two stone arches painted with pictograms. The goblins have set up tents around the pagan temple. The inquisitor's gift of tongues is powerful enough that he can slowly read the words of the goblin prophets written on the archway walls and encampment banners.

Inquisitor Sheen focuses on them prayerfully and as the words form in his mind, it suddenly clicks and the sign flashes out its warning, "Here on these hallowed grounds, you will behold the rites that voices may never share. Thou shalt not talk without speaking. Thou shalt not listen without hearing. Defilers of these stones are doomed."

One goblin wearing a coyote fur draped across his head and shoulders fills a flagon from a barrel and makes the inquisitors and rangers drink it, saying, "Koolaed!"

Brother Umbert refuses. "I will not partake in this heathen ceremony!"

Sir Robert Roger shouts, "Just drink the koolaed, and let's get this over with!"

Brother Crowe takes a swig, then another, and exclaims with a grin, "Hops!"

Among the group of captive rangers is a young apprentice named Nathan Hayle. The coyote goblin passes him by. He asks, "What hops?"

Dame Frances Marian says, "Hops is a bitter seasoning from Bohemia that preserves drinks from spoiling. Whenever available, I add hops and vinegar to my canteen to keep the water from going rancid and ward off scurvy. Actually, I find it tasty. Ahem! Mister Goblin, could I have another swig of your koolaed?"

Nathan Hayle sours his face when he takes a sip. "Tasty? Says the lady who drinks vinegar every day."

Sir Robert Roger looks at one of the goblin acolytes and says, "Over here, let me try some of that."

The goblin acolyte scoops some more out and the ranger captain quaffs the entire flagon. Having all drunk the koolaed, the rangers comply with their part in preparing themselves for the human sacrifice. Brother Umbert, however, folds his arms in protest.

Inquisitor Sheen says, "Brother Umbert, drink the koolaed or they will offer you to their god, Poodoo!"

Brother Umbert wrinkles his face in indignation. "Is this real life or just a fantasy? The inquisitor himself is telling me to take part in a human sacrifice ritual!"

Two goblins drag the wicker basket cage holding the young monk toward the sacrificial altar. He is a tall, lanky human teenager sporting a peach fuzz mustache. His wears a Carmelite brown robe and white cape.

The hulking goblin who seems to be the chieftain's older son pulls the young monk out of the cage with one hand. Towering over the other goblins, this hulking goblin stands an inch or two over six feet tall. He wears little more than a purple loincloth and his bulging muscles make the strongest goblins around him seem scrawny.

He is decked out with white and black tribal paints and carries a ceremonial phoenix claw in his right hand. He shouts, "Malileo gandango scaramanifico!"

All look to Inquisitor Sheen for a translation but the inquisitor says nothing.

Brother Umbert makes the sign of the cross and cries out, "Look, Inquisitor Sheen! That boy is a monk! Spare him his life from this monstrosity!"

The inquisitor remains silent.

The young monk turns his collar to the cold and damp and says, "Don't stir trouble for yourselves over me. I'm just a poor boy. I need no sympathy! If you object too loudly, they will kill you too."

The goblin king approaches the altar wearing a ceremonial headdress with vulture feathers, snake fangs, and coyote skulls. The hulking goblin hands his father the ceremonial phoenix talon. Then the goblin king sprinkles a powder into the altar flame and it explodes with a frightful boom.

The flash of demon light stabs the eyes of the inquisitors and rangers, splitting the night.

The young monk continues to intone the words of the psalm, "Yes, though I walk through the valley of the shadow of death, I will fear no evil. For you are with me, O God. Your rod and staff give me comfort." And in the naked light of that flash Brother Umbert sees ten drowsy people, maybe more, close enough to rescue the boy but no one dares to disturb the sound of the inquisitor's silence.

"Fools," says Brother Umbert. "Don't you know that the silence of good people in the face of evil grows like a cancer? Hear my words. At least we can teach these goblins by our deaths that we do not approve of killing innocent lives."

But his words fall like silent raindrops and run off the stones without soaking in. The only echoes come from the wells in the caverns beneath.

And the goblins bow and pray to the demon gods they made out of stone.

Despite Brother Umbert's protests, the goblin king carries on as if nothing really matters and says, "Basem illa mammia."

They pour koolaed into Brother Umbert's mouth but he spits it out all over the goblin king. Two goblin acolytes grab him and put him on the sacrificial altar. All the courage drains from his face as he blubbers to himself, "Wait! What . . . what are they doing?"

At last, the thought of losing his feisty but dear friend moves Inquisitor Sheen to risk failing his quest of reaching Tuscoraura Mountain for the Holy Office of the Inquisition. Thus, he speaks out to the old war chief in Gobbledygook, "I know that you are powerful, mighty Gog, and that your anger with my friend must be equally powerful. I count on your greatness to bargain for his life. With your wisdom, I'm sure we can work out an arrangement that will be mutually beneficial and avoid any unpleasant confrontation."

The chief grunts, "Heck no, I won't let him go!"

Not understanding the words exchanged between the two but seeing the disappointment on the inquisitor's face at the goblin king's reply, Brother Umbert whimpers, "Too late, my time has come. It sends shivers down my spine. My body aches."

A goblin shaman approaches the altar and throws another handful of powder into the fire. It explodes and seems to put the goblin king into a trance. He begins to prophesy in a sacred goblin tongue that only goblin shamans and Inquisitor Sheen, because of his mystical gift of tongues, can understand. "Hello, darkness, my old friend, I've come to offer you this boy as a human sacrifice as you instructed me in that softly creeping vision. The seeds of long life and a glorious future were planted in my spleen while I was sleeping. May this offering ensure that I always destroy my enemies and may it keep us safe from wendigos."

The goblin king drags the young monk up to the altar and lifts the phoenix talon dagger high over his head, aiming to strike the boy's heart.

Seeing death close in on him, the young Carmelite monk panics. "Mama, ooh, I don't want to die!"

With a sudden smile alighting on his face, Brother Umbert shouts, "Wait! I see a little silhouette of an elf in the trees. We are saved!"

Scene 7: A Long Shot

Shade Gap
Five Miles Northwest of Tuscoraura Mountain
Spy Woden's Day Matins
After Midnight, 5th of April, 1284

The trees do not grow tall on the mountaintops overlooking the Shade Gap, but Lynx perches himself two hundred yards away on an aspen tree with enough foliage to conceal his movements. Zena crouches close behind him still wondering why exactly Lynx invited her out to spy on this goblin ritual. Although the greenish-yellow glow from the tips of the goblin torchbearers' ten-foot poles cast an unnatural hue across the horizon, like a grim dawn, the evening stars are still romantic, so she decides to focus on the starlight and daydream the night away while Lynx figures out what he really wants to do here.

Her thoughts drift to seven wedding plans to match seven different scenarios that she can imagine where Enganyon finally confesses that he loves her. Her reveries halt when she notices the halfling monk—whom we know to be Brother Umbert—pointing straight at them. Most of the goblins turn their heads to look but the goblin king remains entranced, ready to carry out the sacrifice.

Lynx shudders. Two hundred yards away foul spirits gambol and innocent lives are under the knife. The wind blows one way, then the next. He steadies his bow arm, draws the bowstring back, and exhales. Casting fate to the wind, Lynx sends his shot.

The yellow-fletched arrow streaks through the dark toward the heart of the goblin king on a mission of mercy to save the two monks from a diabolical death.

It misses.

The arrow glides high and wide, then unexpectedly buries itself in the goblin king's wrist. Covered with koolaed and spittle, the goblin king drops the ceremonial dagger. Blood drips freely down past his elbow but his trance is undisturbed.

Uncomfortable groans reverberate on the mountaintop and the goblins' faces are covered with worry and discord. For devout goblins, interrupting a human sacrifice is a very ill omen indeed. The goblin king, not realizing he dropped the sacrificial dagger, purses his lips and readies himself to finish it.

Sir Robert Roger's hostage, the goblin with long, dark hair, smiles confidently seeing the confusion well up. With a sudden lurch of his head backwards he breaks Sir Robert Roger's nose. All it takes is a quick flick of his wrist, and he twists the long knife away from his throat. The black-haired goblin gives the ranger a fierce elbow in the chest, knocking the wind out of him, then snatches the steel hatchet from his belt.

The wheezing ranger captain looks on helplessly as the black-haired goblin runs toward the sacrificial altar calling out, "Kwid prow kwow!"

Mass chaos breaks out among the goblins. They hack and slash at each other mercilessly. Not sure if Lynx angered them with his sacrilegious interruption of the ceremony or if they are just too prone to infighting for their own good, Zena snaps into action. She strings her own bow and starts launching poisoned arrows into the wild press of scuffling goblins.

Elves are not particularly fond of goblins, especially these goblins who have been terrorizing travelers in the forests around Tuscoraura Mountain. Being an elve of her times, Zena enjoys the chance to bloody her enemies with too much zeal. Lynx tugs at her sleeve and urges her. "Come on, Mademoiselle Zena! Now we can rescue the halflings and the humans."

Taking great satisfaction in dealing out death and destruction, she brushes him off, "It's still too risky! Let's improve the odds by killing off these goblins."

Back on the altar, straining under the weight of a dead gobliness fallen on top of him, Brother Umbert whirls his eyes around and hatches a plan. He whispers as loudly as he can without attracting attention to the young monk, "What's your name, Frater?"

"I don't know."

"What do you mean you don't know?"

"Brother David was my religious name," he says, unsure of himself. "But I don't think I'm a Carmelite anymore, so I'm supposed to go by my baptismal name. But I was a foundling on the monastery doorstep and no one ever told me my baptismal name."

"Whatever your canonical status with the Carmelites may be, you're still a cleric. I'll call you Brother Clarke."

"Why Clarke?" asks the confused young monk.

Brother Umbert cannot help but throw in some of his knowledge. "Have you ever heard of a cooper?"

"Sure, that's a barrel maker."

"How about a wainwright?"

"Um, I think they're in the wagon business."

"Right. A cooper is trained to make barrels, and a wainwright is trained to fix wagons. Likewise, a clarke

142

is trained as a cleric to heal, counsel, and guide. You're trained. That makes you a clarke, doesn't it, Frater?"

"I suppose it does."

"Good. Now then, Brother Clarke, the ceremonial dagger is right behind you. Just scootch back a bit and cut yourself free."

Brother Clarke rolls onto the ceremonial dagger in an attempt to grab hold of it. He wiggles around so he can slide his fingers around the handle but his blind attempts wind up with him accidentally cutting his ring finger deeply before he finally succeeds in clutching the handle and sliding the blade against the ropes.

The dagger is so sharp that it easily slices through the thick vines used to bind his hands. When he turns to free Brother Umbert, he notices that his right hand is covered with blood.

The dagger itself is nothing more than a four-inch-long phoenix claw fused onto the top of a stick with a glob of melted copper to bind them together. There is no attempt at artistry or even tidiness in the craftsmanship but its sharpness alone explains why it was chosen as a sacred implement in a ritual sacrifice.

Instead of rescuing Brother Umbert, the young monk sways, waving the dagger around recklessly.

Brother Umbert barks, "Hey, watch where you swing that thing! Don't you know that a phoenix talon has powerful soporific effects?"

Brother Clarke yawns and asks, "What does *soporific* mean?"

"That means it will put you to sleep."

Before he finishes his sentence, Brother Clarke collapses back onto the altar, snoring as loud as a lion sleeping in the night.

Back up in the aspen tree overlooking the ritual site, Lynx sees the young human monk tumble over right before freeing the halfling monk. He dreads the worst for them and announces to Zena, who is still sending poisoned arrows into the crowd of goblins, "I'm going to rescue the innocent people down there before the goblins kill them all."

Zena cannot believe Lynx's naïve plan. She whispers back harshly, "No, you can't go! There are still too many goblins. Besides, even if you do free them, the humans would stab you in the back."

"Why would they do that if we're helping them?"

"Humans are the most ungrateful of all the clayborn. If they see your valuables, they wouldn't bat an eyelash at murdering the very same elf who saved them from bondage to steal it all."

Lynx wipes the sweat from his brow. "I'll just free the two halflings and they can free the humans."

"The goblins will hear you and run you down."

"It's my life I'm risking, not yours."

Zena raises her voice, welling up with emotion. "Lynx, I care about you. I really do. You're so precious to me. Please don't risk your life just to save those humans. They're not worth it."

Lynx pauses for a moment, trying to hold back the tears. A black-haired Weemaway goblin appears at the sacrifice site, rifling through the belongings of the rangers and bundling up their spare weapons to take away. One ranger, Sir Thomas, resists, and the goblin stabs him in the ribs with cold disinterest.

Lynx looks Zena in the eye and says, "I know you can't appreciate it, but I can't turn a blind eye while innocent lives are lost, even if they are only humans."

Lynx surveys the scene to find the best path for sneaking over to free the captives. A rocky gully allows him a quick and concealed path to the altar. With his plan decided upon, he quietly slides down the aspen tree and starts to sneak over to rescue the halfling.

Before he gets far, he spots a little nook in a large pile of rocks that would make the perfect hiding spot and slides himself in.

"Hey, watch it!" says an older elf's voice in Eldric from deeper inside the nook.

"Ahhh!" The surprise of getting caught soon fades into wonderment at finding another fire elf in his hiding spot. When his heartbeat settles down, Lynx asks in Eldric, "Who are you?"

"Master Shoemaker Gulliber Swiffson of Clan Adidazar, at your service. Am I safe in guessing you are a fellow wood elf of Tuscoraura?"

"You are, but your name is not familiar to me."

"That's because I disappeared from Tuscoraura Mountain before you were born. Anyway, no time to chitchat. I'm here to rescue these humans."

"Actually, I was just going to rescue the halfling and let him help the humans escape. A good friend warned me not to trust humans. They have a reputation for ingratitude. Besides, my mother always told me that traipsing around with goblins lurking about is not good for my health."

Master Gulliber nods. "All too true. All right then, let's free that garrulous halfling up there on the altar; but be careful! Try to keep in step with me."

Master Gulliber pops his head up to check for goblins. Confident no one has seen him, he waves to Lynx and the two wood elves crawl up on the altar. There is a dead gobliness warrior splayed across Brother Umbert. Her huge frame pins his arms and legs down so that he can't budge an inch.

Master Gulliber moves next to Brother Umbert, lies down on his back, and gets his legs under the dead gobliness. Lynx catches on and positions himself side by side. With a silent heave-ho, they roll her off the altar. The halfling monk seems to be thanking them, but his babbling is in a language they don't understand.

Lynx simply draws his leaf-bladed short sword and cuts through the vines that were tying the halfling monk's hands together. He whispers to Master Gulliber, "Job's done! Let's get out of here."

Suddenly, they both turn their heads and see a goblin running toward them. Master Gulliber lets out a foul word. On foot, goblins are the fastest runners of all the races in Vinland, so both elves duck behind the other side of the altar and try to vanish from sight. Lynx gets down on his hands and bear-walks to a corner of the altar where he can tuck himself inside a small niche.

The sound of the goblin's footsteps moves up onto the altar. Lynx readies his short sword and smears the blade with some poison. He does not have the kind of money to afford an exceptionally fast-acting nerve agent but if he can get in a first prick with a surprise attack and wear the goblin down with a few adroit dodges and parries, he could have a chance at winning the fight.

As usual, nothing goes according to plan. The goblin leaps down from the altar and lands facing Lynx, who is still wedged into his hiding spot. Lynx lunges forward to stab the goblin but a quick swipe from the goblin's war club knocks his short sword out of his hand. Cornered, Lynx tries to slip by him but the goblin snatches Lynx by the scruff of his neck, lifts him into the air, and squeezes slowly to make him suffer.

As Lynx dangles up off his feet above the ground, trying desperately to pry the powerful fingers from around his throat, he kicks and punches to no avail. Just as he feels he is about to pass out, he drops to the ground like a potato sack and bangs his knee on a rock.

Catching his breath, he turns around to see Zena standing triumphantly over the goblin's lifeless body. She does have the money to afford quick and deadly poisons for her sword and arrows. She twirls her sleek blade in the air and asks with a big, friendly smile, "Why do I always have to save your aaaaahhhhh!"

A second lurking goblin, cloaked in a black bear's pelt, crushes Zena's sword arm and right hip with a dreadful swipe of his ashen club. It is a swift and silent blow but the raw power in the goblin's arm crashes into her lithe frame, shattering bones and sending her into shock. The goblin bends down and starts picking the jewelry off her while she moans in delirious agony. Unarmed, Lynx's grief-crazed mind can only come up with one plan—a desperate charge with his bare hands.

The goblin looks up but carelessly swats him aside with a heavy backhand, then gets back to picking the jewelry off Zena's outfit and limbs. Lynx sees stars and can't figure out which way is up, never mind getting back on his feet for another charge.

Master Gulliber whistles at the goblin and calls to him in Eldric, saying, "Yoo-hoo! Over here!" which would have sounded to our modern Aenglish ears more like, "Thou eat trash! Hernia!" had we been there ourselves. Next to him, Lynx sees a vaguely familiar older elve dangle her jewelry like a curbside sales rep.

Having helped himself to the most impressive pieces from Zena's outfit, the goblin swaggers over with the same greedy confidence as an unnoticed five-year-old stealing the prize from an open cereal box down a lonely supermarket aisle. Just as the goblin reaches for the jewelry, the elf lady unfurls a sling, twirls it twice, and hurls the stone at the goblin's masculine parts for an up-close and personal sales pitch.

The goblin keels over. Master Gulliber grabs Zena's poisoned blade and sticks it to him. Their boldness breathes new life into Lynx. He wills himself back into action and hoists Zena's broken body into his arms.

Moving a trauma patient with possible spine, neck, and head injuries is a bad idea but Lynx does not think. He runs on pure emotion—grief, passion, anger, fear, desperation. Holding Zena close to his chest and hoping that somehow getting her back to Tuscoraura Mountain will save her, he runs.

And he runs.

The dark earth haunts his mind. Time takes its toll. His berserker frenzy chills. The thorns scrape his legs. The weight of Zena's body burns the muscles in his arms. His chest heaves. The wind scrapes his lungs. A low-hanging branch smacks his head.

Through an opening in the trees, he sees the garden gnome village on the edges of the marchlands of

Tuscoraura Mountain. Garden gnomes have good doctors. With that one grain of blind hope, he collapses.

Zena wavers in and out of consciousness and moans, "The goblins! Watch out, Mister Lynx."

Lynx, sincerely touched by her concern and utterly exhausted, says, "Hush, my darling, don't fear, my darling. The goblins sleep tonight."

She stammers, "B...b...but where are we?"

"Near the village, the peaceful gnome village . . . the goblins sleep tonight."

"When will we go home?"

"When daylight comes, we'll go home."

Zena asks, "Is it okay if I sleep then?"

"Yes, my darling, to sleep . . . perchance to dream."

With that, they both pass out amid the shrubs of the marchlands.

ACT III

SUGAR AND HEISTS
AND EVERYTHING NICE

Scene 1: Catch an Elve by the Toe

Elf Colonial Marchlands, Tuscoraura Mountain
Maundy Thor's Day Sext
Afternoon, 6th of April, 1284

Florenz looks around nervously and notices Lynx is missing. She left him there. Trembling guilt drips from the corner of her right eye. She left him when he was surrounded by goblins near the altar. She wanted to help but Enganyon had convinced her to run.

Angst. That's what Enganyon called it: angst.

She went out to Shade Gap hoping to save a few humans from the goblin sacrificial rites but instead she abandoned her compatriot—one of the sweetest wood elves she knows—to their blood-thirsty clutches.

But wait! Here he comes now.

Lynx is alive!

His eyes are heavy, his hands are trembling, and his shoulders are stooped. He plops down on the bench and just closes his eyes. Leaning his head back, he breathes such a woeful sigh you'd think it was his last.

Florenz doesn't dare ask what happened. She cannot let the high elves know she's been moonlighting as a hero to save humans—especially not her father.

With a wink to his daughter, Umpire-in-Chief Kibbler Earnestson steps up on a raised platform and announces, "Mesdames, mesdemoiselles, messieurs, ladies, and gentelves, we all have stakes in today's tournament and I doubly so. First, as umpire-in-chief, I want to see our colony recruit the finest and fittest elves to bolster the ranks of the Ivy League. They are our first line of defense, securing our borders against goblin raiders, human poachers, gnome spies, and dwarf troublemakers of every sort.

"Second, as a father, I want to see my daughter perform well so she can pledge her strong hands and nimble body to the service of our great colony. Some of you, no doubt most of you, are feeling put off by the conflict of interest. In years past, an unofficial tradition has developed whereby the umpire's immediate family has had to sit out these tournaments to prevent their family ties from bringing an unfair advantage.

"Even with this precautionary measure in place, many elves still criticize these recruitment tournaments because they feel the judges lean partially toward those who are politically well-connected rather than those who are the most qualified.

"To rectify this imbalance, I am offering to pay for a scholarship—out of my own personal funds—for a commission as a junior officer in the Ivy League to any elf or elve who comes up as the second-place winner, if my daughter takes first place. This way, she will not be depriving anyone of a well-deserved scholarship."

The news startles the crowd and excited murmurs ripple throughout Thor's Base. The dean of the Ivy League himself, Dean Halvard Prinson of Clan Sandford, replaces Umpire Kibbler on the stage and announces in a loud voice, "The rules for this tournament will be the same as always—the first elf to make it to the highest point of Tiw's Tree shall win a free commission as a junior officer in the Ivy League.

"Earlier today I expressed my concern about the unprecedented participation of Mademoiselle Florenz Kibblersdottir in this tournament, but our assembly of senior officers feels the umpire-in-chief's offer to pay for the commission of his daughter's runner-up is a fair way to compensate.

"Before we begin, a warning—the Ivy League is not for the fainthearted, but it is not for the rash or reckless either. It requires self-control and good judgment. Any elf or elve who directly or indirectly causes a fellow contestant to suffer permanent injury or death will be barred from the Ivy League, with no possibility for appeal, on top of the usual civil and criminal penalties.

"And now . . . contestants, take your places!"

They all circle around Tiw's Tree. It is the only one of the seven sacred trees supporting Thor's Base with low-lying branches that can be reached from the platform. The rules are simple—get to the top first. The sport resembles a special mix between gymnastics and martial arts because the competitors punch, kick, knee, and elbow each other while climbing—a vertically ascending wrestling match with a touch of acrobatics.

"Contestants, ready? Three . . . two . . . one . . . go!"

Florenz, Lynx, and Screech, a small but tenacious high elve from Clan Antmiony, scramble to the west side of the tree where the branches are spaced farthest apart, making the climb more difficult but giving their ascent less chance of getting stymied by a fistfight.

On the east side, where the branches interweave like a tidy set of monkey bars, the main pack of elves clusters up for an easier climb but with more violence in the fray. Only a few yards up from the starting block the pushing, shoving, grabbing, elbowing, and scuffles get desperate and ruthless.

On the west side, Screech takes the lead quickly. She is only an inch over four feet in height, but she has unusually large hands and feet. She climbs quickly and without thinking. Florenz and Lynx follow close behind.

Despite his fatigue after having saved the humans from the goblin ritual, Lynx seems to be powered by some unearthly rage and strains his way up, neck and neck with Screech. His ferocity draws too much attention as a fist comes slamming across his face. He hears his nose crack and slips down a branch. The elf who punched him is a reject from the east side scuffle and retreats from the tournament altogether to avoid retaliation, but Lynx has no time to waste on revenge. He quickly wipes his nose with his left sleeve—luckily, only snot. *No blood, no foul!*

With Lynx out of the way for the moment, Florenz races past him, hot on the heels of Screech. Umpire Kibbler's generous offer has had the side effect of keeping the most dangerous roughhousing away from her since she poses no threat by winning. When Screech reaches a branch that dead-ends, Florenz realizes she has made a terrible mistake.

Like a flying squirrel, Screech leaps off the branch to another that hangs quite a way off, covering a distance Florenz can't jump across safely. Reluctantly, Florenz backtracks and loses second place.

Although the east side is a much quicker climb, the scuffle has taken a steep toll in attrition among the competitors. In overall first is Dyre. Although both his parents are wood elves, his physique is bulky and dark-haired, suggesting some dwarf ancestry. He is by nature a friendly sort of chap but having grown up constantly picked on, slow with words, and gifted with exceptional physical strength, Dyre has learned to use his fists to settle arguments.

As they climb higher, those on the east side are forced by the arrangement of branches to move west.

When Screech's eyes meet Dyre's, she desperately surges upwards, hoping to outpace him. Unfortunately for her, the easy climb on the east side has given Dyre too much of a lead to be easily outmaneuvered. He knows she is the quicker climber and that his only chance at staying in first place is with brute force.

Seeing him close in on her, Screech leaps away to a far-off branch that will put a safe distance between them but Dyre snatches Screech's ankle in midflight. Had Screech just let him pass, she might have outpaced him on the final sprint upward.

She does not think. Being grabbed at the ankle triggers a vicious defense mechanism in her muscle memory and Screech struggles so hard to break free that she falls. Fearing for her safety, Dyre holds on to her ankle. He lets her dangle upside down until she finally calms down.

Had he just let her free fall, he might have stayed in first place, but his chivalrous act in making sure she stayed safe gives Florenz and Lynx the chance to catch up to him.

Realizing he has lost his chance, Dyre bottlenecks the route up and allows Lynx past. "Go, Lynx! I'll hold them off. At least one of us wood elves has to win!"

In a heartbeat, the race has narrowed down to Florenz and Lynx, with Lynx in the lead thanks to Dyre's cooperation. Now the wild animal in Florenz comes out. If Lynx wins, she loses everything—the race *and* her reputation as a warrior, and no one will vote for an elve who does not know how to put up a good fight. In the heat of the moment, Florenz pulls out her silver dagger, the same one Enganyon recovered from the gobliness, and pins Lynx's left boot to the tree.

Technically an illegal move, the adjudicators below pretend not to notice. Lynx has the clarity of mind to realize there is no point in fighting with her or blaming the adjudicators. He can still win second place. Quickly, he kicks his boot off and veers onto a divergent branch to avoid further conflicts.

With the route ahead of her cleared away, Florenz shimmies up the homestretch branch, the one that is painted red and has a small knife gash notched into it. Every Ivy League champion climber in the past twenty years has considered that marker the top notch. With five feet left before Florenz's victory, Lynx swings his legs out and uses the springiness of the divergent branch to pole-vault himself up to a nearby branch that leads almost as high as Florenz's top-notch branch.

Although he is close enough to leap onto Florenz's branch and wrestle her for first place, Lynx instead wraps his arms around the tip of his branch and twists his whole body until his legs stick straight up into the air like a defiant flagpole. Immediately afterward, Florenz reaches up and taps the top notch.

The victory horn blows.

Lynx swings himself around and looks at Florenz. She looks at him and realizes that by making himself a living elf flagpole, he technically reached the highest point above Tiw's Tree first. To ensure her victory, she wraps her arms around the branch and tries to swing her legs above her head as well.

But the last twenty years have not been gentle on the top-notch branch. Year after year, violent scuffles have weakened its integrity. When Florenz swings her legs out, the bough breaks and sends her sailing in free flight two hundred fifty feet above the forest floor.

Seeing the danger, Lynx reaches out with his right arm and prays for a miracle. Before either of them even start to process the physics of her trajectory, their hands wrap around each other's wrists. Florenz dangles from one arm. The panicking audience gasps and shrieks.

Thrashing about, Florenz finally grabs onto a branch and starts to climb down slowly.

Once Florenz and Lynx reach the platform at Thor's Base, the crowd cheers wildly in relief and celebration. Some even start chanting Lynx's name; but the adjudicators confidently shove through the densely packed bodies and lift Florenz's hand in the air, proclaiming, "The winner! The Ivy League offers Mademoiselle Florenz Kibblersdottir a well-merited commission as a junior officer in the Ivy League!"

Unsure about his fate and feeling pressure in his bowels, Lynx heads towards the privy. Umpire Kibbler calls for silence. "Hear ye! Hear ye! I have an important question. Dean Halvard, do the rules not state that the first person to reach the highest point wins?"

"A feat your daughter accomplished admirably."

Kibbler boldly says, "It seems to me that Mister Lynx Cougarson reached the highest point first."

Barely able to believe his keen ears, Lynx freezes when he realizes he is peeing in his pants.

Dean Halvard is not happy. "You can't be serious! If you allow him to get away with that stunt, then it will set a precedent. Winners will have to stick their feet in the air from now on."

Umpire Kibbler folds his arms smugly as he speaks. "A good skill to have for a tree climber, wouldn't you say, Monsieur Dean? Young Mister Lynx reached the highest point first, performed an incredible acrobatic stunt, and single-handedly saved my daughter's life; yet you did not hesitate to disqualify him."

Florenz is shocked out of her wits upon hearing her father trying to rob her of her victory. He's sapping the political momentum that such a prestigious win would give her campaign! She hears the dean insist, "Young Mister Lynx has abandoned our company and has thus disqualified himself."

"Not at all, he is right over there!"

Several hundred elves turn and stare at Lynx. The front of his pants are all wet. He sheepishly lifts his left hand and wiggles his fingers at them. Anyone who saw him leave with what appeared to be frustration and bitterness written all over his face would have assumed he was a sore loser when, in fact, finding a restroom was his most pressing concern.

Sparing Lynx from the unflattering spotlight, Umpire Kibbler then announces, "True to my word, I shall pay for Mister Lynx Cougarson of Clan Highrune to be commissioned as a junior officer in the Ivy League in hopes that he will bring to the prestigious military unit entrusted with the defense of our borders a new level of excellence."

The wood elves go crazy, recklessly stomping up and down, whistling, squealing, cheering, whooping, and slapping each other on the back. None can remember the last time a wood elf won a commission in a major military league.

At that moment, Florenz realizes that her father just won over all the wood elves to her side. *Zena's wood elf ancestry won't win voters now.*

The one who has fared worst of all from Umpire Kibbler's confrontation is Dean Halvard. Humiliated at having his judgment called into question so publicly, he nearly chokes on the news that the umpire-in-chief is sponsoring a wood elf as a junior officer in his elite Ivy League.

His voice cracks with emotion as he forces himself to speak. "The Ivy League is proud to welcome this year's tournament winner, Mademoiselle Florenz Kibblersdottir of Clan Ithelion. The Ivy League has been the great guardian of our colony along its borders. Never have we been defeated, because the Ivy League only admits the best and the brightest elves. We have detected the echoes of the subtlest burglar-gnomes' footsteps and heard the breath of dwarves from far enough to shoot them in the dark. We have felt the shadows of the Magog goblins fall on—"

The dean's voice trails off as a heavily bound goblin is led into Thor's Base by longhouse humans.

The dean snarls, "Who let that beast up here?"

Umpire Kibbler nudges the dean aside and takes center stage. With more thespian artistry than sincerity of feeling he announces sadly, "It is with deep regret that I announce a report from my security staff only moments ago—a goblin has penetrated Tuscoraura Mountain, lurking past the Ivy League patrols undetected. If it had not been for our allies, the longhouse humans, he might have rampaged through the wood elf villages unchecked."

The longhouse human war chief tugs on a hemp rope tied to the hulking, green goblin's neck, taking him through the dense crowd of elves toward the stage. Although tightly bound from neck to toe, the goblin snaps and bellows at the elves as he passes, clearly taking great delight in how easy it is to scare them. Florenz and Lynx recognize him as the son of the goblin war chief performing those human sacrifices.

Umpire Kibbler continues his speech. "Not only did this hulking goblin sneak past the Ivy League patrols, but so did the entire band of longhouse humans who tracked him down. Even after pricking it with sedatives, it took seven of their strongest to wrestle this monstrous goblin to the ground and not a single Ivy Leaguer showed up to help them. This battle took place inside the marchlands near Weaving Widow's Peak."

Umpire Kibbler waits for full dramatic effect as the elves shiver with fear and outrage. Hearing that a goblin reached the marchlands is like hearing that an armed criminal sat on your front porch and no one noticed. Goblins are not supposed to be able to get so close to their elven settlement.

"We owe these allies our lives and our thanks. Out of my own funds I have already paid a reward of five thousand dollars in Tuscoraura double eagles to these warriors who captured the goblin. I hope the Ivy League will be willing to match my donation to the longhouse humans to make sure our friendship and treaties with them stay strong. If, Thor forbid, another more dangerous enemy should find a way to bypass the Ivy League's defenses, we ought to be able to count on human military support, just as they know they could count on us elves.

"Without further ado, I present Chief Skaruren."

Chief Skaruren holds up a hand and says in a thunderous voice, "Se'g Honyaweh!"

To Florenz's great surprise, Enganyon's father, Gandorf Mithranderson, steps up next to the tall human, completely unafraid of appearing short. Chief Skaruren stands a full-bodied six and a half feet above the stage. Despite the chief's muscular physique and height, the six-footer goblin's chest is so broad and his bulging pecs, shoulders, and biceps are so intimidating that he looks much larger than the chief, despite being a half-foot shorter. Meanwhile, Enganyon's father stands there next to them both, puffing out his chest and waving his skinny arms with not the slightest hint of shame at his puny height a few inches below five feet.

Enganyon's father is skilled in the language of the longhouse humans and translates the chief's words into Runic for the benefit of the high elves in the audience. "The big, blue sky above has wept tears of compassion upon my people for centuries untold. In daylight, the sun rises from the east and moves west.

161

"Every day a new wave of affliction rises in the east and pushes westward, but every night the stars come out again fixed in the heavens.

"Tuscoraura Mountain is our home. Every inch of its soil is sacred to us. We will not be moved from here. The Magog goblins come like clouds to cover the night sky. The next day, we shine again. The Frankish and Aenglish humans come like lightning and thunder and to dim our eyes and deafen our ears. The next day, we see and hear again.

"These hillsides hide the ashes of our ancestors. The mountain peaks remember their footsteps. The streams and rivers run with their blood.

"When the elves climb up in trees and keep watch above our heads with the squirrels, they honor our ancestors. When the halflings burrow under the soil and pile up food under our feet with the chipmunks, they honor our ancestors. When the dwarves tunnel deep into the mountains finding the waters whose springs give us cool drink, they honor our ancestors. The spirits of the generations past and the Great Spirit, who speaks to us in dreams, protect us all.

"But those who come to walk over our lands that did not welcome them; those who come to take away our food that we did not lay before them; those who come to spoil our water that does not recognize their reflection—against them, the fight is ours. Against them, allies are strong. Against them, united we stand."

The roar of applause is deafening. Even Florenz cannot restrain herself from cheering the noble and ingenious chief who has proven himself such a loyal and effective ally to the elves.

Kibbler laborers, stewards, and household guards file into Thor's Base and adorn the longhouse human warriors with leatherwork headbands, golden bracelets, and jeweled necklaces. They drape gold filigree woven velvet capes around their shoulders and wrap embroidered silk sashes around their waists. They buckle elegant silver blades with gem-encrusted scabbards to their hips.

When Umpire Kibbler finishes decorating the longhouse humans, the crowd eyes Dean Halvard, expecting similar pomp and fanfare. Completely taken unawares, Dean Halvard does his best to improvise a suitable reward. He removes from around his neck the symbol of his office as dean of the Ivy League, the Carcanet of Light and Truth Flourishing.

Exquisite and more valuable than all of Kibbler's gifts combined, the gift of the Carcanet provokes mixed emotions among the elves. On one hand, it certainly exempts the dean from having to come up with any more gifts to balance out Umpire Kibbler's display of generosity. On the other hand, giving away such a masterpiece of the jeweler's art, such a significant icon of their cultural heritage, such a major portion of their patrimony—to a human! It boggles their minds, offends their proprieties, and rakes against their values.

The umpire-in-chief waits for the elves in the audience to vent their outrage before continuing. "Although the praise in subduing the goblin rests so squarely on the shoulders of our human allies, the blame for overlooking it belongs to each and every one of us. We elves are so proud of our individual skills that we forget the value of collaboration.

"To remedy this problem, I have decided to create a new post on the Council of Perfects—an overseer for all the military leagues in our colony. In an emergency session just before this tournament, legislation was approved naming Monsieur Gandorf Mithranderson the first Major Leagues Umpire in fire elf history. His role will be to coordinate and direct homeland security, making sure all three major military leagues, the Justiciar League, the Ivy League, and the League of Licornes work together for the good of the colony."

Fortunately, Lynx has already soiled his pants so there is no new shock when he wets them again. In a single afternoon, not only has Umpire Kibbler suddenly become his patron in purchasing a commission for him in the Ivy League, thereby elevating his social standing in Shentalpee City to that of a high elf, but now Enganyon's father is his new boss!

Scene 2: The Odd Party

Gorsline Mill at High Falls, Town of Rofchester
in the Aenglish Lordship of Vinland
Tiw's Day Lauds. Dawn, 18ᵗʰ of April, 1284
Eve of the Feast of Saint Aelfheah, Bishop and Martyr

A beautiful human rogue folds her arms in a huff. She has long, straight, black hair, leather armor, and plenty of daggers strapped about her hip, arms, and legs. Losing patience, she complains, "So what are we doing here? I think it's about time you started sharing some information with us, Mister Silence Dogood. You've been a little too tight-lipped about this whole operation for my liking."

Benjamin Frankelyn smiles. "You know what they say, 'Well done is better than well said.'"

"Well said, Mister Silence," replies the snarky rogue. She is also the leader of the party.

A half-goblin cleric agrees with the pretty young rogue. "Silence can be a virtue, but the line between virtue and vice is growing thinner. We are starting to get the impression that you're not so much here to help us as to spy on us."

"You are obviously the prophet in this party of adventurers, Brother . . . what's your name?"

The half-goblin cleric makes a loud blowing sound with his wide, greenish-red lips and says, "Brother? I'm a much higher-level cleric than a brother. My name changes with every monastery I get kicked out of, but you may address me as Monsignor Oscar Meyer."

"Well then, Monsignor Meyer. How about lunch?" Benjamin Frankelyn opens up a sack and hands out trenchers of bread, cold meats, and small wheels of cheese to the party of adventurers. The relaxed environment and the scenic view strike up some lively chitter-chatter between a dark elf magicultor and a human fighter. Together with the human rogue and the half-goblin cleric, they make up the party of adventurers that Amhirst sent to assassinate the last surviving heir to the throne of Fort Duquesne.

Amid the din of the waterfalls and grist mills behind them, Benjamin Frankelyn talks over their chitchatting in an assertive but discrete voice. He announces, "My secrecy is for your own safety. Three can keep a secret, as long as two of them are dead. I intend to keep you all alive. It is of utmost importance to your success—and indeed, to your own survival—that curious ears do not hear the details of your quest."

"Hey, it's your quest too," butts in the dark elf magicultor. Dressed like a pirate with a bandana on his head, a bright-red sash, puffy, black pants, and tall leather boots that fold over at the knees, he carries an assortment of knives wide enough to make him look like a wandering cutlery salesman and holsters a magica wand. "Our success is your success. That's what being a party of adventurers is all about."

Benjamin Frankelyn replies, "Not really. I am mostly here to spy on you, as Monsignor Meyer so accurately prophesied. The last time my patron gave you a quest, you took about three years too long and came back with nothing but an amulet; rather unconvincing evidence that you had accomplished the quest successfully. Nevertheless, he paid you for your services in full. If you fooled him once, shame on you, but if you fool him twice, shame on him.

"I am here to make sure you get the job done with no excuses. If I don't return to vouch for you, no reward. Understood?"

All of a sudden, the party of adventurers gets significantly less chatty.

Benjamin Frankelyn appreciates their undivided attention and continues. "It is supposed that you don't know anything about the quest-giver. If you stumble upon any hints about his identity, please practice every diligence in feigning ignorance. The job is extremely dangerous and extremely important. Any foul-ups would cause a fury and a menace like—"

"Yeah, yeah, yeah," interrupts the beautiful rogue. "We know the spiel. Just cut to the chase."

Benjamin Frankelyn straightens himself up and says, "All right. A special sword was deposited in a Templar safe deposit box, but a thief stole the deposit slip. Our patron needs us to recover that sword before the thief does."

The fighter in the party has long, white hair and a well-trimmed, white beard. He is equipped with heavy chain mail, a brimmed chapel-de-fer steel hat, and a steel-rimmed heater shield. A heavy, winged mace, clings to his belt along with his arming sword and war dagger. He says, "You don't have to play those games with us. Our regard for the law is neutral. We don't mind stealing a sword from the Knights Templar vaults before the real owner gets it first."

"Not at all. I meant what I said," counters Benjamin Frankelyn. "The safe deposit slip has been stolen, and your job is to recover the sword for the true owner

167

before the thief can use the stolen safe deposit slip to lawfully steal the sword.

"We have several ways to do this. One, we could counterfeit a fake safe deposit slip, or two, we could break into the vault and take it for ourselves."

"What do we know about the thief?" asks the beautiful rogue.

He points to her and says, "Hey, you, why don't you give me a name so I can address you properly?"

"'Hey, you,' is fine with me. Proper is not my thing these days."

"Did I mention that you get no reward if I don't feel like I can vouch for you at the end of this quest?"

She rolls her eyes. "Let's go with Ariel."

"Okay, Miss Ariel, to answer your question about the thief, we know practically nothing. The owners of the safe deposit slip caught a glimpse of her as she was jumping out of the window. She was the size of a human child and had large, blond curls. They have code-named her Goldilocks."

"Are you sure the thief is even human or are you just assuming?" asks the piratey dark elf. "I mean, dark elves sometimes have blonde, curly hair. Just saying."

"Possible, but extremely unlikely," replies Benjamin Frankelyn. "Now, may I ask your name, sir elf?"

"How about 'Yeehaw'? No, wait, that's too obvious. I've got a better one, 'Whoopee'! My name is Whoopee. I like the sound of that."

Benjamin Frankelyn rubs his brow. "Do you expect anyone to take you seriously with a name like that?"

"No, but if you've got a name like Moneybags or Mountain of Gold, people take you too seriously. So I'm sticking with Whoopee, thank you."

168

"All right, then, Whoopee. My guess is that Goldilocks is just some poor, innocent, helpless girl that the real crooks pressured into doing their dirty work for them. Speaking of which, Miss Ariel, we'll use your good looks to avoid suspicion. Can you put on an innocent, helpless girl act?"

She snarls, "That's me—innocent and sweet."

"Okay, great. Like I said, you just need to pretend, Miss Ariel. I don't mean to presume there is anything innocent or sweet about you. Your role will be to create an account with the Templars and store an item in one of their safe deposit boxes.

"First off, an authentic deposit slip will serve as a template for counterfeiting one of our own, and second, creating the chance to walk through the vaults will allow us to map it out so we can figure out which safe deposit box we need to crack, if need be. You could tell them you inherited a few gold bars and will need to put them somewhere for safekeeping."

The white-haired fighter asks in a loud voice, "And when do we come back to get the gold bars?"

"Never," replies Benjamin Frankelyn. "I purchased a few pyrite-coated lead bars on the way. They should be the right color and weight to pass off as gold."

The white-haired fighter objects, "Mister Dogood, pyrite is fool's gold. Templar bankers are no fools."

Benjamin Frankelyn is not the least bothered by the objection. He replies to the old fighter with a confident tone, "Then just leave the bars in the sack. Bankers don't ask questions. It's their job. So what's your name anyway, old man?"

"Willis."

169

The dark elf whines, "Willis, we're supposed to be using code names. Now he knows your real name!"

"He didn't know that until you told him. He would have thought Willis *wasn't* my real name."

Benjamin Frankelyn interrupts their little side spat and says, "All right, whatever. Sir Willis, you and I are going to—"

"Please, please, please!" Willis halts him in mid-sentence. "I'm not a knight, just a champion. You can call me Willis the Champion, or just plain old Willis, but none of this *Sir* stuff."

"Okay, Willis the Champion, as I was saying, you and I—"

"On second thought, let's keep it to Willis. The whole champion thing is for special occasions only."

"Fine, fine. Willis it is. So you and I—"

"And don't call me Miss Ariel. It's just Ariel. I'm not fond of getting confined in ladylike society."

Benjamin Frankelyn pauses for a deep breath and asks, "Anyone else have comments about names or characters before we proceed?" He looks around; all project innocence at the disruptions. "Okay, if that's all settled, then let's continue with the heist. Willis, you and I will pose as Knights Paladin passing by on a holy quest. We recently lost track of a necromancer who claims to have purchased his sword from a thief who stole it from a Templar vault."

Willis asks, "Why would a necromancer need a sword? They usually stick to rune-inlaid staves and enchanted daggers."

"It's a flaming sword."

Willis objects again, "Sorry, buddy, but I've been in this business a lot longer than you have. Flaming swords are for guys like me to fight the undead, not for necromancers who want to reanimate them."

"This sword does blackflame."

The dark elf looks at him suspiciously. "Are you making this up? If this story gets too far-fetched, they won't believe us."

"Getting them to believe the story is my job. Your job will be to follow the Templar vault-keeper back into the vaults and stay hidden."

The dark elf notes, "Hey, you! I've got news—they don't let nobody back there. It's called security."

Benjamin Frankelyn looks at the dark elf, then points to the half-goblin cleric. (The other half of his family is dwarf.) His shoulders are massive but his gut is trim. "A goblin-dwarf that wide should have a paunch belly. You will go in as the cleric's belly."

Willis jumps in. "Wait! That's brilliant—use their own security measures against them! Templars believe outhouses are a security threat so they dig cesspits for their privies indoors. Monsignor Meyer can just say he needs to use the privy and Whoopee can jump out and hide in the cesspit all day."

"Wha'choo talkin' 'bout, Willis?" snaps Whoopee.

Benjamin Frankelyn works up emotion as he thrills about the genius of the plan. "Yes, that's it! After you jump off, Whoopee, we'll inflate a leather wineskin to replace the paunch belly."

The dark elf says, "No way! Your plan stinks."

Monsignor Meyer adds, "It won't work. The privy's in the dungeon. He'll be trapped behind prison bars."

Benjamin Frankelyn hands Whoopee a wire with a wooden handle at each end. "Unwind the wooden handle like this, slip the wire around any bolts or bars,

171

and then just keep working it back and forth. This wire will cut through just about anything, eventually."

Ariel says, "If the Templars find their dungeon cut open, they'll lock down the fort until they find him."

Benjamin Frankelyn looks at her with penetrating eyes. "They won't find him. It's our good fortune that the Thieves' Guild has already constructed a tunnel most of the way into the fort and were willing to sell us access to it. Once we've located the safe deposit box, all we have to do is pick the lock and break out through the tunnel. Ariel, you up for picking Templar locks?"

Ariel purses her lips. "Yeah, with the right tools."

Whoopee says, "I object to my role in this."

Willis replies, "Welcome to the party, pal."

"Sorry, team, but the water clock is dripping. We start tomorrow at first light."

"Tomorrow? I need to know what kind of lock it is and get the right tools to crack it. It will take all day today just to find places that sell that kind of equipment. Then I'd need another day to test it out."

Benjamin Frankelyn raises a finger. "Never leave for tomorrow what you can do today."

Arial cannot believe all the aphorisms. She tries to make her point. "That's what I'm saying. I can't get it all done today. I'll need both today and tomorrow."

"One today is worth two tomorrows. Use your downtime to fill in the gaps, but we start tomorrow."

"Look, good thief tools are expensive, and I don't have that kind of money on me."

Benjamin Frankelyn puts an end to the excuses. "Then borrow it from the Templar bank."

Scene 3: The Oregan Tale

Amphitheater at Thor's Base, Shentalpee City
Hock Moon Day Terce. Morning, 10th of April, 1284

"Monsieur Lynx, I wanted to thank you for saving my life and I need to tell you that my father was right, even though I didn't want to hear it at the time. You deserved to win. You improvised a new solution to an old problem, and I'm sure you will make one of the finest officers the Ivy League has ever seen."

Lynx's eyebrows soften and he stares at his feet for a few moments to hide the gush of flustered emotions. When he recovers, he looks Florenz straight in the eyes and says, "I was wrong about your father. I assumed he was just a dishonest, power-hungry politician like the rest of them, but your father had the courage to break nearly every social convention among the Tuscoraura elves to stand up for me in public. You have that kind of courage too. I'm sure you'll make one of the finest umpires-in-chief the Tuscoraura elves have ever seen."

Zena stomps up from behind them both and says, "Mister Lynx, dear, what was it you were saying about becoming the finest umpire-in-chief? The mademoiselle umpire-in-chief's daughter is just about to deliver an important announcement, isn't that right?"

"Mademoiselle Zena!" Dungaree Jeanne calls out from the middle of a crowd of her bravos pushing Johnny Appleseed up in a medieval version of a wheelchair. Though he puts on a brave face, it's clear his leg is still in a lot of pain. "Keep it down, Zena dear! I can see that you're gloating from way back here!"

Zena gives her mother a full-on teenager huff and says, "Mother, we were simply having a discussion about future policy here. There is no mudslinging involved, is there, Mademoiselle Florenz?"

Florenz hesitates. She knows she's supposed to play dumb but Zena's gloating gets under her skin in a way that would make lice and maggots jealous.

Zena presses on. "We've been best friends since childhood. We wouldn't sink so low as to make baseless accusations against each other, would we?"

Dungaree Jeanne is humiliated by her daughter's behavior and says sharply, "Mademoiselle Zena!"

Struggling to maintain her self-control, Florenz decides it's time to change topics. "Why, Reverend Appleseed, what happened to your leg?"

Johnny Appleseed doesn't understand a word of Eldric, so Dungaree Jeanne translates into Aenglish.

Before he has a chance to respond, Lynx says, "The monsieur Enganyon pushed him over the edge."

Florenz forces a laugh. "Oh, that jokester tries my patience all the time; but what happened to his leg?"

Lynx presses on. "No, he literally shoved the good reverend over the edge of Thor's Base. Miraculously, a branch caught him, but the fall twisted his leg bad."

Florenz can't believe it. "He can be devious at times but the monsieur Enganyon would never do anything like that!"

"Never say never, dear!" With a big, cocky grin, Enganyon rushes forward on his crutches to greet them. At Enganyon's heels walks Old Mother Hubbard's dog.

The shock has not washed off Florenz's face when she stammers, "But . . . you could have killed him!"

"You know, the thought had occurred to me," says Enganyon, as if he were incapable of taking anything seriously. "I was just giving him a friendly pat on the back to welcome him to Shentalpee City and I slipped."

Lynx looks at Enganyon's leg and asks sarcastically, "So is that why you decided to fake a leg injury? After all, misery loves company."

Enganyon cannot be outdone in sarcasm. "Exactly. Mister Lynx, you are the only one who understands the way I think. Besides, these crutches happen to match my new jacket."

He is wearing a plain, black leather coat. As the scion of a family of immense wealth, he normally wears a considerably more elaborate white coat, studded with jewels and embroidered with gold filigree.

"Are we supposed to ask what happened to your old coat, Monsieur Enganyon?" asks Dungaree Jeanne.

"As a matter of fact, I sold it and used some of the money to buy this one, and I gave the rest to poor old Madame Hubbard. She was so happy that she ran to the baker to buy her dog some bread, but it died while she was out. Then she called the undertaker to measure it for a funeral, but the dog just got up again and started laughing. She was too spooked-out to keep him, so I told her I'd look after him for her."

"That's quite a story, young elf," says Dungaree Jeanne skeptically.

Johnny Appleseed points to the dog and rambles on in Aenglish. Enganyon asks, "What's he saying?"

Dungaree Jeanne looks at him seriously. "He says your dog's undead. He's worried that if the Inquisition finds out that certain Tuscoraura elves have been using his gift of blackflame to dabble in necromancy—"

Enganyon interrupts her, "You don't say! I'd love to hear all about it except that I want a good seat for this Thor's schtick. Those three magi look nerdtastic."

After the group wanders off their separate ways, Dungaree Jeanne breathes a sigh of relief. Her hired bravos roll Johnny Appleseed into the amphitheater while she hustles after Florenz. Johnny Appleseed loves children, and he asks the bravos to wheel him closer. The big human and the scuzzy bravos make some parents nervous, but Johnny Appleseed comes ready with tricks to delight them all. He pulls the tip off his thumb, plucks coins out of their pointy ears, and snaps a rope in two then connects the halves back together.

When she catches up to her, Dungaree Jeanne pulls Florenz aside. "I just want to apologize for my daughter's behavior. She seems to think that she'll appear more confident in herself if she walks around as smug and haughty as—"

"As the monsieur Enganyon?" Florenz finishes her sentence, knowing that Dungaree Jeanne would never say it out loud. "I know that the mademoiselle Zena looks up to him in every way: the good, the bad, and the ugly. But I am the one to owe you an apology because I accused you publicly of treason without there even being an official case against you. The garden gnomes are furious that I ruined Bartlebee's reputation without a fair trial. It has harmed the trust that many high elf families put in their garden gnome employees.

"They demanded that I resign from the elections."

"Posh! What do garden gnomes have to say about our electoral processes?"

Florenz looks at her with a grim seriousness that ages her face far beyond her nineteen years. "Reverend

Appleseed was right. My father has been toying with necromancy, and the Inquisition is here."

"Impossible!"

"Well, it turned out well for your daughter—the inquisitor healed her from a nasty injury. For the rest of us, it's not going so well. The Inquisition is demanding that we extinguish all our blackflame braziers and that my father turns over all his necromantic artifacts."

"And what did your father say?"

"He planned to kill the inquisitor, but the inquisitor is a dwarf, and now the dwarves are angry as well. They insist we comply with his demands."

Dungaree Jeanne touches her lip. "Oh dear, this is serious. How can the mountain dwarves and garden gnomes help an outsider encroach upon our rights and our sovereignty? We have an ancient alliance."

"Apparently, they consider necromancy a weapon and feel that we have violated the terms of our alliance by secretly developing a new weapon without sharing that information with them."

"Hmmm." Dungaree Jeanne, a natural negotiator, is straining her brain to find a way out. A part of her hopes that Florenz wins the election because she cringes at the thought of Zena's haughtiness on a power trip like that. Another part calculates the benefits of being the mother of the reigning umpire-in-chief.

Either way, if Florenz withdraws from the ballot, Zena would be the only candidate left and, by law, the Council of Perfects would have to call off the elections and start the nomination process over from scratch.

Dungaree Jeanne says, "But, Mademoiselle Florenz, you can't quit the race. You've come too far!"

With studied calm Florenz replies, "Yes, I can."

Appleseed is on his way to stealing the show when Florenz walks past him up onto the stage. Something is clearly bothering her, but she puts on her game face and speaks. "Mesdames, mesdemoiselles, messieurs, ladies, gentelves, and guests, I have often had the privilege of introducing the Thor's Enlightenment Discourse on behalf of my father whenever the affairs of state have conflicted with his ability to attend this pleasant occasion to learn and socialize. Sadly, this will be the last time I have that honor."

She pauses as if doing her best not to cry, then takes a deep breath and continues. "The great dwarf warlord Gimsteinn Hardbones, after repulsing multiple assaults of the five armies against his heavy infantry, said, 'I am constant as the northern star of whose true-fixed and resting quality has no fellow in the firmament.'

"My seafaring dark elf relatives have told me that even the best sailors at times lose track of the course they have plotted, and can only find their way once night settles and reveals the North Star.

"We all lose our way now and then. First, we welcome these polar elves as our guests for this TED. Before they begin, I must make an apology for one way in which I was blown off course and hurt the innocent.

"At our last umpirical election debate, I accused the dungaree's stewardess of stealing the secret to elf fire. That accusation was false. The entire Bartlebee affair was a simple misunderstanding, which I inflated to unreasonable proportions.

"It all started when Bartlebee came up with a fabulous recipe for acorn pie and got so excited about it that she wrote it down for a gnome friend of hers who happened to work for us at Vandsee Estates.

"My knowledge of Gnorrachi is informal at best, and when I read its heading, I misinterpreted the letter that she sent to her friend on our estate. She wrote at the top of her note, 'Fire Elf Recipe for Acorn Pie.' The Gnorrachi word for acorn, *deargan*, is similar to the word for secret, *deargal*. On top of that, the word order in their language is completely different than ours.

"So I thought she wrote, 'Secret Recipe for Elf Fire.' It was all a big misunderstanding. I jumped to conclusions and pounced upon the opportunity to discredit my political opponent. In the process, I ruined the professional reputation of Mistress Bartlebee Scrivener and hurt the good name of the dungaree's family. For that, I am deeply sorry."

Zena is standing at the edge of the stage and comes over and gives Florenz a big, theatrical hug, weeping and stating loudly in Runic, "Naturally, I forgive thee, my dearest, kindest, best friend. Oh, how it burdens my soul to think of the weight these elections have put upon our lifelong friendship. But I know that thou wouldst never—"

Their exchange is cut short by a roaring scream. Lynx Cougarson comes riding down the serpentine aqueduct on a dwarven shield, leaning into the twists and turns like a pro. He lets out a full-bellied, "Yeehaw!"

Scene 4: Quest: Impossible

Templar Priory, Town of Rofchester
Woden's Day Prime. Morning, 19th of April, 1284
Feast of Saint Aelfheah, Bishop and Martyr

The next morning, Benjamin Frankelyn and his team start off early with the sunrise. The Templar priory is a modest fort made of brownstone. Ariel wants to get her sweet girl act over with as fast as possible so she'll have the rest of the day for purchasing a nice set of vault-cracking tools. Her leather armor and daggers do not exactly match up with the sweet and innocent stereotype. She ditches the armor but keeps the daggers, tucking them in even more intimately than before—after all, a nice girl can never be too cautious these days!

Visiting a few shops, she finds some surprisingly stylish and zesty outfits, but she does not indulge in trying any of them on. A long, modest dress calls to her. Imagining what a nice girl should look like, she asks herself, *All self-respecting, sweet, and innocent girls wear modest clothes, right?*

To resolve her doubts, Ariel shows the half-goblin/half-dwarf cleric a dress and asks, "Do I have to wear a modest dress to look innocent and sweet?"

Monsignor Meyer raises his hands like it's a police holdup and says, "Don't ask me. I don't check out girls anymore. But before I became a cleric, my mommy told me that shapely hips won't guarantee a happy family life. Even if I were in the marrying business, I wouldn't let a little skin overly influence my decision."

"Just answer the question about the outfit."

"That's more like a nun outfit than a sweet girl next door outfit. Not sure that's what you're supposed—"

She squints her eyes. "Okay, let's start over. Tell me this outfit makes me look frumpy."

"That outfit makes you look frumpy."

"Perfect! That's exactly what I wanted to hear."

Together, they go to the rendezvous point. Benjamin Frankelyn takes one look at Ariel and frowns. "I said innocent and sweet, not a nun!"

"Nuns are innocent and sweet—at least they're supposed to be."

Benjamin Frankelyn pulls at his sideburns dramatically and moans, "But even if they're not innocent and sweet, they know a lot about religion. If you get jittery about the liturgy or snarky about the hierarchy, they'll see through you at once. The Templars aren't just warriors, they're monks! That's like walking into a wine shop dressed like a vintner and asking where's the grape juice."

Monsignor Meyer says, "Oh, that reminds me of the time we caught an old lady walking out of the sacristy with a bottle of altar wine. The abbot stopped her and asked, 'Where are you going with that?'

"She pointed to an old guy snoring on the church steps and said, 'I got it for my husband.'

"The abbot looked at the snoozing old man for a moment, then said, 'Good trade.' And he let her go! Ha! Uh-ha! Uh-ha! *Snort!*"

They all start laughing—some because they get the joke, others because his snorting laughter is contagious. It takes the monsignor a while to recover from his own joke. He says, "Don't worry, Ben. I'll cover for her."

Frankelyn looks at him awry. "How did you figure out my name?"

Monsignor Meyer shrugs his huge shoulders. "I might be a bad one, but I'm still a cleric. Once you have the gift of prophecy, you always have the gift of prophecy. God didn't take it away when I . . . er . . . fell from grace. He's funny like that. How do you think I got signed on to a party of adventurers that specializes in hide-and-seek quests like this?"

Benjamin Frankelyn gets cheeky. "I always figured it was just your big nose. But that's not important now. Can you just use the gift of prophecy to figure out which vault the sword is in?"

"No, I can't. The Templars have clerics of their own. They've got special protective blessings that keep guys like me from taking advantage of the system."

"Well, I can tell you that the sword is evil. Can't your gift of prophecy detect evil?"

"Yeah, but it's still a long shot. It's a bank, after all, and money is the root of all evil. I'm going to get a lot of false positives if I send up a detect evil prayer. Let's get moving. Whoopee's in position and doesn't want this to take any longer than it has to."

Ariel adds, "I second that."

"Wait. Where's Whoopee?"

"He's already hanging onto my belly, and the leather pouch is strapped on as a cushion for him to fill up with air once he drops off so I won't walk out of there looking like I lost a hundred pounds after one dump."

"Right." Benjamin Frankelyn pats the cleric's fake belly and calls down to the dark elf inside, "How you doing in there, buddy?"

From under the monk's robes a voice moans, "Let's just get this over with."

Monsignor Meyer says, "Ariel, you go in first and I'll come in a few moments later to make it seem like we're not traveling together. While I'm waiting for you to finish up your business, I will ask to use the privy and then I'll let Whoopee out. You're going to have to try to delay them long enough so they don't bring the fake gold bars into the vault until after he's ready to sneak in after them."

Ariel snaps her fingers and psyches herself up. "Okay, I got this. Innocent and sweet. What could possibly go wrong if I just do the sister act?"

Ariel walks into the brownstone Templar fort. The inside is dark and stuffy. The few narrow windows are barred with heavy iron rods, allowing little light or air to get in. Wealth is apparent everywhere. The large number of candles burning all day long, polished hardwood floors, and granite teller counters were all extravagant luxuries in the Middle Ages, even though they would be considered standard for a bank these days. Two Templar clerks, one human and one dwarf, sit at separate desks.

Ariel groans to herself as she realizes Benjamin Frankelyn's plan will get shot to pieces as soon as Monsignor Meyer steps in. *There is only supposed to be one clerk! How am I supposed to distract both of them?* She turns around to go out and warn him.

The human clerk on the left looks at her quizzically and says in Latin, "Pax Domini tecum."

Remembering she is wearing a nun outfit and is supposed to know Latin, she plays dumb and answers in Aenglish, "Ah, yes, holy brother! I think I'm not supposed to be here."

He switches to Aenglish and asks, "What have you got in the sack?"

"Oh, you know, just some silly old gold bars, but it's none of your business, really."

"Actually, I'm a banker. Gold bars *are* my business. There's plenty of thieves out there and you just walked into one of the safest banks in Vinland. You won't get to the end of the street before they steal it. God has brought you here, not by accident. Take the hint."

"I'll take my chances. Thanks. Bye! I mean, God be with you." She opens the door and Monsignor Meyer walks right in and exclaims with a cheerful outspreading of his hands, "Sister!"

The dwarf clerk on the right says to the lumbering half-goblin/half-dwarf brother in Dwarvish Runic, "Lakunto Tesaged."

Monsignor Meyer replies in Aenglish with his porcine Santa-Claus-like jovial manner, "Peace of Christ be with you, brothers. Sister Wendy here is really an extern—a novice extern—so we'll speak Aenglish for her sake."

"There are two of us. We can help you both in your own languages."

Ariel says, "Well, that's a blessing, isn't it, Brother . . . uh . . . Brother Francis . . . Footer?"

Monsignor Meyer tries to stall, saying, "What a blessing indeed! God's providence is everywhere if only we have the faith to see it."

The human clerk says, "Would you like me to take a look at those gold bars, Sister Wendy?"

Ariel shakes her head. "Oh, no need. My abbess told me I needed to be as discreet as possible about this. I'll just get a safe deposit box."

"Small, medium, or large?"

"What would be the right size if I, say, wanted to store a sword in a safe deposit box?"

Human clerk doubts he heard that right. "Do you have a sword with you as well?"

"No, no, no! Our convent is hoping to obtain the sword of Saint George from the Holy Land. You know, the one he slew the dragon with? So I might as well get one big enough to fit a sword, just in case."

The dwarf clerk squints his eyes. "You just said your abbess."

"My abbess what?"

The dwarf clerk voices his suspicions. "How can you live in a convent if you have an abbess? An abbess is the head of a monastery, not a convent. In any event, I recommend you bring the sword in for authentication before your abbess purchases it. There are many hucksters in the relic trade these days. We have a very thorough authentication team."

"What, you think I took vows yesterday? I know a real sword when I see one!"

The dwarf clerk grows very suspicious. "So your abbess trains the nuns in your convent in the use of swords? Is this a convent for adventurers, perhaps?"

Monsignor Meyer slaps Ariel on the back. "Goodness gracious, no! I guarantee you she is no adventurer! Sister Wendy is a famous artifact critic. Nuns from all kinds of different convents and monasteries bring her in to consult about the authenticity of various relics and artifacts. That's why she got confused and called her mother superior an abbess! She is from a monastery, but she is temporarily on assignment in a convent."

The dwarf clerk replies, "Sister, you ought to ask your mother superior for a penance to curb your haughty attitude."

Ariel goes at him. "Why, I oughta—"

Monsignor Meyer covers her mouth and says, "Speaking of penances, a guy walks into a canonry and tells the prior, 'I want to become a canon regular, the monastery up the road is too strict.'

"The prior tells him, 'My son, you are welcome to join us, but we use the discipline daily here.'

"He says, 'No problem, when can I begin?' The prior says, 'Today, thanks be to God!'

"For the rest of the week, the prior notices his new postulant's back is all wet every morning and finally he asks him, 'Brother, why is your back all wet?'

"The postulant points to the sacristy and says, 'You said to use the discipline every day!'

"The prior follows his finger and says, 'Oh, that's not a flagellum, that's an aspergillum!'"

The two Templar clerks roar with laughter and Monsignor Meyer can hardly contain himself laughing and snorting. Ariel's face is stone cold until Monsignor Meyer looks right at her. She pretends to laugh.

Whoopee can hardly take it anymore and makes a splurting noise with his lips.

When his laughter calms down, Monsignor Meyer groans and says, "Excuse me, gentlemen, I was fasting for a novena in reparation of sins when our provincial visited us. I ate a full meal with him and now it's disagreeing with me. Do you have a privy I can use?"

The human clerk says, "I'll show him the way. Brother Bifur, would you tend to the young nun over there? Those gold bars look heavy."

The dwarf clerk waddles over to Ariel, still chuckling to himself, and says, "Okay, so you'd like a medium safe deposit box for the gold bars, correct?"

"Yes, Brother Bifur."

He looks up at her. "How do you know my name?"

"The other brother just said it."

"Right, and what is your name, Sister?"

Ariel looks away from him for half a breath.

"Uh . . . Sister Shensi."

"Brother Frank Footer over there just called you Sister Wendy. Which is it?"

"Um . . . both, really. He knew me before I entered the convent, I mean monastery. Wendy's my baptismal name and Sister Shensi is my name in religion. Saint Shensi is the patron saint of . . . er . . . adventurers."

"So you *are* an adventurer?"

"No way!"

The dwarf clerk takes the sack of gold bars and says, "That'll be fourpence. Do you have a groat?"

Ariel deeply regrets trying to pull off this sister act. "Absolutely. It's great for prayer."

The dwarf Templar shakes his head. "A groat is the new four-pence coin. Since you seem to get around, I figured you might have one on you."

Ariel says, "Actually, about that—I heard Templars are great money lenders. Can I borrow, say, twelve dollars? You know, one for each of the apostles."

"For that kind of loan, you'll need collateral." In the blink of an eye, the dwarf Templar unstrings the sack and dumps the gold bars on the counter before Ariel can stop him.

She grabs for the bars and starts stuffing them back into the bag, saying, "Oh, never mind then."

He takes one look at the pyrite and says, "These are fake. I don't know what you're playing at, but this ain't real gold and you ain't a real nun."

Ariel gathers her bars up and storms off in all the mock outrage she can muster. "Well, I never! How dare you disrespect a woman of the cloth like that!"

Around the corner, Benjamin Frankelyn, dressed as a Knight Paladin, asks her eagerly, "How did it go?"

Ariel curls her lip. "What's an aspergillum?"

Frankelyn's face falls. "Oh no! That bad, was it?"

"Monsignor Meyer got into the privy, so at least Whoopee's in place, but they wouldn't take this stupid fool's gold back into the vault."

"Hopefully, the monsignor got some useful intel."

A few moments later, Monsignor Meyer comes out smiling and says, "By all the saints, those Templars are swell guys, let me tell ya!"

Benjamin Frankelyn looks at him expectantly and asks, "What happened to Ariel?"

"Yeah, so, the sister act didn't quite work out, and we have no idea where the vaults are. The good news is, I lowered Whoopee into the cesspit. He'll have to hide out there until we can cook up a plan to get him out. I say we start first thing in the morning."

"It's first thing in the morning right now."

"I meant tomorrow. No sense pushing our bad luck now. Dark elves are comfortable in cesspits—it reminds them of home." Monsignor Meyer laughs until his face turns red and tears well up in his eyes.

Benjamin Frankelyn gets worried. "Did your gift of prophecy reveal anything about the sword?"

"Well, I spoke with the tongue of angels, but it felt like I was holding the hand of a devil. All I got was a cold, brooding evil."

"Yes, yes, that must have been it. The sword has a cold evil to it. It is a blackflame sword, after all."

"But I still haven't found what we're looking for."

189

"Why not?"

"You, Mister Silent Willy Dogood, have told us nothing about it. How am I supposed to find it if I have no idea what I'm looking for?"

Flurrrppp.

Benjamin Frankelyn asks, "What was that?"

Monsignor Meyer removes the inflated leather wineskin from under his robe and says, wiping a tear from his eye, "Oh, it's Whoopee's cushion. It makes this annoying sound, but it only helped lend credibility to my story about needing to use the privy. That's the only part of your plan that's gone right so far."

Benjamin Frankelyn looks at Willis. The white-haired adventurer is wearing blue robes with a silver cross, signifying the order of the Knights Paladin. "We can still pull this off. Ready for part two, Willis?"

Willis moans, "Are you sure it's a good idea to be posing as warrior monks? I don't know what an aspergillum is either."

Benjamin Frankelyn shakes his head. "Just follow my lead."

The two phony Knights Paladin walk into the bank. The human clerk asks, "May I help you, brothers?"

Benjamin Frankelyn puts on his most authoritative voice. "We have come here urgently from Salim. Our patron has reported that a vault slip has been stolen from his residence. He paid an ungodly fortune so that the Templars would get the item to him safely. We're here to ensure that sloppy security procedures don't endanger the safe transfer of the item."

The dwarf puts his elbows on the desk as if offended and says, "So the big cardinals in Salim are sending Knights Paladin to make sure the Knights

Templar are doing their job right. Is that how it goes these days?"

Benjamin Frankelyn keeps his calm. "The fact that we are Knights Paladin is irrelevant to the matter. We just happened to be the only trusted sons of the Church that were heading toward Rofchester."

The dwarf Templar keeps interrogating them. "And what business brings you to Rofchester?"

"We're investigating reports of wendigo elves wandering out of Tuscoraura Mountain."

The human Templar says, "Yes, I have heard such reports. It's getting worse, not better."

The dwarf Templar is not appeased. "Did the cardinals in Salim trust you enough to tell you precisely what item it was that had its vault slip stolen?"

Benjamin Frankelyn leans in close and says, "This is for your ears only. Gather around."

The human and the dwarf Templars huddle in together. Willis leans in as if he were in on the secret. Benjamin Frankelyn raises an eyebrow and whispers slowly, "The Sword of Layban . . ."

Willis stands back slowly and squints his eyes, nodding as if that just made total sense to him. The dwarf Templar genuinely seems relieved to hear it and says, "Well then, we have good news for you. We got the warning by Pony Express before Goldilocks arrived. She presented the vault slip and we arrested her. She came in wearing a red cloak and an elven dagger. Tomorrow we will cart her off to Salim for trial.

"You can tell the cardinals our security procedures are quite rigorous. We will not hand over the item until a fully authenticated vault slip is reissued."

Benjamin Frankelyn gawks. "Goldilocks is here?"

The dwarf points to a cabinet overhead. "Her cloak and dagger are up there in the evidence chest. We removed them carefully so as not to spoil any clues."

Benjamin Frankelyn slaps his hands together and starts to head out. "Splendid! You know what we Knights Paladin always say . . . leave the cloak and dagger stuff to the Templars. Well, that'd be all. Thank you so much! God bless us, everyone!"

As soon as Benjamin Frankelyn reaches his party of adventurers, he starts jamming out on an imaginary air lute. Ariel looks at him as if he's crazy. But Monsignor Meyer has seen it all before and does not betray the least bit of surprise. He says, "So, I'm guessing that part went better than the first. I don't need the gift of prophecy to know you walked out of there empty-handed. What's got your spirits up so high?"

Benjamin Frankelyn strums a fast-paced cadenza on his imaginary lute and says, "They captured Goldilocks and she's right inside there with Whoopee!"

Ariel looks around, trying to feel the joy. "Whoopee! Yeah that's great, I think. What'd you have in mind? You want Whoopee to kill her?"

"No, no, no! Don't you see? She'll steal it for us."

"Why would she do that?"

Benjamin Frankelyn recovers his calm and announces solemnly, "I'm going to make her an offer she can't refuse."

Scene 5: Lynx to the Rescue

Amphitheater at Thor's Base, Shentalpee City
Hock Moon Day Terce. Morning, 10th of April, 1284

"Yeehaw!"

Leaning back on the dwarven shield, Lynx sticks out his feet and trails a hand behind him to brake his speed down the watercourse. He's going too fast. Two ornate wooden flowers guard the lip of the aqueduct and his feet slam into them so hard the wooden petals fly off. The shield gets swamped with water on one side, flipping him upside down. As his legs dangle over the reflecting pool, Lynx grips the base of one wooden flower with his right hand and keeps hold of the shield, flapping in the spray, with his left.

Down below, the spectacle upends the audience, but the three polar elves prove their scholarly prowess by pulling out source stones and magica wands to help Lynx back up onto the aqueduct.

Florenz knows exactly what he is doing so she announces to the crowd, "Illustrious fire elves! I beg you, keep your calm. In the wake of the goblin's attack, my father has decided to tighten up our security procedures and introduce some radical reforms. He has received credible reports that the Inquisition has arrived at Tuscoraura Mountain and has contrived a number of ingenious traps to ambush them.

"Please remain seated and calm. All these measures will make sense shortly. Monsieur Lynx, do you have a progress report for us?"

"Um . . . yes. I've got an important public service announcement to make. Our noble umpire-in-chief, who has personally sponsored my commission in the Ivy League, has come up with a cunning plan in mind to . . . ah . . . eliminate the threats to our homeland security. Right now, the current project I'm working on is top secret but will. . . ah . . . eliminate those threats."

His words make no sense, but public service announcements rarely do, so no one notices. He continues, "Right now, we are experiencing some technical difficulties, so you can go right along with the program for this Thor's Enlightenment Discourse, and I'll—I mean, we'll—finish up this important public service project shortly."

Florenz resumes. "So now, without further ado, I introduce three elves renowned for their wisdom— Hakeem Melchior, Mage Gaspar, and Sage Balthazar."

With brown skin and black hair, a stout chest, long arms, and pointy ears, Hakeem Melchior's physical characteristics defy all ethnic stereotypes. On his head sits an ornate red silk turban and he wears a decorated red leather vest and red velvet sash over a green silk shirt. His green pants are puffy, while his red shoes stick out far enough to flop at the toes. He says in Runic with a thick polar elf accent, "May the gods bless ye, merry fire elves of Tuscoraura Mountain! Tidings of comfort and joy to one and all! We three elves from Oregan are bearing gifts—we have traveled from afar. Across snowy tundra, through torrid valleys, and over grand canyons we have followed the northern star, leading us unto ye, our cherished fire elf cousins.

"Instead of one big gift to your community, we decided to hand out a few little gifts to each of your families. To keep them together, we tucked the gifts into a new stocking, which we offer as a bonus gift.

"Now, let us explain the first gift—a needle. Beneath the earth run ley lines that harness and channel the power of the elements. Sorcerers call the site where these ley lines converge the North Pole.

"The needle we bring unto ye is actually a thin piece of lodestone. When perfectly balanced and suspended from a string, it will unerringly point the way to the convergence of those ley lines.

"We, the Yulenisse, now call ourselves polar elves because over a century ago, a group of dedicated mages, philosophers, sages, alchemists, geomancers, and astrologers teamed up and founded an underground city with a complex of workshops on our pole, the northernmost convergence of ley lines.

"This oasis of learning includes an observatory, a prismatic greenhouse for growing magica trees, a vast library of books in every field of learning, and a research station with workshops in the fields of sorcery, alchemy, noetics, tectonics, and astrology.

"Any scholar would need nothing more than to follow that needle and the light of the North Star to calculate where to find us at the North Pole. For nearly a hundred years we have given each visitor a share in our knowledge, without price.

"In recent years, the number of visitors to our workshops has declined drastically, for several reasons. In the first place, most races prefer to dwell in middle earth, where clement weather prevails and seasonal changes are pleasant. Polar north can only be found in upper earth, that inclement region of our world where adventurers seldom dare explore.

"Several well-meaning scholars have hired parties of adventurers to escort them out to the North Pole to visit our workshops. Since these needles will always point to the convergence of the ley lines until they crisscross over the North Pole itself, they assumed that they would traipse across upper earth along the Oregan Trail until their needles fell into an X shape.

"Unfortunately, their calculations were off. Their learning was superficial, and their adventurous spirit was easily chilled. They did not heed our maps, which clearly stated, 'Warning! Ley lines pulse and shift.'

"Each year the convergence of ley lines migrates and, unlike the adventure tales, in real true sorcery, X never, ever, marks the spot.

"The most important part of sorcery is done in the library. A hundred years ago, our workshops were directly over the North Pole. Had they done their research, they could have tracked the ley line drift over the years and traced it back to our exact location.

"Instead, they found the polar wastes barren and empty. Disappointed, they returned home and began spreading rumors that our sorcery, alchemy, noetics, tectonics, and astrology workshops do not even exist."

Hakeem Melchior steps down off the stage and Mage Gaspar moves forward and speaks in a melodious voice. "In order to revive the flow of visitors, our nomocratic prefect, the monsieur Kris Kringleson, has decreed that every year on the winter solstice we will distribute an updated almanac containing articles on our research, star charts, current maps of ley lines, and geomantic fluctuations, and a mail-order catalogue of our latest inventions.

"Therefore, our second gift unto ye today is a copy of this year's almanac. At the back, we have a current list of all the known elf communities in Vinland that will be receiving a free almanac this upcoming winter solstice. This knowledge base is for non-military purposes only. Weaponizing our ideas is forbidden.

"So remember, we are making this list and checking it twice to ensure that all those receiving these almanacs are truly committed to playing nice with our new technologies. Likewise, naughty elves who dabble with necromancy or carelessly release toxins into the environment or provoke unjustifiable wars will be removed from this list."

Mage Gaspar steps down and Sage Balthazar replaces him on the stage. "Finally, since those gifts already mentioned are not enough to stuff those stockings full, we added a special treat from the North Pole for the children—a sweetened mint stick with a hook at the end."

The little elf children burst into a joyful noise as they dig their hands into the nearest stocking and pull out candy canes. They are made from two sprigs of peppermint, one red, the other white, twisted together, soaked in sweetened honey water, and sunbaked until crispy. These original candy canes were not edible. The children all quiet down to suck on their treat and chew on the ends without swallowing.

Now that the three wise elves have finished, all eyes look up to Lynx, who is still sitting at the lip of the aqueduct awkwardly waiting for something. Feeling the audience's attention on him, he waves at them.

The crowd is about to leave when a Justiciar League officer comes shooting down the aqueduct headfirst, barely managing to keep his face above water. Lynx bounds to his feet and lets the officer zing past him, splashing down into the reflecting pool below.

While the Justiciar League officer flopping around in the pool draws the crowd's attention, few notice that the water from the aqueduct suddenly stops flowing. Taking his cue, Lynx sets the dwarven shield down and positions it above the blackflame brazier.

In a few moments, a stream of amber liquid flows down the empty aqueduct. With the shield, Lynx diverts its flow onto the blackflame brazier. Snap, crackle, and pop! The blackflame fizzles out.

When they notice the blackflame has been quenched, an uproar surges through the crowd. Some elves are relieved—finally able to voice their fears about the blackflame. Others writhe with indignation at the quashing of a gift dedicated to the statue of Thor. Arguments break out throughout the plaza; a few elders call it sacrilege and demand atonement—with Lynx's blood.

To make matters worse, two humans come sliding down the aqueduct and get dumped in the reflecting pool soon after Lynx himself jumps down into it. New outrage flairs up. How did those humans get here? What are they doing in our water? It's not a swimming pool! It is the primary source of drinking water and aesthetic peace for the colony. Now confusion reigns.

Seeing Florenz, the Justiciar League officer trudges out of the pool and says to her, panting, "The goblin! The goblin killed your father!"

Scene 6: Handcrank Redemption

Templar Priory, Town of Rofchester
Woden's Day Compline. Night, 19th of April, 1284
Feast of Saint Aelfheah, Bishop and Martyr

The security has been much tighter than anything he could have imagined. Templar sergeants follow a tight schedule keeping watch over every imaginable corner of the vaults—the corners inside the latrines happily escaped their imaginations.

After the Templars locked it all up for the night and after having stewed in feces all day, the dark elf code-named Whoopee cautiously creeps out of the cesspit and washes his hands and face off with the pitcher and basin provided for the privy. Monks were some of the cleanest people in the Middle Ages, and washing the hands and face regularly was required by their rules.

Now he begins the impossible task of trying to locate the vault that might contain this blackflame sword. Benjamin Frankelyn has been so tight-lipped about the whole operation that Whoopee would not even recognize the sword if he tripped over it. Still, he is a professional and knows his business well. He looks around, memorizing every detail of the walls, the doors, and the layout of the vault. He paces out the hallways and scans for potential access points, making a mental note of one spot ideal for an escape tunnel.

With impeccable timing, a small section of that very section of wall starts making a harsh grinding noise.

The wall starts to shake and then crumble until a six-inch bore bit pokes its way through. It retracts, leaving a cloud of powdery dust and a small tunnel just big enough to fit his fist into. A voice calls through the hole, "Whoopee!"

Still miffed about the cesspit, the dark elf calls back, "Glad you're having fun, Benny. I spent the day crouching in poo. You humans always make us dark elves do the dirty work."

The hole is too long and narrow for them to see each other but it carries the echoes of their voices well. Benjamin Frankelyn says, "You can take it up with the complaints department. Right now, I need to know if you've figured out which vault has the sword."

The dark elf hears a movement. Something black and furry skits around a corner. Benjamin Frankelyn calls out but the dark elf hushes him. "Shhhhhhh!"

Benjamin Frankelyn calls out again, "What is it?"

"I thought I saw a kitty cat. I'm going to go check it out." Whoopee sneaks over and peers around the corner. He sees a big, bushy mop of curly, blond hair on a girl with furry, black boots locked behind some bars. She seems to be asleep. He tiptoes back to the hole and says, "It's a little girl with curly, blond hair."

Ariel's voice comes piping through the hole. "Goldilocks! You found the cat burglar we need!"

Benjamin Frankelyn says, "Listen, this girl knows where the sword is. We need to cut a deal. Can you get her over to this hole to negotiate?"

"She's locked in a cage with iron bars."

"Use the wire I gave you. It's made by the Akmy dwarves. It should cut through iron fairly easily."

"Don't worry! I got this." The dark elf goes back and asks in Aenglish, "Hey, you! Goldilocks! You awake?"

No response.

She must be really tired because she does not look all that comfortable the way she is sleeping. He looks around and sees a tin plate with leftover corn and lima beans on it. He reaches in and bangs the plate against the bars and it makes a racket.

The girl is not happy to be woken up and she moans. When her eyes focus in on his dark face, she instinctively addresses him in Drowish, the language she spoke with her mother, "Peh-peh-le-pee yew! It smells like you spent the day in a cesspit."

A huge smile broadens across his face as he realizes the blond, curly hair hides a young, cute, aristocratic, dark elf lady. He loosens up and reaches out a hand and replies in Drowish, "I did, sister! I'm a dark elf too and I'm here to rescue you. Give me some skin!"

She whips him with her chains so hard it hurts.

"Suffering succotash! What was that about?"

She warns him sternly, "No touchie! There's one rule when talking to princesses and it's no touchie!"

"You're a princess?"

"Technically, yes. My mother was a dark elf commodore. If you knew anything about sea elves, you'd know that makes me a princess."

Whoopee applies the charm. "Indeed, it does, Princess. Indeed it does. So then, how did a gorgeous princess like yourself end up in a nasty cage like this?"

"I took a wrong turn at Albuquerque."

Trying to make friendly with her, he chatters away in Drowish. "Well, you see, I'm a member of the Ducaine Magicultors' Guild—named Magicultor of the Month last December. Anyhow, I'm with this cool group of adventurers who want to crack a vault that's got a dark flaming sword inside it. The chubby human peeping through the hole back there wants to talk."

"If you haven't noticed, I'm behind bars."

"That's the nice thing about magic. Locks, bars, traps, guards—no big deal." He takes out his magica wand and sings a magic word, "Poisson!"

Nothing happens. The princess wrinkles her lips and says, "Very impressive, Magicultor of the Month."

Whoopee chuckles, "Obviously, it's warded. No big deal. As they said in magic classes, 'Your magica wand is only the first of many tools it takes to be a great magicultor.' Check this out. This is a wire that can cut through iron bars. If you agree to hear the human out, I'll cut you out of that cage. Deal, sister?"

"Fine, but I am not your sister. Now cut this lock."

"Aye, aye, Your Highness."

He files furiously back and forth at the lock with the Akmy wire. Once he has cut through most of the lock, she leans back and gives the cage door a tremendous kick. The door slams into Whoopee and knocks him off his feet with a loud, "Ouch! That hurt."

She walks past him without offering to help him back onto his feet and finds the hole on her own. She calls down through in Drowish, "So what's the deal?"

Unruffled, Whoopee gets himself up and shouts past her to his friends, "So your human Goldilocks girl is actually a beautiful Drowish princess!"

Benjamin Frankelyn replies in Aenglish and Whoopee translates his words into Drowish, "Princess, we are honored to make your acquaintance. I am a frankelyn to a very important personage in Vinland and it has come to the attention of my patron that you are seeking the Sword of Layban."

202

The dark elf princess snaps back, "I didn't come all the way out here to get the sword for you!"

"Oh, agreed!" says Benjamin Frankelyn. "When I get into a bind like this, I like to find a solution that is, shall we say, a win for the both of us."

The princess folds her arms and says, "Before we even begin, tell me how this is all supposed to end up as a win-win scenario. Other than my leftover succotash, I don't have anything to offer you except the sword, and that's the one thing I'm not willing to negotiate about. I'm not seeing a win here."

Whoopee relays her concerns to Benjamin Frankelyn, who continues, "Well, you see, I did some reading up on the Sword of Layban, and apparently it means a lot to the Ammonite Christians. A group of them are here in Rofchester and they are willing to help you. The only price they are asking is that you listen empathetically to what they have to say."

"Fine. Get me out of here."

Whoopee tells her, "Good, now step back a bit."

"Why?"

"This is going to be loud and messy."

Before Whoopee gets her to stand back, the stones of the wall crumble and disintegrate. A tunnel opens all the way out of the Templar vault. It's a long and uncomfortably narrow passageway, just wide enough for a skinny elf to wiggle through like a worm. The rocks inside are still crumbling.

The princess orders Whoopee, "You first."

Whoopee isn't even paying attention. He's upset. He sticks his head through the hole shouting to his fellow adventurers, "Where was the kaboom? There was supposed to be an earth-shattering kaboom!"

Slithering through the tunnel is twice as awful as it sounds and doesn't help the princess's sour mood any.

Once she gets through to the other end, she sees a jovial Benjamin Frankelyn dressed in plain medieval civilian clothes; the broad-shouldered half-goblin/half-dwarf Monsignor Oscar Meyer wearing his clerical robe; Ariel, who has dyed her hair red and stuffed some wool fleece around her gums to change her facial features; and the white-haired Willis, now back in his suit of reinforced mail armor, singling him out as a fighter-class adventurer.

Benjamin Frankelyn smiles proudly. "You've heard of elf fire, right? Imagine what happens to solid stone when you heat it with elf fire then quickly freeze it with blackflame. Impressive, isn't it?"

Around them stand four figures in simple, white robes—two women and two men. Their faces are austere but gentle. An older woman introduces herself using the mystical gift of tongues so all can understand each other despite the language barriers. "I am Sister Elmyra and this is my associate, Sister Penelope. We think you ought to know the truth about Jesus Christ."

Goldilocks snaps back, "Oh, don't worry, I already know all about him. Can we move on to discussing why you are going to give me the Sword of Layban or should I just start running now?"

Sister Elmyra's gift of tongues is powerful enough that all present hear Goldilocks's Drowish words in their own native language. Benjamin Frankelyn replies to her in Aenglish, but she hears his words in Drowish. "The deal was for us to break you out in exchange for empathetic listening. You're just assuming you already know what they're going to say. Give them time to explain and we can find a solution where we all win." Benjamin Frankelyn bows to Sister Elmyra and yields the spotlight—or in this case, the moonlight—to her.

Sister Elmyra resumes speaking. "No worries, my dear. Let's talk about what matters most to you right now—the Sword of Layban. It is significant to Ammonite Christians because without it, the true faith would never have come to Vinland. Layban had it forged as a weapon capable of great evil, but God has used it by his command to accomplish a greater good.

"We are a peaceful people, and we are not here for the sword itself, but our prophet believes God has a plan to use it to lead us to a treasure without price."

"What makes you think I know anything about this treasure you are seeking?"

"Pure faith. A certain prophet, seer, and revelator foretold evil on a scale that would make the Thieves' Guild look like a gathering of modern-day saints unless we follow this path. The Sword of Layban is worthless to us, but we believe its bearer will save Vinland."

The blond-haired dark elf princess looks at her intently. "So you're saying you would agree to let me have the Sword of Layban because of some prophecy, but I have a hunch this guy over here wants it too."

Benjamin Frankelyn puts a hand on her shoulders but she snaps, "No touchie! Rule number one with princesses—no touchie!"

Frankelyn backs off and says, "You're right, princess. All I'm saying is that we agreed to some empathetic listening. You keep assuming you already know what we're going to say. Do you know a way to get the sword out of that vault? Because if you do, by all means, go ahead. It's all yours."

"No, I don't know how to get it out."

He continues. "You know which vault it's in, but you don't know how to get it out. We have a plan to get it out, but we don't know which vault it's in. Let's figure out our differences before the Templars find us."

Sister Elmyra says, "This is going to take some trust. All of us, including Mister Frankelyn here, fear the evil of the Sword of Layban. But if we give it to you, you must promise to lead us to the bronze plates that contain the Law of God. Only by learning and obeying the Law of God can we hope to keep this nation from dwindling and perishing in unbelief.

"The power of the blackflame is enough to engulf this entire continent from sea to shining sea in war, strife, and sin, but our prophet has told us that although you seek it for the evil powers it will grant you, you will eventually turn from your evil ways."

The princess crosses her arms and states, "So let me get this straight; you know I am going to use this sword for evil, but you are going to help me get it anyway because your prophet says that I'll eventually lead you to some kind of bronze plates."

"Yes. It's the only way."

The dark elf princess suddenly becomes apologetic. "So let's just say hypothetically that I have no idea where these bronze plates are. Do I still get to keep the sword—hypothetically speaking, of course?"

Sister Elmyra replies with great patience and kindness in her eyes, "We know that you are ignorant of the bronze plates right now but we firmly believe in God's plan that you will lead us to those plates one way or another."

She turns to Benjamin Frankelyn and asks, "Okay, but it kind of sounds like a stretch to me. Is that what you believe too, Mister Frankelyn?"

Benjamin Frankelyn smiles cheerfully. "Nope. Not at all. I work by reason, not by faith. Let's just say when it comes to the battle between good and evil, I steer the middle course and keep neutral about it all."

Goldilocks groans. "I've heard that line before."

Frankelyn continues. "The reason I invited the Ammonites here is that they have preserved in their oral traditions important information about how the sword works. Getting the sword to work is key to our plans for getting it out.

"The Sword of Layban has the power to billow out freezing blackflame, even in small, confined spaces without fresh air. All we have to do is ignite the blackflame inside its vault and it will freeze-burn the vault. Once the metal has frozen through, we'll heat it with elf fire. The alternation will make it brittle enough to shatter it as easily as if it were made out of glass. If you agree to turn over the Sword of Layban to us so we can complete our quest with it, we'll give it back to you when we're done with it."

She squints with suspicion in her eyes. "And how long is that going to take?"

"A few days, perhaps; a few weeks at most. Once we complete our quest, we won't need the sword anymore. It'll be all yours. Win-win scenario."

"How am I going to know you'll keep your end of the bargain? You could just keep telling me, we need one more week, and before you know it, years go by."

Benjamin Frankelyn cuts to the chase. "Think of it this way. You get your hands on the sword first, so we're the ones taking the biggest leap of faith in trusting you. If you don't trust us, you're welcome to go back and take your chances with the Inquisition."

"So why are you taking a leap of faith with me? You just said you work by reason and not by faith."

"That's my ideal. As a realist, I accept the fact that ninety percent of our decisions are based more on faith in someone or something than hard facts or rational explanations. That's just the way life goes."

"So let's fit this deal into the ten percent that makes perfect sense to our reason."

"No, the other ten percent is pure emotion."

The princess thinks for a while. "Fine, what are the magic words to make the Sword of Layban work?"

Sister Elmyra says, "They are not magic words at all, but rather a dark incantation for an unholy ritual— words that bring great evil upon those who speak them. Consider well before you—"

Goldilocks interrupts, "Yeah, yeah, blah, blah, blah. Just tell me the words and let's get this over with."

"By the power of Layban . . . I have the power!"

Goldilocks shrivels. "That's kind of dorky."

Willis cuts her off. "Don't knock it! For some people, it's really cool. Maybe it's a guy thing."

Benjamin Frankelyn resumes. "You and Whoopee are the only ones who can fit through the tunnel. He'll bring the elf fire. All you have to do is put your hand on the safe box holding the Sword of Layban and recite the ritual words. After he heats it with elf fire, just keep tapping at it and it'll break."

"What if I had a hammer and I'm hammering until morning? I wouldn't hear the Templars coming back."

"Don't worry, we've got a hammer of our own. We'll hammer out a warning if there is danger around. Once you break through, stop the sword from flaming by calling out, 'Let the power return!' Be careful, it'll be extremely cold in there."

Goldilocks thinks for a moment. Despite all her misgivings, she runs out of objections. This frankelyn has answers to everything. She says, "I don't like it, but whatever—I'm going to go with it. You have a deal."

"Splendid!" exclaims Benjamin Frankelyn. "Let's shake on it!"

"Tut, tut! No touchie!" She points to herself and reminds them, "Princess. No touchie!"

They all look at her silently. She remembers she once heard a preacher say that the path to evil starts from 'whatever.' With those words still ringing in her ears, she intentionally chooses to brush aside all the warnings of her conscience. "Whatever."

She then shakes hands with the devil.

Scene 7: Dear Lynx

Council Chambers at Thor's Base, Shentalpee City
Hock Moon Day Vespers. Evening, 10th of April, 1284

Just when the crowd reaches its breaking point and verges on anarchic violence, Major Leagues Umpire Gandorf Mithranderson shows up with a large contingent of armed elves combined from the Justiciar League, the League of Licornes, and the Ivy League.

Elf standard bearers from each of the leagues blow their horns furiously, demanding that the crowds quiet down. Officers and sergeants from the leagues wade into the reflecting pool to bring Lynx and the two humans before the Major Leagues Umpire.

Enganyon's father treats him with the utmost respect. "Monsieur Lynx! Can you tell us what happened to the monsieur umpire-in-chief?"

Lynx knows he could be in big trouble. "No, I have no idea where he is. But we had to extinguish the blackflame to save the colony! The inquisitor —"

"Calm down, monsieur! We'll hear your story out in due time. Right now, the monsieur umpire-in-chief is missing. His safety is our first priority. Do these humans know anything about his whereabouts?"

Lynx asks them in his crude Aenglish and then he translates their response for Umpire Gandorf. "They said that the goblin killed our leader. They must mean the goblin that the longhouse humans captured for us."

Umpire Gandorf thinks for a moment, then waves his hands to beckon some soldiers. "This is an emergency of the first order. Calm the crowds down!"

The officers and sergeants press through the crowd using elbows, batons, and the flat of their swords to get the hysterical elves to submit. Enganyon's father shouts above the crowd, "Reports have confirmed that our umpire-in-chief has died in defense of his homeland! As Major Leagues Umpire, I am exercising my prerogative to declare martial law and assume leadership of the government until the Council of Perfects decides on a provisional head of state!

"Due to the current political crisis, the Council of Perfects will be holding an emergency council session at sundown. All those not invited to the session are ordered to return to their homes until the council has announced its decisions. Anyone found roaming the walkways after sundown without a pass will be arrested as a rabble-rouser!"

Suspecting foul play, Florenz gives instructions to Officer Bunzi, the soaking-wet Justiciar Leaguer who told her about her father's death. "Go tell the monsieur Major Leagues Umpire that I am too distressed over my father's death to attend the emergency council session; then, meet me at Woden's Tree."

After delivering the message, Officer Bunzi looks for Florenz at Woden's Tree but can't find her.

"Psst!" she hisses at him. "Over here."

He moves to where the sound came from and a hand grabs him into the tree trunk. "Where are we?"

"This is a secret entrance into the council chambers that only the umpire-in-chief knows about."

"Then how do you know about it?"

"Duh! You really think Zena could win the election? My father started showing me the ropes early."

"Yay democracy! And why take me along?"

"My father told me once, 'That Officer Bunzi is a low-life thug, but you can count on his loyalty.'"

"Thanks for the compliment, I think."

"Climb this ladder. I suspect the Council of Perfects is going to be a lot more honest about what happened to my father if they think I'm not listening."

"So you have a secret room where you can spy on everything that goes on in there?"

"Exactly. And if you betray that secret, you'll be put to a horrible death."

"Don't worry. Your father was right about me."

"That's reassuring; but not at all comforting."

"Hey! I'm loyal, okay? The other part—"

"Shhhhh!" Florenz puts her hand over his mouth.

Through the spy holes they hear Dungaree Jeanne say, "By my bushy eyebrows, you do seem to be taking these unexpectedly catastrophic events rather well."

It's Enganyon's voice that responds. "Oh, Madame Dungaree, you're always so dramatic! There's nothing catastrophic or unexpected about this turn of events. My father's been planning it out all along."

Florenz blurts out, "That rat!"

Officer Bunzi jumps back. "Where?"

"Shhhh! Keep it down. It was only a metaphor."

"Do metaphors bite?"

Florenz waves him to follow. "Only when you don't want to hear the truth. Come on!"

They climb through some tight tunnels and walk over rafters until they reach a dusty, unpolished, dark room with a screen that allows them to look down into the council chambers and hear what is going on. There are no chairs or cushions, so they sit on the raw planks.

Officer Bunzi gets antsy. "So how's a rodent supposed to know if I don't want to hear the truth?"

"Shhhh!" Florenz breathes right into his ear. "They'll hear us down there with all your chatter."

Still trying to digest Enganyon's comments, Florenz settles herself against the screen to watch and listen.

Dungaree Jeanne sits in the front row next to Johnny Appleseed in his wheelchair. The civic summoner reads the names of those summoned to the council session. To Florenz's surprise, the names Johnny Appleseed, Zena, and Lynx are on the list.

Zena is seated next to Enganyon's father, Major Leagues Umpire Gandorf Mithranderson, who has taken his place next to the umpire-in-chief's chair. Once the civic summoner has finished issuing summonses, the high commissioner commissions the meeting by going through the formality of inviting the umpire-in-chief to speak. Then, at his request, the entire council chamber pauses for a moment of silence out of respect for the umpire-in-chief's death.

The high commissioner announces, "In the absence of our dearly departed monsieur umpire-in-chief, I call upon the acting head of state for the Tuscoraura Elves, the monsieur Major Leagues Umpire Gandorf."

A burst of applause erupts as Umpire Gandorf makes his way onto the stage and addresses the high elves in the audience (no wood elves were invited) in Runic. "Mesdames, mesdemoiselles, and messieurs, esteemed high elves of our noble race around whom the cosmos turns, on this day, a tragic day, we gather to honor the life of our dearly departed monsieur Umpire-in-Chief Kibbler Earnestson, and to ensure that the fire elves of Tuscoraura Mountain will carry on his legacy.

"Superlative high elves, read through the history books to understand what this great elf accomplished. Never has our military felt more confident. Never has our economy been so strong. Never have our relationships with the longhouse humans, the mountain dwarves, and the garden gnomes been so reliable and productive as they are now at the end of these twelve years of his umpirage. Ask yourselves: would the longhouse humans have turned over a lurking goblin to Monsieur Drayton while he was umpire-in-chief?

"He was a second father to me and appointed me Major Leagues Umpire because he knew that our military needed a strong leader to unify its power.

"I remember the day when Mademoiselle Florenz announced to him she would run for umpire-in-chief. At first, he refused. He wanted her to take over his business and have a happy life with no other concerns than taste-testing chocolate chip cookies.

"'What is the point,' I asked him, 'of spending thy whole life fighting to open the path to happiness for thy children when thou must bar them from the career they see themselves most happily pursuing?'

"I reminded him that, although it goes against precedence for the children of umpires to run for office, no law forbids it. By the time the sorbet was served at that dinner, our dearly departed monsieur umpire-in-chief promised his daughter he would support her candidacy in private as her father but not in public. If she was going to win the chief umpirage, she would have to earn it on her own merit.

"Her dedication to the campaign trail and her stellar performance in the Ivy League Tournament proved that she was a worthy candidate. However, superlative high elves, it pains me to say that Mademoiselle Florenz is no longer on Tuscoraura Mountain. She has gone into voluntary exile."

Florenz gasps. "What? I never said that!"

Umpire Gandorf continues. "The first reason is obvious: her grief at her father's loss. The second reason is less obvious but equally public: her embarrassment over the Bartlebee affair."

Florenz can't believe her ears! "Why that—"

Officer Bunzi leans into her ear. "Shhh! They'll hear us down there with all your chatter."

"When her staff first intercepted the letter implying that the garden gnomid stewardess Bartlebee might have leaked the secret recipe for elf fire, she did not want to act on it out of her love for her dear friend, Mademoiselle Zena. The poor taste of her campaign manager pressured her to go public with the scant information available, claiming that it would be the only way to protect Shentalpee City. After hours of agonizing over it, she felt she had no choice.

"We now know Bartlebee handed over a simple acorn pie recipe. In a single day, Mademoiselle Florenz realized that she lost both her best friend to dirty politics and her father to a security breach. Such strokes of misfortune one at a time have shattered stronger persons, but all together on a single day . . .

"She needs time to grieve. But that timing leaves us in a delicate predicament. Right now, Mademoiselle Zena Jeannesdottir is the only candidate for the chief umpirage left in Shentalpee City."

A few gasps ripple through the audience as the ramifications of the current political situation sink in.

After a rhetorical pause, Umpire Gandorf continues. "Without a second candidate, according to the Magnificent Charter, we cannot hold an election. If we postpone the elections, it could be months, perhaps years, before candidates of sufficient quality step forward."

Florenz rolls her eyes. Now she sees where Umpire Gandorf has been going with this. He is going to angle the whole situation so that his indecisive son can get back on the ballot, even after spitting on the opportunity when it was first presented to him.

Umpire Gandorf calls out, "Mister Lynx Highrune, wilt thou please approach the stage?"

Surprise and shock hit every last soul in the council chambers. Absolutely no one saw this coming.

Lynx stands, surprised and nervous. When he walks up onto the stage, Umpire Gandorf turns him around with an affirming pat on the back and announces, "To honor the memory of our dearly departed monsieur umpire-in-chief and to fulfill one of his last promises, as acting head of state, I hereby grant Monsieur Lynx Cougarson of Clan Highrune a paid commission as a junior officer in the Ivy League and enfranchisement as a high elf of Tuscoraura Mountain."

Umpire Gandorf hands him a scroll and the chamber hall offers a reluctant round of applause.

"Monsieur Lynx, all the other high elves on Tuscoraura Mountain have declined to run for the office of umpire-in-chief. Wilt thou be willing to put in thy bid for candidacy to maintain the democratic process?"

Lynx hesitates. It's all too much to take in.

Zena stands and asks publicly in a loud voice, "Monsieur Major Leagues Umpire, art thou not intending to prosecute him for sacrilege? After all, the blackflame was dedicated to Thor."

Lynx looks at Zena with bulging eyes, feeling utterly betrayed. *How could you bring that up at a moment like this? With a friend like you, who needs enemies?*

Umpire Gandorf announces to the council chambers in Runic, "If thou dost accept the candidacy, Monsieur Lynx, as acting head of state, I would grant thee an umpirical pardon for thy act to keep these disruptions from scuttling the ship of democracy."

Her glare makes Lynx realize Zena doesn't want him to become her equal. He rebels. "I accept!"

Satisfied, Umpire Gandorf ushers Lynx off the stand with the disinterest of a newspaper reader suddenly realizing the edition in hand is yesterday's news. He nods to the civic summoner, and the warder goes down and wheels Johnny Appleseed to the front. Dungaree Jeanne stands next to him as his translator.

The high commissioner asks Johnny Appleseed, "Dost thou swear to tell the truth, the whole truth, and nothing but the truth, or else invite the wrath of Woden upon thy head?"

After hearing Dungaree Jeanne's translation, Johnny Appleseed replies, "The good Lord in the Bible forbids us from swearing, but I solemnly affirm before the One True God that I will tell the truth, the whole truth, and nothing but the truth."

Dungaree Jeanne translates his statement word for word. The high commissioner looks to Umpire Gandorf with worry on his face.

The Major Leagues Umpire nods and asks him in a commanding voice, "Reverend Appleseed, the two humans have informed us that before his death, our dearly departed monsieur umpire-in-chief figured out a way to weaponize the blackflame by shooting it out of a siphon. Armed with this advanced technology, he used it to ambush and destroy the inquisitor. Little did he suspect that the captured goblin had forged an alliance with the Inquisition and brought death to many brave high elves, including our dearly departed monsieur umpire-in-chief.

"In thy expert opinion, is it possible to weaponize blackflame in a manner similar to what the two humans claim our dearly departed monsieur umpire-in-chief managed to do?"

Dungaree Jeanne waits for Appleseed's reply and says in Runic, "Yes, Monsieur Major Leagues Umpire."

The chamber audience mumbles and comments to each other. Umpire Gandorf continues interrogating him through Dungaree Jeanne. "Canst thou replicate the military applications of blackflame that the two human witnesses described?"

"No, Monsieur Major Leagues Umpire. He cannot."

Umpire Gandorf calls out, "I propose legislation establishing a commission to thoroughly investigate the blackflame findings of our dearly departed monsieur umpire-in-chief. These discoveries could be the key to maintaining elf military superiority in the near future!

"My thanks to thee, Reverend Appleseed, for thy testimony. Thou mayest return to thy place."

She starts to roll Appleseed back to the front row of the audience but he whispers to Dungaree Jeanne and she says in a loud voice, "Begging thy permission, Monsieur Major Leagues Umpire, Reverend Appleseed wishes to make a final statement regarding his gift of blackflame to our community."

"Permission granted."

Johnny Appleseed speaks as Dungaree Jeanne translates his words into Runic. "In my childhood, famines were common in Vinland. Our soil is fertile, but nutritious food often spoils quickly. I have seen families and entire communities on the brink of starvation because their vast supplies of food had rotted before anyone could eat them.

"When I learned of apples—how easily they grow in almost any climate and how easy they are to preserve as apple jelly, apple sauce, apple butter, and dried apple chips—I decided the first step to combatting hunger in Vinland would be to make apple seeds readily available. I traveled far and wide, offering the gift of free apple seeds and using my family's patrimony to establish apple orchards across Vinland.

"Through my travels, I saw how alcohol drove mothers and fathers to spend money that should have gone to feeding their hungry children on inebriating drinks instead. Dogfennel was the only effective remedy to alcoholism I could find, so I began to distribute it along with the apple seeds.

"But when I came upon a group of outcasts who fostered the secret to blackflame, I realized I had discovered the best solution to keeping food from spoiling. It seemed to me that hunger and famine were on their last legs in Vinland. If only I could make blackflame available to every community, then we could support twice the number of people with half the food production that is required now due to the amount of spoilage that wastes food stocks so easily.

"Regretfully, the military applications of blackflame have caused quite an uproar among Church authorities. The Inquisition has tracked me down and forbidden me to distribute dogfennel, blackflame, or even the Bible.

"If you do choose to cultivate blackflame and investigate its military applications, understand that you must prepare for a terrible war. The Crusades have brought to their knees fortresses previously considered impregnable. Think of what happened to the town of Donora when it tried to shut its gates to the crusaders."

Hearing his grave warning, the high elves break out into laughter. They hold the pope's battalions in utter contempt. Umpire Gandorf quiets them down and asks, "Is it not true that the Inquisition fears most the power of blackflame to recall the dead from the netherworld?"

"It is."

"Could blackflame recall our dearly departed monsieur umpire-in-chief from the netherworld?"

"Not without the Sword of Layban."

The high commissioner smacks his gavel. "I wish to second Monsieur Major Leagues Umpire's proposal to establish a blackflame commission. Any opposition?"

Silence.

"All in favor, say aye."

The raucous shouting of the power-hungry high elves drowns out the gavel.

"Motion carries!"

Satisfied with how that went, Umpire Gandorf turns to Lynx. "Now then, there remains only the formality of Monsieur Lynx's candidacy. Please repeat after me. I, Monsieur Lynx Cougarson of Clan Highrune, high elf of Shentalpee City, do hereby tender my candidacy for the position of umpire-in-chief over the fire elves of Tuscoraura Mountain."

Lynx repeats the formula, but barely does he sit down when one high elf stands up. "Objection!"

The high commissioner bangs his gavel. "Your objection, Monsieur Toadly?"

With bombast on his lips, Toadly says, "A good number of us are wondering why we are banking the future of Shentalpee City on a nouveau riche, former wood elve mademoiselle and a young upstart, former wood elf monsieur when we have before us in these very council chambers the perfect candidate: one who has merited his commission in a major league through his own competence and who has never committed a sacrilege or been embroiled in a scandal, and one whose bloodlines do great honor to our elfin pedigree—Monsieur Enganyon Gandorfson."

Murmurs of agreement make Toadly even bolder. "I make a motion to draft ad hoc legislation in this emergency council session allowing Monsieur Enganyon Gandorfson to reconsider his candidacy for umpire-in-chief!"

Applause washes over the assembly. Before hand-clapping stops, the high commissioner has already seconded the proposal and the audience has carried it.

All of a sudden, the Toadly Act paving the way for Enganyon to offer his candidacy for umpire-in-chief is now law under the Emergency Provisions Act of 1284.

When Enganyon walks up to his father's umpirical chair, he acts as if he is totally taken by surprise and has no idea what to do. Enganyon steps up to the stage, where he addresses the chamber audience in Runic. "Mesdames, mesdemoiselles, and messieurs! While I am deeply honored by the high regard ye hold me in and I would do anything within my power to honor the legacy of our dearly departed monsieur umpire-in-chief, my heart desires to see only one elve in that role—Mademoiselle Zena Jeannesdottir."

He kneels on one knee before her and pulls out a ring. In a loud, manly voice he says for the whole assembly to hear, "Mademoiselle Zena, thou art the only elve I ever truly loved. Wilt thou marry me?"

Jumping up and clapping and flushed red in the face, she says, "Yes! Yes!"

Some elves in the chamber audience take no delight in this spectacle. Lynx, hurt, confused, and humiliated, storms out of the council chambers. Florenz fumes.

Officer Bunzi taps Florenz on the shoulder and says meekly, "Maybe we should get going, Mademoiselle."

Straining every nerve to calm herself before speaking, Florenz states, "Please tell the Major Leagues Umpire I've gone away. In my absence, you must recover my father's body, put it in a barrel of vinegar, and hide it here. Take the key to my father's coffer and bribe anyone who tries to stop you."

"You're not leaving for exile, are you?"

"No. I'm going on a quest to bring back the Sword of Layban—and my father's soul."

ACT IV

I SPY

WITH MY ELFY EYE

Scene 1: Meet the Heresiarch's Family

Village of Carthage, Long Falls
in the Confederacy of the Seven Nations
Tiw's Day Vespers. Evening, 25th of April, 1284
Feast of Saint Mark the Evangelist

Ariel's party of adventurers has new-found respect for Benjamin Frankelyn. For a nineteen-year-old, he has unbounded energy, dazzling people skills, and an uncanny knack for improvisation. Not only did his plan for cracking open the vault work, but he got Goldilocks to hand over the Sword of Layban without issue.

After a week of journeying, they reach an Irokian village called Long Falls where a group of Aenglish Blackflame Cultists has taken refuge from the inquisitors seeking to put them on trial for heresy. They have named their settlement Carthage.

Once inside the cultists' secret temple, Frankelyn tells Whoopee, "Introduce the princess to her new best friends, if you please. This is Heresiarch Joagbert, the head of the Blackflame Cult in Vinland. His archdeacon is Elmer the Fadet. The Fadets are cliff elves from Vaucluse in Languedoc, now controlled by the Frankish king. His other deacon is Hugo the Troll. Unlike the stereotypes about trolls from his Sasquatch tribe, he is a very sensitive and philosophical believer who was deeply touched by the religion of Heresiarch Joagbert."

Whoopee translates the introductions for the princess into Drowish. When Deacon Hugo notices the conversation turn to him, he holds an undead rabbit in his hands and says in simplified Aenglish, "I always wanted my own little bunny rabbit. I like to hug him and pet him and squeeze him. I named him George. One day George stopped moving, but Joagbert made him good again. I like Joagbert."

Whoopee explains the gist of the troll's conversion story and she stares up at the giant, hairy deacon. She's not quite sure how to respond so she just smiles and agrees. "Right . . ."

Deacon Elmer says in Runic, "Princess, our beloved heresiarch would like to see thee ignite the sword to test if thou truly hast the power."

She replies in Runic, "What is it with ye people and power?" She asks Whoopee for the Sword of Layban and at his request Frankelyn hands it to her.

She holds it up and exclaims, "By the power of Layban . . . I have the power!"

Black puffs of flames like dark thunderclouds crackle with blue sparks. She then recalls the flame saying, "Let the power return!"

The sword's flaming blade settles down to a low rumbling of shadows at play which then disappear completely.

The heresiarch smiles with sinister satisfaction and speaks to Deacon Elmer, who then tells her in Runic, "The heresiarch is greatly pleased with thy mastery of the sword. He still has much to teach thee before thou canst unlock its full potential. He shall teach thee how to reanimate the dead with it, if thou art willing to call him thy master."

The princess tries to stifle her smile of eagerness and says modestly, "I am ready to learn, master."

The heresiarch guides them deeper into the secret temple. They come to a crypt, and the heresiarch orders the troll to open the large, stone slab covering one of the sarcophagi. Deacon Hugo puts down his undead bunny and slides the stone away to reveal a decaying giant dwarf. His shoulders alone are nearly five feet wide and he stretches from head to toe roughly six and a half feet tall. His massive body makes him seem much more powerful than any giant she has encountered.

"Behold! The last of his kind," says Deacon Elmer. "The Jintel were a race of dwarves of unusual size. Their language and facial features are similar to their cousin Pyrinoak dwarves, but their colossal strength made them reckless and slower to apologize than common sense would dictate. They fought war after war and their population dwindled in Europa. A century ago, a Jintel clan sailed to Vinland but they fared no better.

"Their race has since finished. Markest thou my words, this Jintel is a good candidate to become thy thrall not because of his large size, but because of his strong will. In the undead state, a thrall's abilities in the physical world depend more on their qualities of mind and spirit than any physical characteristic. A strong will translates into great physical strength, and an agile mind grants a body that was once clumsy in life more dexterity than Gordo the Thief. A weak-minded ogre in life becomes a weak-limbed ogre after reanimation.

"This Jintel you see here, Balrock, was strong-willed. It is not by coincidence that he survived longer than any of his kinsmen. The heresiarch offers thee the gift to enthrall him so he may serve thee in thy noble quest of seeking revenge against the Inquisition that slew thy father. In return, thou wilt welcome missionaries of the blackflame into thy homeland."

"Fine. Now show me this ritual."

Deacon Elmer says, "Before we begin, thou must know the rules. Thou shalt not allow thy thrall to get wet with holy water. Thou shalt not subject thy thrall to get sliced or diced with silver weapons. Thou shalt not allow thy thrall to get blessed by holy clerics or druids. Thou shalt not snack after midnight."

The princess grimaces and says, "I thought joining up with the evil side would mean that I do not have to worry about the thou-shalt-nots anymore."

"Not snacking after midnight is just my personal recommendation for thee. The rest of these thou-shalt-nots have more to do with the immutable nature of the cosmos. There is nothing good or bad but that thinking makes it so; but there are some rules you just cannot break without breaking thine own coccyx bone."

She huffs and says, "Okay, fine. Let's just get on with the part where I enthrall this giant dwarf."

"Thou must first learn the Dark Tongue of Caldor."

"Drat! And how long will that take?"

"An instant but it shall reveal thy secret thoughts."

"I only have one thought on my mind—revenge."

Deacon Elmer says in Aenglish, "She is ready."

Heresiarch Joagbert lays a hand on her head and says, "Receive the power to speak the Black Tongue of Caldor, Florenz Kibblersdottir."

Suddenly, the princess is able to speak directly to the heresiarch in the Black Tongue of Caldor. "Okay, you figured me out. Now show me how to use this dumb old sword to bring back my father."

"Call me master."

Florenz shrugs and says, "Okay, master. Show me."

The heresiarch goes through the ritual in the Black Tongue of Caldor. Her memory is keen, and it is not long before she is able to perform it perfectly by heart.

Once she is ready, Florenz taps both shoulders of the giant dwarf with the Sword of Layban, saying, "Arise, Balrock! I dub thee a servant of the black fire, a dread knight of the flame of Layban. I bid thee come back from the shadows. Arise, Sir Balrock!"

The dull-yellow eyes of the reanimated giant open. His throat gurgles and a convulsive motion agitates his limbs. Oh, his twitching fingers! The humungous body shivers as his yellowed skin tightens. It scarcely covers the work of muscles and arteries beneath.

His lustrous, black hair hangs limp from his head as he sits himself up. His mouth opens with a garbled moan, displaying his pearly white teeth, but there is nothing healthy about them. Behind his shriveled lips, the whiteness of his teeth only forms a lurid contrast against his dried-out eyes, sunken back into dun-yellow sockets and emitting a strange, reddish glow.

Breathless horror and disgust fill Florenz's heart until a rush of power intoxicates her mind. "Arise, Sir Balrock!" she shouts. "Bow to thy new master!"

The giant studies her for a moment, then works his way out of his sarcophagus and bows before her. A surge of pride and superiority wells up in her. She swears to herself she will bring back her father and gather a great army of undead warriors against the Inquisition who orchestrated his death.

As if reading her thoughts, the heresiarch lets out a sinister laugh. He speaks to her in the Black Tongue of Caldor. "Good, my young apprentice. I can feel thy anger. Take up thy weapon. Strike down the next inquisitor thou seest with all of thy hatred, and thy journey with the blackflame will be complete."

Not wanting to ruin the moment but needing the Sword of Layban back, Benjamin Frankelyn announces cheerfully, "Welcome to the family, Balrock! It's been a real treat to watch you two bond so quickly. Now, Your Highness, could you please return to me the sword so we can complete our quest?"

The heresiarch tells him in Aenglish, "According to the power of blackflame gathered within the Sword of Layban, this giant dwarf is now a Dread Knight and as such, deserves the style of respect *Sir* Balrock."

Clearing his throat, Benjamin Frankelyn corrects himself. "Ahem. Yes, well, then. My apologies, Sir Balrock. We are glad to have you with us. And thank you for the clarification, Your Holiness . . . um, Your Evilness . . . how should I address you, Heresiarch?"

"Please, please, just plain Joagbert. We despise hierarchy and aspire to create an egalitarian society."

Benjamin Frankelyn does not appear unsettled in the least by his words. "Wonderful! Just wonderful! You must send me a pamphlet someday about all those ideals and aspirations you have. In the meantime, I should really like that sword back so I can complete my quest. You know the deal. We'll only release the funds for our contribution to your cause if we succeed in our quest as well.

"So how about it, Joagbert?"

The heresiarch turns to Florenz and nods, but she seems to like possessing the sword too much to give it up. Benjamin Frankelyn gets edgy. Ariel and Willis put their hands on their weapons — they are not in the least inclined to let this quest fail after they have come so far.

The heresiarch commands her in the Black Tongue of Caldor. This time, the sound is horrible. She screams and covers her ears until she gives in. "Yes, master."

Clearly battling with her own will, she drops the Sword of Layban with a clank upon the stony ground. Wrapping it in a cloth, Benjamin Frankelyn asks politely, "Excuse me, Joagbert, one last question. Um . . . with no hierarchy and all, I'm just curious why everyone keeps calling you master."

"I said we despise hierarchy, Mister Frankelyn, but make no mistake about it — once a person fully commits to evil, I am very much the master."

Scene 2: War Never Changes

Township of Salim
in the Aenglish Duchy of Masswachoosut Bay
Woden's Day Terce. Morning, 3rd of May, 1284
Holy Rood Day (Crouchmas)

They travel by day on a horse-drawn wagon and at night they load the horses onto the wagon and let Sir Balrock pull the harness. After another week of journeying, the party of adventurers reaches the township of Salim, the seat of the Holy Office of the Inquisition in Vinland.

Benjamin Frankelyn holds one last huddle to make sure the plan is clear in everyone's mind. Relying on his dark elf Whoopee to translate his words into Drowish, he says, "Princess, thank you for your cooperation so far. I'm glad this is working out for you. Ariel has a replica of the Sword of Layban, which the Hill Dwarves of Cumorah forged for us after we left Rofchester.

"We won't be able to fool the high inquisitors with a fake sword because of their prophetic gifts, but right after presenting the real Sword of Layban, Ariel will switch it out using sleight of hand with the fake one. If that fails, Whoopee will swap it out using magic.

"Sir Balrock has been very useful so far but the downside to having an undead giant in our company is that he won't escape the notice of the guards at the city gates. He'll have to stay here. We'll use this place as a rallying point to fall back on in case of an emergency.

"Princess, please make sure he knows he is supposed to stay put right here. If we get caught outside the residence of the high inquisition with an undead thrall—yeah, I don't even want to think about it. So I'm only going to ask this once—can Sir Balrock obey orders and stick to this spot?"

Confident, Florenz replies, "He can."

When he hears Whoopee's translation, Frankelyn snaps his fingers. "Good! That's what I like to hear!

"Monsignor Meyer, you will come with us to lend a veneer of holiness to our group. Meanwhile, Willis, here's a few pennies. Take Whoopee and the princess to dinner at a tavern called the Leaky Carvel, my treat. You'll find it down the road on the right from the high inquisitors' residence at the Holy Office headquarters.

"Princess, once we get the real sword back, you're free to head home with the Sword of Layban. Any questions? No? All right, let's move out."

Almost from the first moment, the plan falls apart. Benjamin Frankelyn, Ariel, and Monsignor Meyer approach the Holy Office headquarters and the security measures are about triple in size and scope of what Frankelyn was expecting. A Swiss guard patrol snags them from behind and interrogates them. "Who are you two, and what's this tramp doing here with you?"

Benjamin Frankelyn turns around with a patient smile and says, "Good evening, dearly beloved brothers in Christ. We are friars seeking an audience—"

The Swiss guard interrupts. "Dolts! This is the precinct of the high inquisitors' residence! No women!"

Assessing the official heraldic markings on the patrol and the unbending expressions on their faces, Benjamin Frankelyn quickly calculates the most likely outcomes for various responses that come to mind and he says, "We are grievous sinners and have been told that only one of the high inquisitors in person can absolve us from our unspeakable crimes. Can you point out to us the way?"

"For starters, you have to show proper penitence for your sins by disassociating yourself from the company of women."

As casual as can be, Benjamin Frankelyn turns to Ariel and says, "My dear, treat yourself to some dinner at a local tavern. It seems this will be our last conversation before we enter a life of righteousness."

She shrugs her shoulders and heads off, still carrying both the fake and the real Sword of Layban. Immediately, Benjamin Frankelyn realizes he made the right call. The patrol leader escorts him to the high inquisitors' residence himself and calls on the captain of the inquisitorial household guard to receive them. The captain comes out with a halfling master thief who pats them all down. No way would they have gotten away with the old switcheroo in front of a guy like that.

The captain looks like he is ready to have them all locked up in the stockade. He shouts, "You gentlemen have guilty looks on your faces!"

Benjamin Frankelyn smiles as if the captain were his long-lost rowing buddy from the Cambridge crew team and says, "Tell the high inquisitor that we are very guilty indeed. We have stolen from the Templars of Rofchester and have come to do penitence."

"Come back in the morning. The Holy Office closes after Vespers."

"Let us say that restitution for our sins must be made immediately."

The captain folds his arms. "I said tomorrow."

"Tell you what, Captain. We'll be on our way. We'll come back in a few days after the high inquisitor has executed you and made his choice about your replacement. In the meantime, we're not going to guarantee that we will be able to return the object we stole so iniquitously from the Templars. I can only guarantee you that the high inquisitors will be furious with you when they hear they missed out on this opportunity to get it back for the Church."

The captain stares at him, trying to assess if he is bluffing. He asks the master thief, "What have they got of value on them?"

"These guys are used to playacting and they have nothing of value on them, but that doesn't mean they're bluffing. If they had something truly valuable, they wouldn't be carrying it on their persons. If I were on the beat, my instincts would tell me to follow these guys around for a while. They'll eventually lead us to something extremely valuable."

The captain huffs, "Wait here while I get your story checked out. What's your name anyway?"

"Mister Silence Dogood."

The captain goes in and comes back out a short while later. He says abruptly, "Walk this way."

The captain leads Benjamin Frankelyn and Monsignor Oscar Meyer inside with four guards surrounding them as if fearing them to be assassins. They walk through hallways paneled in carved wood with scenes from Graec and Roman mythology—not all of them are as pious as one might presume for a residence of clerics. The guards open the door to a dining room with a long table capable of entertaining a large number of guests. Instead, there are only three men seated—one in a large chair, the next in a middling chair, and the third in a small chair.

From their cardinals' robes and obvious family resemblance, Benjamin Frankelyn does not need more than one guess that the three men facing him are the Cardinals Orsini—the three bears of the Holy Office of the Inquisition in Vinland. They are eating a meal. The shortest of the three, Piccolo Cardinal Orsini, seems the friendliest. He says, "Ah! Mista Dogood, so kind of you to pay us a visit. Pwease, you and ya fwiend awe wewcome to join us fa suppa. Any good news?"

Benjamin Frankelyn takes a seat, unfolds a napkin, and places it on his lap as if he ate here every night. He says in his most charming voice, "Good news indeed, Your Eminence! The Templars have once again proven themselves reliable bankers. Your Rofchester refund is ready and awaiting your approval."

The serving boy brings him three dishes. One is piping hot, the other is cold to the touch, but the third looks and smells deliciously warm. Benjamin Frankelyn indulges in a nice, warm bowl of porridge.

The biggest of the three brothers, Paterno Cardinal Orsini, puts on a sour face and says, "That is not the way we understand it. We received an urgent message by Pony Express from the Templars that the bank was destroyed by blackflame and nearly all the valuables inside turned to glass and shattered. Our investment was lost."

Benjamin Frankelyn pats his lips with the silk napkin and says, "Your Eminence, the line 'nearly all' is the most important one to take away from that brief. Since the Templar clerks were being less than reasonable with our honest request, we took liberties with the quest details and found a way to recover for you what is rightfully yours. It's not a sin to steal what belongs to you in the first place, is it? As for the blackflame, it's not our fault the vault lacked a proper sprinkler system or um . . . flamethrowers to put it out."

The middle brother, Maderno Cardinal Orsini, joins in. "Not at all. The captain of our guard informed us you claim to have something for us. Our loremasters and a few monks with special gifts in these matters would like to examine it. Where is it?"

Benjamin Frankelyn gulps down another spoonful of delicious porridge, then leans back and says, "Nearby, Your Eminence. Before we get to that, may we discuss the reward you had offered my patron? It would be foolish of me to deliver the goods before making sure that no misunderstanding of the quest reward should inhibit our working relationship. After all, my patron went to great expense to hire an adventurer of my caliber for this quest; at this late stage, it's not my policy to bungle it for him."

Instead of responding to this kind of petulance, the three Orsini brothers begin to pray. They open their eyes and Maderno Cardinal Orsini says, "The gift of prophecy is telling us that the Sword of Layban is not far away. And also, the girl."

"What girl?" asks Benjamin Frankelyn, putting on an innocent face.

"Goldilocks. The Templars apprehended her when she was trying to collect the sword, but she escaped the wreckage. No doubt your handiwork as well."

"The name does not sound familiar."

"The size of a child; blonde, curly hair. Please do not delude yourself that you could get away with lying to us. Even a low-level cleric could use the gift of prophecy to see through a flat-out lie like that."

Benjamin Frankelyn strokes his chin and looks up into the air as if thinking intently. "*Familiar* then is probably not the best term. Yes, indeed, we found a dark elf there, but she is not a child and she does not go by that name. She identifies as a princess."

Paterno Cardinal Orsini says, "Play all the word games you please, Frankelyn, just deliver to us the sword and the girl. Life is always simpler and less painful when you cooperate with the Inquisition."

Benjamin Frankelyn measures his words carefully. He cannot get away with lying to such powerful clerics but he cannot tell them the truth, either—too dangerous. He says with deliberately constructed wording, "The Sword of Layban is in the possession of some of my associates who are waiting to hear word from me that you are going to uphold your end of the deal for my patron. As for the girl we rescued, I have a feeling she is not far from here, doing everything in her power to recover the Sword of Layban for herself."

Maderno Cardinal Orsini says, "Perhaps she has tempted you to betray us."

Benjamin Frankelyn holds up his hands and says with a defensive chuckle, "Every day I pray the Lord's Prayer, 'Lead us not into temptation.'"

Paterno Cardinal Orsini says, "Stalling is futile. Our household inquisitors will easily locate them. The Holy Office of the Inquisition is not just another faction—it's the mother of all factions and we can destroy your reputation across Vinland. You'll never receive another quest from anyone again if you so much as think about double-crossing us."

Benjamin Frankelyn does not flinch at how easily their prophetic gifts cut through his schemes and he immediately goes on the offensive. "Speaking of double-crossing, we must discuss my patron's new status as viceroy. When will he be crowned?"

Maderno Cardinal Orsini says, "As soon as we receive the sword and take Goldilocks into custody, you will receive a royal decree appointing the baron of Amhirst Aengland's crown governor-general of Vinland. He will have extensive authority but no crown, no royal privileges, and no hereditary title."

Benjamin Frankelyn is visibly flustered. "That wasn't the deal. He was supposed to be *crowned* Aenglish viceroy of Vinland."

Paterno Cardinal Orsini says, "We are altering the deal. Pray we do not alter it any further. We have an agent in Ithica who described how overeager the baron of Amhirst was to usurp the Crown's authority for his personal interests. A viceroyal crown in Vinland would tempt even the most loyal servant to declare independence from the royal crown in Mother Aengland. King Eddard is an honored Crusader and a friend of the Holy Office of the Inquisition. He looks after our interests, and we look after his."

Benjamin Frankelyn leans forward and says intently, "If loyalty is your basis, then you will appreciate the fact that I look after the interests of my patron. I repeat—no deal until I receive word from him that he agrees to your changes."

"Too late," says Paterno Cardinal Orsini. "Our household inquisitors have just used the gift of tongues to report that your friends are already in our custody."

Benjamin Frankelyn replies, "How do you think the people would respond to hearing that the Holy Office of the Inquisition is using blackflame necromancy in its war against heresy?"

Maderno Cardinal Orsini laughs dismissively, saying, "No one would be so bold as to believe you—not in public, anyhow. Up until this point you have handled yourself well, so it comes as a surprise that you should risk all on such a clumsy threat. However, it does seem that you are exactly the kind of efficient, loyal, and unscrupulous adventurer we are looking for to fulfill an important quest. Perhaps we can compromise."

"I respectfully decline. I am actually a student of sorcery and must return to my studies."

"We beg to differ, young Frankelyn," replies Paterno Cardinal Orsini. "You have come this far. I regret to inform you that you have crossed the point of no return. From here on out, you will do as we say or join the next crop of heretics being burned at the stake."

"This deal is getting worse all the time."

"Glad we can all agree. Captain Ronaldo, bring Miss Sacagawea in, if you please."

"Right away, Your Most Reverend Eminence."

A beautiful young woman with bronze skin and black eyes appears from the inner hallway. Her gentle steps and deliberate gait tell Benjamin Frankelyn and Monsignor Meyer that she has endured many hardships and pulled through them with great courage. Instinctively, they both stand up to greet her when she walks into the dining room as if she were royalty. Her bearing is confident but modest, devoid of pretension but evincing a strong sense of self-worth.

239

Maderno Cardinal Orsini explains, "A confederacy of Algonkian and Irokian nations allied with the former Frankish viceroy Samuel de Champlane a long time ago and are not happy that the new Aenglish settlers flooding into the west are refusing to honor the treaties they brokered with the Franks. The situation is escalating rapidly, and they have sent Miss Sacagawea to us as the representative of their cause.

"The unofficial leader of the confederacy, Sagamore Pontiak, has written down sworn statements from a large number of leaders inviting us to send missionaries and agreeing to a military alliance with the Holy Office of the Inquisition if we help them recover from custody the former Frankish viceroy, whom they call the Great Uncle."

Piccolo Cardinal Orsini says excitedly, "This is a wunce-in-a-wifetime chance fa us in Vinwand! We want you to intwoduce Miss Sacagawea to the bawon of Amhiwst and teww him how gweat she is!"

Maderno Cardinal Orsini continues, "After you vouch for her, she will recover Uncle Sam and deliver him to Pontiak's confederacy. In return, we will overlook your indiscretion in trying to threaten us — and pay you thirty pounds sterling for your troubles."

Benjamin Frankelyn groans, "Thirty silver pieces to betray my benefactor. I'm loving the irony here."

Maderno Cardinal Orsini says, "The Lord chastises the son he loves with an iron rod indeed. We had promised the baron of Amhirst the privilege of denouncing any of his political enemies to us. We will honor that pledge and extend a custom offer to you.

"On that table is a signed and sealed unconditional pardon with papal authority. If you ever find yourself detained or in trouble with the law for any reason, you have only to present that pardon and you will be freed from custody or punishments immediately."

Piccolo Cardinal Orsini adds, "That's a huge gift fwom us, Mista Fwankewyn. Just think of aww the things you can mess up and just wak wight out of the dungeon! Besides, you can wash ya hands of tweason — you awe not gonna betway the bawon, we awe . . . I mean, Sacagawea is."

Piccolo draws stern looks from his brothers, who both shout at him, "Stai zito!"

Maderno Cardinal Orsini says, "You are not betraying the baron of Amhirst. He wanted supreme authority in Vinland, and that royal edict on the table confers it to him. He wanted the friendship of the Holy Office of the Inquisition and he shall have it. By doing this little favor for us, you guarantee that the baron of Amhirst gets what he wants. If you refuse, we keep the sword, Amhirst's title as governor, and throw you in our dungeon, just to keep our little secret safe."

Frankelyn asks, "What do you intend to do with our princess, whom you call Goldilocks?"

Paterno Cardinal Orsini replies, "She will stand trial. If we uncover any foul play, she'll be burned at the stake. If she's innocent, we'll cook something up to burn her at the stake. Get it? Cook something up — burn at the stake! Ha, ha, ha!"

Piccolo Cardinal Orsini joins in laughing but Maderno Cardinal Orsini does a facepalm.

When the one-sided laughter dies down, Maderno Cardinal Orsini concludes the discussion. "The choice is yours, Mister Frankelyn. Behind door one is the royal edict declaring the baron of Amhirst Aenglish crown

241

governor-general of Vinland, thirty pounds sterling silver, an unconditional pardon for any future misunderstandings, and the friendship of the Holy Office of the Inquisition."

Paterno Cardinal Orsini wipes the drip from his nose and adds, "Behind door two is our dungeon. We feel confident we've already got all we need to know from you, but I do have a few techniques for extracting confessions that I'd like to try out. You could give us feedback from your firsthand experiences."

Benjamin Frankelyn gulps. "Well, Your Eminences. It's been a tough decision, but I've decided to go with door one."

Benjamin Frankelyn stands up and bows. "This has been a pleasure, really, but I must be going. Miss Sacagawea, would you care to join Monsignor Meyer and myself on a tranquil stroll through this beautifully moonlit evening?"

She bows her head gently.

"You can lay out in detail all you need from us to complete your quest as we walk, my dear. Come along, Monsignor Meyer, we have work to do for our new friends."

Once they reach the Leaky Carvel tavern, Sacagawea asks, "Where's your party of adventurers?"

"Over here, come meet them. You already know our cleric, Monsignor Oscar Meyer. This is our fighter, Willis, our rogue, Ariel, and our magicultor, Whoopee."

Sacagawea looks at them. "Those names sound kind of fake."

Willis raises his hand. "Mine doesn't."

Whoopee mutters, "That's 'cause it's your real name."

"Come on!" he huffs. "You keep giving it away. She would have thought it was a clever code name if you hadn't said anything. You want me to come up with a name as silly as yours?" He takes a sip of his drink and says, "How about we call you Heiniekin?"

Benjamin Frankelyn asks, "Where's the princess?"

A wave of shame washes over Ariel's face. "They took her and the real sword. They had powerful clerics with the gift of prophecy. I had no chance."

Monsignor Meyer grunts, "What does it matter to us? We fulfilled our quest and now that the princess has been arrested by the Inquisition, that cancels our obligation to fulfill our promise to her."

Ariel shoots him an angry look. "Is that the kind of drivel you learn in your theology classes?"

Seeing the party about to explode in an ugly argument, Sacagawea says, "Do not worry. I know where she is."

They all look at her, astounded. Sacagawea continues, "I understand that my current quest requires you to steal something from your quest-giver. You are a man with a deep sense of loyalty, Mister Frankelyn. So here's the deal—if I help you rescue the princess and steal this sword back from the Inquisition, will you help me rescue Uncle Sam from captivity?"

"Deal."

Ariel is confused. "So you are going to steal from your patron? That's bad business in my book."

Benjamin Frankelyn replies, "Monsignor Meyer was on to something. You see, my patron agreed to engage my services only occasionally while I study sorcery at Silvermorn. Now that I have completed the quest he assigned to me, I am no longer in his service."

Ariel huffs, "I don't like it, but if we have to resort to technicalities to rescue the princess, then technicalities will have to do for now. I'm in."

Sacagawea cuts off any further discussion. "Deal. Now listen. There's no time to waste. I overheard the inquisitors say they intend to send the sword on the next ship to Frankland. There's a dwarf whaling vessel docked at Baston heading back to Bayonne at dawn."

"Bayonne? That derelict port city in New Gersey?"

Sacagawea acknowledges Ariel respectfully and says, "Actually, I was referring to the port city in the Duchy of Aquatania in Europa at the northern base of the Pyrinoak Mountains. The high inquisitors have already sent for a messenger from the Pony Express post in Salim. If we can intercept the Pony Express rider after he makes the pickup, your magicultor can locomutate away this sword of yours."

Whoopee says, "Brilliant plan. Unfortunately, I'd have to be within fifteen feet to get it right the first time. I could probably pull it off from as far as sixty feet, but I might just as easily flub it up."

Benjamin Frankelyn says, "Don't worry, Whoopee. We'll get you close. What about the princess?"

Sacagawea says, "She'll be in the dungeon. There's a chimney that leads all the way down to it from the roof. It's only wide enough to fit a skinny elf."

They all look at Whoopee and he puffs out his chest proudly. "You guys make fun of me for being skinny all the time, and now you see how many times I get to rescue the princesses on these quests!"

Willis says, "You've only done it once so far. I see two problems with going down a chimney. First, we have to get up on the roof without being noticed. Second, there's usually a fire going on at the bottom."

Whoopee says, "Don't worry! I can work my magic with the fire, but getting past the guards will be a real problem. We cased the joint and there's no gap in the patrol routes. If one false step of ours tips the guards off that something funny is going on, they'll call in their high-level clerics. We won't be able to hide from their gift of prophecy."

Ariel says proudly, "Leave that to me. I grew up in a castle with overprotective parents. Sneaking past guards is what rogues like me do best."

With that, they commence the first part of their plan—recovering the Sword of Layban. Ariel and Whoopee jog back to the Holy Office without drawing too much attention. They maneuver themselves behind an empty butcher's stall and arrive just in the nick of time; the Pony Express rider is knocking on the door.

Ariel says, "Quick! They're handing her a package."

Whoopee says, "Okay. I'm doing my best. Let's see, the metal seems to be a more ancient version of steel—probably just wrought iron—with a gold hilt. It'll be sloppy, but this magic word just might do the trick . . . presto change-o!"

He waves his magica wand.

"Nothing happened," says Ariel.

Whoopee looks closely and whispers, "That pony rider's got an apotropaic charm."

Ariel gasps, "What does that mean?"

"See that dreamcatcher on her saddle? It's made of unicorn ivory—very powerful at warding off magic. We've got to get rid of it."

Ariel rolls out from under the butcher stall and walks across the intersection to make it seem like she is coming from the next alley over. She staggers and sways as if she is drunk and walks up to the halfling pony rider. "My family lives in Baston and I haven't got a dime. Can you give me a lift to Baston? I'm in no condition to walk."

The halfling Pony Express locks the package in a security saddlebag and mounts up quickly. She flips Ariel a dime and snaps her reins.

Ariel throws her body in front of the pony and it rears. "How about a quarter?"

She pretends to stumble over the spooked pony and swipes the dreamcatcher as she falls to the cobblestone.

A guard calls out, "Wait! Arrest that woman!"

Two Swiss guards come out and apprehend Ariel. The guard in the doorway calls to the Pony Express rider, "Let me inspect the package to make sure she didn't steal the sword."

The rider unlocks it and hands the package to a Swiss guard who takes it back inside for inspection. After a close examination from their cleric and master thief, the Swiss guard hands the authenticated package back to the Pony Express rider.

No sooner does she secure the Sword of Layban back into her saddlebag than whoopee sings out from behind the butcher stall, "Presto change-o."

The other Swiss guard puts manacles (the medieval version of handcuffs) on Ariel and starts leading her inside for interrogation. Weary of trouble, the Pony Express rider gallops off into the night while two Swiss guards head over to the butcher stall to investigate.

The next instant, Whoopee displays the full scope of his virtuosity as a magicultor. Seeing his friend about to get tortured, he whips his magica wand around and chants, "Mancala hexa hold'm, mancala niney morris."

Ariel's manacles are gone! The Swiss guard next to her is now wearing them.

Whoopee whirls around and intones, "Hnafatafl chataranga latrunclarum, majong bagammon go!"

The fake sword on her hip vanishes and the real Sword of Layban takes its place. She elbows the Swiss guard in the nose and scampers off into the shadows.

Whoopee turns around to dash away, but the Swiss guards catch up to him. He barely has enough time to reach into his pouch and shove a few magica leaves in his mouth before the Swiss guards corner him and take him into custody.

Knowing when a situation is lost, Ariel does not stick around for the swarming Swiss guards to detect her hiding spot. As quietly and swiftly as she can, she slips from shadow to shadow until she makes her way back to the Leaky Carvel.

When Ariel sees her companions in the tavern, they ask, "Where's Whoopee?"

"They arrested him."

Benjamin Frankelyn asks, "Did you manage to swap the swords?"

"No, but Whoopee did say a lot of magic words before he got caught. I think he locomutated the real Sword of Layban into my scabbard."

Benjamin Frankelyn draws the sword from her hip and comments, "I put a little scratch into the real one to help me tell the difference." He inspects the blade briefly. "Yep! This is it. Whoopee pulled it off before they got him! Now that's team spirit. I'm really starting to like that little guy."

Ariel snorts, "Well, we don't just like him; we all love him because he's family. We're going back!"

Benjamin Frankelyn is too practical for chivalrous rescue attempts. "Wait! We need to get the Sword of Layban far away from here before those snooping clerics start doing their prophecy trick again."

Ariel argues, "You might be okay with waiting for them to torture him until you work out your plan, but I'm not going to wait. As leader of this party of adventurers I call the shots, and I say we move out now. You're just here to spy on us, remember?"

"Okay, fine, I guess I did say that," concedes Benjamin Frankelyn. "We'll split up. You go find Whoopee without a plan. I'll go bury the sword at our regroup point so Sir Balrock can keep a watch over it. Then I'll meet you back here."

Ariel groans. "What adventurers' guild did you train in? Haven't you heard the old adage, 'Splitting up is the best way to turn a questline into a horror story'?"

It's starting to get late enough that the tavern empties. The innkeeper puts his big hands on the table and says, "The inn's closing, so unless you're going to rent a room, I'm going to have to ask you to leave. It's a penny a night per person; a tuppence each if you want your own room."

Benjamin Frankelyn hands the innkeeper a groat but the innkeeper asks, "What's this?"

"A groat. Newly minted fourpence piece. We won't stay long, but this should cover your discretion."

The innkeeper eyes the coin to figure out if it is legit or not. Benjamin Frankelyn adds, "Or we can leave."

The innkeeper takes the groat and walks away.

Benjamin Frankelyn smiles and says, "Now then, where were we?"

Ariel takes charge of the rescue operation. "Monsignor Meyer, pray and see if your gift of prophecy can tell you where they've taken Whoopee."

Monsignor Meyer prays for a while, then looks up and says, "Halleluiah, praise the Lord!"

Benjamin Frankelyn comments, "Monsignor Meyer, your piety is inspiring, but we really haven't got the time for a worship service at the moment. Did you find Whoopee or not?"

"Had a vision," replies Monsignor Meyer. "Whoopee got some magica leaves in his mouth before they arrested him. He managed to locomutate himself away before they put him in a warded cell, but he didn't get very far. He's still hiding behind a butcher's stall adjacent to the high inquisitors' residence.

"The place is still crawling with guards. They're sending a group here to apprehend Ariel. We don't have much time before their clerics find Whoopee too."

Willis pounds his fist in his palm. "Let's move out!"

Sacagawea interrupts their fervor. "I'm your best chance for getting in and out of there alive. I know the butcher stall you're talking about. Follow me."

Monsignor Meyer and Willis look to Ariel for her say in this. She nods and motions with her hand for Sacagawea to take the lead.

Sacagawea looks at Ariel and says, "We'll draw less attention if it's just the two of us. Mister Frankelyn is right. You need to get that sword as far away from here as possible. I suggest the two big guys stay with him in case he runs into any trouble. Ariel and I need to go alone if we are going to sneak past all those guards."

Willis objects, "What if it's a trap? She works for the Inquisition. How do we know she's not going to hand us over to them one by one?"

Ariel swallows hard and looks Sacagawea straight in the eyes to get a sense of her motives. She sees nothing but a young woman who is an expert at masking her own feelings.

After a short pause, Ariel says, "We don't have time to come up with another plan. It's all or nothing. Willis, Monsignor, escort Mister Frankelyn and the sword back to Sir Balrock. I'm with her."

Willis hands her the party's climbing rope. "The Monsignor will know if you get double-crossed. We'll come for you even if we have to raise an army."

They split up and head out to face the dark terrors of the night.

The guard dogs are already sniffing around the butcher stall and barking. One of the Swiss guards smashes open a barrel and they all cover their noses at the stench. Another guard kicks it over. Oozing intestines, gooey brains, dangly sinews, and stinking entrails spill across the floor. The puddle of muck seems to take the shape of a little person.

Ariel tosses a coin across the cobblestones. The sudden *clink-clank* startles the edgy Swiss guards and she dashes off in the other direction.

"It's her!" One of them yells and the rest of the Swiss guards ply their skills at parkour in chasing after her. In full armor, they display less skill than a stack of sixty-gallon steel drums.

Sacagawea scoops Whoopee out of the sludge he's been hiding in and they slink off into the darkness.

When they come to a secluded spot along the Salim harbor walk, Whoopee whines. "Next quest I sign up for is going to including a clause stipulating extra pay if I get stuck with all the yucky work again."

Sacagawea points to the waterfront and says, "You need to get cleaned off."

Whoopee is not thrilled about a cold dunk. "Wait! Where's everyone else? What happened to Ariel?"

"I'm right behind you, you little stinker. Sacagawea's right. You'd better wash yourself off. I could smell you from two blocks away."

Whoopee knows she's right and takes his chilly bath like a brave dark elf. After drying off for a bit in the cool night air, Sacagawea leads them back towards the high inquisitors' residence.

"Ariel, if you can pick this lock, the attic of this house leads out to a scaffold. We can use it to get onto the roof of the residence."

Ariel twirls a lockpick in her fingers and says, "Let me show you how it's done, sister!"

Her pick does the trick. Soon they are on top of the high inquisitor's residence. Sacagawea points out the chimney that leads to the dungeon. Still wet and feeling the evening chill, Whoopee says, "It's mighty nice of them to keep their prisoners warm like that at night."

She replies, "I think the purpose is to heat up the hot pokers for their victims' feet."

Whoopee gulps as he pulls out his magic wand. "Sound like nice guys. I'm going to have to assume they'll be hard at work when I get down there. All right, give me some room to concentrate. Making all that fire locomutate from way up here will be a chore."

Whoopee closes his eyes to concentrate, then he swirls his magic wand around and sings, "Oo ee oo ah ah ting tang walla walla bing bang."

The smoke from the chimney thins out and Ariel lets down Willis's rope. "Quickly, before they relight the fire."

Whoopee slides down the rope swiftly but cautiously. As he gets farther down, the bricks inside the chimney get hotter and hotter. He drops down the last few feet, singes his fingertips on the way down, and rolls out of the fireplace into a dimly lit torture chamber.

A torturer and his assistant are getting two fire pokers ready, having already tied Florenz to the rack. Fortunately for her, Whoopee's appearance interrupts the torture session before it really heated up.

Drawing his dagger with his right hand and keeping his magic wand ready in his left, Whoopee charges at the torturers with the wild ferocity of a momma bear defending her cub. The torturer's assistant's first reaction is to swipe his hot poker at the raging dark elf, but it is a slow and clumsy weapon and he swings wide. The torturer himself grabs some hooks with extremely sharp points attached to chains and swings one at the dark elf with deadly accuracy.

The attack is spot-on. The hook buries its tip into the back of Whoopee's left leg. The torturer yanks him off his feet but once on the ground, Whoopee waves his wand, chanting, "Izzy wizzy!"

The hook disappears. Whoopee gets back up and runs with a limp at the torturer, who blocks a chop from the magica wand in Whoopee's left hand with the length of chain he has been holding. The torturer realizes too late that a magica wand isn't sharp. Having diverted his foe's guard in the wrong direction with the feint, Whoopee slashes the torturer from hand to elbow with the dagger in his right hand.

The assistant torturer decides to help his mentor, stabbing at Whoopee with his fire poker, but the dark elf uses his small size to roll underneath the bed of a torture rack. Whoopee watches the assistant's feet carefully and when the assistant walks past, Whoopee slashes at the back of the assistant's ankle, hamstringing him. The assistant tumbles to the floor and lands on his own hot fire poker. It hisses against his skin and burns in deep. The big baby cannot stand the pain and rolls on the floor, crying hysterically.

The torturer, seeing the dark elf's skill with his wand and his blade and the dexterous movements that took his assistant down so quickly, realizes he cannot win the match by force of arms, so he resorts to a different tactic. He grabs the other hot poker and holds it over Florenz, shouting, "If you want to see your girlfriend live, drop your weapons!"

Whoopee looks at him anxiously and raises both hands in the air. The torturer smiles with cruel satisfaction, reassured his ploy worked—but too soon! Whoopee flicks his wrist and trills, "Jantar mantar!"

Not bluffing, the torturer jabs the poker toward Florenz, but it has disappeared. With another flick of his wrist Whoopee sings, "Jadu mandu!"

The hot poker reappears above the torturer's head. He looks up and it drops down onto his face. Whoopee dashes forward and drives his dagger between the screaming torturer's ribs, quieting him for good.

Whoopee frees Florenz and says to her in Drowish, "Hey, Princess, welcome to our party of adventurers! We've got the Sword of Layban for you, as promised."

Florenz is in no mood for cheerful reunions. Immediately after her hands are loose, she sees the blubbering torturer's assistant trying to flee, grabs a fire poker, runs over, and finishes him off.

Whoopee is horrified by the act of vengeful violence and waves her toward the fireplace, warning her, "Okay, that's enough. Let's split before anyone comes to check out who's been doing all that screaming."

Florenz looks at him sardonically and says, "Seriously? It's a torture chamber. People scream down here all the time."

"Right, let's just leave. All this freaky torture stuff makes me want to go home and unwind with a nice cup of hot cocoa."

At last, she smiles. "Ever heard of the Kibbler workshops? I'll get you a lifetime supply of hot cocoa if we make it out of this alive."

"Seriously, girl! You're my hero."

She gives him a wink and heads into the still-hot fireplace to climb the rope up the chimney.

Once they make it to the top, Sacagawea is already worried that their escape route has been cut off. "It's getting bad down there. The Swiss guards are edgy and the captain just sent someone to wake up a high-level cleric to make sure that there are no intruders left in the vicinity. We are going to need one heck of a distraction to get out of here in one piece and we need it now."

Whoopee says, "Oh, don't worry, lady. Just sit back and relax. You know all that fire in the chimney? I had to put it somewhere."

It doesn't take long for the smoke to start puffing out the windows of the high inquisitors' residence. Soon enough, the inquisitors are racing out of the house in a panic and barking instructions to the guards. More worried about the priceless works of art going up in flames than their own safety, they instruct the Swiss guards to form a fire brigade.

For an expert like Ariel, adding misinformation and misdirection to the smokey confusion is second nature and the adventurers walk out of the vicinity unnoticed while the guards scramble about all around them.

Sacagawea leads them through Salim's back roads and dark alleys to a house built next to the town wall. The owner is an entrepreneur who moonlights as an escape artist. For three dollars he hoists up a ladder onto the wall after the night watchman paces past the house and lowers a rope down the other side.

When they reach Sir Balrock's hiding place, their fellow adventurers greet them with warm hugs. Benjamin Frankelyn notices Florenz backing away from the profusions of affection and switches to a love language that he knows she'll appreciate. He gives her a gift—the Sword of Layban. He asks Whoopee to translate for him and says to her, "Now you see that we have kept our end of the bargain. We consider you our friend and we hope that you will count us among your friends. Please know that you can call on us for a favor in the future if you ever need anything. We just might do the same."

Whoopee talks to her in Drowish briefly and looks up at the entire party of adventurers and tells them her answer. "She says she only needs one thing—revenge."

Scene 3: The Return of the Martinet of War

Malarkey Market at Thor's Base, Shentalpee City
Whit Sun Day's Eve Compline
Night, 27th of May, 1284

Gone is the sweet, loveable young elve who was so pampered by her father. Tonight, a different Florenz steps onto Thor's Base. There is anger in her eyes, a mystically evil sword on her hip, and a party of undead thralls at her back. Her red cloak is dirty and prickled with dead leaves and broken twigs. Her curly, dyed-blond hair has lost its bounce and its black roots show.

"Hey, beautiful! I heard my girlfriend's back."

It's Enganyon, dressed in a dashing military uniform. Not far behind him stand Officer Bunzi and another Justiciar Leaguer who was one of Enganyon's former cronies when he was nothing but a rebellious teen. Enganyon's got a confident and affectionate smirk on his face, hiding his guilt behind a romantic mask.

"Hey, liar. Your girlfriend's back and you're gonna be in trouble."

Enganyon looks around as if Florenz must be calling someone else a liar. It's late at night. The plaza is empty, but Enganyon feels the need to put on a show.

Florenz isn't in the mood for nonsense. "I've been gone for a long time, but I know about your cheating."

"Has someone been spreading lies that I was untrue to you, darling?"

"Let's put it this way: if you don't break off your betrothal to Mademoiselle Zena tomorrow, you're going to be sorry you were ever born."

"Tomorrow? The paperwork alone'll take a week!"

Sir Balrock grabs his cheeks, lifts him, and squeezes.

Florenz's patience runs thin. "Monsieur Lynx was engaged to Mademoiselle Zena when you proposed to her. Should we ask him to sign off on your registry?"

Enganyon struggles but cannot break Sir Balrock's grip on his face. He tries to speak, "Hey la day la!"

"What did you say?"

"Hey la day la!"

"What's the matter? A wight's got your tongue?" She snaps her fingers and says, "Drop him."

Sir Balrock lets go. Enganyon gasps for air and mutters, "He's kind of big and he's awful strong."

Florenz sneers, "So what about the paperwork?"

Enganyon is still clutching his face. "Monsieur Lynx died in an ambush on an Ivy League quest."

"That's a pity. I really liked that kid. Hmmm, that means that Mademoiselle Zena is the only candidate left. Did they call off the election yet?"

"Actually, there *is* another candidate."

"What? Who?"

"Me."

"You? But you were like, 'Oh, I don't want to be umpire-in-chief. I only want to see the love of my life, Mademoiselle Zena, become umpire-in-chief.'"

"That was the love potion talking! She gave me a love potion. I wasn't in my right mind. You know that I only—"

She slaps his face. "Stop! In the name of love, before you break my heart. That really hurt, and your lame excuses are only making it worse. Never mind how it started. End this infatuation or Sir Balrock here will cut you down to size. I've tried so hard to be patient, but it's over. Capisce?"

"Oh, darling, you know I only have eyes for you! Are the stars out tonight? I can't tell. You sparkle—"

"Oh, cut out the poetry. Just hold me tight and tell me you love me."

"I love you, and I promise I'll never let you go."

Florenz gives him a sly grin. "Never say never."

"I'll never win with you."

"Never."

Their tender reunion is interrupted by Officer Bunzi, who points to his comrade. "Excuse me, Mademoiselle Florenz, but do you want Junior Officer Parris and I to, you know, mosey on home while you two enjoy your moment in the still of the night?"

She unfurls herself from Enganyon's arms and asks, "Actually, Officer Bunzi, you are exactly the person I need right now. Did you recover my father's body and hide it where I asked?"

"Yes, Mademoiselle, I did. It ended up costing—"

"Never mind the cost," she snaps. "Now I'm back and things will be fine. Follow me."

She takes them all into the secret room overlooking the council chambers and has them open up the barrel full of vinegar.

Florenz ignites the Sword of Layban and chants, "Arise, Kibbler! I dub thee a servant of the black fire, a dread knight of the flame of Layban. I bid thee come back from the shadows. Arise, Sir Kibbler!"

Her pickled father emerges from the vinegar barrel with his flesh bleached white. The damage from the fall has marred his face, having knocked out all his front teeth except his canines. The damage to his mouth is so severe his words are all garbled. Instead, he projects his thoughts to those nearby using the Black Tongue of

260

Caldor. To ordinary folks it just sounds like a horrid, shrieking noise inside their minds. Only Florenz understands what the Dread Knight is saying.

She replies in Eldric, "When I left you, I was but the learner. Now, I am the master. Even the heresiarch will have to bow to the power of the Sword of Layban."

The undead Umpire Kibbler points to Enganyon and speaks to him forcefully in the black tongue of Caldor. Enganyon writhes in pain at the cacophonous utterances ringing inside his head.

Florenz stops her father, saying, "He's as clumsy as he is stupid. He *must* obey me as his master."

Her father speaks again and she replies, "I will go speak with the high elves. They will not rebel. This will be a day long remembered. It has seen the return of the monsieur umpire-in-chief and it will soon see the end of the Inquisition." She turns to Officer Bunzi and says, "Tomorrow call all the high elves of Shentalpee City for a special Thor's Enlightenment Discourse."

Enganyon does not like the way events are developing and he points to the monstrosity that was Umpire Kibbler and asks, "How do you know it's really him? I mean, that could be some kind of demon or foul spirit animating your father's body."

Florenz growls and chides him. "I find your lack of faith disturbing. My father wishes to punish you for your faithlessness, but I have other plans. You will bring us Dungaree Jeanne's archon stone."

"It's a priceless treasure, darling! She'll never—"

"Never say never. Failure is not an option."

Officer Bunzi cringes. Enganyon tries to blow it off and pretends to be joking, "Yes, master."

No one is fooled.

The next morning, the high elves gather in the outdoor amphitheater beneath the colossal statue of Thor, the Mighty Hammer Bearer. Florenz steps up onto the stage and says in Runic, "Mesdames, mesdemoiselles, and messieurs. I am here to set the record straight. I left Tuscoraura not because of my grief at my father's death, but because of the overwhelming evidence piling up before my eyes that my father was intending to subvert our democracy.

"In public, he encouraged all elves to collaborate in unlocking the secrets of the blackflame to update our military technology. In private, he had been secretive about his own experiments with the blackflame so that he could raise up an undead army with unquestioning loyalty to him alone."

The crowd gasps.

"My father intended to use me as a puppet umpire-in-chief. To that end, he bullied all my rival candidates out of the race except Mademoiselle Zena, because he figured he could use the scandal involving her gnomid stewardess to discredit her without knocking her out of the race. That tactic backfired. It so enraged the garden gnomes and mountain dwarves that they aided the inquisitor in orchestrating my father's death.

"During my exile, I endured many hardships and have had much time to think about the injustices my father was committing. I have resolved to set them all straight. There is no time to go into all the details now. The bottom line is, I succeeded. I have mastered the blackflame and I intend to share that power with you, o superlative high elves of Shentalpee City."

Florenz draws the Sword of Layban and intones the words, "By the power of Layban . . . I have the power!"

As the blackflame erupts from her blade, wild applause and cheering erupt for the return of their exiled princess and her newfound power.

Florenz continues holding the flaming sword above her head and says, "I have paid a heavy price to obtain this weapon for ye, o famed high elves of Tuscoraura Mountain. Our enemies resent our superiority. Even now, the Inquisition is gathering a Crusade to take this sword away from us. Who among ye chooses to surrender this new technology and throw ourselves on the mercy of the Inquisition?"

The audience looks at her, watches her, listens to her, and hears her, utterly stunned. *Is this the same Florenz who left Shentalpee City only a few weeks ago?*

The skin on Florenz's hand holding the flaming sword starts to redden. It cracks and blisters. She pays no attention, nor does the crowd. Instead, she shouts, "With this blackflame, I have reanimated long-lost warriors, including my father. Behold!"

From the back of the crowd, a heavily battered version of Umpire Kibbler, with white skin and no teeth except his canines, presses through the audience. The giant dwarf is right behind him, crushing benches and scuffing the polished hardwood floors with his heavy boots as elves dive out of his way in panic.

In the giant dwarf's wake follow twenty or more undead wights. Umpire Kibbler and the giant dwarf, Sir Balrock, go down on one knee and bow their heads to the blackflame. Florenz shouts, "Who among ye chooses to surrender these new undead warriors and throw ourselves on the mercy of the Inquisition?"

Now hisses and boos circulate through the crowd at the thought of cowering before the Inquisition.

Florenz shouts over their voices, "I say let the fire elves master both the unquenchable elf fire *and* the mystical blackflame. Who among ye chooses to stand with me and fight?"

The crowd gets up on their feet and applaud wildly.

Louder she shouts, "Who among ye chooses to stand with me and fight?"

The elves are jumping up and down and screaming in a mad frenzy—delusions of grandeur infect their minds and they are ready to relinquish all their rights as elfin persons for the sake of latching onto the power they now see before their eyes.

As if thundering with the voice of Thor himself, Florenz places an amulet into her undead father's mouth. It has an archon stone in the middle inlaid next to a large chip of pyrite, a big glob of amber, and a dark clump of lodestone. Her father dutifully swallows it.

Florenz shouts, "I have obtained an archon stone, which will render my father invincible. Shall we surrender it to the Inquisition or shall we fight?"

They claw at their faces and wriggle around hypnotically, letting loose a wide range of emotions. They cheer and hoot and holler. They weep and cover their faces. They chant, "Florenz, hail! Florenz, hail!"

At last, she sheaths the freezing-cold sword and states with the dignified authority of a war-hardened commander, "Your choice is made. As of today, I declare martial law. We prepare for war."

Scene 4: Bend it Like a Buttercup

Shentalpee City on Tuscoraura Mountain
Whit Moon Day Terce. Morning, 29th of May, 1284

As his background in blackflame, miracle-working, and magiculture attracts more gossip on Tuscoraura Mountain, Johnny Appleseed receives an ever-growing stream of visitors. He is honoring his promise to instruct the elves in the non-military applications of blackflame, and thanks to his generosity and humble service in helping the colony, a good many elves are open to hearing him tell them stories from the Bible. A few even request baptism into the Christian faith.

On this fine, sunny morning, Florenz knocks on the door at Betzy Rose Mansion and Enganyon stands proudly behind her. Dungaree Jeanne opens the door and says in Runic, "Why, Mademoiselle Florenz! Such a pleasure to see thou hast returned. Please come in!"

She steps in but Enganyon politely waits outside. Florenz notices the slight at not inviting him in and seeks to rectify it. She asks in Eldric, "Would you mind if the monsieur Enganyon joined us?"

Dungaree Jeanne wears a stern face. "I don't believe the monsieur Enganyon and I have any business to discuss. If he wishes to apologize to my daughter for his behavior of late . . . ah, here she comes now."

Zena creeps down the steps, red-eyed from hours of crying. She sees the visitors and whimpers, "Monsieur Enganyon . . ."

Enganyon steps forward and says in Runic, "I do wish to apologize, Mademoiselle Zena. I have treated thee most unfairly. What business had I to propose marriage to thee when my heart was all along bound to the mademoiselle Florenz? I have come to set things aright and call off our hasty engagement."

Straining to hold her nerve together, Zena replies in Runic, "Thou canst not, Monsieur Enganyon. I have not agreed to a cessation of our betrothal contract."

Enganyon shows no pity or remorse. "As it stands, thy consent is irrelevant. Since thy betrothal contract with Monsieur Lynx was on record when I proposed to thee, the scribe at the council chambers never even entered the contract we submitted to the registrar. For the future, please remember that before thou wilt be free to enter into a new betrothal contract, thou must obtain a public copy of Monsieur Lynx's death certificate and present it to the registrar."

Zena's eyebrows curl with intense frustration. She switches back into Eldric. "But that's the love potion speaking, not you! I have the recipe; I can fix this!"

Dropping down into Eldric as well, Enganyon waves it all away, saying, "Oh, don't be ridiculous! Most love potions are fakes, hawked to unsuspecting and desperate teenagers who cannot deal with rejection." He then looks at Florenz lovingly and says in Runic, "Even the real ones can at best simulate a passing ardor. My love for the mademoiselle Florenz, I assure you, has never faltered since the day I first laid eyes on her."

To wonder if Zena is crushed at hearing those words is like wondering if a crusty pretzel sitting on an anvil is still edible after a grand piano has fallen twelve storeys down upon it. If only Enganyon were frantic and emotional, she could process his reaction as a gut-wrenching predicament that he is struggling to escape with a bout of bizarre, erratic behavior. But the dispassionate rationality behind his words makes her realize it's over for good.

Her normal reaction to not getting her way is to throw a temper tantrum, scream and shout, and say hurtful words to her loved ones. This time around she just stands there, dizzy and unable to speak.

With the unpleasant formalities accomplished, Florenz steps forward and says in Eldric, "Madame Dungaree, Master Leevai and Captain Gunnar have arrived from Fort Loudon with their mercenary companies. The Council of Perfects would like you, as acting dean of the League of Nations, to convince them to stay and help us fight off the Crusade. You will have a budget of five hundred dollars for their expenses.

"The council is also willing to promote non-elves to the order of silver elves if they prove themselves exceptionally valiant in battle, but please be aware that as of now, no official protocol for inducting them has been approved. No guarantees.

"You have come up with some clever ideas. I hope for your sake that you manage to put them into effect to aid Shentalpee City in this upcoming war."

Dungaree Jeanne says, "That sounds like a threat."

Florenz continues in Eldric, "It is. By the way, if we do survive this attack by the Crusade, the Council of Perfects is now convinced that Bartlebee did in fact sell the Athabask recipe to Master Chief Engineer Tom Thumb. Before confirming you in the office of dean, they want you to kill him and make sure no one else has gotten a hold of that recipe. If you fail, you will be executed for treason and your family will be banished.

"That is also a threat."

Dungaree Jeanne stares wide-eyed and speechless at Florenz while her heart skips a beat or two. What happened to the sweet girl who was Zena's best friend for so many years? Zena, for her part, is still so stunned that she shows no reaction whatsoever.

Dungaree Jeanne finally finds her voice. "You publicly announced it was all a big misunderstanding."

"The Council of Perfects would not allow me to publicly humiliate your family without hard evidence. Since I could not produce any, they forced me to come up with some excuse to recant my accusations. Thanks to the Thieves' Guild, we now have conclusive evidence—and other information damaging to your family's good name. If you eliminate Tom Thumb, we'll lock that all away in the secret archives and confirm you as dean of the League of Nations."

"Lock it away? Why not destroy it?"

Florenz cannot fathom why such an intelligent person cannot see the obvious, so she states it clearly with fire in her eyes. "To make sure you do not give them a reason to unlock it."

They gaze at each other in silence for a menacing moment like two lionesses pacing in circles around each other without breaking eye contact to so much as blink. Dungaree Jeanne's mind spins furiously to come up with a counterattack and then she pounces. "The Monsieur Major Leagues Umpire has stated that the League of Nations is to include a unit of undead warriors. Will you be transferring the undead warriors you summoned at Thor's Base to my command?"

"Yes," says Florenz with a snarl. "As soon as this issue with Tom Thumb is resolved and the Council of

Perfects officially confirms your appointment as dean of the League of Nations. Not all the Perfects are convinced the League of Nations is a good idea. Since its only official member right now is a spellbound Pinne Mage University dropout," pointing to Zena, "I highly recommend you take the council's advice to recruit Master Leevai and Captain Gunnar for the war effort before they figure out that your leadership here is nothing but a waste of time and resources."

Dungaree Jeanne gasps at the rudeness of the insults and presses on. "In Thor's Base, after Master Gulliber's talk, you placed an archon stone in your undead father's mouth, rendering him invincible. They are quite rare and hard to come by. May I ask where you got that particular archon stone?"

"No." Florenz waves her hand and dozens of Justiciar League police barge into Betzy Rose Mansion. Dungaree Jeanne's hired bravos intercept them with their swords and knives drawn. They are all brilliant duelists but have no discipline for fighting in ranks, and their fancy footwork would be useless in such confined quarters. Dungaree Jeanne orders them to stand down.

The Justicar Leaguers seize Johnny Appleseed's wheelchair and push him out to Florenz, who holds up a letter and announces in Runic, "Johnny Appleseed, I hereby place thee under arrest for espionage and subversion against the Tuscoraura elves."

Johnny Appleseed asks, "What's she saying?"

Dungaree Jeanne ignores him and speaks directly to Florenz in Eldric. "What is the meaning of this? Reverend Appleseed is our guest. Arresting him is an insult to our honor as his hosts."

"Precisely." Florenz grins and flaps a letter in front of her face. "We have intercepted a letter written by Johnny Appleseed informing the Inquisition of our military technology. He will be hanged as a spy."

"No! He wrote that letter to avoid a war! He was trying to save Tuscoraura Mountain from a Crusade! How could you do this to a sweet, old man?"

"You may recall that he affronted my father's honor after he delivered his TED."

Zena chokes, then cries out, "That was me! You never figured it out, but I put him up to it."

"If I have learned anything from your two-timing ex-fiancé, never say never. I knew all along."

"So you knew all along and never had the nerve to do anything about it?"

Officer Bunzi shackles the crippled missionary and wheels him out.

Florenz concludes, "Never say never. I just did something about it. Aren't you proud of how grown-up I am now?" She walks out the front door.

Scene 5: Cleanup Hitter

Vandsee Estates
Shentalpee City on Tuscoraura Mountain
Ember Woden's Day Vespers
Evening, 31ˢᵗ of May, 1284

Florenz is sitting at her father's desk while Umpire Kibbler stands unblinking behind her. His eyes have a faint glow of red in them, but he does not move them to look at any of the people sitting in the room. In fact, he does not move at all. His chest does not heave to breathe, his feet do not shuffle, and his face does not twitch a muscle, even when flies land on his eyelids.

In front of her desk, like two schoolboys sitting in silent detention before the principal, Enganyon and Umpire Gandorf fidget while Florenz reads through a scroll on her desk.

When she finally rolls up the scroll, Enganyon jumps in first and says in Eldric, "My beloved Mademoiselle Florenz, Reverend Appleseed is clearly favored by his God. His God listens to him when he calls upon his name. Is it really wise to antagonize both the Inquisition and his God over a trivial letter? He insists he wrote it to dissuade the Inquisition from sending the Crusade against us."

Florenz gives him a stern glare and says harshly, "First of all, Captain Enganyon, during the state of martial law, the Magnificent Charter bids us address each other by our military ranks. Since the Ivy League and the Justiciar League were wise enough to promote us, we must address each other as captains.

271

"Second, Johnny Appleseed should not have survived that fall. The Tuscoraura elves were to be the last nation to learn the secrets of blackflame. Not only did you let Mister Appleseed live, but you let him report information on our military technologies to the Inquisition. He must die.

"Third, my father appointed your father Major Leagues Umpire for one purpose and one purpose only—to orchestrate the ambush at Forge Hill Gap and rid the colony of the madame Dungaree and her daughter. The madame Dungaree's daughter was more popular than expected and her network of business and military contacts could enable her to spark a rebellion after my father is declared supreme umpire for life."

Enganyon hems and haws, saying, "Technically, your father is dead now, so supreme umpire for life would be a rather short term. I was expecting us to change tack and slot you in as supreme umpire for life instead, after you get elected through the normal—"

Florenz cuts him off abruptly. "It's too risky. The monsieur Lynx was supposed to be the only non-viable candidate left on the ballot by election day. Instead, the mademoiselle Zena is still alive and has too many supporters. She could easily sway her constituency into her mother's camp in case of a civil war. We'd be forced to execute half the colony for sedition. It's no fun being the supreme ruler over the fire elves and if there are almost no fire elves left to rule over."

Enganyon bobs his head around as if trying to be modest. "Well, there's always my constituency. You wouldn't have to execute them since we'd support—"

"Yes! Thank you! Thank you for bringing up the most painful topic of all. What in the sigelwar fires of lower earth possessed you to run for umpire-in-chief? You made yourself my rival instead of my ally. Do you know how I deal with my rivals?"

Enganyon puts his fist to his mouth and clears his throat. "Your flair for getting rid of them inspires awe."

Florence gives him a patronizing nod. "Good. Good. That's exactly the way it should be. So how are we going to fix this?"

"Well, you know, I could always speak to—"

She cuts him off. "For starters, we're going to require your father and all the Shentalpee City umpires to transmogrify into undead thralls."

Up until now, Umpire Gandorf has been lolling his head in boredom, aware that nothing he says will make any difference. Suddenly, at that last statement, he looks up with terror in his eyes. "You can't! I'm still in my prime! My mind is sharp as an assassin's blade.

"After all, I was the one who figured out the whole stormcrow thing. Without it, your father would never have gotten the blackflame siphon to work. It would be a horrible waste of my technological genius to turn me into an expressionless zombie like your father—no offense intended."

"None taken, Monsieur Umpire," replies Florenz. "But don't be too proud over that technological terror you introduced as the stormcrow. The ability to squirt blackflame is insignificant compared to the true power of the Sword of Layban.

"After you transmogrify into my undead thrall you will be in charge of monitoring your own son's activities. If the monsieur Enganyon fails me again, you shall execute him with your own hands. Your will shall be unable to resist my commands as Master of Layban."

Enganyon looks at his father's face rising with anxiety and says, "The solution is simple. I'll just announce that we've come across a legal technicality that makes my candidacy invalid. Now that you are back, I don't need to be on the ballot anyway."

Umpire Gandorf adds, "Besides, your blackflame nearly killed off that magica tree that the mademoiselle Zena was counting on to get admitted into Pinne Mage University. It vanished to save itself and Johnny Appleseed claims he can help her find it.

"So there it is. We just tell Johnny Appleseed to take the mademoiselle Zena off to search for her magica tree. Bam! It's that simple. Everyone is happy and our plan . . . I mean . . . your plan, gets back on course. No one has to die."

Florenz stares with an expression that tells them she is deeply unimpressed with their thinking skills.

She says, "There's going to be a new rule around here—you don't throw your useless opinions at me unless I ask for them. And when I do ask for them, it will just be for show—to make it look like I actually care what other people think, this being a democracy for the time being and all that blibber-blabber.

"In the future, you'd better learn how to come up with opinions that sound a lot more like the ones coming from my mouth than the drivel coming from yours. Appleseed has to die so no one else can get their hands on the blackflame. The mademoiselle Zena has to die because your son made the mistake of proposing to her in a plenary session of the Council of Perfects. The madame Dungaree has to die because she has the power and influence to rally the fire elves against us.

Enganyon runs his fingers through his hair and leans back for a deep breath before saying, "Captain Florenz, this is not you speaking! It's the Sword of Layban! It's corrupting your beautiful soul!"

She narrows her eyes at him. "No darling, it's the angst speaking. You liked me a lot better when I was naïve and easy to manipulate. You and your father have been playing games behind my back this whole time doing anything and everything you could think of to seize power for yourselves.

"Now you wonder why a girl like me doesn't trust you? I've just come to terms with the fact that I was born into a powerful family. That was reason enough for Umpire Drayton and his goons to deprive me of my mother as a child, for my best friend to humiliate my father in public, and for my boyfriend to propose to her on the day my father was murdered.

"So it comes down to this—you and your father learn how to take orders, or I'll kill you both and find friends that won't be so quick to stab me in the back."

Enganyon gulps. Umpire Gandorf puts a hand on his son's shoulder and stands up, saying, "We understand our instructions and we will obey, master. Let's get out of here, son. We've taken up enough of Captain Florenz's time for one day."

Scene 6: The Democratic Big Bang

Shentalpee City on Tuscoraura Mountain
Tiw's Day Sext. Afternoon, 13th of June, 1284
Morrow of Saint Gervase (Nordlandic Midsummer)

Two weeks later, Captain Florenz is sitting at her desk, reviewing reports and writing briefs to various elected officials and clan leaders reassuring them that her undead father is still perfectly capable of ruling Shentalpee City as umpire-in-chief. Blunderbore enters her office. "Kindly excuse the interruption, Madame Captain, but Johnny Appleseed has escaped."

"Send out search parties."

"No need. We know where he is."

"Why haven't you arrested him?"

"It seems elections were held today. We did not want to infringe on the jurisdiction of the electoral deputies."

"But it's not election day."

"Someone convinced the high commissioner that election day should be held on Midsummer as reckoned by the old Alfheim calendar instead of the Julian Calendar of Roma."

"I'll put a stop to that! Bring me my armor."

Florenz marches into the square dressed in a new suit of black leather armor and followed by her undead warriors robed in black with silver death masks hiding their decaying faces. Florenz breathes heavily, seething with anger. Johnny Appleseed is sitting with Zena by the reflecting pool, while Umpire Gandorf harangues the crowds from the amphitheater stage.

Enganyon and Dungaree Jeanne stand near Zena as if waiting to congratulate her. Deducing from the scene that Zena has won these fake elections, Florenz points the Sword of Layban at Umpire Gandorf, clearly the mastermind behind it all, and yells, "Arrest him!"

Her undead warriors take off, shambling toward him. Some shuffle like elderly convalescents in long pajamas, but others sprint forward with the ferocity of saber-toothed tigers. Umpire Gandorf runs.

Whizzing by Johnny Appleseed and Zena, Umpire Gandorf is drenched with sweat and flushed red on his face and neck. A few steps after having passed them, he turns back and looks at them, bewildered. His cheeks twitch as he croaks out the words, "Run, fools!"

Madame Dungaree, Enganyon, Zena, and Johnny Appleseed feel the heat of Florenz's anger breathing down at them. They join Umpire Gandorf and flee.

Having anticipated undead resistance, Enganyon and his father are armed with silver blades. They push their way through the crowds and run into the outdoor Malarkey Market. One undead warrior gropes for Dungaree Jeanne but Umpire Gandorf doubles back and strikes off its hand. The undead warrior stops and picks up its hand. It tries to jam the hand back onto its wrist but the silver in the blade impedes it from bonding. The undead warrior gives up in short order and chucks its own hand at Umpire Gandorf.

The hand nails him square in the back of the head and Umpire Gandorf topples over. Within a few heartbeats he is swarmed by undead warriors, grabbing his ankles, poking at his face, and twisting his arms.

Enganyon is the swiftest runner of the group but he hangs back with his leaf-bladed silver sword to protect the others. For all his bravery and for all his skillful strokes severing limbs, he is quickly overwhelmed too.

The undead warriors claw at his face and tangle their limbs between his arms and legs. Subdued, Enganyon finds himself being dragged back through the crowd as a vengeful Florenz walks toward him imperiously.

Johnny Appleseed sees what is happening and begins to pray his restoration prayers. Each undead warrior tries to resist him in a battle of wills but they are no match. One by one, the knot of undead limbs wrapped around Enganyon and Umpire Gandorf untangles. Soon, Enganyon hacks his way out.

He runs over to help his staggering father back up onto his feet. Umpire Gandorf, frightened out of his mind, somehow manages to push his body back into gear, fleeing with a heavy limp and a wheeze.

Enganyon and Umpire Gandorf follow Dungaree Jeanne and Zena across the bridge to their home base — Red Giant's Base. With the undead warriors stunned, Johnny Appleseed finds the silver sword that Umpire Gandorf abandoned on the floor and uses it to start cutting away at the ropes on the bridge connecting Thor's Base to Red Giant's Base.

Ashamed that he did not think of such a heroic idea himself, the injured Umpire Gandorf calls out to Madame Dungaree, "Tell Reverend Appleseed that I can cut off the bridgehead. Let him keep praying or doing whatever he did back there to save my life."

After hearing the translation, Johnny Appleseed replies, "That kind of miracle requires a lot of prayer and fasting. I'm getting exhausted."

Hearing Dungaree Jeanne's translation of that last comment, Enganyon shouts, "Now's the time to give it all you've got, Reverend! I'm too young to die!"

Seeing the next round of thralls making their way toward the bridge, Johnny Appleseed sits on Dungaree Jeanne's front porch so he can concentrate in prayer.

The undead thralls come charging at them and Appleseed prays with all his heart. The first few thralls drop like bags of bones but shortly afterward, Johnny Appleseed collapses from the strain, unconscious.

From behind the basilica, Florenz marches forward, surrounded by Ivy League sergeants and officers, shouting, "Traitors!"

Enganyon desperately saws at the suspension bridge ropes with his silver sword. (As you probably know, silver cannot hold its edge as sharp as tempered steel, so cutting those tough ropes with it takes a little extra elbow grease.) When he sees Florenz storming her way across Malarkey Plaza toward him he shouts out to her, "But, my love, you won! The Tuscoraura elves elected you their umpire-in-chief! I was just helping you win the election!"

Florenz looks shocked. "Wait, what?"

The Ivy Leaguers stop in their tracks. Florenz can't help but think out loud, "The high elves are all too arrogant and conceited to vote for someone who does not look like them or who fails to live up to their superficial and unrealistic standards of perfection."

Enganyon's knee-jerk response comes out wrong. "Apparently not . . . I mean . . . of course, you look like us and live up to our superficial and unrealistic standards of perfection. What does it matter?"

That was not the answer Florenz wanted to hear.

Umpire Gandorf redoubles his efforts to cut the bridge cables. Meanwhile, one undead thrall drags itself forward with a total lack of enthusiasm, as if it would rather be taking a hot bath right now. Florenz is too flustered with conflicting emotions to give a clear command to direct its enslaved will decisively. It simply obeys her last command halfheartedly and steps onto the suspension bridge, wiggling its arms like a slug in a purple finch's beak.

The frayed cables holding up the suspension bridge start to snap. Umpire Gandorf grabs his son and shoves him back across the bridge toward safety while he himself runs back to intercept the thrall, shouting, "You shall not pass!"

Seeing the turmoil, Florenz tries to resolve the conflict in her heart. She asks tentatively, "Wait, wait! Are you trying to say that you really love me for who I am, Captain Enganyon?"

As his father hacks at the undead thrall, Enganyon fumbles a bit to find the right words. "It didn't hurt that your father was the most powerful elf in Tuscoraura, but I could genuinely see us marrying and living together happily ever after."

Apparently, that was not the answer Florenz was hoping to hear either. Her lips curl, her nose wrinkles, her fingers clench the bare skies. She gives a mental command to Sir Balrock, the giant dwarf now holding a whip. It comes lumbering forward from behind the basilica, picking up impressive speed as it goes. When the Ivy League sergeants realize what is coming their way, they dive to the sides to avoid getting trampled.

Enganyon shouts, "Quickly, Father! Come back!"

Umpire Gandorf sees the giant dwarf hurtling at him and hacks ever more vigorously at the last few strands of the suspension bridge cables. The giant dwarf's huge bones and rotting flesh still weigh an incredible amount. Seeing it coming, Umpire Gandorf makes a dash for safety on the far end. Sir Balrock's first ponderous step snaps the last cords. The suspension bridge gives way and the giant dwarf plummets down to the forest floor.

As for Umpire Gandorf, he feels the bridge boards slacken and leaps forward just as his feet start to lose traction. With a lucky reach, Umpire Gandorf grabs hold of the ledge with his two hands and hangs on for dear life.

BUT!

Before Enganyon and Dungaree Jeanne can reach down to pull him up, the giant dwarf Balrock lashes out with its whip and snags Umpire Gandorf's ankle, pulling him down with it. They both fall one hundred fifty feet to the forest floor.

Enganyon screams, "Noooooooo!"

Dungaree Jeanne pulls Enganyon, screaming and crying hysterically, away from the ledge. Meanwhile, Zena plies every muscle in her body to drag the unconscious Johnny Appleseed into Betzy Rose Mansion but makes little progress.

After getting Enganyon safely inside, Dungaree Jeanne runs out to help her drag the unconscious human inside her front door. Zena locks the front door while her mother dashes from room to room, bolting and reinforcing all the doors and shutters.

Enganyon rushes about frantically, but instead of helping them, he seems to be looking for something.

Once calmed down, Enganyon announces in Runic, "Madame Dungaree, I have resolved to surrender myself to the authorities and plead for clemency. I shall wave this white flag out the front window and request a parley with the mademoiselle Umpire-in-Chief-elect."

Dungaree Jeanne can't believe her ears. "Monsieur Enganyon, that's not a white flag! That's my best quality red-and-white striped guest bedsheet!"

"If I hold out a dirty old dishrag, what do you think my chances of surviving an audience with the mademoiselle Umpire-in-Chief-elect Florenz will be?"

Getting up, Dungaree Jeanne wipes the tear from her eye and grabs the striped sheet from him. "Okay, okay. If we're going to demand a parley, we might as well do it in style. Go grab the starry blue pillowcase from the linen closet and meet me in the sewing nook."

"What's the point of the pillowcase?"

"Captain Enganyon, go fetch me a broomstick from the kitchen that we can use as a flagpole. You're forgetting that I'm the dean of the League of Nations. We're not going to surrender; we're going to wave high the flag of freedom!"

Scene 7: The Grand Detour

Shentalpee City on Tuscoraura Mountain
Tiw's Day Sext. Afternoon, 13th of June, 1284
Morrow of Saint Gervase (Nordlandic Midsummer)

The red-and-white striped bedsheet grabs Florenz's attention as soon as Enganyon carries it out of Betzy Rose Mansion. She calls out to him, "What's that?"

Enganyon says, "We wish to parley."

Florenz scratches her ear and calls across the chasm, "You know I'm such a soft touch that I'll probably regret it later on, but right now the only terms we're going to discuss regard the manner of your execution."

Dungaree Jeanne yanks the flagpole out of Enganyon's hands and waves its star-spangled banner. "Excuse me, Mademoiselle Umpire-in-Chief-elect, but you must have gotten the wrong impression. We're not here to surrender; we're here to share some good news.

"Both Master Leevai and Captain Gunnar have agreed to join the League of Nations. I'm not going to let the heresiarch and his undead minions overrun our beautiful colony on my watch."

Florenz glares. "Oh yeah? You and what army?"

Horns go off beneath them.

The anxious elves all rush to the ramparts of Thor's Base to see what's going on down below.

Haughty hosts of Crusaders are mustering in a pell-mell of mad confusion in the wood elf villages on the forest floor. Trumpet blasts burst in the air, signaling the oncoming havoc of war.

A dread silence reposes over Shentalpee City.

At length, Florenz looks up and rages. "Your blood will wash out the pollution of their foul footsteps."

Dungaree Jeanne still gazes over the railing. "Praise the power that has preserved us from your cult!"

Florenz is so angry she spits as she shouts, "Traitor! I should have known you've been siding with our foes all along!"

"Not at all, Mademoiselle Umpire-in-Chief-elect. You are the one who has allowed outsiders to seize control of our fair city. We will not let the heresiarch dictate our freedoms. Until a moment ago, the League of Nations was the only group of elves brave enough to stand up to you with that blackflaming sword of yours but now heaven has rescued our land.

"Swear that you will expel the heresiarch and I will summon the League of Nations to assist in the defense of Shentalpee City. Refuse and I'll rally every freedom-loving elf on Tuscoraura Mountain to depose you."

Florenz fidgets with the scabbard of the Sword of Layban, calculating a solution to her predicament. If Dungaree Jeanne starts a civil war now, she just might win. Florenz decides to cut a deal. "Okay, okay, fine. He has terrible bad breath anyway. If you bring the League of Nations into the fight on our side, I'll kick the heresiarch out of here after we win—I swear it."

"Kick him out now."

"That would be foolish. We've been preparing to fight the Crusade ever since he got here. He's got a bag of nasty tricks all ready for them. Let him unleash the Aeolian winds upon our enemies before he leaves."

"Agreed, but remember—we will fight for you only as long as your cause is just."

The earth groans under the trampling feet of dwarves, men, and gnomes as each company of warriors seeks a place of honor on the battlefield without exposing themselves to too much danger. Dozens of heralds go about shouting orders amidst the tumult until at last they are arranged in a formidable battle line.

Although Amhirst's contingent is small in number compared to the duke of Philadelphia's many vassals, allies, and mercenaries, the cardinals immediately notice the baron's absence. Suited up for war in armor adorned with the papal insignia, Paterno Cardinal Orsini canters briskly into Amhirst's camp on his warhorse and calls out, "What is going on here? Didn't you hear the trumpet call for the general muster?"

Amhirst exits his tent and casts a smug glare at the cardinal, saying, "I'm sorry, Your Eminence, but you have failed to deliver on your promise to make me the new viceroy. Fool me once, shame on you. Fool me twice, shame on me. I'm sitting this one out."

Paterno Cardinal Orsini growls, "Be warned, Amhirst—if you abandon this Crusade, you will incur an excommunication."

"Abandon the Crusade? Heavens no! I promised to *accompany* the Crusade, not to fight in it."

Paterno Cardinal Orsini is not amused. "Suddenly you think you can go playing at being a lawyer with me? I could destroy you in the course of a leisurely afternoon's siesta if I wanted to."

"Your Eminence," sighs the baron of Amhirst, "The memory of the killings at Fort William Henry has engraved in my mind a deep caution about war leaders who feel bound to nothing more than the letter of a treaty. We all have to do a better job in managing expectations if we are going to work together."

The cardinal clenches his fists. "This is treachery!"

"At least I'm an honest traitor who plays by the book, Your Eminence. My herald, Sir Sean, is still trying to make sense of your playbook. Until then, no game."

Paterno Cardinal Orsini gallops off, seething with rage. Sir Sean turns to the baron and asks, "My lord, do you think it was wise to irk the cardinal thus?"

Amhirst shrugs. "The man betrayed me. The world is not big enough to hold both of us. My Achilles' heel is my ambition, and he holds Paris's arrow in his quiver. We can't both walk out of here alive. Right now, we should be looking into every possible stratagem to make sure the elves crush the cardinals."

Unlike the high elves up in the imposing tree-lofted bases and towers, the wood elves have no protection against the invaders. Some flee toward the marchlands, but most crowd around the elevators, screaming for a chance to be hoisted up to the safety of Shentalpee City. The dwarves working the cranks strain to get the overloaded elevators up while shoving off desperate hangers-on, slowing the process down. Parents pass their screaming children to anybody lucky enough to make their way onto an elevator. Chaos rules over their terror with gloating tyranny.

The wind smells slow and sour while the high elves watch the crusading army march toward them in unending ranks, trampling down the scutch grass and uprooting the dandelions. A few old crows caw out the sounds of their morbid curiosity and add to the palpable tension.

The high elves safely tucked inside their thick wooden barricades lean over the railings to mock the invaders, but the panicked squeals of the wood elf refugees take away some of their thunder. The Justiciar League officers busy themselves knocking on doors, asking for high elf volunteers to take the unsheltered wood elves into their homes—vagrants can become a security liability in the event of an assault.

Leading off Thor's Base, the major dignitaries of the non-elf communities arrive—the mountain dwarf Lawspeaker Sturl Snorrison; the garden gnome High Bailiff Harfud Fellowhide; and the longhouse human War Chief Skaruren—also known as King Hancock to the Aenglish.

Representing the high elves, High Commissioner Kordon Bleuson rides down in one of the larger elevators. He steps off before touching down and it jangles behind him. A detachment from the League of Licornes rides over to him and helps him mount his battle reindeer.

Once the green-and-brown League of Licornes' reindeer honor guard has formed up with the high commissioner, they unfurl their white flags and escort him across the scorched wood elf village to a parley with the duke of Philadelphia and the Cardinals Orsini.

With his teeth sounding gray, Maderno Cardinal Orsini greets each delegate in his own language. "Hale ant sail, Monsieur Kordon! *Se'g Honyaweh*, Skaruren agigo rekweh! *Kaishu*, andrea nanoa Sturl! *Beannach*, tighern Harfud gnormach!"

Then he says in Latin, relying on his translators to make his words understood, "The Holy Office of the Inquisition has no ill feeling toward your peoples. We are only here to arrest the heresiarch and his blackflame cultists, including the renegade Florenz Kibblersdottir. We personally assure you that she will get a fair trial. We will offer the fire elves a truce and safe-conduct to our tent and back for the sake of negotiating terms."

The elf high commissioner, compared to the others, is shortish, brownish, oldish, and mossy. With a voice that is sharp and perfunctory, he says in Latin, "Salve, patres conscripti cardinales!" Sensing he didn't get it quite right, he switches to Elvish Runic, saying, "We accept your offer to negotiate, as long as you withdraw your army past the marchlands. We demand restitution for all the mayhem and destruction you have caused before we discuss terms."

The lawspeaker's command of Latin is quite strong, so he delivers his words entirely in Latin. "Your Eminences, we do not recognize Florenz Kibblersdottir as the legally appointed umpire-in-chief, and we have no love for the wendigo-creating cult leeching off her opulent city-state. Nonetheless, you have recklessly violated our territorial sovereignty and threatened our blood-sworn allies without inviting us to mediate the conflict. A diplomatic affront of such epic proportions cannot be ignored."

King Hancock says in the Irockian dialect of the Tuscoraura tribes, "You say that the fire elf leader walks with the turtles and runs with the rabbits. Today the rabbit sleeps and the turtle finishes the race. You bring axes to chop down our trees and torches to raise our homes, but the sequoias above do not burn; the caves below do not split. United we stand."

Maderno Cardinal Orsini sneezes with a sawdusty sneeze and says in Latin, "Our armies have merely chopped down a few trees. We have done no harm, esteemed lords of Tuscoraura Mountain, and we have not invaded your territories. We are the high inquisitors of Vinland, and our business is hunting down heretics. Princess Florenz harbors the heresiarch of the great and abominable Blackflame Cult. As soon as we arrest them, we will—"

The high commissioner cuts him short. "We will not discuss terms unless you withdraw your army and make restitution! You have no hope of winning a war against us. Leave, before we demonstrate our fury."

With a grim look on his face, Maderno Cardinal Orsini suddenly lapses into his Italian dialect, common only on the city streets of Roma. "All right then, here's our condition—unless you hand over Princess Florenz Kibblersdottir and the other blackflame heretics, we'll whack them down off every scrofulous tree growing on top of Tuscoraura Mountain and smoke them out of every smogulous hole beneath it."

The translators struggle to decipher the message. When they communicate the gist of it, the high commissioner is so enraged he can only gargle and croak out a few nonsense words. Suddenly he looks behind him and says in Eldric, "You're asking for it and boy oh boy, you're gonna get it. Here's our umpire-elect on her way now to show you what's what."

Florenz trots up on a war reindeer followed by her father on foot in a dark cape. His face is pale and his jaw hangs open. The whiteness of the two canines on his upper jaw spooks them from afar.

Lawspeaker Sturl Snorrison turns around and seethes with outrage, shouting in Elvish Runic, "Mademoiselle Florenz! How dare you violate your parole by returning to Tuscoraura Mountain!"

Florenz keeps a stony-hard face and rebuts his accusation. "You condemned me without a trial for condemning Bartlebee without a trial. I have come back to set the record straight. Now the fire elves have elected me umpire-in-chief. Any attack on me as head of the state is an attack on Shentalpee City itself."

The lawspeaker's fury boils with exasperation. "We told you we would not recognize you as head of state. A political stunt like this is reckless in peacetime and sheer madness in time of war."

The high inquisitor's translator tries to explain to the cardinals what is going on, but it is all hopelessly confusing.

Maderno Cardinal Orsini shouts out, "Enough! War has been averted. Mademoiselle Florenz and her father are here. The Holy Office of the Inquisition always gives heretics a chance to repent. Come with me, heretical elves, and answer to the tribunal."

The lawspeaker turns back to the high inquisitor and declares, "If you have a mind to vacate our lands, we won't stop you. But, be warned! Dwarves hold grudges. If you bring any more pandemonium to our homeland we will roll you over so hot and heavy that your widows will use your corpses as yule logs."

The dwarves and gnomes send their criers who speak Eldric to the panicking throng of wood elves around the elevators, asking them to calm down and proceed in an orderly fashion to the burrows and tunnels beneath Tuscoraura, where they will be given refuge until the crusading army withdraws. Most forget about the elevators instantly and head for safety among the dwarves and gnomes underground. Those wood elves who desperately sent their children up the elevator now plead with the dwarf operators to help get them back down again.

The undead umpire-in-chief, Kibbler Earnestson, walks toward the high inquisitors imperiously. The high inquisitors are well prepared for dealing with the undead, and low-level clerics bring out a pair of silver manacles. They chain the umpire's wrists together behind his back. A pair of silver manacles come out for Florenz as well, just in case. The Inquisition's guards escort the two prisoners into the tent.

Once inside the tent, the gathered lords all have a common language, Aenglish, so the high inquisitors order the proceedings to be conducted in Aenglish. They form a tribunal and give Florenz an opportunity to publicly confess her wrongdoings and declare her repentance. Her testimony is long and complicated.

The Inquisition's translator, a Toutonic cleric who knows Latin, Elvish Runic, and Dwarvish Runic perfectly—though his Aenglish is still a little weak—tries his best to explain to the gathered lords the convolutions of her political discourse through his thick

Toutonic accent. It comes out something like this: "Mademoiselle Florenz, she says zat she vants no schlaughter of innocent lives. She says zat zee Eldritch elves voted her ... how do you say ... First Vampire, but she is schtill no vampire. She says zat she vill come to schtand judgment. She says zat her fazer is zee eldritch First Vampire. Her fazer vill also come to schtand judgment. Her fazer vill say to us about ze schvartz fire."

The duke of Philadelphia looks at him, baffled. "What is an eldritch vampire?"

The translator points at Kibbler and says, "Zat!"

The duke of Philadelphia, William Pinne, speaks as the highest-ranking noble among the military forces. "Whatever. Just tell the eldritch vampire that we accept his repentance, but unfortunately cannot leave without an indemnity. Fighting this pesky heresy is expensive — two hundred silver marks for my battalions, two hundred for the Inquisition, and two hundred for our allies and mercenaries should be sufficient."

Florenz hears the translation and asks, "How about a fist full of dollars?"

The translation has less spunk, but Paterno Cardinal Orsini catches the drift and says, "Don't get too cocky with us, miss! With one wave of my hand I can turn your undead father back to the realms of oblivion forever."

Florenz replies, "Don't try to frighten us with your clerical ways, Inquisitor. Your sad devotion to that ancient religion has not helped you conjure up the Sword of Layban, or given you clairvoyance enough to find the heresiarch's hidden base —"

Before she has a chance to finish that thought, her eldritch vampire father darts forward with incredible speed and force. Though his arms are still chained behind his back, they forgot to muzzle him. He leaps over a tall guard in a single bound and bites Paterno Cardinal Orsini in the neck.

Duke William Pinne shouts, "That eldritch vampire is biting the cardinal's neck! Someone get it off!"

Using the power of the archon stone in his chest, Vampire Kibbler polarizes the three source stones in the amulet to repel fire, lightning, and metal. The steel-clad and steel-armed soldiers around him flip backwards as if an invisible fist has punched them where it counts. The braziers and candles in the tent flicker out and the darkness adds to the chaos while the eldritch vampire wreaks bloody havoc.

Before any guard reaches the tent flaps to let more light in, Florenz jumps back over her chained wrists to bring her hands to the front and she draws the Sword of Layban from a special concealed sheath she had constructed specifically for this payback strike. "By the power of Layban . . . I have the power!" she thunders.

Having memorized the middle cardinal's position and rehearsed this covert operation with her father many times, she strikes Maderno Cardinal Orsini in the thigh with the Sword of Layban, freezing his innards and setting his armor ablaze with the blackflame surging out from its blade.

Hearing the commotion, the outside guards pour into the tent. Once sunlight shines in through the open flaps, the light infantry guards—immune to the sorcery because they wear no steel—step forward. One brave swashbuckler with leather armor, a wooden buckler, and a silver sword chops at Vampire Kibbler just before a cleric uses his Turn Undead prayer. The silver sword severs his right arm at the shoulder. Although the Turn Undead prayer cannot destroy the vampire's unnatural bond of soul to body thanks to the archon stone, the effect of the prayer sends Kibbler flying back as if he got hit with a wrecking ball.

Florenz quickly realizes that in a den of clerics, Knights Paladin, and fighters who specialize in countering magic, sorcery, and the undead, her father's invincibility has severe limitations. With his evil will enfeebled by the prayers of the holy cleric, Kibbler loses control of the source stones in his amulet. The next moment, Vampire Kibbler's chest is a pincushion of medieval darts and missiles.

Florenz beats a hasty retreat behind her father just in the nick of time. The leather-clad swashbucklers and a few light-armored guards lunge in to attack with wooden and silver weapons. Vampire Kibbler whirls his severed arm on the silver chain like a flail and smacks the nearest swashbuckler with tornado force, flipping him over the inquisitors' lunch table. Florenz reaches back and drags her father out of the tent.

Not a moment too soon, because a Knight Paladin steps forward with a blessed cross. The power of the cross clobbers Vampire Kibbler and knocks him senseless. His body slumps over his daughter's, but she does not stop. Florenz hoists him up onto her shoulders and carries him off at a run.

Before pursuing them, the Crusaders turn to the last surviving high inquisitor. Clutching his dying brothers, Piccolo Cardinal Orsini crumples his tear-washed cheeks and shouts, "Kill them all!"

Duke William Pinne objects, "But, Your Eminence, many of these wood elves are good Christians!"

Suddenly having lost his speech impediment, the hysterical inquisitor screams, "Kill them all, and God will recognize his own!"

The horns blow and the Crusaders rush forward to a terrible massacre of innocents.

ACT V

YOU'RE IT

Scene 1: Monstrous Mash

Shentalpee City on Tuscoraura Mountain
Tiw's Day Sext. Afternoon, 13th of June, 1284
Morrow of Saint Gervase (Nordlandic Midsummer)

At the reckless command of the enraged little cardinal, all the Crusaders rush forward to attack the helpless wood elves who have not yet reached the safety of the dwarf tunnels or the gnome burrows. Even without the elaborate jewelry of a high elf, a wood elf's day-to-day getup still has enough linen fabrics, copper buckles, high-grade steel tools, and homemade finery to make looting their belongings a profitable business model for the rank-and-file Crusaders. Moreover, elves always earn a good price on the slave market.

Back at the cardinals' tent, Florenz and her father run for their lives—or in the case of her father, for his undeath. She mutters breathless curses upon the heresiarch who severely overestimated the archon stone's effectiveness in rendering her father invincible. It did not take long for the Inquisition's forces to prove themselves quite capable of dealing with the threat.

Even the legendary Sword of Layban failed to make her the kind of super-warrior the heresiarch led her to believe she would become.

As they retreat, her father's will revives little by little. Still, the active source stones inside her father's chest provide little protection against the gnome sling stones and the human silver arrows from the cardinals' elite guard. Her father tries but fails to reattach his right arm, severed with a silver blade. He runs close behind her but staggers around as if punch drunk from the Turn Undead prayers and the blessed crosses they have directed at him. As he runs, he does manage to position himself to absorb the missiles flying in at Florenz.

Thanks to his protection as a mobile meat shield, Florenz only suffers a few minor flesh wounds on the way back to Shentalpee City, despite the torrents of arrows, crossbow bolts, and sling stones falling down upon her at every step.

But her luck soon runs out. Several light-armored swashbucklers from the high inquisitors' tent catch up to her before she reaches Thor's Base with her father. They are armed with silver swords and know how to use them well . . . very well.

Unable to outpace them in the footrace, Florenz desperately parries their blows with the Sword of Layban. Her father does his best to ward them off by flicking his chained hand at them, but his imprecise swings offer little relief. Her swordsmanship is simply not up to par, and she knows it will only take them a few more strokes to bypass her guard.

But Florenz has never put much stock in swordplay —a waste of time. Organization and planning, as far as she is concerned, will always win the day, and she has carefully laid out and rehearsed a plan for escape.

The elevator operator dwarves have been keeping one elevator, reinforced with sturdy boards, dangling about ten feet above the battlefield with a large brass bell buried upside down directly beneath it. The swashbucklers move to corner her just as Florenz hops down into the bell with her father holding onto her tightly. He then uses the archon stone to flip the polarization of the lodestone in the amulet to repel metal as vehemently as possible.

Kibbler's lodestone magnetically propels them both upward out of the bell's skirt like a railgun or a sorcery-charged blunderbuss. A dwarf elevator operator makes ready to reach out and grab them as they fly by, but their trajectory is so perfect that they both make a clean landing inside the elevator's platform without any help at all. Impressed, the dwarf compliments her in Eldric, saying, "Quite a bell hop, Mademoiselle Umpire!"

They are not safe yet. Crossbow bolts, longbow arrows, and sling stones come flying up at them. Florenz does not want to wait around to test how long the elevator's improvised shell of maplewood planks will last against so many missiles. She gives him a terse reply. "Okay, bellhop, just get us out of here."

The operator dwarves ply their muscle strength and quick hands to the pulleys. The elevator glides upward swiftly. Vampire Kibbler continues to swat at sling stones and intercept arrows aimed at his daughter until they rise up beyond their range.

Once they're at the top, the heresiarch walks over to them, surrounded by his entourage of cultists and blackflame fanatics. With triumph in his eyes, he curls his fists together and announces, "Welcome back, Lord Vampire and my young apprentice, Florenz. From here you will witness the final destruction of the Inquisition and the last of its pathetic Crusades."

Florenz grabs her father's arm, still dangling from the silver chain, and says in the Black Tongue of Caldor, "What gives with this? My father is not as invincible as you promised. The high inquisitors had a lot more tricks up their sleeves than you ever bothered to tell me about. I'm starting to doubt the blackflame will do much good against this Crusade."

The heresiarch ignores her doubts and says, "Little combat tricks are nothing compared to the true power of the blackflame. Behold!"

With a grandiose wave of his hand, the heresiarch summons undead reinforcements. Out of the forest charge hundreds—nay, rather thousands—of undead animals, big and small; woolly mammoths, cave bears, saber-toothed tigers, moose, deer, opossums, rabbits, squirrels, chipmunks, field mice, and garden snakes.

The stampede of undead animals crashes into the Crusader front lines like gusts of hurricane winds—it flattens them, but does not completely destroy them. The Crusaders desperately attack the undead animals only to find themselves gored, clawed, bitten, gnawed, trampled, and butted by that monstrous fury.

The valiant soldiers hack the undead animals to pieces, but only those appendages severed by silver blades stay severed. Those animals attacked by steel recompose themselves into strange new horrors.

The duke's son, Sir William Pinne the Younger, bravely chops the antlers off an undead antelope lunging toward him. At that moment, a scalped jackrabbit hops by and attaches the antlers to its own head. The undead jackalope harries the Crusaders with such speed and precision with its antlers that it leaves a trail of death and destruction in its wake.

The battlesages in the duke's employ conjure up ensorcelled tornadoes with their wind and water source stones to vacuum up the monsters while the battlemages whip around their magica wands uttering every manner of incomprehensible magic incantations to locomutate the monsters away from the battlefield. But the vast number of undead animals overwhelms their endurance, and soon the front lines of Crusaders are put to flight in a mad panic.

Only the three orders of military monks keep their calm as they strive to devise a tactic to clear these abominations of nature away. The Knights Templar are renowned for their prowess with weapons and use blessed maces and silver swords combined with brute force to break the forward momentum of the monstrous onslaught. True to their untarnished military fame, the Templars follow Brother Jack de Molay into the jaws of hell and pass through unharmed.

The Knights Hospitaller, the pious warrior monks of compassion, add prayers and holy invocations to their attack. They protect not only the Crusaders but also—and especially—the innocent, unarmed wood elf refugees. Though bound by their vows to obey the high inquisitor, they conscientiously object to war crimes. Peace and healing follow wherever they go.

For all the hard work and the valuable tactical achievements of the other military orders, it is the Knights Paladin who save the day. Their temperate lifestyle allows them to heroically wade their way into the worst of the fighting. Armed with prayer and fasting according to the Lord's command, they burst through the festering horde of monsters with righteous fury in their eyes.

The human Paladins ride warhorses, the dwarf Paladins ride war donkeys, and the gnome Paladins ride war ponies. They all couch their holy lances and hone in on the largest and most ferocious monsters before them. When their lances break, they pull out holy water and blessed crucifixes, silver blades and relic-filled maces, staves carved with saints' effigies, and shields painted with icons.

Though surrounded by unnatural beasts that outnumber them a hundred to one, they cast themselves into the fray fearlessly. Still, the odds are so dismal that it would take a miracle for them to succeed—and yet, somehow, these holy warriors dish out just such miracles with sugar and spice.

After an hour of brave strokes, fervent prayers, and mighty miracles, they demolish and scatter the frenzied undead before them. Body part after body part, slabs of meat, dismembered limbs, splattered organs, gristle, and bone twitch and ooze across the forest floor—a horrid sight but a threat no more.

Having retreated back to their camp, the bloodied Crusaders stand together, huddling against each other and trembling like children under a blanket having just come inside after being caught in a thunderstorm.

The duke of Philadelphia can almost hear all the coins tumbling out of his coffers while picturing for himself a protracted siege. He hopes they can give it one last hurrah and says, "We still have the element of surprise! If we press our advantage—"

"Whoa, whoa, whoa!" interrupts Brother Radisson, the Commander-elect of the Knights Hospitallar. "The elves have been preparing for this attack long before you even summoned us. There is no surprise here and we have no advantage—we are getting picked off like mosquitoes in a flock of bats . . . uh-oh!"

"What?"

The Elect Radisson points to the skies. "Holy bat guano! Look up there!"

Along the edge of Thor's Base, Vampire Kibbler leads the other notables and high elf leaders whom he has forced to undergo transmogrification into the undead state. Among their ranks is the enthralled revenant Gandorf Mithranderson, the unwilling but subservient Major Leagues Vampire. Wearing long, black capes as a sort of primitive parachute, they throw themselves off Thor's Base one after another.

Riding next to Duke William Pinne of Philadelphia, the rogue adventurer Ariel—whose real name is Lady Philippa, the duke's daughter—sees their black capes flutter as they come flying down and turns to the Hospitallar knight. "Look up there! Are they sending undead bats to attack us? They look too big to be ordinary bats—they're like bat . . . men."

The Elect Radisson follows her finger and the undead umpires come quickly into view. "Holy Adam laid to rest west of paradise! Those aren't bats; they've got more undead elf vampires!"

The first to crash to the ground, Vampire Kibbler's flattened body billows out and upward like a tube man sky dancer at a luxury car dealership. Likewise, as if reinflated by the electric fans of their own willpower, the other sky-fallen vampires uncrumple their limbs to a macabre rhythm.

"Look! They're dancing!" The Crusaders stand around mesmerized, watching the pulverized vampires wriggle and churn as if featured artists in some horrific ballet. No sooner do they recompose themselves than the vampires smash, rip, fling, and batter the Crusaders with no mercy. They spin them around, pound them down, and toss them up in the air like a pizza man kneading thin-crust pizza dough.

Suddenly Ariel, *alias* Lady Philippa, calls up her party of adventurers. Monsignor Oscar Meyer charges to the rescue. His war mallet comes down with such force that it knocks one vampire's right arm clean out of its shoulder socket. He then chants a Turn Undead prayer that immediately drains the battle frenzy out of another vampire.

Ariel wedges herself between two vampires and severs a left arm off the first and a right arm off the second with her silver knives. Before the one-armed vampires can retaliate, Willis chops off the legs of the first with his longsword while Whoopee taps his magic wand on the second's knees to make them disappear, humming out his magic words, "Ekki tang zoo boing!"

Hard behind Ariel's party rides a detachment of Knights Paladin. They are armed with clay bombs filled with holy water, exorcism oils, and blessed salts. They foist these sacred petards on the vampires and neutralize their ferocity.

Even from afar, Vampire Kibbler senses the strength of this group's holiness. His bloodlust has not been slaked, but he knows that another assault by the Knights Paladin will annihilate his undead thralls.

He simply does not have enough vampires to put up a fight against such a holy foe. Far too few elves volunteered to undergo transmogrification. He uses the Black Tongue of Caldor to order his thralls to retreat from the battle.

Next time, he will return with a massive undead elf army. It will take time, patience, and most of all, a brilliant lie to convince enough high elves in the power structure to force transmogrification upon the citizens of Shentalpee City whether their private, individual consciences agree to it or not.

Not far away, Vampire Gandorf seethes with loathing as he watches Vampire Kibbler run away. His heart burns to take revenge for his death and political demise but his mind allows him no respite except to obey Vampire Kibbler's commands. Vampire Gandorf retreats and the other vampires follow close behind.

Seeing the vampires retreating, Ariel shouts to the surviving Crusaders, "Fall back to the camps!"

They unanimously follow her.

Scene 2: The Odyssey Policy

Shentalpee City on Tuscoraura Mountain
Saturn's Day Nones. Afternoon, 24th of June, 1284
Nativity of Saint John the Baptist
(Christian Midsummer)

"Amhirst!" shouts the little cardinal as he storms into the baron's camp. "Your little pouting session will come to an end right this instant. We're languishing here and the Duke of Philadelphia doesn't have enough troops left to mount a proper assault. Those undead monsters and vampires crippled his army. This is the last time I'm going to say this. You'd better put your troops in the field or I'll excommunicate your army and release them from their feudal vows to serve you."

"Tut, tut, Your Eminence," replies Amhirst, sipping his wine by the campfire. "If the rest of Vinland does not hear about it, your excommunication won't bother my career aspirations much. You are deep in enemy territory, surrounded by elves and cultists who are hell-bent to reap vengeance upon you; I wouldn't give you one chance in thirty to make it out of here alive.

"In my business as a successful military leader, one in thirty makes for some very shabby odds and in war, the only bookie is the grim reaper. The last I heard, he doesn't extend credit to anyone, not even clerics. What this Crusade needs is coordination. Appointing a single leader as, say, crowned viceroy of Vinland, might streamline the chain of command, allow us to drive home the final punch—the coup de grâce, as the defeated Frankish viceroy of Vinland would say."

Piccolo Cardinal Orsini stomps his feet and pouts. "Okay, okay already! I get your point. It was all just a big misunderstanding. The capture of the Frankish viceroy of Vinland does grant you a claim to his title, but my advisors have been telling me that the man you captured is not the viceroy, merely an innocent, poor old man who happens to resemble Lord Samuel de Champlane. After a brief interview to verify his identity, I will crown you Aenglish viceroy of Vinland. Please bring the prisoner forward."

The baron of Amhirst nods to Sir Sean Madigan, who approaches him and whispers into his ear.

Amhirst turns red with anger and humiliation. He calms himself and announces, "It seems the viceroy is indisposed at the moment. Could we resume this meeting at another time?"

"If you are afraid your prisoner will not pass the test, I must declare your claim to right of conquest null and void. The duke of Philadelphia, however, has proposed a compromise. Even though he is the highest-ranking noble in Vinland and most deserving of supreme command, whichever of you two lords is first to have his troops seize one of the elf tree-lofted platforms shall be named governor-general. Agreed?"

Barely able to hide his outrage, Amhirst walks out of the tent. Sir Sean, seeing through the ploy and not wanting to get squeezed out, quickly says, "We agree."

Sir Sean then races out of the tent to catch up with the baron and confesses, "My lord, I took the liberty to speak on your behalf and told the cardinal we agree. He obviously wants to offer the title to the duke of Philadelphia even though it rightly belongs to you. That goes without saying, but I thought—"

Struggling to control his anger, Amhirst snaps, "You thought wrong, Sir Sean. As a matter of fact, we are all going about this wrong. All wrong."

Sir Sean trembles a little as he asks, "What do you mean, my lord?"

Amhirst stops and looks Sir Sean fiercely in the eye and says, "Do you know how I translate *velle est posse*?"

Sir Sean does not want to upstage the baron right now but he does not want to look dumb either. He says tentatively, "Something like 'where there's a will, there's a way,' my lord."

Amhirst sneers and says, "In your world that would be a good translation. In my world, a better translation would be, 'when someone gets in your way, find out which one of his relatives is most eager to read his will.' I assure you, every powerful man has at least one close family member who wants him dead."

"But the cardinal's brothers are already—"

As they walk, Amhirst sees Sir Robert Roger directing his troops in building stockade walls and storms up to him. "Sir Robert Roger! How could you lose my most valuable prisoner?"

Sir Robert Roger looks at him, befuddled. "My lord, you did not entrust the viceroy to my custody, if that is whom you are referring to."

"Someone was sneaking around our camp and took him away. You're supposed to detect intruders. That's what I pay you big dollars for! At the crucial moment, you come up empty-handed!"

Benjamin Frankelyn walks up boldly. "Excuse me, my lord, but we're not entirely empty-handed at the moment." Benjamin Frankelyn bows with great deference, attempting to soothe the wrath of his patron.

"You will find that the missing viceroy is just one of many schemes the Cardinals Orsini have been playing on you. After sniffing around the right places, I found out Piccolo Cardinal Orsini himself sent an agent to abduct the Frankish viceroy from your custody.

"It seems the high inquisitors promised the duke of Philadelphia appointment as crown governor-general of Vinland as well. You should have listened to my advice and accepted the appointment when we first got back from Salim. Now we're back to square one, dancing around while the Inquisition chuckles. The cardinal arranged this whole charade about demanding to see the Frankish viceroy in person, knowing full well you did not have him."

Sir Sean Madigan immediately backs him up, saying, "You see, my lord! It's nothing but a childish ploy to get both you and the duke of Philadelphia strung along on this Crusade without fulfilling any promises to either of you."

Amhirst glares at Benjamin Frankelyn and says, "So now you're going to tell me that your trusted fellow adventurer Ariel—or should I say Lady Philippa Pinne, the blasted duke's own daughter—helped the Frankish viceroy escape even though I paid her a small fortune to retain her services because she's really been working for her father all along!"

Frankelyn responds confidently, "Lady Philippa's integrity is irreproachable, my lord. You hired her to deliver the Sword of Layban to the Holy Office of the Inquisition and she completed that quest admirably. Not even her father knows that she carried out this quest for you. Still, I assure you she was not assigned the quest to rescue the viceroy for the cardinal."

"What makes you so sure?"

Benjamin Frankelyn polishes his fingernails on his tunic after a quick breath and says, "I happen to have stumbled across the identity of the adventurer who did it; also a young woman, like Lady Philippa, and also a frankelyn like myself, but in service to the Ottawan Lord, Sagamore Pontiak."

Skeptical about such a lucky find, Amhirst folds his arms and asks, "So where is the viceroy now?"

Benjamin Frankelyn raises his eyebrows as if deeply sympathetic to the baron's plight. "Alas, could it not be more obvious? The viceroy is resting in the cardinal's tent as we speak."

"Sir Robert Roger!" Amhirst snaps. "I want you to get that viceroy back for me. Do whatever you have to."

Benjamin Frankelyn clears his throat and raises a hand. "A word of caution, my lord. You have already introduced Sir Robert Roger to all the lords of this Crusade as a trusted member of your retinue. If he is caught, or even noticed, while engaged in this quest, it could prove disastrous to all your ambitions."

"So how do you suggest I get the Frankish viceroy back from the cardinal?"

Frankelyn raises his eyebrows. "Forget the Frankish viceroy and forget the Aenglish viceroyship. It was never on the table to begin with. King Eddard's priority is to reassert his authority in Vinland, as you discovered when you met his coroner at Ithica. He has no interest whatsoever in sharing royal prerogatives with a viceroy in Vinland. None. You will only make him your enemy if you press this issue any further.

"Look at the whole landscape with a level head, my lord. The Church was furious with kindhearted Uncle

310

Sam because he wasn't tough enough with the blackflame heretics. The whole reason they agreed to let King Eddard conduct his war against fellow Christians on Vinland's soil was that Uncle Sam was using his position as Frankish viceroy to block the Inquisition from executing heretics.

"The pope does not want a noble who can stymie his orders here or anywhere else in the world. There will be no viceroy of Vinland. Never again. Period."

Amhirst cannot argue with Frankelyn's logic but does not like the picture he is painting. He asks, "So what do you suggest I do instead?"

"Take up their offer to be Aenglish governor-general. I have certain information that both King Eddard and Pope Martin have approved the title since it's not hereditary and it doesn't include any royal privileges. A governor-general has the power to enforce the Crown's wishes, but can be removed instantly by the king's decree. There *will* be an Aenglish governor-general and, with all due respect, unless you act quickly, it won't be you."

Welling up with anger once again, Amhirst says, "Isn't it perfectly obvious that the duke of Philadelphia has a much larger and better-equipped army than I do? He got decimated on his first try. We don't stand a chance of seizing those elven platforms. The whole offer is a ploy to deliver the title to him instead of me."

Benjamin Frankelyn's natural charisma works wonders at calming the baron back down when he says, "Indeed, it *is* perfectly obvious! But why not beat the duke and the cardinals at their own game? All you have to do is be the first one to reach the top of one of the tree-lofted elf platforms."

"Impossible."

"As the Good Book says, all things are possible with God—and I might add, with a little ingenuity. It just so happens that in my adventures, I stumbled across a certain young elve who is the daughter of the leader of the Tuscoraura elves. Send me on a quest to negotiate with her and I am sure we could work out a winning solution to the cardinals' challenge.

"However, my one condition is that you grant me full authority to speak in your name. If I have to run back and forth to get your approval for every stage of the negotiations, it won't work."

Amhirst's reluctance grows softer—but not too soft. He says, "My word is my honor. If you bind me to a treaty in my name, I will honor it. If, however, the treaty costs me too much, you will pay the difference with your head. Are you willing to bet your life that this arrangement will win me the title of governor-general without promising away more than it's worth?"

"Indeed I am!"

Amhirst is not sure how he came around to trusting Benjamin Frankelyn so completely but he says, "You have full authority to speak in my name. Sir Robert Roger, get our frankelyn whatever he needs."

"Thank you, my lord. You might as well start appointing your new gubernatorial staff now. The next time you see me, Vinland will be yours."

Scene 3: The Vandsee Conference

Vandsee Estates, Shentalpee City on Tuscoraura Mountain
Moon Day Nones. Afternoon, 3rd of July, 1284
Morrow of Saint Swithun

Back up on Shentalpee City, umpire-in-chief-elect Florenz Kibblersdottir has invited the deans of the military leagues to her mansion on Vandsee Estates. She addresses them with these words: "Esteemed deans, as you know all too well, we have not been able to drive the Crusade off our lands as quickly and as easily as you originally thought. I have spent the last few days planning the final solution."

Dean Norwall, head of the League of Licornes, interjects, "With your permission, Mademoiselle Umpire-in-Chief-elect, the League of Licornes would like to participate in the final assault against the Crusaders, even if we have to fight dismounted. We believe that our unflagging—"

Florenz cuts her off. "There will be no final assault."

"But you just said—"

"I just said that I have finished planning the final solution to the Crusade, not the final assault against it."

"Excuse me, Mademoiselle Umpire-in-Chief-elect," says Dean Kallel, head of the Justiciar League. "We must attack. Ever since the bankruptcy of the Kibbler workshops, our economy has teetered on the brink of ruin. Our treasury cannot endure the financial burden of a protracted siege! It is better to expend a few extra lives and reduce the surplus population than to have our standard of living collapse."

Florenz chews her nails while the dean talks. When she is done, she spits out the distal edges. "This is why the high elves elected me umpire-in-chief. It seems everyone else fails to see the obvious. The Crusaders are not attacking us because they know *we* will win if they do. We are not attacking them because we know *they* will win if we do. If we do nothing, it comes down to whoever runs out of resources first. High elves are heavy consumers, and the wood elf refugees up here are only making it worse. Right now, the Crusade is poised to win the waiting game.

"As you so clumsily put it, Shentalpee City is encumbered with surplus population. Throwing their lives away will certainly stretch out our supplies a lot longer, but your reports all agree that ridding our city of enough population to win the waiting game would leave us with too few defenders to repulse an assault."

Dean Halvard, head of the Ivy League, points out, "And even if we do defeat the crusading army below us today, they'd just send another one in a few months' time. Is it really worth—"

Florenz cuts in. "As I was about to say before you so rudely interrupted me, I've just made a deal that will keep the Crusaders out of here forever."

She opens the door and behold! Benjamin Frankelyn steps out and delivers an elaborate bow to salute the shocked elf military leaders.

Scene 4: Holy War Mania

Shentalpee City on Tuscoraura Mountain
Tiw's Day Prime. Dawn, 4ᵗʰ of July, 1284
Third of Saint Swithun

As rosy-fingered dawn stretches her arms out at the break of the new day, Sir Robert Roger wakes his rangers from their cozy dorms up on Vandsee Estates, the sycamore platform holding up the Kibbler workshops. Although she trusts Benjamin Frankelyn enough to go along with his plan, Florenz has ordered both bridges leading up to Thor's Base destroyed, just in case the rangers have ideas of their own.

Once the rangers are up and ready, Sir Robert Roger orders his bards, Sir Humbert of Denk and Sir Gilbert Sullivan, to sound their trumpets with the fanfare and pizzazz of an epic, earth-shattering struggle. All the rangers carry empty jars and torches.

He calls out to his rangers, "Look at me and do the same. When I go up to the edge of the platform, do as I do. Shout, 'For the Lord and for Amhirst! God wills it!' Smash your jars on the ground and wave your torches."

The blaring trumpets, the din of crashing clay jars, the whirling of torches, and the wild shouting above rouse the sleeping Crusaders. They come out and climb up on the palisade wall of the camp to spectate.

From below, Sir Sean Madigan, having carefully stationed himself in the middle of the crowd, hypes up the battle with a running commentary: "Oh look! I can't believe it! The Queen's Rangers have made it to the top of one of the elven treetop platforms. And what a battle it is, folks! There goes Sir Robert Roger up against the ropes. Ouch! What a punch! That black-masked elf nearly smacked him over the ledge!

"Here comes Sir Benedict Arnold, his faithful friend, to the rescue. If anyone can teach that heel of an elf a lesson, it's Bonking Benny. The black-masked elf climbs up on the ropes and does a backflip. He flattens Sir Benedict Arnold . . . and that's terrible!

"Wait! I see a comeback brewing like a storm. All those rangers up there are teaming up like superstars!"

Suddenly, Sir Benedict Arnold gets up and bangs his derrière into the oncoming dark-masked elf, knocking him over backwards. Sir Benedict Arnold extends a hand to Sir Robert Roger. He tags him back into the fight.

The Crusaders chant, "Vic-to-ry! Vic-to-ry!"

Meanwhile, high up behind the scenes, Florenz watches the choreographed fight at the edge of the platform next to Benjamin Frankelyn. He hollers, "Oh, look at that suplex finisher! The elves are supposed to pretend to lose by now and there goes your fiancé, hijacking the show!"

Seeing Enganyon's stunning performance, Florenz cannot help but root for him. "Take that!"

With one giant, acrofatic [sic] leap, the ponderous ranger, Sir Febold Feboldson, squashes Enganyon, face to the mat. Cheers rise up from the Crusader camp below. As far as they are concerned, the match is a total and complete victory for the rangers.

Scene 5: A String Quartet

Shentalpee City on Tuscoraura Mountain
Tiw's Day Terce. Morning, 4th of July, 1284
Third of Saint Swithun

Back in the tent of the high inquisitor, Piccolo Cardinal Orsini holds a conference with the duke of Philadelphia and the baron of Amhirst. Despite the apparent victory, the cardinal is displeased and rants, "How did your rangers get up there?"

The baron of Amhirst puts his hands together piously and says, "As it says in the sacred Scriptures, we called upon the Lord, our Rock, and he answered our prayer!"

"We have the holiest clerics in Vinland on our team and our prayers were not answered so dramatically."

Amhirst plays innocent. "Oh, you know how it goes; you get some friends to vouch for you, slip a few coins under the table, drop a few names worth mentioning . . . it smooths the process, even in heaven."

Piccolo Cardinal Orsini leans in and consults with his team and says, "My high-level clerics heard the voice of the Lord, your Rock, and they are saying that the Rock says the Rock has not been mentioned yet! Do not forget that you cannot lie to the Inquisition. We specialize in detecting lies."

"I wouldn't dream of it, Your Eminence! If you want to go into specifics, we had help from a high-ranking elve who was disgruntled with the status quo, blah, blah, blah—I don't need to bore you with the details—"

Piccolo Cardinal Orsini interrupts, "God is in the details, Lord Geoffrey."

"Speaking of details, whatever happened to the . . . you know . . . the way you talked before?"

The high inquisitor is in no mood for chitchat. "What do you mean . . . the way I talked before?"

"'Wascawy wabbit' and all that rot. It's gone."

"If you must know, the tragedy of my brothers' loss spurred me to overcome my speech impediment. Where there's a will, there's a way."

Amhirst whispers loudly as if letting the cardinal in on a special secret, "You're absolutely right, Your Eminence. That is how we are going to capitalize on this victory and bring success to the entire Crusade. Great minds think alike."

"Ha!" laughs the cardinal sarcastically. "Speak for yourself!"

"Trust me, I do, Your Eminence, I do. In fact, I was just telling myself that a promise is a promise, and one long overdue promise is enough to ruin—"

Piccolo Cardinal Orsini stomps his feet. "Okay, okay already! I get your point. You want your reward for completing this quest. My clerical advisors, however, still fear you might have entered into league with some unholy powers to pull this off."

Amhirst sits down and sips the beverage laid out on the table for him, soaking up the moment—he knows he's got the cardinal by the biretta. "In fact, I was going to invite our elve special agent for you to interview."

"I'd prefer to meet no more elves in person. The pain at the loss of my brothers is still too fresh."

"Oh, nothing to worry about there, Your Eminence. I will simply describe her to you. After all, the Holy

Office of the Inquisition knows better than any other human institution how to read the secret thoughts of the clayborn. If I were lying, you would find out in short order, would you not, Your Eminence?"

"Go on. Tell us about this special agent of yours."

"A disgruntled politician. Her name is Zena. She aspired to high office among the fire elves and was betrayed by their current vampire-in-chief. When she's not hell-bent on revenge, she is quite a lovely young elve, and very open to hearing you preach the word of God. Who knows? You might make good Christians out of these pagans. Your common policy on vendetta might help you two get along famously."

The high inquisitor rubs his chin. "Hmmm. *Hell-bent* is a strong term among clerics, but not entirely inaccurate in this case. My inclination is to turn their forest paradise into an inferno. There's a certain poetic justice in destroying Fire Elf City with fire."

Amhirst rubs his chin, mimicking the high inquisitor, and says, "Hmmm, I do see the poetry in that, Your Eminence, but I must warn you that setting it all on fire might not be as productive a strategy as your armchair theologians imagine. I highly recommend having a good conversation with our insider elve. She will tell you the REAL weakness of Fire Elf City. She is hell-bent on revenge—"

Piccolo Cardinal Orsini says, "Could we please stop bending hell so much? Revenge is not as effective a strategy as most people think, and hell does not bend over backwards to help you. It only breaks your back with fruitless desires."

Amhirst comments, "If only your wisdom extended far enough for you to practice what you preach."

Piccolo Cardinal Orsini folds his arms and curls his bottom lip. "When it comes to clerics, it's a totally different issue. 'Vengeance is mine,' sayeth the Lord, 'and I will repay them in due time, that their foot may slide. The day of destruction is at hand, and the time makes haste to come.' As the high inquisitor, it's my business to right the wrongs inflicted against the Lord."

"Forgive me for being such a paltry theologian—being such a successful war leader leaves me less time for books than I would hope. But I might propose the thesis that God is quite capable of handling all that vengeance stuff for himself."

Piccolo Cardinal Orsini is irritated. "You might as well nail ninety-five such theses to a door and see how far that gets you. Regardless, let us get back to more pressing issues. His Lordship, the duke of Philadelphia here, has his dwarves ready to set up weapons of mass destruction to bombard fire and doom upon the entire—"

"Tut, tut, tut," interrupts Amhirst. "We still haven't resolved the matter of my appointment as the crown governor-general of Vinland."

The cardinal waves his hands. "That, of course, goes without saying. We'll have an elaborate inaugural ceremony for you after the—"

"Nope," the baron of Amhirst states firmly. He gets up and tosses his drink on the floor. "Not going to happen. Fool me once, shame on you. Fool me twice, shame on me.

"If I leave this tent without your promised appointment, I am going to order my rangers to withdraw from the platform they conquered and I'm taking the rest of my contingent out of here."

Piccolo Cardinal Orsini threatens, "If you abandon us, I'll excommunicate your fanny from here to the place you like to bend so much."

"Excuse me, Your Eminence, you already tried that threat and it doesn't work, especially not here, one hundred fifty feet below an enemy *hell-bent* on bringing vengeance down upon your head. You won't survive."

At last, the duke of Philadelphia intervenes. "Your Eminence, the baron of Amhirst has a point. Wars aren't cheap. As a feudal lord, I pay wages and have to replace fallen horses. A quick victory makes war profitable, while a prolonged siege can lead to financial ruin, even if we do ultimately win.

"You gave your word that whichever of us should make it to the top of an elven platform first should be named governor-general of Vinland. The baron of Amhirst won that race fair and square. I expect you to honor your word and proceed with the appointment. If you keep breaking your promises, none of us will make it out of here alive."

Piccolo Cardinal Orsini consults with his high-level clerics and says, "My advisors concur. If you don't want an elaborate inaugural ceremony, then we'll simply name you as governor-general of Vinland with a handshake. Satisfied, Amhirst?"

The baron of Amhirst, still standing, replies tersely, "No. I want the paperwork."

The high inquisitor's secretaries busy themselves scribbling up an official scroll and seal it with the pope's own sigil. Piccolo Cardinal Orsini hands it to the baron of Amhirst and asks, "Satisfied now?"

The baron of Amhirst takes his time to scrutinize the document and to consult with his advisors.

With Brother Tuck's guarantee that the document is sound, Amhirst finally turns to the duke of Philadelphia and says, "Done. Your Grace, you may instruct your dwarves to commence operations and burn Fire Elf City to ashes."

Duke William Pinne bows. "With your leave, Your Eminence, I wish to oversee preparations in person."

Piccolo Cardinal Orsini nods and then says, "Does anyone have a fidel or a viol? I think we'll also need a lyre and a harp or . . . um . . . a dulcimer, and maybe a gittern as well."

Puzzled, the duke of Philadelphia asks, "What's all that for? It's a little early to celebrate victory, is it not, Your Eminence?"

"Nero played the fidel while Roma burned, to mourn the loss of all the art and culture around him. We'll need at least a string quartet to properly commemorate the loss of all the learning and artistic treasures up there on Fire Elf City."

Scene 6: Seabiscuits

Shentalpee City on Tuscoraura Mountain
Tiw's Day Terce. Morning, 4th of July, 1284
Third of Saint Swithun

Laughter and merriment abound among the rangers and the elves. Putting on a show of such grandeur and import has formed a sense of camaraderie among the actors, directors, and producers of the spectacle.

Officer Bunzi comes up to Florenz. "Mademoiselle Umpire-in-Chief-elect. The heresiarch summons you."

"Did he say what he wants?"

"No, but he has ordered his acolytes to prepare the transmogrification ceremony."

Florenz's heart is heavy. It's easy to be mean and cruel when everyone else has a shovel full of put-downs for you. But here, the rangers and the military leagues are all celebrating her. If the heresiarch wants to transmogrify her into an emotionless undead state, she'll lose all the joy—and her free will.

She sighs. "It's been a great show so far. Perhaps the final curtain call is coming."

Officer Bunzi asks, "You mean, it's time to smash the Crusaders once and for all?"

"Or lose ourselves to the same lust for power that led the Inquisition here."

She excuses herself from the feast and heads into the brownie workshop where the heresiarch has installed himself, transforming the premises into a sort of blackflame temple. When she opens the door, the heresiarch beckons her to approach his throne. She kneels and bows low, saying in the Black Tongue of Caldor, "What is thy bidding, master?"

Hooded and creepy, the heresiarch replies, "It is time to unleash the full power of the blackflame. The entire Crusade Army must be frozen solid at the very stakes where they intended for us to burn alive. With the destruction of the Crusade, our heresy will spread like wildfire across Vinland. Its cooling flames will give umbrage to generations of minds and spirits who have hitherto been sweltering from the oppression and superstition of the Christian faith."

Florenz recites words of submission. "Reveal to me thy plan, master, and I shall see to it."

The heresiarch says, "The Sword of Layban is now the ultimate power in Vinland. I suggest we use it. The Crusaders will be coming; hoping to claim the Vandsee Estates. Order the human rangers and your military leagues to transmogrify into your faithful thralls. When they do, you will order the attack to begin."

Florenz looks up. "I'm confused. How can I induce them to accept transmogrification, my master? They are lusty men and have a strong love of life. They know it will drain away all feeling and emotions."

The heresiarch lets out a maniacal laugh. "They will have no choice. You will use the Sword of Layban to set all of Vandsee Estates on blackfire. They will have to transmogrify or perish!"

Not liking the sound of that plan, Florenz points out the obvious flaw and hopes plan B will not involve annihilating her childhood home. "This platform is made entirely of wood. There is not enough metal or stone to set the entire estate on blackfire."

"You forget, my pretty, that a good dousing with oil will make almost any object burn with yellow fire. So too, soaking Vandsee Estates with water will make it dark-flammable."

"Where will we get so much water?"

"Johnny Appleseed is a Christian druid with a miraculous gift for calling down rain. Once the rains have fallen for a short while, you will go through every nook and cranny of these estates that you know so well and set them adark."

Florenz squirms inside without showing it on the outside. "The Reverend Appleseed would never cooperate with such a plan."

"He will have no choice. One of my most trusted heretics is none other than the last high inquisitor, whom I told you not to assassinate. He has used his position to convince the feeble-minded Crusaders to set Shentalpee City on fire from below."

"Ridiculous!" snaps back Florenz. "Sequoias are immune to fire."

"We are sitting in the colony's only sycamore grove. Sycamores will burn, with enough kindling. You have already ordered the elves to cut off access to Thor's Base because you didn't trust the rangers. When the Crusaders' fire threatens to engulf Vandsee Estates, Appleseed will have no choice but to call down rain from the heavens. They will all come to you begging for an escape and you will transmogrify them into thralls— perfectly submissive to my bidding!" Already tasting complete triumph on his wormy tongue, the heresiarch cackles. "Go and see to my plan."

Florenz walks out of the blackflame temple feeling rather downtrodden. When she first met the heresiarch, it sounded like using the Sword of Layban would put insane amounts of power into her own hands. It hasn't. Now the heresiarch wants her to destroy her own home, betray her friends and allies, and submit them all to *his* will, not hers.

At the bottom of it all, she really hates the person she has become. She thought that she could fix her problems by getting a little more assertive and pushing back on all the bullies. Now *she* is the big, bad bully that everyone hates and she still has no more control over her problems than she did before.

Slouching around under the weight of these thoughts, the first elf she happens upon is her fiancé, Enganyon. For as pathetic as he can be at times, she's still glad she hasn't executed him—so far.

Feeling like a champion from his rousing performance in the staged fight, Enganyon spots her from a distance and comes over to cheer her up. "Hey there, my beautiful dove! What's got you down?"

She snaps at him, "Doves are white. I'm a dark elf. Couldn't you have thought of a better metaphor?"

Enganyon takes it in stride and says, "Always eager to please, my beautiful raven."

"Ravens make a horrible cackling noise."

Enganyon is puzzled but does not give up. "My sweetly singing nightingale!"

"Nightingales never sing when you need to hear their songs the most."

"Never say never, darling."

"Whatever. I need to speak to the madame Dean of the League of Nations immediately."

He holds out his arm and says gallantly, "Then at least permit me to escort you to her."

Together, they walk toward the storage room where Dungaree Jeanne has set up her headquarters for her budding League of Nations. Enganyon has figured out by now that saying anything is only going to make things worse, so he just holds her and hopes that supporting her physically will help her feel supported emotionally.

When Florenz enters inside, everyone comes to attention and salutes her. Dungaree Jeanne welcomes her, saying in Runic, "Mademoiselle Umpire-in-Chief-elect, you bring light to this place."

Hearing the formulaic fire elf greeting Florenz breaks down sobbing. Her orders are to engulf this place in darkness.

When she recovers from her fit of weeping, she reveals to Dungaree Jeanne the heresiarch's plan to force them all to transmogrify into undead thralls.

A woman of action, Dungaree Jeanne gets up and immediately rushes out with Florenz to warn Johnny Appleseed not to pray for rain; but the raindrops are already falling. She smells the smoke and runs over to the ledge of the platform. Down below, she sees the huge Crusader bonfires burning around the trunks of the sycamore trees holding up Vandsee Estates.

It is worse than she expected. The heresiarch's plan is already in full motion. She asks anxiously around for Johnny Appleseed and they point her to the far end of Vandsee Estates. She shouts, "Reverend Appleseed! Can you stop it from raining?"

He looks at her exhausted and says, "I just prayed for rain to put out the Crusaders' fires."

"The heresiarch is going to use the rain to set all of Vandsee Estates on blackfire. You must stop the rain immediately!"

Johnny Appleseed shakes his head and says, "It's not up to me. God performs the miracles, but I must prepare to invoke his holy name with prayer and fasting. I've prayed and fasted to the edge of my endurance. The bonfires are already raging below. Without the rain, the whole platform'd come tumbling down in short order anyway. I suggest we stop the heresiarch before he sets the blackfires."

Dungaree Jeanne exclaims, "That's the whole problem! He wanted Mademoiselle Florenz to do it for him with the Sword of Layban. She wants to give it to me for safekeeping but I don't trust myself with that kind of power. Could you hold onto it for us?"

Johnny Appleseed backs away. "No, druids aligned to goodness shouldn't even be touching an artifact of such evil. We need someone whose alignment is chaotic enough to hold it and yet whose moral character is somehow selfless enough to use it for good."

Veins bloat on Florenz's temples and neck as the internal struggle with the Sword of Layban puts immense strain on her body and soul. "Please, someone needs to take the sword from me. It is ravaging through my mind, trying to force me to obey the heresiarch!"

Johnny Appleseed says, "He must have the Breastplate of Layban."

"What's that?"

"Layban was immensely wealthy, and not at all stupid. He feared that if he imbued the sword with too much power, it could one day be used against him. So, he had a breastplate secretly forged that subjugated the

328

sword's owner to his will as a thrall. Little did Layban suspect that he would be slain in his sleep by his own sword's blade after passing out drunk."

Florenz groans, "It's making me forget who I am!"

"Wait, that's it!" shouts Zena in Eldric. "Let's give it to the human cleric who doesn't know his name!"

Dungaree Jeanne balks. "Who?"

Zena looks around to get everyone's attention. "Our dearly departed monsieur Lynx dragged me out to the Shade Gap to rescue these same rangers that are up here now from getting sacrificed to the goblin god, Poodoo. The goblins had also captured a young cleric who grew up in a monastery that never told him his real name. That's the one they call Clarke."

Dungaree Jeanne thinks for a moment. "There's no evidence that he has adopted an alignment that will allow him to hold the sword without becoming evil, but we're out of options. It's worth a shot."

Florenz's will is giving out. "Find him quickly! The sword . . . it's freezing my heart."

Appleseed says, "I'll use the gift of prophecy to find him." He closes his eyes for a brief moment and says, "I see him among biscuits—seashell-shaped biscuits."

Florenz crumples to the ground as she urges her will to defy the heresiarch's commands. "The seabiscuit workshop! It's right over there, but I'm feeling so weak. I can't walk a single step farther."

Johnny Appleseed lifts her up, saying, "I can't carry the sword, but I *can* carry you!"

With Johnny Appleseed carrying Florenz cradled in his arms and the Sword of Layban in her hand, she points the way to the seashell biscuit bakery. Inside, a few naughty rangers and elves have set up a fight club with spectators smoking longbotham weed and gambling on the outcome of the fights. Clarke, formerly known as Brother David, is sprawled out on the flour bags sleeping like a baby, but Louis is in the ring trading fisticuffs with Officer Bunzi.

Officer Bunzi leaps to one side of Louis and swivels an arm around his neck, putting Louis in a chokehold. Louis does not even gag. Calmly, he plants two feet on the ground, jumps up as high as he can, tilting backwards, and lands flat on Officer Bunzi with a tremendous thud.

With his body weight and the force of the fall, the impact knocks the air out of Officer Bunzi's lungs.

Cheers go up until suddenly the crowd realizes that the dean of the League of Nations is standing there watching them. Guilty looks and shushing hisses ripple through the seabiscuit bakery.

Zena rushes over to wake Clarke from his sleep and to get the Sword of Layban to him before it chills Florenz's heart. The groggy young monk looks around bewildered at all the attention. Johnny Appleseed lowers Florenz down next to him and asks, "Can you take the sword that is strapped to this elve's back?"

Clarke asks, "What is it?"

"It is a very evil sword that is about to destroy us all. We want to get rid of it but none of us can hold it. Please see if you can handle it."

"Why me?"

"Because your're not a cleric anymore and you're still a good person. Perhaps it's evil won't affect you."

"Not very reassuring." His hand trembles as he reaches for the sword's grip and recoils suddenly when it nips him with its cold evil.

"No," Clarke replies. "I can't touch it either."

Zena looks around and sees some of the members of the improvised fight club trying to sneak out before they get caught for their breach of military discipline. Suddenly she takes inspiration from the moment and barges into the ring. With the flourish of a true showman, she holds up Louis's arm, announcing in her elvish-accented Aenglish, "Big winner!"

They all look around, puzzled; most of all, Louis.

Zena grabs his hand and leads Louis to Florenz. Then she says to her in Eldric, "He's the one! I know it. Give him the sword."

Florenz winces and blinks her eyes as if someone were shining a flashlight in her face. Slowly, weakly, she draws the Sword of Layban from behind her back and holds it out to Louis. He kneels down on one knee before her to receive his prize.

The sword hovers above Louis's outstretched hand. Finally, Louis reaches up and grips it. At that moment, Florenz clutches it even more tightly and rips it out of his grasp, growling, "My precious."

Suddenly, a faint glow of red fills her eyes. Her willpower snaps and the sword takes over. With unearthly vigor, Florenz holds up the sword and shouts, "By the power of Layban . . . I have the power!"

She runs out of the seabiscuit bakery and starts setting her home ablaze with blackflame.

Scene 7: Precious Goods

Shentalpee City on Tuscoraura Mountain
Tiw's Day Terce. Morning, 4th of July, 1284
Third of Saint Swithun

Dungaree Jeanne calls out to the naughty rangers and elves first in Eldric, then in Aenglish, "We must stop her!"

Too late!

By the time they open the door, the blackflame is billowing around them in every direction. Barely does the blackflame touch a crate, a wall, or a puddle before it ignites with chilling violence. The water soon freezes with a hissing, crackling sound. Like a patchwork quilt on a winter's morning, sections of Vandsee Estates here and there whiten with frost and slick over with ice.

The rangers and elves start to run after her but they slip and slide all over the place, scattered like marbles, helpless as turtles spinning on their backs.

The heresiarch marches out of his Blackflame Temple with his acolytes carrying torches of blackflame. The glee of triumph encircles his head and his belly jiggles with scorn and gloating chuckles.

Using the power of the blackflame, his voice booms. He speaks in the Black Tongue of Caldor, but his acolytes translate into Aenglish and Eldric. "Today begins a new world order, where you shall become deathless champions of the Blackflame Cult. Forget whatever you heard about good or evil. Fate has in store for you only two alternative roles—masters and slaves. Come to me and become the masters! I will grant you powers that you never before imagined possible. You will have no fear of death and earthly blades; sickness and injuries will do you no harm. Receive the blackflame!"

The heresiarch's eyes glow red and blackflames sprout from his fingertips. As impressive as the show is, no one volunteers. He continues, "The blackflame is coming whether you like it or not. It surrounds us and is closing in on us. There is nowhere to run, nowhere to hide. Death and cremation are all that await you over those ledges. The only way for you to survive this day is to submit to the blackflame."

Despite their aversion to the blackflame, several elves and rangers reluctantly move toward the heresiarch, seeing no other way to escape death.

Dungaree Jeanne pleads with Johnny Appleseed to share his wisdom. "Please, Reverend Appleseed, tell us how we can stop him!"

As if racked with doubts for the first time since they met him, Johnny Appleseed shakes his head. "Only a weapon forged out of a material intrinsically imbued with fire, blessed by a holy cleric, and charged with the relic of a saint renowned for great ferocity in fighting evil will be powerful enough to destroy the heresiarch."

Dungaree Jeanne asks, "A material imbued with fire? Like what?"

Johnny Appleseed says, "Flint or obsidian or pyrite, or even a wyvern tooth or a phoenix talon."

A drowsy Clarke pulls out his ceremonial dagger. "Did someone say they need a phoenix talon?"

Dungaree Jeanne grabs the dagger from his hand and holds it up to Johnny Appleseed. "Will this do?"

"Yes, but we still need a relic."

Dungaree Jeanne pulls a ruby ring off her finger. "This was the engagement ring that Zena gave to our dearly departed monsieur Lynx. He was wearing it when he laid down his life to save his friends from the ambush that Umpire Gandorf set up for us."

Johnny Appleseed winces. "Sort of. It's only a second-class relic. Holy body parts are much more effective in turning the undead. Still, it won't matter unless we find a holy cleric to bless the dagger. As a druid, blessing objects is not a class skill for me. Only clerics sanctioned by the institutional Church can bestow blessings on objects. The holier the better."

Clarke asks, "What about that big, half-goblin cleric in Benjamin Frankelyn's party of adventurers? He's a canon regular, right?"

Johnny Appleseed says, "Yes, I remember him. As a canon regular, Monsignor Oscar Meyer could do it; but he's not particularly holy. We're only going to get one chance at this and if the dagger fails to turn the heresiarch, we're all going to end up undead thralls, enslaved mind, body, and will to his evil whims."

Dungaree Jeanne settles it once and for all. "If that's what we've got, then that's what we've got." She twists Lynx's engagement ring onto the dagger's handle and gives it back to Clarke. Then she instructs them. "Louis and Clarke, you two go get Monsignor Oscar Meyer to bless this as fast as you can. Time is running out. He should be in Benjamin Frankelyn's headquarters at the end of that alley. The blackflame is spreading quickly, and the rest of us need to find a way to put it out."

No sooner do Louis and Clarke take off than Vampire Kibbler and his team of undead vampires surround Zena, Dungaree Jeanne, and Johnny

Appleseed, and drag them kicking and screaming into the Blackflame Temple. The acolytes bring a pillow for smothering victims into an undead state.

The heresiarch hunches over and says, "Come now, Jeanne, it's time to be a good girl. You will be the first to transmogrify and inaugurate the new world order as my undead servant."

ACT VI

ASHES ASHES
WE'RE ALL SMALL NOW

Scene 1: Return of the Vampire

Shentalpee City on Tuscoraura Mountain
Tiw's Day Sext. Noontide, 4th of July, 1284
Third of Saint Swithun

The platform itself protects most of the fires from the rain, and the bonfires are big enough that those that do get wet billow with blinding, gray smoke. Amid the suffocating clouds, the heresiarch uses the Black Tongue of Caldor to announce his plan in a terrorizing, ear-splitting voice while his acolytes translate. "Hear me, my friends! A manifest destiny has brought you all together up here on this sycamore platform today. Now, you will witness your leader undergo transmogrification into the undead state. When you follow her example, you will become more powerful than you could have ever imagined possible.

"Then together, as my undead warriors, we will march throughout Vinland spreading heresy and liberating the clayborn from the mindless superstition that Vinland's Christians now believe in."

"Never!" shouts Dungaree Jeanne.

Behind the heresiarch, the undead Vampire Gandorf picks Zena up by the throat and holds her over

336

the ledge. The heresiarch says, "Submit, or your daughter dies."

Dungaree Jeanne cries out, "No! Don't harm her. Promise me you won't harm her and I will willingly submit to your transmogrification."

Johnny Appleseed, bound up in ropes, warns her, "Don't do it, Madame Dungaree! The heresiarch is a master of lies. He will promise you anything and once you give in, he won't keep his end of the bargain—but he'll make you pay off your end a hundredfold."

"I'm a mother. I can't let my daughter die."

"Better to be dead and to rest in peace than to be undead and enslaved to the will of that monster."

The heresiarch interrupts, "Theologically speaking, I am a wight—an undead person is a wight. An undead animal is a monster."

"Let her go!" The stern voice comes from the duke of Philadelphia's daughter. She is leading her party of adventurers toward the steps of the Blackflame Temple, backed up by Benjamin Frankelyn, Louis, and Clarke.

The heresiarch laughs at Ariel with scorn. "I have nothing to fear from a little old lady like you."

Out of nowhere, Enganyon comes swinging down on a rope, yodeling with all his might. "A liddle ole ladi hoo?" As he whizzes by, he cuts off his father's hand with a silver dagger. Zena drops over the ledge.

After a few feet of freefall, a rope tied around her ankle runs out of slack and yanks her back up for a short rebound. Officer Bunzi underneath the platform tied a lifeline around her foot during Enganyon's distraction with impeccable timing.

For a few moments, Vampire Gandorf stands still, as if computing the unexpected new data to figure out what to do next. Enganyon smiles cheerfully at the undead effigy of his father and says, "It's me, Enganyon! I'm your son."

The undead father draws his sword and brings down its blade upon his living son without any remorse. Enganyon, armed only with his silver dagger, counters his father's attacks with dodges, parries, and jumps. His father's blows are coming in heavy but slow enough for Enganyon to deflect the attacks and maintain his footing.

Enganyon sidesteps in front of a sycamore tree and Vampire Gandorf chops at him with so much force that his sword lodges itself in the tree trunk. Vampire Gandorf struggles to pry it out. Enganyon takes advantage of the distraction to grab a large, wooden board and slap it over the back of his father's head. He hits so hard that his father's eyeballs pop out.

Enganyon swoops down and tucks the eyeballs away into his belt pouch, thinking it will blind his father. Instead, red lights flicker inside Vampire Gandorf's skull and with two glowing, red orbs in place of his eyes, Vampire Gandorf resumes his attack against his son.

Meanwhile, Willis, Louis, and Monsignor Oscar Meyer charge at Vampire Kibbler and the acolytes holding Dungaree Jeanne down. The combined mass of their body weight alone is enough to bowl them over like so many duckpins, and the acolytes all end up piled on top of each other. Wriggling, squirming, scratching, and slashing at the acolytes, they manage to free Dungaree Jeanne from their clutches.

Watching his plans fall to pieces, the heresiarch screams with thunderous fury, "Destroy them!"

Vampire Gandorf lets go of the sword stuck in the sycamore tree and grabs a hook off a pulley from one of the workshop lifts. He jams the hook into his severed wrist and hisses two words, "Die, son!"

Enganyon rolls behind the sprawling acolytes just as Vampire Gandorf takes another swing at him. This time, his hook sinks into the back of one of the acolytes. An unsettling relief spreads through Enganyon's soul to hear his father acknowledge him as his son. Enganyon calls out, "To die would be an awfully big adventure, dad. How's it working out for you?"

Vampire Gandorf flings the squealing acolyte away to free up his hook and snarls, "Fool!"

Enganyon grabs a black banner resting on a crate and throws it over his father, replying, "A fool, am I? Well then, you're a codfish."

Still more nimble than his undead father, Enganyon dances around him, slashing at him here and there with his silver dagger but not managing to land a direct hit.

Not far off, Florenz, exhausted from her blackflame binge, recovers some shard of her normal self. When she realizes what is going on, she shrieks, "Oh no, watch out for father! Run, Monsieur Enganyon, run!"

Enganyon, chipper and lighthearted as ever, tips his hat and says, "Faint hearts never won a fight, fair lady."

Unfortunately, he doesn't realize that Florenz's warning was not about *his* father, but hers. Vampire Kibbler comes up from behind and clobbers Enganyon with an empty crate, splintering it over his back. The surprise attack sends him down for the count.

Vampire Kibbler drags Enganyon to the heresiarch, who sneers, "Now your transmogrification through the blackflame will be complete."

Helpless, Enganyon shouts, "No! I'm too young to be undead! I love life."

The heresiarch grins, "Oh, but you'll love being undead too! You'll have the joy of bowing to my will."

He places the ceremonial pillow over Enganyon's face to begin the transmogrification ritual. The acolytes chant with a strange droning hum in the background while the heresiarch recites formulaic words in the Black Tongue of Caldor.

Throughout the ritual, the other vampires pin Enganyon's arms and legs to the floor. All he can do is tap on the ground with his left hand. Whoopee sees Enganyon's call for help amidst the tumult and confusion of the fight and uses his magica wand to locomutate away the pillow covering his face. The next moment, Enganyon takes in a deep breath and the transmogrification ritual is broken.

That same instant, the three rangers' apprentices—Louis, Clarke, and Hayle—come charging in recklessly to save the day. Louis buries his two-handed battle-axe in Vampire Gandorf's back. The vampire, barely noticing the blow, spins around, grabs Louis's wrists, and flings him away with an ease that frightens even the most seasoned veterans on the front lines.

Hayle attempts to sneak up on Vampire Kibbler with a wooden stake in his left hand and a mallet in his right. The plan is futile. Vampire Kibbler turns casually around and slaps the implements out of his hands so hard it knocks his whole body to the ground. Hayle rolls to avoid a wicked stomp of the vampire's foot.

Eager to save his friends, Clarke charges straight at the heresiarch, holding his newly blessed phoenix talon infixed with the engagement ring relic of Lynx. The heresiarch grabs him by the neck, but Clarke's right arm is long enough to get behind his foe's neck. With a swift sawing motion back and forth, the phoenix talon chops off the heresiarch's head.

Enganyon crawls over and scoops up the severed head. He rolls it towards the ledge of the platform. Like a painfully slow bowling ball, the head barely reaches the last plank, teeters back and forth three times, then drops over. The heresiarch's head laughs hideously as it plummets, slowly rotating one hundred feet down into the crusader bonfires below.

The headless heresiarch, however, does not die, but his undead body runs off the ledge in search of his head. Everyone looks around, not sure what's next.

Enraged, Vampire Kibbler lets them have it. He holds out his hand and shoots a short burst of blackflame, covering Enganyon with a coat of rime frost. Enganyon squeals worse than if someone dropped an ice cube down the back of his shirt on a hot summer day. "Ahhhhhh!"

Vampire Kibbler kicks him again and sends another spray of blackflame at him. Enganyon rolls and writhes in pain. After another burst of blackflame, Enganyon is shivering pathetically. He calls out to Vampire Gandorf, "Father!"

Johnny Appleseed taps deep into special druid prayers and prays for his enemy—in this case, Vampire Gandorf. A moment of grace awakens compassion in his torpid, undead soul.

Amid the agony of his son's torture, something snaps in Vampire Gandorf. A tear trickles down the glowing orb in his eye socket. Spotting Hayle's wooden stake and mallet, Vampire Gandorf creeps up behind

Vampire Kibbler and places the wooden stake between his shoulder blades. With one tremendous blow, he drives the stake through Vampire Kibbler's chest with the mallet. The archon stone amulet bursts out through the front of his rib cage.

Though missing a hand, Vampire Gandorf hoists the now vulnerable Vampire Kibbler over his head and tosses him over the ledge. Staggering to the ground as the druid's continued prayers restore his soul to its natural state — death — Vampire Gandorf says, "Son, let me see you with my own eyes one last time."

Enganyon takes the eyeballs from out of his belt pouch and hands them back to his father, saying with a worried face, "But you'll die — I guess you are already dead, but I mean, like, for good this time."

"Nothing can stop that now."

Vampire Gandorf pops the eyeballs back into his head and looks at him lovingly. "I love you, my son!"

Enganyon starts to cry. "I love you, Dad!"

As he fades, Vampire Gandorf says, "My son, be honest, even when it hurts . . . or your spirit will spend all eternity running from the truth."

With that, his body slumps back, motionless. Enganyon holds his father's lifeless body and weeps. Although the rains have died down, a tickle of cold reminds him that the blackflames are close to freezing over all of Vandsee Estates.

The rangers and elves are getting hemmed in and huddle up closer to each other for warmth and safety.

Enganyon spots a narrow passageway through the bitter-cold flames and quickly formulates a plan to rescue the survivors but first, he must run a gauntlet through the most grueling ordeal of all — the truth.

Scene 2: Fudging the Truth

Shentalpee City on Tuscoraura Mountain
Tiw's Day Sext. Noontide, 4ʰ of July, 1284
Third of Saint Swithun

Worse than having the sky fall on his head, Enganyon realizes it is time to fess up when Florenz puts an arm around his shoulders. With both tender sympathy and outraged menace, she asks him, "What did your father mean when he said that thing about running from the truth? Is there something you're not telling me?"

With the skill of a master chef, Enganyon cooks up some zesty excuses fast. "First, we need to rescue Zena! Look, she's dangling below the ledge, barely hanging on for dear life. Next, we need to get everyone out of here before they all get frozen solid by the black wildfires you set. Then we need to stop the high inquisitor from taking over Thor's Base.

"When all that's done, we'll have a heart-to-heart."

The rangers and major league elves are already hauling Zena up. Barely escaping the blackflames at her back, Zena rushes to Enganyon and comments, "That was like a crazy trust exercise."

Florenz asks, "But how did she not fall?"

"When our dearly departed monsieur umpire-in-chief ordered my dad to kill Reverend Appleseed, Officer Bunzi came up with a plan to use these emergency escape lines to make it look like we tried to get rid of him but that he miraculously survived. I'm at my best when faking it, so I volunteered for the job."

Enganyon polishes his fingernails on his chest with a smug wink.

Zena asks him, "Speaking of faking it. Were you faking that you were in love with me or are you faking that you're in love with the mademoiselle Florenz?"

"That's 'Umpire-in-Chief-elect Florenz' to you!"

Zena ignores her and focuses on Enganyon's eyes as if to read the truth from the subconscious signals of his body language. Florenz gets curious too and asks, "Yeah, how about it, Captain Enganyon? Are you faking being in love with me?"

Enganyon gets back up on his feet. "Now, now, ladies, if you just give me enough time, I can make you both see the big picture. The problem is, we don't have time right now. We've got to get everyone off Vandsee Estates before the blackflame freezes us all!"

Florenz says, "We're stuck! When we allowed the rangers up here, I had all the suspension bridges on Vandsee Estates destroyed as a safety precaution."

The annoying Officer Bunzi walks up as if he were the savior of the day and proudly announces, "The Justiciar League has a series of emergency chutes and ladders spread throughout Shentalpee City. I was the one in charge of installing them on Vandsee Estates. With the Crusader fires burning down there we can't use the chutes, but just crank that lever over there and it will bring up an escape ladder to Thor's Base."

Dungaree Jeanne is already coughing as the frozen air scalds her lungs. She asks Johnny Appleseed in Aenglish, "We're cut off from that escape ladder. With your vast knowledge of blackflame, can you tell us if there is any way to keep these blackflames at bay so we can make it over there before being engulfed?"

Reverend Appleseed wraps a blanket around her shoulders to warm her and says, "The answer is all around you. Ever notice how Kibbler chocolates always seem to melt in your hand but not in your mouth? Refined cocoa beans are highly susceptible to heat but almost totally resistant to the cold. If we just scatter refined cocoa powder, it will create a safe zone where the blackfires can't touch us."

Brightening with hope, Dungaree Jeanne exclaims, "I know exactly where the cocoa powder is stored."

Johnny Appleseed cautions her, "We'd need to spread around quite a bit. A few handfuls won't do much against flames this high."

Whoopee interjects, "As a magicultor myself, we could work as a team. All we have to do is run a spell to disperse water on fire and tweak it just enough so that it will disperse cocoa on blackflame."

Johnny Appleseed strokes his white beard for a moment as a great philosophical paradox comes to mind. "Magic would work the charm but we face Meno's problem—we don't know what the magic word for spreading cocoa powder is, so we wouldn't recognize it even if we guessed it correctly. Normally, trial and error can solve the paradox, but the imminent danger around us doesn't afford us the luxury of guessing wrong even once.

"If we locomutate the cocoa powder incorrectly, everyone either freezes to death from the blackflame closing in on us or burns to death from the bonfires raging below us."

Zena steps forward and says in Aenglish, "I know it! I know what is magic word for spreading cocoa powder everywhere!"

The first to doubt is, of course, her mother. "How's that even possible? You haven't even begun your studies as a magicultor!"

A subtle trembling sound soon turns into a mighty rumble as the wooden flooring shakes beneath their feet. The bonfires down below have weakened major sycamore branches and consumed vital support beams. With the alternations of freezing-cold blackfires up top and burning-hot yellow fires beneath, the very foundations of Vandsee Estates crack and shudder. Large chunks of floorboarding splinter upwards nearby while faraway buildings collapse.

The forces of nature rending wood and toppling sycamores reverberate with deafening fright, like the pulsed shrieks of a blue whale whose calf is beset by orcas. What little space is left to the survivors from the dark wildfires around them just got cut down by one-third from the crumbling planks and floorboards. Rangers and major league elves scramble and roll away from sharp slivers and widening gaps, desperate for a stable place to fix their feet.

Frightened by the upheavals, Zena lets nonsense syllables dribble out of her mouth. "Oh, fudge!"

Keep in mind, dear reader, that as of the year 1284, fudge had not yet been invented, and the word itself at that time had no meaning.

Whoopee looks at Johnny Appleseed, shrugs, and says, "Oh, fudge? Zena's magic words sound good enough to me. On my mark, we will cast her spell in harmony for maximum effect."

Dungaree Jeanne points to a warehouse, now separated from them by a gaping chasm. "All the cocoa bean powder is in there, but we can't get to it!"

Whoopee says, "If the magic word is good enough, we'll be able to grab the cocoa powder from back here and locomutate it in puffs so it spreads evenly along the path to those emergency ladders."

Johnny Appleseed pulls out the magica wand that he stores in the handle of the tin pot on his head and nods to Whoopee. "Let's do this!"

They count to three and together shout out in a commanding but melodious tone, "Oh, fudge!"

POOF!

Suddenly, it is snowing cocoa powder and all the rangers and major league elves let out thrilled cheers as the dark wildfires back off, leaving them sneezing but safe all along the corridor to the escape ladders, with a delicious chocolatey aftertaste in their mouths.

From there, it's not long before Enganyon and Officer Bunzi hoist the emergency escape ladders and start guiding the survivors up toward Thor's Base as the rest of the flooring planks and wooden structures collapse behind them on Vandsee Estates.

Being a noble leader, Dungaree Jeanne makes sure everyone is on their way toward safety before allowing herself to escape. Once she is standing on Thor's Base, she shouts out orders, looping her words in Eldric and in Aenglish. "Listen up! We've got work to do, people! First off, Officer Bunzi, take the Justiciar Leaguers, along with Sir Jon Stark's rangers, to post guards at all the chutes and ladders on Thor's Base that you know of. Make sure no one can sneak up on us, and assess which ones offer us the best escape routes.

"Next, Mademoiselle Umpire-in-Chief-elect, I am going to request that you and your Ivy Leaguers take Sir Robert Roger's rangers to the aqueduct. See if you can jury-rig a way to take all non-combatants to the mountain dwarves' vault at the peak.

"Reverend Appleseed, may I ask you to help Lady Philippa's party of adventurers find a way to counter the threat of blackflame up here? We narrowly escaped Vandsee Estates with the cocoa powder. We don't want to find ourselves in double jeopardy.

"Finally, I will work with the League of Licornes and Sir Benedict Arnald's rangers to build barricades to fence off any points of access the Crusaders might use to assault Shentalpee City. We'll also figure out the best tactical locations to set up elf fire siphons in case it comes down to street-to-street fighting. We're safe for the moment, but in a siege like this, the enemy will probably try to find a traitor to open a way—"

Enganyon tugs on her sleeve as sheepishly and as insistently as a little kid asking for apple juice in the middle of a crowded bus.

He stutters, then says, "Um, we're not all that safe up here at the moment."

The comment makes no sense to Dungaree Jeanne, so she asks tentatively, "What do you mean, Captain Enganyon? As far as I can tell the Crusaders' bonfires have had no effect on the sequoias and there's no sign of blackflame in any—"

"Um," he interrupts. "I'm not worried about fire."

Fearing where that's going, Zena flips the archon stone that came out of Vampire Kibbler's heart up in the air and catches it in her palm, saying, "Mother, I believe I owe you one of these. That's the last of the invincible undead we'll ever have to face." Zena glares at her ex-fiancé and says, "Right, Captain Enganyon?"

"Well actually—now that you mention it—it just so happens that the last high inquisitor is coming up a secret passageway with an invincible undead army to destroy Thor's Base."

Florenz doesn't give Enganyon a chance to speak further. "That's impossible! My father was the only one who knew about the secret passageway and he would never betray that secret—alive or undead."

Enganyon starts to fidget. "Well, you see, where there's a will, there's a way. I found out about it so when your dad was still alive . . . or still undead . . . I was kind of angry with you and him for killing my father, so I sort of—"

"Yes?"

"I sort of cut a deal with the Inquisition."

Scene 3: Three isn't Company

Shentalpee City on Tuscoraura Mountain
Tiw's Day Nones. Afternoon, 4ᵗʰ of July, 1284
Third of Saint Swithun

"You what?"

Staring at the floor, Enganyon mutters under his breath, "I hate telling the truth."

Florenz gets in his face. "You betrayed us to the Inquisition? How could you?"

At last he looks her in the eyes and says, "Well, not us. Just you. I only wanted to betray you."

Florenz throws up her arms. "So you really love Zena after all? I thought you loved me!"

"I do love you . . . and kind of hate you too. You're awfully mean sometimes. This is awkward. Not that you're awkward, but because we're . . . I'm awkward. You're gorgeous. Wait, what?"

Zena tries to help him. "Mademoiselle Florenz, you did send that giant undead dwarf to kill us all. As far as I know, you haven't bothered apologizing yet."

"That's Umpire-in-Chief-elect Florenz to you, missy," she reiterates, and then adds, "Besides, true love means never having to say you're sorry."

Dungaree Jeanne drops her jaw and says, "That's the dumbest thing I ever heard."

Florenz ignores her and continues ranting at Enganyon. "So just because of a little misunderstanding like that, you betrayed me?"

Enganyon starts to find his footing and says more confidently, "Yes! No! I wouldn't call that a little

350

misunderstanding, more like a dynastic feud. I was also pretty peeved that you got elected umpire-in-chief instead of me. Somewhere between revenge and ambition, I figured it was time to make a deal."

Zena pulls his shoulder to point him in her direction and says to his face, "You said that you wanted *me* to get elected umpire-in-chief."

"Well, my political ambitions evolved."

Florenz pulls him in her direction and shouts in his face, "So you made a deal with the enemy? Traitor!"

"No, no, no! I'm a patriot! I couldn't let an undead wight seize control of the government and throw out the Magnificent Charter. My primary goal was to restore our way of life according to the vision of our Founding Mothers and Fathers."

Zena pulls him back her way and says, "Okay, forget all that rhetoric for now. Let's get back to the essentials—what exactly is this deal that you made with the high inquisitor?"

Enganyon turns to look at Florenz straight in the eyes and says, "So I was sort of supposed to show them a secret passageway up to Thor's Base in exchange for arresting you and making me the next umpire-in-chief of Shentalpee City."

Florenz exclaims, "I knew it! You betrayed me!"

Zena interrupts, "Does that mean you really love me? You said your heart always belonged to Florenz."

Enganyon replies, "No! Yes! I mean, my love is really . . . look, can we deal with the fact that the high inquisitor is going to come through that secret passageway any moment now? When we are all safe and alive, I'll tell you both anything you want to hear."

Although she was invested in her relationship with Enganyon, what is really causing turmoil in Florenz's heart is her struggle with the revelation that he might have outmaneuvered her politically.

It's one thing to have a gutless, sleazy, two-timing boyfriend. It's another thing entirely to get outwitted at the game you've always believed you play the best. She looks him straight in the eyes and says, "Look! It's not a problem anymore. My dad's secret passageway has been destroyed by the fires."

"There's another one you don't know about."

Florenz gives him a wry face. "My dad would never build a secret passageway that I don't know about."

"Never say never."

"You just did, twice."

"By Thor's beard, I can't win with you, can I?"

"Nope."

"Unfortunately, I did win this time." Instead of arguing any further, Enganyon throws his silver dagger at the trunk of Frige's Tree. It stands there trembling.

From deep inside, drums pound. The silver dagger keeps on vibrating as the pounding grows louder and faster. *Boom! Boom! Boom!*

Like rowdy football players bursting through their team banner, crazed undead ghouls burst through the bark and rush onto Thor's Base.

Scene 4: A Song and a Dance for the Lord

Shentalpee City on Tuscoraura Mountain
Tiw's Day Nones. Afternoon, 4th of July, 1284
Third of Saint Swithun

For as untamed and as savage as their pep rally seems, as soon as Piccolo Cardinal Orsini makes his entrance, the undead ghouls show perfect discipline in lining up in two straight rows beside him. Arrayed in his red cardinal robes, red satin slippers, and wide-brimmed red cardinal hat, the cardinal has added one piece to his wardrobe that escapes no one's notice—the Breastplate of Layban. It is charred from the heresiarch's plunge into the bonfires but otherwise fully intact and exuding a chilling evil.

When the high inquisitor's eyes fall on Florenz he shouts in the Dark Tongue of Caldor, "Well if it isn't Miss hoity-toity Umpire-in-Chief Florenz Kibblersdottir herself! You've escaped us for the last time! Never again will your pointy ears prickle our plans for the people of Vinland."

Florenz pounds her index finger on Enganyon's chest and says, "I'll deal with you later." Then, turning to face the high inquisitor, she yells in Dark Tongue of Caldor, "Thou art supposed to be a lawful cleric—praying and preaching the word of God. Thou hast no business dabbling in necromancy. How darest thou play at being a god by commanding all these undead thralls!"

The high inquisitor replies, booming his voice out as the heresiarch did. "Oh, they're not thralls at all, dearie. They're *ghouls*.

"Without freedom, you can't inspire a true fighting spirit among the clayborn. The Crusaders learned that lesson from infidels in the Holy Land. Instead of serfs, they rely on elite freed slaves called ghoulams to fight their battles for them. While my brother cardinals were busy fighting heretics, I've been interviewing them.

"My stroke of genius has been to raise up an army of undead warriors behind their backs. But my legions are not abject slaves. These ghouls have embraced their undead condition and fight with free will. They are more than a match for your enthralled vampires."

While he is speaking, Dungaree Jeanne leans into Florenz's ear and says, "Keep him monologuing as long as possible. I've got a plan, but I need you to buy me some time."

Florenz nods and replies to the traitorous high inquisitor in the Black Tongue of Caldor, "You speak the Black Tongue of Caldor so fluently. Only those of an evil alignment can do so . . . it's as if you've been evil for a long time. How could your brothers, the high inquisitors, not notice?"

The high inquisitor takes the hook and he starts to monologue away the element of surprise from his surprise attack. "It started with my speech impediment. None of the holy Christian healers could help me. They said God wanted me to endure this defect as a thorn in my side, like Saint Paul.

"Then one day, a blackflame missionary cured it with a single touch. It was then that I knew there were untapped powers in the Blackflame Cult that I could never master as a Christian cleric, but I had to be cautious. I played dumb. I pretended I still had the speech impediment and intentionally made lots of idiotic comments. My brothers were so convinced I was stupid that in their arrogance, they did not bother to investigate my strange behaviors any deeper. My power grew right under their noses. Now I am more powerful than the heresiarch ever was."

Florenz is playing him, but she is also genuinely curious how he got his powers. "More powerful than the heresiarch? How's that even possible?"

Somehow, he seems to grow bigger and louder. "Ever heard of a wolf in sheep's clothing? By betraying my holy calling, I have reached lower levels of evil much faster than the heresiarch ever could, because he was openly evil. Now I'm a big, bad wolf and I'm going to huff and puff and blow your houses down!"

The high inquisitor heaves his chest and his breath explodes with blackflame—not just one or two feet in front of him, but dark fire streams forward with unnatural power twenty, thirty feet in front of him, igniting the wet planks and merchant stalls around him. As he blows, a hoary frost crinkles over his beard.

"Not by the frosty hairs of your chubby little chin," says Florenz as she raises the Sword of Layban and signals to the remaining vampires to attack the high inquisitor. "Time to avenge this reckless assault on Shentalpee City!"

Though wild and ferocious, the high inquisitor's ghouls nonetheless form up ranks and fight with discipline and coordination. As promised, they are more than a match for the elf vampires who come at them helter-skelter. The elf vampires never counted on fighting undead peers. They have no silver weapons, no holy relics, no fire attacks. The cardinal's ghouls are equipped with all three.

The combat is brief. The best and the brightest from among the undead elves, the vampire avengers of Shentalpee City, the cream of the crop from among high elf society, the fieriest of all the fire elves—lay scattered and dismembered, piece by piece, across the floorboards of Thor's Base. Seeing how easily the high inquisitor's ghouls cut down their vampires, the Major League elves scream to each other in a desperate panic, "What shall we do?"

Dungaree Jeanne reappears and holds up her hands, waving for their attention, and says in both Aenglish and Eldric, "Everybody, listen up! Calm down! I've got a plan that will save us!"

Sir Robert Roger shouts, "Quick, put it into action! The high inquisitor is hell-bent on revenge!"

Dungaree Jeanne says, "As the dean of the League of Nations and the founder of the real New World Order, I encourage you all in this moment of crisis to stick to our motto. In God we trust! We must put our trust in the Lord!"

Sir Robert Roger sours his face. "What kind of plan is that?"

As the high inquisitor's ghouls march relentlessly forward, the Major League elves and rangers step back, feeling utterly helpless. As he goes, the high inquisitor blows forth streams of blackflame across the still wet platforms of Thor's Base. Though the rains have stopped, the freezing darkflames turn the soggy wood into brittle ice. The high inquisitor places his blackflame attacks so precisely that he seems to intentionally herd the survivors into a smaller and smaller area.

Taking up Dungaree Jeanne's rallying call, Johnny Appleseed sings and dances. "Oooooh, the Lord is good to me, and so I thank the Lord for giving me the things I need; the sun and the rain and the apple seed. The Lord is good to me. Amen! Amen! Amen! Amen!"

They mock and insult him for looking so silly at such a crucial time when their lives are nearing the ropes' edge of Thor's Base.

At that moment, Amhirst's independent-minded ally, Lord Samuel Maverick, comes sliding down the aquifer hollering like Tarzan and leading a train of swashbucklers who specialize in combating the undead. It's time to even up the score.

Scene 5: The Battle of the Four Armies

Shentalpee City on Tuscoraura Mountain
Tiw's Day Nones. Afternoon, 4ᵗʰ of July, 1284
Third of Saint Swithun

Lord Maverick's swashbucklers are all equipped with blessed silver blades and bucklers with holy icons painted on them. From behind the high inquisitor and his ghouls, the great dwarf Lawspeaker Sturl Snorrison emerges from the same secret passageway in Frige's Tree that the high inquisitor and his ghouls used. Behind him step forth several ranks of crossbow dwarves equipped with hammerhead bolts doused in holy water.

Johnny Appleseed says, "An answered prayer."

Sir Robert Roger replies sharply, "It had nothing to do with prayer! You just happened to be praying moments before we got rescued."

Lord Maverick calls out, "O ye of little faith! No time for palavering. Let's nip these ghouls in their undead hienies!"

A perfectly coordinated volley of dwarven hammerhead crossbow bolts flies out and blows large chunks off the ghouls' flesh with each hit. The line of ghouls falters and loses cohesion.

Taking advantage of the muddle, the swashbucklers leap at the ghouls with their silver swords. Swaying gracefully around them with the synced rhythms of grandfather clocks, the swashbucklers cut the ghouls down a notch, then fall back while the crossbow dwarves shoot off another volley of holy water bolts.

Keeping focused, the cardinal sends out more blackflame to wreak destruction upon the brilliant art and culture enshrined around him upon Thor's Base.

Seeing their tactical situation deteriorating, the ghouls drop their weapons and tear strips off their shirts to wave as flags of surrender. Lawmaker Sturl Snorrison calls out in Latin, "Your ghouls have surrendered. It's time for you to yield. I wish to thank you, Your Eminence, for monologuing long enough for our warriors to get into position. You are now quite surrounded."

"No, Lawspeaker, it is you who have allowed me time to surround you!" His laugh is more like the high-pitched squeal of a pig eager to roll in manure.

As he speaks, the Knights Templar, the Knights Hospitaller, and the Knights Paladin emerge from the same secret passageway in Frige's Tree behind the dwarves. With the ghouls in front of them and the most elite fighting force in Vinland behind them, the dwarves' tactical advantage evaporates.

Johnny Appleseed calls out to the holy warriors with these words in Aenglish, "O brothers in Christ! You know that the Inquisition has been chasing me for years because I have been distributing blackflame as part of my mission against hunger in Vinland. I knew that blackflame could have destructive applications, but I have never used blackflame for any other purpose than to give relief to the feverish and preserve food from spoiling.

"Your high inquisitor has chosen to use blackflame both as a weapon, though it is banned by Church law, and for necromancy, which God forbids in the Bible. Ask yourselves—are you serving God by killing innocent clayborn for no other purpose than to win for the Church a monopoly on blackflame weaponry?

"By attacking us, you would be making the One, Holy, Catholic, and Apostolic Church no better than the great and abominable Blackflame Cult."

The Elect Radisson speaks for the rest when he says in Aenglish, "Reverend Appleseed, your words ring true and cut us to the heart. However, you must remember that we are both warriors and monks. In both capacities, our highest obligation is to obey the commands of our superior officers, even if they ask us to forfeit our lives. We cannot disobey orders simply because our individual, private consciences tell us that our commander is in the wrong."

While the elect speaks, Brother Clarke runs over to Lawspeaker Snorrison and explains Appleseed's words to him in Latin since he knows almost no Aenglish. The Lawspeaker nods and then calls out to the holy knights in Latin, "As lawspeaker for the Tuscoraura Mountain dwarves, my training has made me proficient not only in the ancient Axenhower Code of the Whaler Dwarves, but also in the Alfheim legal tradition. I am also familiar with Aenglish Common Law and Roman Civil Law. Finally, I spent several months memorizing Canon Law and discussing it with the most learned clerics in Vinland.

"If my memory serves me right, Canon Law states that using blackflame for necromancy is an act that can be punished by excommunication. An excommunicated prelate has no authority to give commands to faithful Christians. That means that Piccolo Cardinal Orsini is no longer your legitimate commanding officer. You are free to decide what is right for yourselves."

Brother Jack de Molay, leading the Knights Templar, replies, "You make a good point, but you forget that he must be tried and found guilty by an ecclesiastical court before we can be released from our vows of obedience to him."

The lawspeaker clears his throat, thinks for a short while, then calls out in Latin, "Correct me if I'm wrong but, as I recall, when Pope Gregory instituted the Papal Inquisition, he had it officially codified in Canon Law and explained in the *Liber Extra* of 1234. In it, he states specifically that anyone who transmogrifies a living person into an undead state, or even oversees any such ritual, incurs a *latae sententiae* excommunication. That means that the act itself automatically excommunicates him without the need for an ecclesiastical trial."

Brother Oliver Roland, leading the Knights Paladin, says, "As you know well, we don't fight for the sake of approval or honors among the clayborn. We fight because it is just and right in God's eyes. Although we have overwhelming circumstantial evidence before us, there is no solid proof that he transmogrified these ghouls or that he oversaw any transmogrifications."

Hearing this, Johnny Appleseed announces in Aenglish, "That's a simple matter to settle! We'll ask them." Johnny Appleseed calls out, "O ye ghouls! Speak, friends, and tell us true. Were you transmogrified to your current undead state by Piccolo Cardinal Orsini? If so, raise your right hand."

Nearly half of the ghouls raise their hands. Johnny Appleseed folds his arms and nods. "Any questions?"

Brother Oliver Roland of the Knights Paladin turns and announces in Aenglish, "There is no more room for doubt. Piccolo Cardinal Orsini has chosen to side with infernal powers and has brought upon himself an excommunication by Holy Mother the Church.

"As the highest-level cleric in the present company, that makes me the commanding officer of the crusading forces at Tuscoraura Mountain." Then, turning to the ghouls he addresses them, saying, "O ye ghouls! Choose your side! The cardinal has no authority to give you orders in the name of Holy Mother the Church. Will you join the Knights Paladin under my command, or will you persist in following this excommunicated cardinal down the path of perdition?"

The ranks of ghouls waver. Eventually, one ghoul steps forward and joins the Knights Paladin. One by one, the voice of reason calls a large minority of ghouls out from service with the fallen high inquisitor to the Order of the Knights Paladin.

Though not all are fully aware of the momentous historic event taking place before their eyes, a loud cheer rises up among the clayborn on Thor's Base—all the rangers, the crossbow dwarves, the swashbucklers, and the Major League elves celebrate the first time in history that ghouls have been counted among the clayborn in the fight against evil.

Scene 6: Ghoul Busters

Shentalpee City on Tuscoraura Mountain
Tiw's Day Nones. Afternoon, 4th of July, 1284
Third of Saint Swithun

Still, the majority of ghouls remain firm to their pledges of service to the fallen high inquisitor. Not in the slightest intimidated at having part of his army of ghouls defect, the high inquisitor claps sarcastically and laughs with scorn. "Oh, very clever. Very clever indeed. You know, choosing evil was a hard decision at first, but what I love most about being wicked is that *I always get to win.*"

With that, he blows a stream of blackflame at the Knights Paladin, staggering them all back and freezing the breath from their lungs until they are gasping for air. The Hospitaller Commander-elect Radisson gets enraged at his insolence and charging in with a spear, surges forward for a personal attack against the high inquisitor. The Elect Radisson jams his spear clear through the Breastplate of Layban.

With mocking derision, the cardinal exclaims, "Oh! Look at that! I've been impaled."

The high inquisitor pulls the spear out of his chest and slaps Brother Radisson on the head with the spear's handle so hard it knocks him out cold. As the Elect Radisson sleeps soundly on the platform floor, the high inquisitor taunts them, "Remember when I said I'm even more powerful than the heresiarch, and nobody believed me? The Breastplate of Layban does more than stop pointy sticks. Watch and weep!"

The whole earth trembles and shakes as the high inquisitor stretches out his arms. From near and far the hacked limbs and chunks of ribs and slabs of raw meat and shattered skulls from all the dead animals and clayborn on the battlefields on high and down below recombine into one huge, hideous collection of rotting flesh and bone, encasing him like armor. So much carnage from the death and destruction of the last two days clings to his body and the padding around him that he grows five feet all around. With the cadaverous armor, the high inquisitor transforms into an undead titanoghoul fifteen feet tall.

"What is that?" asks Zena.

Clarke comments, "It's heinous. It looks like he's covered himself in a million watermelons."

Louis asks, "How does he stay puffed up like that? The body parts should just cave in on themselves, shouldn't they?"

Johnny Appleseed says, "If I remember the lore of Layban correctly, the Breastplate of Layban weaves together carnage to form an undead suit of armor."

The stay-puffed watermelon wight belches out blackflame from its muzzle, instantly freezing all the holy warriors within range. The survivors charge with selfless courage. This time around, the Knights Paladin have met their match. Its huge arms swipe at them with sharp, bony claws, dismembering them instantly. Although their weapons gouge large holes in its meat-bone armor, its dismembered victims are sucked back into the gaps, filling them up and boosting its strength.

Florenz draws the Sword of Layban and asks Dungaree Jeanne, "Can we defeat this stay-puffed watermelon wight with this?"

Dungaree Jeanne consults with Johnny Appleseed and then replies in Eldric, "He says it's too dangerous. If those streams of blackflame from the Breastplate of Layban hit the stream from the Sword of Layban, you would be instantly killed, and it might rain blackflame over the entire span of Shentalpee City."

"But would it kill the cardinal too?"

Dungaree Jeanne repeats Florenz's question in Aenglish and Johnny Appleseed replies, "You bet your bottom dollar it'd kill him; but the sun won't come out over Tuscoraura Mountain for a long time!"

Although the dwarf hammerhead bolts pummel the behemoth wight with each volley, it crashes into them with a horrid stomp, crushing even the finest armored dwarves with the sheer weight of corpses. The Knights Hospitaller clamber forward on the icy floorboards, half of them slipping and skidding on the ground before they even attack.

The stay-puffed watermelon wight spits a long stream of blackflame and freezes one after another. Then it steps on the frozen Hospitallers, shattering them like icicles crashing down from broken shingles and it adds their remains to its abominable hide.

Florenz weighs the options and comes to the only possible conclusion. "So many lives lost . . . we have to cross the streams."

Enganyon butts in, "Wait! Reverend Appleseed just said that crossing the streams is bad. That would be suicide."

With a swat of its arm, the mega-wight knocks over the aqueduct's spout and splashes the water in every direction. It then ignites the growing puddle with its blackflame breath. As the aqueduct pours more water into Thor's Base, the flames rise higher and the chill bites deeper into the bones of the living. With a burst of bulbous laughter, the stay-puffed watermelon wight heaves its belly back as it watches Thor's Base ice over.

Florenz announces without taking her eyes off her adversary, "The evil cardinal is unstoppable. It's the only chance the Tuscoraura elves have to survive this."

Enganyon thinks it over for a second and suddenly grows very supportive. "You know what? I love this plan. I'm excited about this plan. Where do you get these amazing ideas?"

Florenz hoists the Sword of Layban over her head and cries out, "By the power of Layban . . . I have the power!"

Johnny Appleseed waves his arms and calls to her in Aenglish. Dungaree Jeanne translates, "He says the only way to destroy the cardinal is if he blows his stream of blackflame directly onto the stream from the Sword of Layban. If the cardinal kills you any other way, you will have given your life for nothing."

The stay-puffed watermelon wight continues to trash Thor's Base by freezing the outdoor amphitheater with streams of blackflame. Florenz charges in with the Sword of Layban flaming, but the stay-puffed watermelon wight swats her with a backhand and knocks her senseless into the Gazebo Cafe's garden.

Louis and Clarke see her go sprawling. Aware of what's at stake, Louis takes up the sword but he doesn't know how to make it go flaming. He shouts over to Johnny Appleseed, "How do I get it to work?"

Johnny Appleseed tells him the formulaic words and Louis repeats them carefully, "By the power of Layban . . . I have the power!"

The sword kicks up a puny blackflame that soon peters out. Louis tries it again and again with the shaky fingers of a chain-smoker who cannot get a lighter on long enough to keep up his streak.

As the stay-puffed watermelon wight rampages on, it grabs a vegetable stand and hurls frozen tomatoes at the rangers. Louis loses patience and lets out a lion's roar as he charges forth. In his rage, the paltry blackflame of Layban suddenly leaps out and hits a new high with its ferocity.

The stay-puffed watermelon wight belches out blackflame across Thor's Base and Louis swings the sword to cross the streams. Right before contact, Louis steps on a slick patch of ice and his feet go flying up in the air. With a nasty *boink*, the back of his head rebounds off the ground twice before settling and the Sword of Layban goes skidding off in another direction.

Enganyon figures out that Louis's plan B is not going as well as hoped. He cradles Florenz in his arms and slaps her cheeks gently. "Come on, baby! Wake up! Don't leave us yet."

She blinks a few times, then turns to Enganyon with a weak voice. "Yes, you're right. I started this mess, I have to finish it. Before I go, I just want to know if you truly love me, Monsieur Enganyon."

Enganyon stutters, "I'd enjoy kissing you. I mean, I'd like to. Is that love? Wait, what?"

Dungaree Jeanne says, "Love is putting someone else's needs before yours. Lynx charged into the maw of the wyvern to keep it away from Senior Officer Onashelf. Lynx never had romantic feelings for her, but he loved her enough to lay down his life for her."

Enganyon sneaks over and picks up the Sword of Layban. He shivers violently from the cold, then drops it. Wrapping his hat around his hand, he picks it up again and says, "If that's what love is, then some people are worth freezing for. I will cross the streams for you, Mademoiselle Florenz."

His hands tremble and he drops it again. Even using his hat as a mitten, the sword is just too cold and inwardly chilling for him to hold onto it for long.

Tears well up in her eyes and she says, "You can't. Your neutral alignment won't allow it. Only I can do this. Just kiss me before you go."

They share a passionate kiss. Enganyon whimpers as if waking up to a whole new world that he never knew was right in front of him all along.

Zena gives her a deep hug and says, "For all those years we played together as little girls, I've loved you and envied you as only a little sister knows how. Florenz, please don't go. You'll freeze!"

She takes up the Sword of Layban with an unshakable resolution in her eyes and says, "The cold never bothered me anyway."

As the stay-puffed watermelon wight rampages toward the last of the beautiful buildings on Thor's Base—the basilica—it pauses before the colossal statue of Thor as if to admire its workmanship for a brief moment. Then it heaves its putrefied chest and belches forth such a tremendous tidal wave of blackflame that snow flurries billow out like a mushroom cloud around it. Then it pummels the statue until it collapses.

Florenz catches up to her foe just as it lays into the tympanum of the basilica with its right foot. Outraged, she shouts, "Nobody steps on the basilica in my city!"

With that, Florenz Kibblersdottir ignites her sword and charges with unflinching courage at the undead giant. The stay-puffed watermelon wight turns and wrinkles its hideous face with unmitigated hatred. Out of blind spite, it unthinkingly blows out a concentrated stream of blackflame that crosses streams with Florenz's flaming blade.

Both freeze over instantly.

A gentle calm blankets the scene.

Silence.

Clarke's voice rings out, "He said he always gets to win but evil always loses in the end!"

Johnny Appleseed cautions them all, "Step back, everyone! It's not over until the flat navel spins."

"What?"

From the middle of the frozen watermelon wight's belly button, cracks start to appear with a *poing*. They start spider-webbing all over his frozen body. The first part to break away is the flat part around its navel. It starts spinning slowly, then faster and faster.

Johnny Appleseed looks up and shouts, "Run! Run for your lives!"

Scene 7: Fallout

Shentalpee City on Tuscoraura Mountain
Tiw's Day Vespers. Evening, 4th of July, 1284
Third of Saint Swithun

Thanks to Officer Bunzi's Justiciar Leaguers and Sir Jon Stark's rangers, most of the escape chutes have been deployed by now. The survivors evacuate Thor's Base in a quick and orderly fashion. Everyone makes it safely to the wood elf villages below in the nick of time.

KABOOM!

After a long wind up, the high inquisitor's frozen corpse explodes, spewing blackflame up and over the forest canopy. Clouds of dust and frozen vapor stifle the skies.

The force of the explosion rattles Tuscoraura Mountain down to the bedrock beneath the dwarven tunnels. Wreckage from the black wildfires collapses, shards of ice rain down, and frozen debris comes crashing from above upon one and all. Elves, humans, gnomes, and dwarves huddle under whatever shelter they can find.

As the fallout starts to settle, Enganyon sees Louis and Clarke. One of them is carrying the Sword of Layban but he can't tell which one. (All humans look the same to elves.) Though not sure exactly why he is outraged by the sight, it bothers him to the core. He runs over and starts shouting at the human in Eldric.

"He doesn't speak a word of Eldric, Monsieur Enganyon." It's Zena. She stews with anger at him.

"But he's got the mademoiselle Florenz's sword!"

"The mademoiselle Florenz is gone! Why can't you get that between your pointy ears?"

Dungaree Jeanne steps in and says, "Because she's not gone. In fact, she's right here."

Enganyon stares at her in silence for a moment.

Zena gasps, "What?"

Dungaree Jeanne points to the sword and explains in Eldric. "I asked Reverend Appleseed to pray for a miracle to bring the mademoiselle Florenz back to life. He prayed and informed me that she is not dead. Apparently, crossing the streams trapped her soul inside the Sword of Layban.

"It also trapped the high inquisitor's soul inside the Breastplate of Layban when he exploded, but the force of the blast must have flung the breastplate several miles from here. When Florenz's body shattered, the Sword of Layban landed at Louis's feet. It's as if she wanted him to have it next."

Enganyon replies, "With all due respect, Madame Dungaree, I could never believe such nonsense."

Dungaree Jeanne says in Aenglish. "Reverend Appleseed, he says he could never believe that the mademoiselle Florenz is inside the sword."

Appleseed prays for a moment and looks up. "Tell Enganyon that Florenz tells him never to say never."

Enganyon gasps when he hears the translation.

Zena stammers a bit then asks in halting Aenglish, "Mademoiselle Florenz, she is really in sword?"

"Her soul is bound to the Sword of Layban, yes."

"That is so very bad!" says Zena.

"It is a mercy," replies Johnny Appleseed. "She chose to delve into great evils during her lifetime, but the Lord Jesus said, 'There is no greater love than to lay down your life for your friends.' She has been given a second chance at salvation now."

Zena asks, "What can she do from inside sword?"

Anxious to learn more, Enganyon pleads for a translation. When he hears the news, he grabs for the sword, vowing to free her. Before he can take hold of it, blackflame erupts from its grip and flash freezes his gloves. He yelps, "What on middle earth!"

Johnny Appleseed explains, "She can guide and defend Louis as he completes the quest destined for her. She promised to find some bronze plates. She will have to honor that promise from inside the sword."

Enganyon demands, "Tell the humans to give me the sword and I'll make this right."

Dungaree Jeanne conveys his words to Johnny Appleseed and he replies, "No. Florenz saw Louis wield it bravely in an attempt to take her place in sacrificing herself. She wants him to carry it. She feels a kinship with him for tasting the same temptations she had and yet carrying the same spark of goodness that led her to sacrifice her own life to save others."

Enganyon cannot wrap his mind around all this. He asks in Eldric, "But what is Mister Louis going to do?"

Dungaree Jeanne asks Louis in Aenglish what he intends to do with the Sword of Layban. His face draws a blank. "I have no idea."

Seeing his confusion, Johnny Appleseed offers sound advice. "Keep it a secret. We have already seen too many ways that the sword can be used for evil, but it was given to Florenz to be used for good. What good will come of it remains to be seen. Until then, her only advice to you, Louis, is to keep its power a secret so that evil people cannot get their hands on it.

"And this is my advice to you: do not be afraid! You don't have to figure out the great mysteries, or even your purpose in life, before adventuring out there. Just go forward with a heart full of trust in God's goodness. The hand of Providence will lead you to wherever you're supposed to be one blind step at a time. As followers of Christ, we walk by faith, not by sight."

Clarke says, "Louis and I decided to join up with Sir Robert Roger's rangers as apprentices. Is that okay?"

Johnny Appleseed replies, "You don't need to ask me. As long as you keep praying every day, you'll find what it is God's calling you to, sooner or later."

Louis adds, "We both feel it's the right decision. We've become good friends with the only other apprentice in the company, Nathan Hayle, and several rangers have taken us under their wing. It's the first time for both of us that we feel like we have a family we can trust."

Dungaree Jeanne asks them, "Do you know where the rangers are headed to next?"

"There's been talk about a quest in Fort Detroit."

Johnny Appleseed strokes his beard and speculates. "Archbishop Bozo has long been accused of sympathizing with the Blackflame Cult. Rumor has it the Inquisition has ordered death to come for the Archbishop. If the baron of Amhirst is in league with the Inquisition, the rangers might have been tasked with fulfilling those orders.

"Still, it's a blessing. Chances are high that Zena's magica tree has locomutated itself somewhere along the shores of Lake Eerie. With your permission, Madame Dungaree, Zena and I can keep an eye on our two young friends here while we look for her tree."

"Permission granted," replies Dungaree Jeanne.

Zena is about to object but she realizes she has no objections. She tells her mother in Aenglish, "There is nothing for me here in Shentalpee City. My magica tree is gone. I lose elections and I not care what high elves think of me.

"My soul wants to believe in real God and my heart wants to learn magica trees. I not think of better guide for me than Reverend Appleseed."

Dungaree Jeanne gives her a hug. "You've been through a lot, dear, but I have to admit that my motherly instincts are telling me it was all worth it to finally see you come to your senses. Reverend Appleseed will be like a father to you, more so than Umpire Kibbler could ever have been."

Enganyon is the only one in the group who speaks no Aenglish but he suspect that last conversation did not go his way. As soon as her mother lets her go, Enganyon grabs Zena's hand and says to her in Eldric, "Mademoiselle Zena, I know my behavior has not made much sense to you, but with his dying words my father instructed me to tell the truth and the truth is—I love you. I love you and I've always loved you. I can explain everything if you just give me the chance."

Zena looks at him in disbelief. "Yeah, about that. My mother and I were just saying—"

"What ho!" shouts a commanding voice in Aenglish.

They all turn around and realize they are surrounded by the Crusader army.

374

ACT VII

WHAT HO!

Scene 1: All Together Now

Shentalpee City on Tuscoraura Mountain
Tiw's Day Vespers. Evening, 4th of July, 1284
Third of Saint Swithun

At that moment, the duke of Philadelphia rides forward on a large, sturdy warhorse, accompanied by his heralds, squires, champions, and his daughter, Lady Philippa, code-named Ariel. He calls down, "What ho! Are the elves capitulating?"

Dungaree Jeanne is standing right next to the duke's horse and, although her command of Aenglish is nearly flawless, she is shocked by the realization that she has no idea what the duke is trying to say.

She turns to Johnny Appleseed for a translation. "Capitulating . . . what ho? I don't get it."

"What ho!" replies Appleseed. He then turns to the duke and says to him, "The name's Johnny Appleseed. What ho, Duke!"

The duke politely replies, "What ho!"

Picking up Appleseed's cue, Louis and Clarke both start calling out, "What ho! What ho!"

The duke grunts and says, "It seems rather difficult to go on with the conversation under the current, adverse circumstances. May I propose a truce?"

Finally comprehending his words, Dungaree Jeanne replies in Aenglish, "There is no need, sir knight. The Crusade is over—the heresiarch is dead, and the high inquisitor burned all the riches of the elves to icicles."

"I am Duke William Pinne. As commander in chief of the crusading army, Madame Elve, I beg your pardon, but the war isn't over until I say it's over. A noble of my standing cannot depart empty-handed."

Dungaree Jeanne says in Aenglish, "Then all is well. Your Grace is seated on an excellent horse and you hold the bridle in your left hand. You are neither standing nor empty-handed. You may take your armies and leave Tuscoraura Mountain for good."

The duke of Philadelphia tries again. "Perhaps something got lost in the translation. Normally, a victorious army pillages the spoils of the battlefield to cover its payroll. We have done no pillaging and if you want to keep it that way, I expect payment. Unpaid soldiers do very nasty things, if you catch my drift."

Dungaree Jeanne stands up and says, "Let me translate this for you. Thanks to your high inquisitor's abuse of the blackflame, all our assets are frozen. As dungaree of Foreign Trade, I could work out a profitable trade pact between the fire elves of Tuscoraura Mountain and the wall humans of Philadelphia if you agree to a simple condition."

Bowing his head slightly, the duke says, "I am all ears, Madame Dungaree."

"You must tell the truth. Spread our story honestly. The world needs to know about what happened here. They need to be made aware of the dangers of the blackflame, the betrayal of the high inquisitor, and the futility of waging a Crusade against fire elves."

"Agreed. My court in Philadelphia is home to the finest bards and the most revered loremasters on this side of the Ocean of Atlantis. The clayborn of Vinland will know your story and we shall tell it true. As a token of goodwill, I invite you to come to Philadelphia as an honored guest of mine.

"At my court, we can iron out the nitty-gritty of a truly revolutionary free trade pact. Moreover, I shall give you final say in how the chronicles record the events that have transpired here today for the memory of the land of the free and the home of the brave."

Dungaree Jeanne eyes him and says, "Agreed. You may now leave in peace, and I shall find you in Philadelphia in one month's time."

"Begging your pardon, Madame Dungaree, but business is business. First, I must request a retainer for our trade agreement. The expenses of this Crusade have already emptied my coffers. I'd need two thousand dollars if I'm going to be able to keep my army under tight discipline on the march home. Unpaid troops are wont to riot and plunder the locals."

"I see." From a grimace to a twinkle in her eye, Dungaree Jeanne lights up and asks Johnny Appleseed, "Do you think you could work your magic for this noble lord and provide him with, say, two sacks of refined cocoa powder?"

With a wave of his magic wand, Johnny Appleseed intones, "Oh, fudge!"

A puff of brown smoke and delicious, brown powder floats in the air. Like a little boy trying to catch snowflakes on his tongue, the duke of Philadelphia arches his head back and tastes the chocolatey fog.

He nods and says, "Adieu, Madame Dungaree! My magicultors should be skilled enough to gather all this cocoa powder into gunnysacks. Your down payment on our future friendship will not be forgotten. For now, we depart in peace, and I look forward to your arrival in Philadelphia."

Dungaree Jeanne's face washes over with relief — and cocoa powder. "It will be a trip to remember."

The duke sighs, "I don't know if Philadelphia has much to offer compared to the wonders of this place."

Dungaree Jeanne assures him, "Oh, no worries, my lord. My heart tells me that this is just the start of many adventures grand and marvelous for both our peoples."

He waves his retinue to fall back and starts turning his horse around while he says, "You are obviously a lady who trusts her heart. I have no doubt that all will happen as you say."

After the duke departs, Dungaree Jeanne looks around and announces in Aenglish, "Reverand Appleseed, do you see that fruit and vegetable stand at the base of that sequoia tree down that road? It's got a warehouse we can use as a make-shift hospital for all the wounded. May I ask you to go and start setting up inside? I'll gather elves to help." She turns to Louis and Clarke, asking, "Can you two get the rangers to put together a few stretchers for those that can't walk?"

Clarke bows his head as if taking orders from the Father Prior of his monastery, while Louis remains on the ground staring at the Sword of Layban.

At that moment, Ariel approaches with her party of adventurers and points to Louis. "Young man, you are carrying a sword that belongs to a princess of these people. I promised her she should have it, so I must insist you return it if she's still alive."

Louis replies, "She's inside the sword."

"What?"

Johnny Appleseed explains, "She sacrificed her life to stop the evil inquisitor by crossing the streams of the blackflame. It brought about the dark clouds above us and a strange fate for her. Her soul is now trapped inside the sword awaiting redemption."

Louis adds, "She has chosen me to fulfill her promise. I'm supposed to find some bronze plates."

Ariel is astonished. "You couldn't have known about her promise unless all you are telling me is true."

"Help! Help!" A young woman bursts into the scene. They all turn around. It's Sacagawea. She cries,

"Monsignor Meyer! We need a miracle. Uncle Sam is dying. Come quickly!"

The Monsignor replies, "Calm down, dear. I can only heal minor wounds. If it's serious we might need to move your uncle to some expert healers."

Sacagawea says, "No. We can't let any of the Aenglish here see him. They might arrest him and time is running out. We can't let him die!"

Johnny Appleseed sees her distress and says, "Jesus healed the centurion's servant from afar. If it's that urgent, we'll all pray together right here for your uncle to be healed no matter where he is." He points to Clarke and Monsignor Meyer, sensing that they are clerics as well. "Brothers, please join me in prayer."

Monsignor Meyer and Clarke kneel down to pray, folding their hands together but Johnny Appleseed remains standing and stretches his arms up to heaven. After they have all prayed for a while, Appleseed opens his eyes. "I'm sorry, daughter, but the answer is no."

"What?" Sacagawea turns to the Monsignor.

Monsignor Oscar Meyer nods his head. "I got the same answer to our prayers. God's saying no."

Sacagawea asks, "Is there a more powerful miracle worker around here who can save him?"

"No miracle workers have any power on their own," replies Johnny Appleseed. "All miracles are gifts from God. He uses them to strengthen our faith and lead people to salvation, not to meddle with politics or make people rich. Viceroy Samuel de Champlain has had to carry a heavy cross over the past few months. He has sincerely repented of his sins and has prayed for a holy death. God has said it's his time to go home and nothing in this world or the next can change that."

Tears leak from her eyes.

Clarke adds, "Yes, God has plans for his salvation. He's going to a better place now."

Sacagawea rebels. "No! I worked too hard to save him; I'm not giving up on him now. If your God can't do it, then I'll find a more powerful god who can." With that, she runs off.

A heavy silence hangs in the chocolatey air for a short while as the cocoa powder settles and everyone sympathizes with Sacagawea's plight.

Duke William Pinne's magicultors interrupt the mood as they move in to collect the scattered cocoa powder into gunnysacks. They intone magic words and ply all their magic tricks but it's not working out too well for them.

The head magicultor whispers something into Ariel's ear and then she calls to Johnny Appleseed. "Reverend Appleseed, it seems gathering all this cocoa powder into gunnysacks is not as easy as you made it look. Could you please tell us the good word that makes it all possible?"

Johnny Appleseed swings his elbow upwards and hollers, "Oooooh, the Lord is good to me, and so I thank the Lord for giving me the things I need; the sun and the rain and the apple seed. The Lord is good to me. Amen! Amen! Amen! Amen! Amen!"

Florenz Nightingale and the Sword of Layban

Once upon a time, the fire elves of Tuscoraura Mountain invited the famous Christian druid Johnny Appleseed to deliver the opening speech for their extravagant New Year's Eve party to welcome in the year 1284. On a mission to end the hunger and bloodshed plaguing Vinland, Appleseed freely offers the elves the good spell of the Lord Jesus, the apple seed, and the secret to blackflame.

But something is rotten in Vinland! Fearing the blackflame's potential as a weapon of mass destruction, the Inquisition launches a manhunt to haul in this ragamuffin preacher before his gifts fall into the wrong hands.

With undead wendigos plaguing the forests around Tuscoraura Mountain, Gog, the war chief of the Magog goblins turns to human sacrifices in hopes that the goblin gods will protect them from the rampaging wendigos. Johnny Appleseed begins to suspect that the fire elves' umpire-in-chief, Kibbler Earnestson, might have dirty hands in all this.

But Kibbler's daughter, Florenz, has a plan to make it right with the songs of nightingales until her father demands that she find for him the blackflaming Sword of Layban. Her heart is heavy and unsure whether or not she can trust her rich, charming, and cowardly boyfriend, Enganyon, with her secret as she sets out on epic adventures in this humorous alternate history of how medieval Vinland came to be modern Amerika.

Author's Bio

Gilchrist Keyes Revel Lindenberg was a twentieth-century scholar of Medieval Dwarvish and Elvish languages and culture. After lengthy schooling, he traveled the world as a young gnome, seeking not wisdom but proficiency in foreign languages. Realizing that wisdom would have been the better choice, he tucked himself away in a small cottage hoping to retell the stories that best remind us what matters most.